THE SOTÍRAS

NOUHA JULLIENNE

THE SOTÍRAS
NOUHA JULLIENNE

Editing by Jennifer Innamorati, Sleepy Night Owl Edits
Cover Design by Dream Echo Designs
Formatting by Danielle Sarah
Character Art - ART by ALEKSA

AUTHOR'S NOTE

Dear Reader,

I wanted to take a moment to address some important aspects of my book. Within these pages, you will encounter themes that are deeply challenging and may be distressing, including death, suicide ideation, drug abuse, and domestic abuse. These topics are not approached lightly, and they are integral to the journeys of the characters you will meet.

The characters in this story undergo therapy, navigating the complexities of their traumas. I am not a mental health professional, but I have made every effort to depict these sessions with as much realism and sensitivity as possible. This involved extensive research into trauma, PTSD, and substance abuse. Despite my best efforts to ensure accuracy, please remember that I am not an expert. Therefore, I ask that you take the portrayals and opinions in this book with a grain of salt.

I really hope that those who resonate with the characters and their struggles find some peace and understanding within this story.

TRIGGER WARNINGS

Graphic violence, gun violence, torture, assault, kidnapping, death, stalking, mention of parental death, verbal and physical abuse, domestic abuse/violence, traumatic events, mental health issues (panic attacks, anxiety, PTSD, suicidal thoughts/ideation), substance abuse (alcohol and drugs), sexually explicit scenes (nudity, masturbation, blood (period) play, gun play, breath play, primal/prey, enema play, anal).

PLAYLIST

Sleepyhead - Jutes
All Around Me – Flyleaf
Last Resort – Papa Roach
Chemical – Post Malone
eyes don't lie sped up – Isabel LaRosa
Obsessed – Jutes
I need - Lithe
Numb to the Feeling - Chase Atlantic
One Day The Only Butterflies Left Will Be In Your Chest As
You March Toward Your Death - Bring Me The Horizon feat.
Amy Lee
Granite – Sleep Token
Bitter – FLETCHER, Kito
Bruises - Lewis Capaldi
Hate Me! - MASN
bad decisions - Bad Omens
Novocaine - Too Close To Touch, Bad Omens
die for - Maggie Lindemann

PLAYLIST

My Fault - Shaboozey feat. Noah Cyrus
Panic Attack - Liza Anne
Birds of a Feather - Billie Eilish
Obsession – Melina Tey
Be Alright – Dean Lewis
Those Eyes – New West
I Fall Apart – Post Malone
Blood Sport – Sleep Token
Angels like You – Miley Cyrus
Bring Me To Life – Evanescence
Sex & Palo Santo – Jutes
If u Fall – Lithe
Like I Want You – Giveon
Alkaline – Sleep Token
NIGHTS LIKE THIS – The Kid LAROI
HELP – Isabel LaRosa

GREEK PLAYLIST

AGAPI – Remix – Sigma, Light
Adrenalina – Sidarta
Blue Iguana – Hawk
Isos – Sicario
Mikri – Mente Fuerte
Voodoo – Hawk, Light
Alithia – Bossilan, Aspa
Vradia – Roi 6/12, Evangelia
Kapote - Kids

GLOSSARY

Adelfé: Brother
Afentikó: Boss
Agápi mou: My love
Angeloúdi mou: My little angel
Astéri mou: My star
Ánte gamisou: Fuck you.
Baba: Dad/Father
Christé mou: Jesus Christ
Diávolos: Devil
Dikiá mou: Mine
Eísai poutána mono gia ména: You are such a little whore for me.
Eísai ómorfi: You're beautiful.
Gamoto: Fuck
Kaliméra, agóri mou: Good morning, my boy.
Kalispéra, afentikó: Good evening, boss.
Kóri mou: Daughter
Mama: Mom/Mother
Maláka: Asshole/Motherfucker
Moró mou: Babe/baby
Ómorfi: Beautiful.
Oo Skatá/Skatá: Oh, shit/Shit.
Oo theé mou: Oh my God
Poú eínai: Where is he?
Poutána: Whore

Poutánas yos: Son of a bitch

Se thélo: I want you.

Signómi: I'm sorry.

Skatofatsa: Fuck face

Ti kánis: How are you?

Ti nea echís: What update do you have for me?

Ti sto diáolo: What the hell/fuck

Ti thelis: What do you want?

Ton brika: I found him.

Vlakas: Stupid

Yassas: Hello

Yassou, liákada mou, pós eísai : Hi, my sunshine, how are you?

Kalá, efkharisto: I'm fine, thank you.

They say a star shines its brightest when it's starting to collapse...

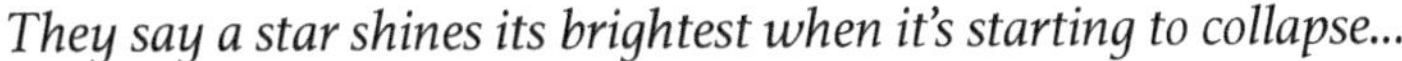

When you feel overwhelmed, remember that your inner blaze burns brighter than the sun.
There's a radiant light beckoning you, a promise of beauty ahead.
Don't give up.
Someday, those flames will become the fires that illuminate falling stars.

*Oh...and if you're not ready to match Dion's freak, turn back now.
I mean it. He's nasty.*

THE SOTÍRAS

(Greek: Σωτήρα, lit. 'savior')

My body is rebelling. There's a burning in my veins, a fiery reminder of my mistake.

My vision blurs, and I can barely make out anything in front of me. The world tilts and spins. I feel Dion's hand on mine. He's talking, but the words are lost in the haze.

The darkness behind my eyelids is a small relief from the sensory overload.

I just wanted the pain to stop, but instead, I've plunged into a new kind of agony.

All I can do is hold on, hoping that I'll make it through to the other side.

PART ONE
The One Night Stand

1

DION

Two years earlier

"Y ou're going to be shitfaced if you keep this up," Xander says from my right, his bulky frame taking up almost the entire booth. His arms are spread along the back of the couch as he eyes me with a disapproving look.

"That's the fucking goal," I murmur, annoyed that I have to spend the night listening to loud, thumping music and watch drunken idiots misbehave. I hate crowds. *Especially* drunken crowds.

I down the rest of my ouzo and slam the glass on the table. "Argh!"

It's my third drink of the night and it's only nine p.m. *Only five more hours to go...*

I'm on babysitting duty—as I call it—at Academia, the nightclub my best friend, Brother from another mother, and boss, Evander Vasilakis, owns.

Even though the manager, Elias, is around and the place is filled with bouncers, Evan still wanted me here.

I get it. He would rather be safe than sorry, given that the threats made against him are becoming serious.

Cebrene is controlled by five main families, and the Vasilakis clan, in which I've been adopted, is one of them. I was born a Loukas. But when tragedy struck, I was taken in by Evander's uncle, Ignatius Vasilakis.

I'll never change my last name, but I'm loyal as fuck to them.

In the many years when Evander was living in the shadows as the *Diávolos*, I was keeping an eye out on the ground, helping Ignatius manage the business.

Now, after his death, Evan has been thrust into the light and has had to get more involved in his family's clan, taking the reins as the heir.

He was never one to seek power, preferring the comfort of the dark. But destiny has a way of dragging even the most reluctant into its grand designs.

Ignatius was like a father to Evander and me, so his death left a permanent mark on both of us, reshaping our lives in ways we could never have anticipated.

The image of his lifeless, bloodied body still haunts me.

It was not just the loss of a beloved family member, but also of a mentor and protector.

For me, it felt like losing a part of myself, a foundation on which I had built so much of my own understanding of the world. He saved me.

I chug another glass of ouzo, the sharp, aniseed flavor blistering its way down my throat, matching the burning I already feel in my chest.

Ignatius's death was also a catalyst, pushing both of us into roles we might never have assumed otherwise.

It lit a fire under me, a determination to see through the vision Ignatius had for our future.

And to see those responsible for his death brought to justice, or better yet, to exact our own vengeance.

Still, tonight, I'd rather be home, in my boxers, playing video games. Or out riding one of my bikes. They're the only things that let me blow off some steam.

That or being balls deep in some cunt.

"Have you spoken to Evan?" I ask Xander.

"Nah. He's been quiet," he replies, taking a swig of his drink.

"It's because of that girl, isn't it?"

Xander shrugs his broad shoulders. "Might be."

I sigh and shake my head. Ever since Evander laid his eyes on our enemy's daughter, he's been a fucking mess. He claims he's only interested in her for revenge, but I call bullshit.

Her father, Peter Kouvalakis, is responsible for the murder of Ignatius. I wanted to simply kill him right away, but instead of starting a full-out war between the clans, Evan decided to take a different approach: convince his daughter to marry him so he can take over Peter's business and clan from the inside. *Then*, kill him.

It was an overall smart plan until Evan asked Xander to get some footage of Angelica Kouvalakis. As soon as he saw her pictures, he became obsessed. *Understatement of the year.*

I grab my phone and shoot him a text.

> Me: Where the fuck are you, vlakas?

The alcohol has definitely kicked in, my head spinning as I wait for a reply. It comes a few seconds later.

> Evan: None of your fucking business.

> Me: Gasp! The least you could do is tell me what you're up to since you've jailed me at your fucking club.

Evan: MY club? As if I don't fucking share everything with you.

He's not wrong. The club and the business might be his officially, but Evander is nothing but generous with his own people. He makes sure that I'm always well taken care of as his second-in-command. I'm responsible for the many warehouses we have around the city, overseeing the import and exporting of our goods. Most of the profits made go in my pocket. I have enough money for two lifetimes.

Me: Fine. Are you stalking that chick again?

Evan: Fuck you. I'm not stalking her.

I let out a deep laugh, startling Xander next to me. His eyes narrow, but I dismiss him with a wave.

Me: Don't lie to me, Brother. You're outside of her house right now, aren't you?

Evan: Text me again and I'm blocking you.

Chuckling, I put my phone away and gulp down my fifth glass of ouzo.

Leon walks in, cigarette in mouth. "*Afentikó*!" he yells.

Xander grunts. "Put that fucking shit away," he says, pointing at the cigarette.

Quickly, Leon grabs an empty glass off the table and puts out the bud. "My bad, my bad! Cyrus is here to see you, Dion."

I roll my eyes so fucking hard, they threaten to roll back in my head. "What the fuck does he want?"

I don't know why Evander hired that dumbass. He's the epitome of a walking ball of stress at all times, and I'm always left dealing with his shit.

Leon shrugs his shoulders. "No clue, but he looks stressed."

"What else is new?" I retort with a grumble. I've been here for an hour, and I'm ready to burn the whole place down.

I force myself off my seat and walk toward the entrance of the club. As soon as I step outside to where Cyrus is waiting for me, he starts speaking. "I'm sorry. I tried to get more info out of him, but he wouldn't budge," he word-vomits. "Then, he started getting suspicious and asked who I worked for, so I darted out of there. I don't think anyone followed me, but—"

"Woah, woah, woah!" I interrupt him mid-speech. "*Christé mou*, take a fucking breath, Cyrus." I rub my temples. The buzz from the alcohol is already leaving me, and I now feel a headache coming on.

Cyrus went to get more information out of Peter Kouvalakis's men. Evander thought it would be better to send someone frail and harmless looking to not raise questions, but judging by the state of Cyrus now, sweat stains and all, I'm thinking it wasn't a good idea.

I take a deep breath. "Start from the beginning."

As Cyrus recounts his experience, my mind cannot focus on anything he's saying. All I want to do is go back inside and have another drink.

"Okay, go home. I'll take care of it," I tell Cyrus when he's done speaking, shooing him away as I pass Leon at the door. Something else I'll have to do tonight.

"Have someone escort him home to make sure he isn't followed," I whisper to Leon, and he nods.

Back inside, I sit down at the booth and take a sip of my drink. Losing myself in the haze, I feel a sudden weight land on my lap.

I look up and see Amber grinning at me. We met at this very club a while back and have been spending some time with her. More specifically, she's a woman I've been fucking.

Her body presses against mine as she wraps her arms around my neck, her pouty lips dangerously close to my ear.

"Hey, stranger," she purrs, her breath hot against my skin.

I grind my teeth, my grip tightening around my glass. This is exactly what I don't need tonight. Amber and I have had our fun, but she's beginning to overstep. I made it clear from the start this was just a hookup, but she's been texting and calling at all hours, acting like we're a thing. I can tell she's starting to believe this is something it's not. She's a decent girl, but I don't do clingy. Clingy means attachment, and attachment means feelings, and feelings are a luxury I can't afford.

I try to lean back to put some distance between us, but she doesn't take the hint. Her hands trail down my chest, fingers grazing the buttons of my shirt. I catch her wrists, holding her still.

"Amber, not tonight," I say, my voice rougher than intended.

She frowns playfully, her brown eyes searching mine. "Why not?

"I'm not in the mood."

"Come on. We always have a good time, don't we?"

I sigh, fighting the urge to push her off me. "We did. But that's all it was—a good time. Nothing more. I already told you."

Her expression hardens, the amused glint in her expression replaced by something darker. "So, that's it? You're just *done* with me?"

I nod, my patience wearing thin. "Yeah, that's it."

Amber huffs. "You can't keep doing this, Dion. Using people and then tossing them aside when they get too close."

I release her wrists and push her off my lap, standing up abruptly.

"Maybe you're right, but I never promised you anything else."

Amber's eyes follow me as I head for the back door, and I ignore the *asshole* she yells at me. I'd rather not leave things like this, but I hate the alternative even more. Feelings mess up everything, and I've got enough complications without adding a woman into the mix.

Outside, the cool night air hits me like a slap, sobering me up a bit. I take a deep breath and debate whether to go back in or ignore Evan's orders and go home.

My phone vibrates in my pocket.

> Evan: Things changed. It looks like I'm coming
> to the club after all.

Oh boy. Here we go.

AN HOUR LATER, I'M SETTLED IN THE VIP SECTION, SEATED AT A booth with Xander, Evander, and his two bodyguards, Sebastien and Gregory.

The place is full of patrons. For being in the Lower District of Cebrene, a less than favorable area of the metropolis, Academia still attracts a crowd, no matter the day of the week. I'm happy it's doing well.

"How did the warehouse visit go?" Evander asks us.

"Everything is clear. No disruptions," Xander replies.

I begin to tell Evan about Cyrus and what happened earlier, but his gaze gets caught on something over on the dance floor, and suddenly, he straightens.

Annoyed that I've been talking to a wall for the past few minutes, I try to get his attention again. "Bro, what is up with you right now? You look as if you're about to pounce on some prey."

"It's Angelica," he responds through clenched teeth.

"*Oo skatá*," is all I manage to say.

My gaze sweeps across the sea of dancing bodies to find the

Kouvalakis girl. She's swaying to the beat of the music with a group of girls. I glance over them and— Like a ray of light amidst the chaos, there *she* is, standing at the heart of the group. A petite, blonde woman with an infectious smile that lights up her face in a way that draws me in effortlessly. With every graceful movement, she commands my attention without even trying. She dances and laughs, waving her hands in the air to the beat of the music, swaying her hips and pumping her chest.

I feel a tug at the corners of my lips as I watch her, an unfamiliar warmth spreading through me. There's something about her that stirs curiosity within me, like the flicker of a flame igniting the darkness in my chest where no woman has ever set foot. Where I've never even let a woman come close.

My heart was ripped away from me years ago and has been closed off to the world ever since.

But in this moment, it's as if everything else fades into the background, leaving only *her* and the electricity that crackles in the space between us. *Who is she?*

I snap out of my daydream when someone steps in front of the girl and I lose sight of her. I turn to Evan. "Did you know Angelica would be here?"

He shakes his head.

Before he has the chance to detonate, I slap him on the shoulder and give it a squeeze. "Hey, please don't do anything crazy tonight. I really don't feel like cleaning up one of your messes." I joke.

Evander grunts, unamused, his jaw ticking as he watches the scene unfolding in front of him.

Angelica is dancing with a man. *Double shit.*

His eyes darken and he clenches his glass so hard, his knuckles whiten.

"For fuck's sake, Evan."

If I don't stop this right now, Evander is going to shoot that motherfucker straight between the eyes in the middle of his own club. That won't be great for business.

"And you say you don't give a shit about her, huh?" I grumble as I stand and head toward the dance floor.

My eyes lock onto the blonde girl, watching her dance, her laugh somehow reaching my ears even across the loud club. I'm unable to resist the magnetic pull she seems to exert as I draw closer and closer.

She stands out like a rare gem, shining brighter than a diamond.

Once I've made my way to the group, I tap Angelica's shoulder. She turns around, and not even a second later, her friend, the blonde, is in front of her, staring up at me with loathing.

"Is this guy bothering you, Angelica?"

Although she's almost baring her teeth at me, her smooth voice makes me go still. My heart quickens its pace, anticipation fluttering in my chest.

"And who's this feisty little one?" I ask after a moment, hoping my smirk hides the chaos running around in my head.

"The name's Aria," she spits. My gaze zeroes in on her mouth. "Who the hell are you and what do you want?"

I try to stifle my smile at her frown. Her attitude is doing the opposite of what it should. I'm mesmerized.

My cock is too, it seems, as it's hardening by the second. *Holy fuck.*

2

ARIA

"You can call me Dion, *astéri mou*," the stranger says with a huge grin. My heart leaps into my throat. I open my mouth to respond, but nothing comes out. *What the hell, Aria? Say something.*

But the words seem to have been snatched from my lips as I stare at this man. This really, *really* handsome man. I hadn't noticed how gorgeous he was until our gazes locked, and I got lost in his green eyes, like stepping into a pair of emerald pools.

Somehow, it's as if I can feel the intensity they hold, secrets waiting to be discovered by those brave enough to venture closer.

His muscular frame fills out his dark suit perfectly. The jacket, tailored to perfection, hangs open, revealing an unbuttoned shirt underneath. I catch glimpses of tattoos peeking out from beneath the fabric.

His short, brown hair is neatly styled, and the light stubble on his jaw looks irresistibly rough. I can't help but imagine how it would feel against my skin.

I blink rapidly, breaking free from my trance. *Woah.*

All I wanted was to have some fun tonight and get Angelica out of her self-induced rut.

She has been struggling to readjust after being kidnapped by one of her father's rivals in Antium City. Yes, *kidnapped.*

She had moved there four years ago, running away from home to escape her life. But ever since coming back to the Metropolis of Cebrene, she often looks distant, her laughter seems forced, and there's a sadness in her eyes that wasn't there before. It's like she's physically back, but mentally is still trapped in that terrifying ordeal.

I wanted to take her out and show her a good time. I wanted my best friend back.

Instead, we keep getting interrupted by sleazy men who just want to grind their dicks on our asses. Exhibit A: mister tall, tanned, and stupidly handsome that just waltzed up to us thinking he deserves even a second of our time and is now *smirking* at me. He's hot, but I could do without the entitlement.

I watch him with a frown as he turns to Angelica to whisper say in her ear over the music, then gives me one last, lingering glance before leaving us.

My breath hitches, and I bring my hand to my mouth.

Aria, come to your senses, damnit. I must be drunk to be this affected by a *look.*

I face Angelica, who has gone pale. "What's wrong, Ang?" I ask, concerned, forgetting all about the suited man. Dion.

"It's him. It's Evan. He's sitting right there, staring at me, and he wants us to join him."

I follow her gaze to a group of men in a VIP booth. Evan is the man she met at the shooting range. Based on what Ang told me, I think she should fist more than just his gun—*if you know what I mean.*

Unable to contain my excitement, I squeal. "Oh. My. God! What are we waiting for?"

I grab her arm and drag her to the table at the back of the

crowded club where Evan, Dion, and another man are sitting. Given their appearance and air of importance, I'm safe to assume they're in the mob—like mine and Ang's families. Maybe I should be a bit cautious, but if these men want to show us a good time and give us free drinks, why the hell not?

Dion has his fingers wrapped around a tumbler of amber liquid that looks like whiskey or bourbon. As I approach, he looks up, his eyes locking onto mine.

"Hey, fellas. You called?" I purr as I hold his gaze, a silent challenge in the air, like we're playing a staring contest. His lips curl into a smirk and, just as he raises his glass to take a sip, I make my move.

I snatch the drink from his hand before it touches his lips.

Without breaking eye contact, I gulp down the entire contents, the burn of the alcohol hitting the back of my throat and making me grimace. I set the empty glass back on the table with a soft clink, winking at Dion.

Dion's expression shifts from surprise to something like intrigue—something *hot*—his eyebrows lifting slightly before he leans back on the couch. "Well, that was unexpected," he says, with a hint of amusement in his voice.

I glance at the empty seat next to him, then slide into the booth, the smooth fabric cool against my legs. "Thought you could use some company." I tilt my head slightly, a playful grin on my lips.

Dion chuckles, shaking his head. "Bold move, Aria. I didn't take you for the type."

I ignore the annoying flip in my chest at hearing him say my name.

"There's a lot you don't know about me.". I lean in closer, resting my arm on the back of the couch.

Dion's smirk widens as he signals the waitress for another drink, his eyes barely leaving mine. "So, what made you come to my table?"

I shrug. "Maybe I was bored. Maybe I wanted to see if you're as interesting as you look."

He laughs softly, the sound rich and warm. "And what's the verdict so far?"

I pretend to ponder, tapping my chin with a finger. "The night's still young. We'll see."

Dion's gaze lingers on me. "Fair enough. Here's to a night of surprises, then."

The tension between us crackles, and I can feel the warmth of his body next to mine, a subtle reminder of the boldness of my move.

Suddenly, I'm hit with nerves like a ton of bricks. I'm not usually the shy type, but being this close to him—this *stranger*—is doing unexplainable things to me. My body is overheating.

I shift on the plush seat, heart hammering against my rib cage like a frantic bird desperate for escape. Beside me, Dion is a presence so powerful it sends shivers down my spine.

Every movement he makes seems calculated, deliberate, as though he knows exactly the effect he has on me. It's dizzying.

My fingers find solace in the delicate fabric of my skirt, tracing the familiar path along the hem. I tug at it, looking down, a weak attempt to ground myself.

Dion places his palm on top of my hand, and the current of energy that courses through my veins almost suffocates me.

"What's the matter, Aria? Nerves getting the best of you?" he remarks, his hand still touching mine. There's a mischievous expression in his eyes.

I inhale a sharp breath. "*No*," I utter indignantly, like a kid who just got caught doing something sneaky.

"Are you sure? You stormed over here, grabbed my drink like you owned the place, and now it seems you're getting cold feet. For a second there, I thought you had guts."

I struggle to keep my composure, still fiddling with my skirt.

"You'll end up unthreading it if you keep twisting the fabric like that," Dion says, looking down at my legs. I notice his gaze lingering a second too long. No matter how hard I try to stifle the heat that's rising to my cheeks, I fail.

I quickly force myself to snap out of it—*he's just a smug asshole who doesn't deserve my attention.* His condescension fuels a spark of defiance in me. I jerk my hand away. "You've got jokes," I deadpan. "Maybe I don't need to prove anything to you. Maybe you don't deserve a lick of my time."

"There she is." Something glints in his eyes, and I roll mine. He's clearly enjoying this.

"*There she is?* You don't even know me," I retort. This man thinks he has me all figured out.

"Let's change that."

"How? You want to talk about our dreams and aspirations in the middle of a loud club?"

The pulsating lights cast shadows across Dion's face, but I don't miss how his lips curl into a smile. "I know somewhere quiet."

I scoff. Of course. Men like him always want one thing. "No, thank you." I knew he was too good to be true.

"We can talk, that's all," he says, feigning innocence, and it's almost convincing.

"I'm not sleeping with you."

"That's not my intention."

My eyes narrow into slits. "You expect me to believe that you're not trying to take me somewhere quiet to get in my pants. Not credible for a second."

"Let me prove you wrong, then." Dion's lips part into a wide grin, and I'm again enveloped by his beauty. *Fuck me.* I can barely contain my smile. But I stand firm.

"I said no. I'm perfectly fine here."

I turn to check on Angelica—but she's no longer in the booth. My eyes search for her in the crowd, telling myself not to be worried, when I spot her on the dance floor alone.

Correction: *not* alone. She's glued to a man who is now grabbing onto her hips, palms flat on her waist. She hooks her arm around his neck and grinds onto him, looking toward us with mischief in her eyes. I follow her gaze and find a *very* angry Evan clutching onto his glass.

Oh my God. Angelica is putting on a show for *him*. What the fuck did I miss? How long have Dion and I been talking?

I have a feeling this will not end well.

Evan gets off his seat in one swift movement and mutters something to the two men standing behind him, who appear to be his guards, and heads toward the dancing crowd.

"What's happening? What is he doing?" I look at Dion for help, but he simply shrugs.

"Trust me, he's far past convincing now. Don't worry, he won't hurt her." He sounds so confident, and I want to believe him, but I still want to go talk to Angelica.

I wiggle my way off the couch, but Dion grabs onto my arm. "Stay here."

"Don't tell me what to do," I spit, jerking away from him.

Evan is now on the dance floor in a heated discussion with the guy. Then, the music abruptly stops. "Everybody. Out. Now," I hear him seethe.

I jump up. Just as I'm about to run to Angie, Dion wraps his arm around my waist, lifts me in the air like a sack of potatoes, and throws me over his shoulders.

"What the fuck, Dion? Put me down, now!"

I try to fight him, but he's too big and overpowering. My protests fall on deaf ears, drowned out by his chuckle and the amused glances from his friend. Dion doesn't even flinch as I thrash against his back.

All I feel are the hard muscles flexing under my palms. His strength radiates through my fingertips, and, for a moment, I just want to run my hands all over him. The temptation is almost overwhelming and—*no*, I need to focus.

"Where are you taking me?" I shout, my irritation growing by the second. The sooner I'm back on solid ground, the better. Then, I will berate him properly.

"Somewhere fucking quiet, you psycho," he laughs. *What an asshole.*

We head upstairs, Dion somehow managing to carry me up a few flights as if I were a feather. He opens a door before gently putting me down.

Disgruntled, I straighten my clothes, trying to regain some composure while shooting daggers at him. My cheeks are flushed with embarrassment and lingering annoyance. *I could kill him.*

I prepare to give him a piece of my mind, but the words get stuck in my throat as he locks the door and leans against it, crossing his arms at his chest with a self-satisfied smile on his face.

"Why did you lock us in?" I ask, now a little concerned about my well-being. Actually, I didn't think about my safety *at all.* I was too distracted by the chaos and his beautiful, green eyes. He could be a bad man and hurt me.

My heart pounds, beating furiously against my chest. He doesn't answer.

"If I don't get home tonight, my fiancé will be worried," I blurt out, hoping it'll put him off. I'm not technically engaged yet, but it's in the works. My father announced a few weeks ago that he'd be arranging a union with one of his counterparts. I'm still trying to convince him it's a bad idea.

At twenty-three years old, I never thought I'd be forced into a marriage against my will. My father always implied that such an option would never be on the table. The news came out of the blue and shocked our entire family. But what *Baba* says, goes, and now I'm just hoping it was a rash decision he made in the heat of the moment. I refuse to believe he would allow his little girl to marry a complete *stranger.* It feels like my world has been turned upside down, and all I can do is cling to the hope that my father will come to his senses and put an end to it.

Right now, though, I'll use it to my advantage.

"Your *fiancé*, huh? And where is he now?" Dion taunts, raising a brow.

I take a quick glance around the space. We seem to be in an office. Behind me, there's a desk and a chair. I slowly back away to reach the solid surface as though it'll make me feel more protected.

Every nerve in my body is on high alert. "Uh, home. Waiting for me," I finally reply.

"Is that so? Your fiancé let you go out without him?"

"My fiancé doesn't *let* me do anything," I snap, suddenly angry again. *Great.* Another man with archaic morals and values.

"That's not what I meant," he says, approaching me, his intense gaze never leaving mine. "If you were mine, I would never let you out of my sight, *astéri mou*."

This time, the nickname catches me off guard, and warmth builds in the pit of my stomach. *My little star*. When he'd said it earlier on the dance floor, I was so disoriented by his arrival that it never sank in. I shake my head to dispel the thoughts.

"Well, thankfully, I'm not yours."

Dion chuckles.

My butt reaches the desk, and I can no longer back away from him. He moves closer, forcing me to sit at the top to keep one last fraction of space between us. Bracing his hands on the table at each side of my body, he brings his nose to my ear. My muscles tense involuntarily, my breath coming in shallow gasps, as if my lungs refuse to fully inflate, fearing what might come next.

"I don't see a ring, Aria." My name rolls off his tongue like melted butter. Goosebumps erupt all over my body.

Mind racing, I try to find an excuse as to why I, in fact, do not have a ring on, but I can't function with him this close to me.

"Hmmm, I think you're a little liar," he adds in a low murmur. "I'm not even sure this *fiancé* exists."

A flicker of determination ignites within me. I refuse to succumb to his games. I steel myself, drawing upon every ounce of courage I possess. "Get away from me, Dion. I told you I won't sleep with you."

He lets out a mocking laugh and backs up. "That's not why we're here," he says, as if the idea is ridiculous.

I give him a disdainful glance. "Sure. And snow falls in summer."

Dion's face contorts into a confused frown. "What?"

I cross my arms at my chest. "You've never heard of that expression?" He shakes his head.

I scoff. "When pigs fly. When fish climb trees. When chickens have teeth. Nothing?"

That annoying eyebrow lifts again. "Definitely not. I'm not weird."

"Fuck off. You just live under a rock."

"I'd rather live under a rock than be weird."

I let out a snarl. "You're infuriating!"

"So I've heard." He shrugs.

He walks around me and sits on the chair; I swivel to not have my back to him. You can never be too safe. I don't have a weapon on me, given they search your bags at the door, so I have nothing to defend myself with. *This reminds me, I should learn self-defense.*

Dion lifts his feet onto the desk and leans back, arms above his head. I roll my eyes. At this moment, he looks like a rich douche bag on his throne.

"If you don't stop rolling your eyes at me, I'll give you a reason to do so, little liar," he threatens with a cheeky grin. I just want to slap it off.

"You're honestly so annoying. I don't know if I can handle being in here with you for another second without throwing something at you," I say, looking around the room as I genuinely consider it.

Dion laughs. All he's done since we met—not even an hour ago—has been smiling and laughing. I want to convince myself that it isn't affecting me. But then, I'd *actually* be a little liar.

"When can I go home?" I ask, exasperated. "I need to check on Angelica." *And I need to put some space between us because you're making me feel like a slut puppy.* I don't say that, obviously.

He waves me off. "She's fine. Evan sent me a text to confirm. You can come see if you'd like," he taunts, waving his phone in the air.

I narrow my gaze. "Right. And I'm supposed to trust you."

"What other choice do you have?"

"Mafia men are all the same," I mumble, more and more frustrated. "Always with the higher-than-thou attitude and power play."

Dion crosses his arms. "Is that so? What else do you know about mafia men?"

I sigh. "Only that I don't want to be around them."

My mind drifts to my father and his plan for my marriage, and I curse the heavens for allowing me to be born into the mob. I'm beginning to understand Angelica's need to escape.

"You know nothing about me either, *astéri mou.* I can almost guarantee I'm not like the others."

I blow out a puff of air. "Isn't that what they all say, Dion?"

With a shit-eating grin, he says, "Innocent until proven guilty."

I resist the urge to roll my eyes at him once more, shutting my lids instead to take a deep breath. I imagine running up to him, strangling him by the throat, his eyes bulging out of his head like a cartoon. The thought is quite amusing.

"Do you want to see, or what?" Dion asks, interrupting my fantasy.

I want to check his phone, but that means I'd have to get close to him again. Although I'd love nothing more than to punch him in the throat, his proximity makes me feel—*weird.*

Good weird. I hate it.

But I decide that Angelica's well-being is more important. "Fine."

I walk around the desk and lean forward to check the text, my hair falling over Dion's face. He stills, as if I've just done something wrong. Then, I hear him inhale. He fucking *inhales.*

"Are you fucking sniffing me?"

"Yes. And?" he replies, no ounce of regret in his tone.

Not realizing how close we are, our noses almost touch when I turn my face to him. I slightly startle, but don't back away. He can't know how much he's affecting me. *I* don't want to admit that to myself. I don't know him. He's a jackass, and I'm getting engaged. *Even though the thought of marrying a stranger makes me sick.*

"So, you really are a dog," I retort.

Dion laughs. *That fucking sound.*

In a matter of seconds, he slides his palm up and around my nape and grabs onto my hair. My breath catches in my throat at the hint of pain. The pull grounds me in a way that feels foreign, yet undeniably comforting.

It's strangely anchoring. Dion's touch is both possessive and reassuring. And I need to get him off me before I do something stupid.

But he brings my face even closer, pulling my head backward enough to stunt my breathing. I hiss, the sting going straight to my eyes, tears pooling. A whimper slips out of my mouth.

A tingling sensation shoots straight down my core. My

center is suddenly pulsating with need. I've never been manhandled like this before.

"You fucking like this," Dion grunts, tugging harder, and I moan. "Look at you, Aria. You're fucking weak, wilting like a leaf for me."

I shake my head. "No," I wheeze.

"You're dying for me to water you, baby," he says, nipping my earlobe with his teeth. *Oh, God.* I have a feeling I won't come out of this unscathed.

"Let me go." I struggle to breathe.

"Not until you stop playing games, little liar. Tell me you feel this. Whatever *this* is between us. Admit it, and I'll let you go." The heat of his breath in my ear causes my skin to erupt in goosebumps.

I gulp. "I don't feel it." *I'm lying.*

He pulls my hair harder. "Liar."

"I'm not a liar." I seethe between my teeth. *Okay, maybe just a little bit, but he's still an asshole.* "Let. Me. Go."

The sound that comes out of Dion's mouth is guttural. Like a beast finally ready to attack his prey. One second, I'm standing next to him, bending down, his fist in my hair. The next, I'm seated on his lap, his erection prodding my backside.

He crashes his lips on mine and my entire world turns on its axis, reality fading into oblivion as I'm consumed by the sensation of his kiss. Firecrackers explode in my chest, every nerve ending tingling. I think I might be dying.

Dion weaves his fingers into my hair, grasping onto it desperately as if to moor himself to me.

I am lost in him. My senses heightened; every touch amplified.

My fingers instinctively reach for his chest, and I clutch onto the lapels of his suit, pulling him closer.

With each heartbeat, the intensity grows, our tongues

battling for control, igniting a fire within me I never knew existed. It's exhilarating, intoxicating, and utterly breathtaking.

When we finally pull away, breathless and dizzy with desire, I realize that this electrifying feeling might just be the beginning of something heartbreaking.

3

DION

Who is this girl and why does she have me so fucked up?

As I break away from our kiss, I breathe Aria in like she's oxygen. I never knew how much I needed air until our lips met.

When she crouched next to me to look at my phone, I couldn't help myself from sniffing her. It was involuntary, almost primal. Her scent was subtle yet intoxicating, like a blend of flowers and warmth.

My fingers are still tangled in her long, blonde hair as I stare into her gray eyes. In their depths, I see reflected my own desires. They speak volumes without her having to utter a single word. *You just fucking met her.*

But her gaze captivates me, drawing me in like a moth to a flame.

No matter how fast this lust has developed, I can't stop it now.

Bringing Aria's mouth back to mine, I suck on her bottom lip, nipping it with my teeth. She moans, and it sends a flutter down my stomach. Are those fucking *butterflies*?

Frustrated by the multitude of unfamiliar feelings I'm expe-

31

riencing, and the deep need to bury myself inside this woman, I let out a low growl and bring Aria's legs around my waist, seating her perfectly on top of my hardened cock. Her skirt rides up her legs, and I squeeze her thighs hard, imprinting her skin with my fingers.

Within an instant, her hips buck forward, and she starts grinding on my dick.

When I look down, I almost pass out at the vision before me: Aria's plump pussy on display through her soaked panties, leaving a damp spot on my trousers. *Good God.*

"Fuck, Aria. What are you doing to me?"

Her breath comes out shallow as she replies, "What do you mean?"

"I need to be inside you," I groan.

For a moment, her body tenses, and she turns her face away. "We can't."

Oh, yeah...her *fiancé.*

Using my hands on her hips, I help grind her pelvis harder on my crotch. She's getting wetter, I'm getting harder. "Why not?"

"There doesn't need to be a reason," she huffs, breathless. "I told you: I'm not sleeping with you." But it's not convincing. Especially as she keeps rocking back and forth against me.

"That was before, when your pussy wasn't dripping on my thighs, baby. Let me in."

Aria looks down at the mess, the rise and fall of her chest mimicking my erratic heartbeat. "Say please," she demands after a moment, a cocky grin spreading across her face.

I chuckle, not believing what she just asked me. "You want me to *beg*?"

Aria's hands come to rest on my shirt. "Yes. If you want it so bad, *big boy*, you'll have to beg for it."

Big boy? Holy fuck, this woman...she's going to make me fucking do it, isn't she?

Taking my silence as hesitation, Aria adds a smug, "That's what I thought."

She tries to lift herself off me, but I pin her down. There's no way I'm letting her get away.

I've never had to beg a woman to get into her pants, but Aria, whose last name I don't even know, could probably get me to do anything with that damn smile.

"Please, baby." I grit out, my voice gruff and deep. "Let me feel you. I'm not sure I'll make it if you don't." *Are you serious, man?* I can't help it, though. I would crawl on my knees if she asked.

Satisfied with my begging, Aria's face lights up into a sultry smile.

It's enough to make me grab her by the back of the head and plunge my lips onto hers. They taste so fucking good. It should be a crime. Her mouth is sweet and smokey—probably from the alcohol she was drinking—and I can't get enough.

"Fuck, Aria. I can't take it anymore. Slide your pussy onto me, please," I groan.

The mere thought of having her wet hole engulf me makes my cock strain in my pants. I need it out and inside her. Stat.

Aria's gaze falters, her hesitation palpable in the way her body shifts. Her eyes fix on mine again, and it looks as if she's contemplating a leap into the unknown. *Did I mistake her intentions?* No. She's kissing me back with hunger, she's soaking, and she made me fucking *beg.* The only other explanation would be her supposed fiancé, though she didn't seem that bothered about him either.

Not able to keep my dick in its confines anymore, I slightly shift Aria to the side and unbuckle my pants, sliding them down just enough to get some relief. Her wetness has traveled through the fabric of my trousers and onto my briefs. The wet spot mixes with the one created by the pre-cum gathering at my tip. I'm so hard, it's almost painful.

Aria looks down at me, her gaze full of heat as she bites on her bottom lip. But her hesitation seems to hold her in place, like an invisible force preventing her from moving. Some kind of inner conflict and indecision flicker in her eyes. Maybe there *is* a fiancé.

Placing both hands on her hips again, I slowly grind her onto my crotch some more and she lets out the smallest of mewls. I need her to stop thinking, to just give herself to me. "Do you love him?" *Why do I even care?*

Aria's posture tenses as she thinks about her answer.

"No," she replies, her tone soft. It's a confident answer, but there's something lying underneath, something that's bothering her.

A spark of curiosity hits me. "Then why are you getting married?"

I know little about Aria, other than that she's friends with Angelica, Evander's new affliction.

Her eyes fixate on me as she brings her hands to my shoulders, her fingers twitching almost imperceptibly, as if debating her next move. Her hips, still swaying against me at a delicious, steady rhythm. There's a play of emotions beneath the surface of her gaze, and I want to uncover them all.

"Why are you getting married?" I repeat, and all her emotions morph into one: anger.

"That's none of your business," she grinds out, and I raise my eyebrows, surprised at her response. Two seconds ago, she seemed worried, soft and small. Now, she's back to that feisty girl from downstairs, and I can't help but grin at her outburst.

"It's not, huh? Well, little liar, I don't think you have a fiancé."

A frown draws her brows together as she crosses her arms at her chest. "How so?"

Letting my fingers crawl up her back, I stop at the ends of her hair, playing with the silky strands. "For starters, you wouldn't be straddling my lap like a cat in heat." Aria gasps, her eyes widening in disbelief.

Suddenly, her facial expression switches into something more like shock, and she shoves my chest. I laugh.

"Second, you'd be wearing an engagement ring. I'm sure you're a woman with morals who wouldn't take it off to go clubbing with her friends," I say matter-of-factly. I might not know Aria, but from her sass and the way she was quick to say she wouldn't have sex with me, I know she has self-respect.

Aria lets out a puff of air, defeat etching across her face. *I knew it.*

Her shoulders slump. "Fine. I'm not engaged...yet."

Relief fills my chest for a moment. "So, you're dating?"

"Not exactly."

"I'm confused."

She exhales a slow, heavy breath. "It's an arranged marriage," she finally admits. There's a vulnerability in her eyes —a stark difference from the air of strength and take-no-shit attitude she's shown me. I'm guessing she's not on board.

Then, it clicks. If she's about to get married by force, she must be from an important family.

"What's your last name?"

A flicker of confusion crosses her face. "Why?"

I sigh. "Just answer the question, Aria."

"Kastellanos." My eyes widen, fists clenching. *Son of a bitch.* She's Philip Kastellanos's daughter, Peter Kouvalakis's right-hand man and partner. An enemy. The whole reason Evander is on a revenge mission and pursuing Peter's daughter, Angelica. A revenge I also want a part of. Aria shifts uncomfortably on top of me, as if wanting to get off, as if sensing my change in mood, but I don't let her. I breathe out and meet her beautiful eyes once more.

Heat comes rushing through me again. This might change things, but nothing will impede us tonight.

The family she's a part of doesn't affect how much I want her.

"You're single, then," I say, resuming the dry humping we've casually been doing for the past little while as though nothing happened. If I don't get inside her as soon as possible, I might fucking lose it.

"Yes," she breathes out, matching my movements.

"Okay. I'm single, too. We're both willing. What's the problem?"

"It's not that simple," she retorts, her breaths getting heavier by the second. "I don't just sleep around." Hmmm...*a good girl*.

"You're the relationship type." It's not a question, but she answers anyway.

"Yes. Something like that." Her voice hitches, a moan escaping her lips. From the way she's withering on top of me, I can tell she's close. I've been edging her for a while now.

"Why aren't you stopping this, then?" I ask, genuinely curious. Aria's already expressed—thrice—that she's not interested in sleeping with me, yet she's doing nothing to stop the kissing and touching.

She stares at me like I'm a puzzle she hasn't quite figured out yet. "I don't know," uncertainty coloring her tone. But I know she's too far gone to stop anything now.

I use my hands to guide her faster on my shaft, the friction causing my dick to twitch. I grunt. I'm getting close to exploding in my briefs like a fucking pubescent teen. I've experienced nothing like this before. A need so intense, I can barely contain myself.

Aria's moans become louder, her breaths shorter. Clinging onto my shoulders to find purchase, she rides me like a professional.

"Come for me, *astéri mou*," I encourage her, breathless. "I'm right there with you."

"Yes!" she cries out. "I'm so close, Dion. Fuck."

My hips buck forward as I chase the high.

And then, our orgasms take over at the same time.

She whimpers. "I'm coming."

I groan in response as my climax erupts from the base of my cock and explodes. "Ahhh," I moan, not able to stop my body from trembling.

Shit. If it's this good to come like this, I can't imagine how it'll feel being inside her. I want to explore every fucking crevice of her pussy and drown in it until I'm grasping for air.

I watch Aria as she tries to catch her breath, her face flushed, a thin layer of sweat glistening on her forehead. She's the most beautiful creature I've ever seen.

I can sense the million and one thoughts swirling in her head, and I want to wipe them away. Why do I even care if she's comfortable with me? It's not like I'm looking for anything more than a good time. I never do. But somehow, with Aria, it feels different.

Our eyes meet, and I take her lips into my mouth. The kiss is electric. Soft—urgent.

I've never been a guy who didn't allow himself to kiss women when hooking up, but those kisses were always brief, forgetful even. Now, it's as if the world has narrowed to just us in this room.

The sensation is overwhelming. I can feel the obsession with Aria already building inside me, and we've just met. This is fucking crazy.

I shake my head, trying to rid myself of these thoughts. Maybe I'm just too into the moment, caught up in the thrill of something new. *Yeah, that's it. It has to be.*

I've always been good at keeping things casual, but with Aria, I'm suddenly second-guessing myself. I can't get carried away. I've seen what happens when you let your guard down, and it's not pretty.

Our bodies press together, as if trying to bridge a gap that would always be too big, and Aria moans into my mouth. Her grip finds its way to my neck, pulling me deeper. My own hands travel up her body, to her nape—which seems to be my favorite place to hold her. When I grab Aria there, it's as if all tension eases from her body and she submits to me.

I stand up from the chair, bringing her with me to the large sofa at the other end of the room. Evander is going to be so fucking pissed that I'm doing this in his office, but I'm not wasting a second trying to convince her to leave with me. "I'm not done with you yet," I say as I place her down on the couch. Her thighs part, giving me a full view of her thong that is now a dark pink shade. It's a sight to behold.

Without hesitation, I drop to my knees in front of her. *Christé mou.* No woman has ever brought me to my fucking knees.

I take her black strappy heels off, and she watches me intently as I kiss my way up her leg, her skin erupting in goosebumps as I near her center. The smell of her arousal is igniting the most feral reaction inside of me. I *have* to taste her.

Grabbing onto her drenched thong, I lift her hips off the seat and pull it down. For a second, I see hesitation flash across her eyes once more, but she doesn't utter a word to stop me. I continue taking it off and bring the fabric to my nose. Aria lets out a low gasp.

I inhale. "You smell fucking divine, *astéri mou.* I want your scent all over me."

Stuffing the thong into my back pocket, I continue traveling up her leg, letting my nose trail a path up to her pussy, her warmth hitting me in the face. My mouth needs to be on her right now.

Spreading her wider, I dive in, taking her swollen clit into my mouth. Aria releases a rough breath and melts into the couch, tilting her head up to the ceiling. It must still be sensitive from before, but I don't give a shit. I'm going to suck, lick, and nibble on her until she becomes limp again.

With the right amount of pressure, I pull on the delicate nub, eliciting a spew of intangible words from Aria's mouth. She tastes even better than I could've imagined. I need more.

"Aria," I growl, frustrated. Not because she did anything wrong, but because I'm wondering how I'll ever want to taste anyone else. "Your pussy tastes like my saving grace, like my fucking redemption."

Aria tastes like a forbidden fruit, better than anything I've ever known. Her sweetness surpasses the purity of holy water, intoxicating and divine.

I just met this woman, and my body calls for her like a sailor beckoned by the sea's irresistible pull. *Irresistible.*

It's not about her physical beauty—her long, silky blonde hair that I want to pull like leather straps on a harness, her unique gray eyes that gleam with a soft brightness, her delectable body, a masterpiece of delicate curves I want to explore with my hands and mouth.

It's her tempting charm, her energy, and her authenticity.

As soon as I saw her in the club, I *felt* her presence, like an aura that enveloped me. Her smile was a magnetic force that drew me in without effort. Aria is unapologetically herself and that's what sets her apart.

How can she have such a pull on me already? Fuck.

I continue to feast on her pussy like it's the first time I've tasted such a delicacy, and it drips all over my mouth and chin. "Good girls like you don't make big messes like this, little liar," I say as I lick up her sweetness.

Aria begins thrusting her hips to find my tongue. "More, please," she whines, and at this moment, I know that I could never say no to this girl.

I dive back into her wet cunt and shove my tongue into her entrance. Aria's entire body jerks at the intrusion, and I move in and out of her as if it were my dick pounding her into oblivion. In response, my cock springs to attention. I grab onto the hardened length, stroking it with vigor.

Taking some of her arousal into my mouth, I spit it into my palm and grab onto the base of my shaft. I rub it up and down as I mimic the movements of my tongue on her pussy.

I revel in the idea of her coming on my face.

Using my free hand, I put a finger inside her, as deep as it could go, and her walls immediately clench around it. "Holy fuck, Aria. Just one finger and you're swallowing me whole."

Letting my digit explore, I make beckoning movements, hooking it up to find her G-spot.

"Oh, God. Dion, that feels so good. Please, don't stop," Aria moans, arching her back into the couch, while I pick up speed.

"Your wish is my command, *astéri mou.*"

Squeezing a second finger inside, I continue hitting her G-spot with a hard and steady pace and suck on her clit until she stills, her climax taking her hostage. "Give it to me, baby. Let it go."

She screams as a jet of wetness squirts past my fingers and into my mouth, her entire body convulsing. *Holy fuck.* I let go of my cock, not wanting to come just yet.

Next time I do, it will be inside her.

She rides out the rest of her orgasm, letting out the most delectable mewls known to humanity. Fuck, I'm done for.

I'm an addict and I'll never come back from this.

4

ARIA

After my second, mind-blowing orgasm, we decide it's finally time to leave Academia.

Dion offers to drive me home, almost having a nervous breakdown when I suggest I find my own ride.

The club is empty, except for two men Dion introduces as Leon and Elias.

Leon is smoking a cigarette while Elias counts the money that was made tonight. They offer me similar smirks and I feel my cheeks heat. Obviously, they know what we were up to.

I awkwardly stay one step behind Dion.

He doesn't seem uncomfortable in front of the other men. Of course, this is probably not the first time he's brought a woman upstairs. The thought causes a flutter of disappointment in my chest.

Dion took care of me, made me come more than once. But I'm not special. I'm just a notch on his belt.

The men exchange a few words while I wait. Then, Dion joins me, putting his hand on my back to lead me outside.

When we step out, I walk behind Dion while he chatters about something, but my attention is elsewhere. There's an uneasy prickling at the back of my neck, a sense that someone's eyes are on me. I glance over my shoulder, scanning the shadows in the parking lot. Nothing. Just the dim glow of the streetlights casting creepy shadows.

I shake my head, trying to dismiss the feeling. It's probably just the aftereffects of the adrenaline, and the dark, empty spaces around us are playing tricks on my mind.

I realize I haven't checked my phone in hours, so I pull it out of my purse to see the time while hopping into the passenger seat. Three o'clock in the morning.

There's a message from my brother, Dimitri.

> Dimo: Mama asked about you. Told her you were at Angie's.

Gamoto. I won't be able to go home.

Dion notices the change in my expression. "What's wrong?"

"It's very late."

He snickers. "Is your *fiancé* going to be mad?"

I scowl at him. "Shut up. It's my parents. They'll ask questions."

My parents don't usually keep up with my whereabouts, but now that I'm getting engaged, they've been insisting on how important it is to *preserve* my reputation. I stop myself from rolling my eyes. Staying out until dawn won't make me look good in the eyes of our community. And in Cebrene, nothing stays unnoticed. I'll try messaging Angie. Maybe Evan took her home and she's still awake—

"Stay at mine, then," Dion says casually, as if it's no big deal.

I whip my head around, squinting at him. "At yours? Haven't you had enough?"

It was meant as a joke, but Dion gives me a piercing look. "It'll never be enough, Aria. However, I'm not asking you over for sex—unless you want to," he says with a wink.

I scoff, trying to hide the heat traveling up my body at the idea of continuing what we started. "Unbelievable! Now, I regret letting you touch me."

"That's not how you felt when you were calling out to God, little liar."

I release an incredulous breath and smack his shoulder. As much as I want to kick his ass, it might be a good idea to go to his place instead. I'll keep up with Dimitri's lie and tell my parents that I stayed over at Angelica's. Besides, I'm not even sure if she's still busy with Evander, and I don't want to risk bothering them.

I make a show of exhaling dramatically. "Fine." Dion smirks and turns on the engine.

I type out a quick reply to my brother.

Me: I owe you one.

With a wide smile on his face, Dion backs out of the parking lot.

The feeling of unease creeps back in, and I glance out the window, scanning our surroundings. Dion shoots me a curious look but keeps driving.

There's nothing there—just an empty lot.

I tell myself it's all in my head, but my skin still crawls as I settle into the passenger seat.

On the drive to Dion's place, I shoot a text to Angelica to tell her I'm going home. I don't want her to worry that I'm with a stranger, and I'd rather not be interrogated about this.

I slip my phone into my purse as we glide down a tree-lined street in a quaint neighborhood.

"We're almost there," Dion says, breaking the silence.

A short while later, he pulls up to a gate. My eyes settle on the house. Its charming exterior exudes warmth and character. It's still dark, so I can't see much, but I notice a large entrance and a neatly trimmed lawn with colorful blooms. Instantly, a wave of happiness washes over me. Flowers are my love language.

Dion notices my smile. "What is it?"

"Huh?" I turn to him. "Oh, nothing. I just saw your flowers."

"Do you like them?"

I nod. "I've always loved flowers."

He cracks a smile. "Tell me more."

I hesitate. Do I really want to share something so personal? But when I look at him, an unexpected feeling of comfort fills me. I take a deep breath and start to speak, my voice growing more confident with each word.

"Well, it started when I was just a little girl. My housekeeper, Magdalena, used to take care of me most days. We'd spend hours in the yard, and she'd teach me about different plants and how to care for them," I explain, grinning at the fond memories. I didn't spend much time with my parents, but Magda made up for it by giving me my love for flowers.

"It became my sanctuary, a place where I felt calm and purposeful, especially when my parents were too preoccupied elsewhere. Seeing the results of my care and effort reminded me that I had the power to create beauty."

I sigh in contentment, looking outside again.

"It's been one of the few constants in my life."

Dion lights up at my words as if I've just spoken the gospel. "Is that something that you'd like to do on a more professional level?" *Was he actually listening to me?* Other guys zone out when I talk about my passion.

"I've always dreamed of owning a flower shop," I begin, my fingers finding the hem of my skirt. "A place where I could design arrangements all day, putting smiles on people's faces. My way of sharing love with the world."

Dion glances over at me, his eyebrow raised in curiosity. "Do you have a place where you work on your arrangements now?"

I nod, a small smile tugging at my lips. "I do. I turned our guest house into a makeshift studio. It's like my own little paradise."

"So why not make that dream a reality? Why not open your own shop?"

I let out a sigh, my smile fading. "You know that women in our world don't really get to have *careers*. It's always about what's safe and manning the household. My family says it's too dangerous for us to lead lives of our own."

Dion shakes his head. "But what if your future husband—hypothetically—was supportive? What if he encouraged you to follow your dreams?"

I stiffen at the reminder of my upcoming engagement. "That would be a miracle."

"Well, you never know," he says. "How about you make some arrangements using my flowers? I could use a professional opinion on my gardening skills. You can tell me if I've done a good job." He winks.

"You planted those?" I ask, surprised.

"Yup."

I giggle. "I'm sorry. The idea of you in messy clothes, knees deep in dirt, doesn't sound right."

"Don't underestimate me. I'm like a Kinder Surprise," he jokes, waggling his eyebrows.

I laugh, the tension easing from my shoulders. "Alright, but don't blame me if I'm brutally honest. Gardening isn't as easy as it looks."

Dion grins, parking his car in the driveway and coming around to open my door. He extends his hand to help me out, and I take it, a sudden jolt of sensation catching me off guard. My skin tingles. I pull away, as if his touch just burnt me. I remind myself why I can't let this happen. My engagement to another man looms in the back of my mind. Even though I have no attachment to my future fiancé, I have to respect our union and my father's wishes.

Dion doesn't flinch at my reaction.

He slips his hands in his pockets. "You ready?"

I give him a small smile as we head toward the house.

Once at the front door, Dion unlocks it and steps back, letting me in first. I find myself in a large and warm foyer.

I slip off my heels, leaving them on the front mat, and walk further into the house. The place is full of windows; the moon casting a gentle glow over the living room where a plush sofa and a couple of well-worn armchairs are arranged around a coffee table stacked with magazines and books. I let my hands graze the fabric as I continue my path.

So far, this place looks lived in and cozy. Somewhere I wouldn't mind spending more time.

No, Aria. This ends tonight.

Dion silently follows a few feet behind, and I don't even feel awkward about snooping around. But it's impossible to ignore his presence. The air seems to heat at his proximity.

I pass a big fireplace, its mantle decorated with photos and knickknacks.

There's a frame with a picture of a young boy and who I assume are his *mama* and *baba*. I pick it up, Dion stopping right at my back.

"My parents," he says, his voice expressionless. "That was the last photo we took together."

I trace their faces with my fingertips. "Your *mama* was beautiful," I say softly, my voice tinged with sadness for him.

"They used to be my everything."

I glance up at him, surprised to hear him open up like this about a clearly sensitive topic. His gaze lingers on the image, something heartbreaking passing over his face. I just want to hold that little boy in my arms and tell him that everything is going to be okay.

"What happened? If you don't mind me asking."

Dion nods, not taking his eyes off the picture, his jaw tensing slightly. "My father was killed in a drive-by. And my mother was so heartbroken, she took her own life a few weeks later."

"Oh my God, Dion. I'm so sorry." My heart breaks in tiny pieces for him. I can't imagine what it must have been like to lose one's parents in such a tragic way. I might not always see eye to eye with my family, but I love them and would be broken if they left me.

"It's been many years." He shrugs, glancing over at me. "I've gotten used to the gap they left, and I've learned to navigate life without them."

"You must miss them," I add, solemnly.

He stares back at the photo for a few moments, not saying anything.

"I had just turned five," he begins, a slight smile forming on his lips. "Back then, I was obsessed with carnivals. I thought they were the most magical places in the world. So, for my birthday, my parents decided to surprise me and took me to a fair right outside the city."

His eyes drift off, as if he's looking through the years, back to that day. "I had no idea where we were going. But I remember how excited they were in the front seat, whispering and smiling, glancing back at me with these big, expectant grins. It was like they were kids too, sharing this secret joy."

Dion chuckles, his shoulders relaxing. "When we finally arrived, I think my eyes almost popped out of my sockets. It was the happiest moment of my life. We did all the rides, played all the games, and ate so much carnival food, I almost got sick. But I didn't care. I was just *so* happy."

He gently traces the edge of the frame with his finger, his brow furrowing. "This picture was taken at a photo booth. I remember squishing into the tiny space, my parents on either side of me, all of us laughing so hard."

Dion's voice falters, and he clears his throat, smoothing out his expression. I reach over and squeeze his hand.

"I wish I had thanked them more," he continues. "I wish I had told them how much I loved them. Because that night was the last time we were all together."

He looks at me, his eyes filled with a mixture of pain and gratitude, his hand trembling slightly. "I just hope they knew how much they meant to me."

I nod, feeling a lump in my throat. "I'm sure they did."

For a moment, Dion remains lost in the memory. Then, as if snapping out of a trance, he inhales sharply and stands up straighter. His expression hardens, all traces of emotion washed away. He carefully plucks the frame from my hands and puts it back on the mantle. "Anyway," he says, his voice firmer. "That's all in the past. No use dwelling on it, right?"

I watch as he composes himself, the vulnerable boy from his story replaced by the strong, guarded man I've just met. "Right. Well, you're so strong for going through that, Dion. Look at how far you've come. I'm sure they would be proud," I assure him.

"Actually, I think my father is rolling in his grave. He always said he wanted me to do better than him and not end up following his path. He worked for one of the families here in Cebrene. Ironically, his death pushed me even deeper into this world. I guess the apple doesn't fall far from the tree," he murmurs.

Dion turns to look at me and smiles. "But perhaps they're still watching over me." A pause. "I think they might have sent you as my shining star."

My cheeks warm as his words catch me off guard, at the intensity in his eyes. My gaze flickers away, and I fumble for a response that doesn't come.

Dion pinches my chin between his fingers to bring my face back to him. "Hey. You don't have to say anything, *astéri mou*. Let's keep touring."

I nod, relieved, and smile softly.

We continue moving through the house, our hands joined. We step into the kitchen—a cheerful room with vintage decor. The cabinets are the most beautiful shade of blue; the countertops adorned with jars of spices and fruits. A small dining table in a nook overlooks the backyard.

This is not what I expected from Dion.

I halt my steps and his body presses against mine, my frame molding effortlessly into his. I take in a sharp breath when he buries his face in my neck, goosebumps erupting over my skin.

"Not what you thought, huh?" he asks.

There's anticipation in the air, drawing me in, making me hyper-aware of every breath, every heartbeat as if we're connected by an invisible thread.

"Not at all," I breathe out.

He chuckles softly and slips my purse off my shoulder.

Suddenly, the tension between us becomes suffocating, wrapping around me like a tight coil. The pull he has on me is too much, and I need some space.

Without excusing myself, I run out of the kitchen, looking for an exit.

My chest constricts, as if I'm drowning in feelings I can't quite understand.

Stepping outside, I inhale the cool air, but it does little to calm the storm raging inside me.

What the hell am I doing?

Was I too impulsive? Did I even think this through? A rush of emotions floods over me. Confusion, disbelief—maybe regret.

My night took a turn I hadn't expected and the weight of what's happened is suddenly too heavy.

Closing my eyes, I try to slow my racing heart. I feel like I'm losing control.

Dion steps outside moments later. "Aria, are you okay?"

I look at him—his intense eyes, his disarming smile.

My head shakes as tears prickle my eyes. I take deeper breaths, but nothing helps.

Dion wraps his arms around me, creating a cocoon, a safety net, and I sob into his chest. I cry in his arms for what feels like ages, then pull away, sniffing.

"God, I must look like a mess. You probably think I'm crazy."

"Not at all." His voice is soft, concerned. "Come, sit," he instructs, leading me to a sofa on the back porch. I sit and curl into myself.

He takes off his suit jacket and covers my shoulders, but not before taking a silver case out of the inside pocket.

"Thank you," I murmur.

"Talk to me." Dion opens the container and pulls out a cigarette, offering one to me. I take it. I'm not a smoker, but I need to shed some stress.

As I bring the stick to my lips, I'm hit with a dose of reality again, like a cruel joke played by fate.

"I'm getting married to a man I don't even know."

Dion lets out a heady sigh and moves closer to light up my cigarette. The tip catches, and I draw in a deep inhale, choking on the smoke as it fills my lungs.

As I exhale slowly, I feel some of the tension ebb away, carried off into the air. A brief escape from the pressure and worry that cling to me.

"Is it a sure thing?" Dion asks, taking a puff of his cigarette. "This wedding?" Though his tone is emotionless, there's something unreadable in his expression, something I can't quite grasp.

I look away and take another drag. "Knowing my father, yes. Unless this other guy refuses, I'm screwed."

"What's in it for him?"

"I don't know. I'm not privy to those conversations, which is ironic given it's *my* life they're messing with."

The burn at the end of the cigarette reminds me to stay present. With each puff, I gain a bit of control over my emotions.

"Have you told Philip that you don't want to get married?" Dion asks.

Philip. He knows my father by name. "Are you acquainted with my *baba*?"

"Somewhat," he replies, not offering any more information. But I don't even care right now.

I finish the cigarette, and Dion takes it from me, crushing it into an ashtray on the ground next to him. "Do you feel any better?"

"A little. I mean, the incessant chatter in my head is quieter now."

"Good."

Silence falls between us for a while. It isn't awkward or uncomfortable, and I don't feel the need to fill it. I wrap Dion's jacket further around me, basking in its scent and warmth.

"Do you know why I call you 'my star'?" he asks suddenly. I shake my head. "From what I've seen, you have a fire in you. Like a star, you carry a light so fucking bright, no one can extinguish it. When I first saw you, it was hard for me to look away." My heart flutters in my chest at his words.

He meets my gaze. "Look, I don't know what you're going through—because let's face it, women have it worse than men in mob families—but never allow others to dim your light."

Dion's words are unexpected, but so genuine.

This man barely knows me and can already touch parts of

my soul I didn't even realize were there, waiting to be acknowledged.

"Thank you for saying that," I say, my eyes welling with tears again. I need to stop getting emotional in front of him. He must think I'm a lunatic.

His gaze homes in on me. "I can't resist putting a smile on my girl's face."

My girl?

I let out a scoff. "I'm not *your* girl."

"Slip up." Dion waves me off, clearing his throat.

I narrow my eyes. "Maybe *one* of your girls, but I'm sure not *your* girl."

"What do you mean by that?"

"You look like the type to have a roster."

It's Dion's turn to scoff. "I beg to differ. I don't have a roster."

"But you don't do relationships either, so…"

"Look, Aria. I'm not the type to play with your feelings. I say it like it is."

"So, what is *this*?" I retort, gesturing between us.

"This is me wanting to spend the rest of the night appreciating you—" Dion gets off his seat and moves closer. My head lifts to meet his gaze. "And your body," he adds, his eyes ablaze, the flame now traveling down my spine, heating me up inside and out.

Dion brings his hand to my legs and parts my knees, exposing my bare pussy. I shiver as the cool air hits me. His fingers start rubbing my clit, and I suck in a breath.

"We shouldn't do this, Dion."

"Tell me to stop then," he replies, teasing my entrance.

But I don't.

Instead, as our eyes meet, I give him a silent nod—a small, reassuring sign to take whatever he wants.

5

DION

The urge to shove my dick so far inside Aria is almost uncontrollable.

Seeing her so vulnerable and sad, her eyes red and swollen from crying, makes my heart ache as much as it turns me on.

There's something about her tears that urges me to lick them off her skin, to touch her and make her feel good. I still crave her—the taste I had at the club wasn't enough to quench my thirst. I need to *feel* Aria around my cock.

Gently, I press two digits inside her pussy, feeling the warmth of her around my fingers. She looks up at me, her eyes full of lust. And a hint of uncertainty again.

Without saying a word, I shift, laying her down on the outdoor couch. As I do, her soft breaths against my neck send shivers down my spine. My desire for her grows stronger with each passing second.

I lean down, pressing a kiss to her forehead. Her lips part slightly, the hint of a smile forming. Tears glisten in her eyes, then flow down her cheeks.

I brush a tear from her cheek, sucking the saltiness off my

57

thumb. "Aria," I whisper, my voice husky. "I can't stand seeing you like this."

She doesn't respond, just leans into me, seeking my comfort. I brush my fingers through her hair, watching as her eyes flutter closed. I hook my hand in an upward motion inside her warm heat and speed up. Aria's back arches, and I revel in the different sounds she makes as I explore each crevice of her pussy. My touch is gentle, but the need within me is fierce.

"Let me take care of you," I murmur, my other hand trailing down her chest. "I want to make everything better."

Aria's body relaxes under my touch, her walls beginning to clench around my fingers. I need more of her, to explore every inch of her being. The reason behind this intense desire is still unknown to me, but I can't seem to control it.

I'm going to embrace tonight and not let myself overthink it.

Come morning, everything will be back to normal, and I'll never see Aria again. I ignore the tightening in my chest at the thought.

I slip my hand under her dress, feeling the smoothness of her skin. Her breath hitches, and she opens her eyes to look at me. I lean in, capturing her lips with mine, tasting the salt of her tears. Fuck. My dick stiffens within an instant.

As our kiss deepens, I can feel her body responding. My heart races, blood pounding in my ears. I pull back slightly.

"I want you, Aria," I say against her mouth, my voice barely a whisper.

A small smile plays on her lips. "Then take me."

With those words, I know that nothing will stop me from erasing every trace of sadness and worry from her face, replacing it with nothing but pleasure and happiness. Wanting to make her forget about the arranged marriage her shitty father is forcing her into.

I reach for my belt, unbuckling it with a sense of urgency,

and slide my pants down my thighs. I position myself on top of her, letting my hard cock slide over her glistening mound.

"Put it in. Put it in, right now," I groan with urgency. Aria grabs the head and levels it at her entrance. "That's my good girl. Now, look at me while I push inside you."

I'm met with resistance. "Goddamn, you're tight," I grunt, the overwhelming sensation sending sparks of pleasure down my spine. Her cunt is clinging to the tip of my cock.

Aria winces as she struggles to take me in.

I've been with many women before, but it's never felt like this. So snug, almost impenetrable.

Her pussy has a firm grip on my cock, and I'm not sure how long I'll last.

"Relax, baby. You're doing a good job."

Lifting her top to expose her breasts, I grab them in my large hands. "Your tits are perfect," I say, squeezing them. I lower myself and take one into my mouth, sucking her nipple and swirling my tongue over the pebbled bud, and her back lifts off the couch. She moans, her body slackening under me, allowing me to slip further inside. "That's it, *moró*. Open up for me."

Slowly, I inch my way in, and when I'm almost buried to the hilt, I slam my hips the rest of the way. She lets out a yelp. "Oh my God!"

I hiss at the feel of her tight walls clenching around my dick, watching her closely as I pull out. Body tense, she relaxes when I stop moving. Each of her labored breaths seems to carry a mixture of discomfort and pleasure.

"Are you okay?" I ask, getting concerned.

Aria nods. "I just feel so full. You're so big," she murmurs, her tone laced with lust.

"You can take it, *astéri mou*."

I continue to inch out, and Aria's face contorts into an

expression that is both strained and blissful. I pause. "Are you sure you're good?" Now, I'm wondering if she's in actual pain.

She reassures me with a smile, and that gives me the go-ahead to continue.

Pulling out fully, I plow into Aria with force, and she screams.

Something's not right. "Do you need me to stop?" I want this to be pleasurable for her. I'm all about getting mine, but I need her to come too. I won't be able to enjoy it if she's wincing every time I pull in and out. "I know I'm big, but it shouldn't hurt. You're soaking wet," I add, breathless.

A crease forms in her brow and her eyes flit around, as if searching for the right words. I can almost see the gears turning in her head. She slightly shifts her body under me, my cock still hard as a rod inside her, and I struggle not to make a move. I'm so close to having her, so close to feeling her pussy pulse around me. This is torture.

When I look down at where we're joined, I notice some red staining my skin. Is that... *blood*? My mind races with questions, wondering if I've been too rough or if there's an underlying issue. I've never made a woman bleed. Not *un*intentionally, at least... "Aria, I'm fucking *hurting* you." My voice is urgent. I pull back, searching her face.

I wait patiently for her response, meeting her gaze. For some unknown reason, I want Aria to feel comfortable and safe around me. "No, I'm fine. I promise," she looks away. "It's just that...I'm a virgin."

6

ARIA

Y ou're what?" Dion whisper-shouts.

He is frozen in place, eyes wide and unblinking, seemingly caught in a state of utter shock and confusion.

I had a feeling he wouldn't take this news well. I don't know why I didn't tell him I was a virgin from the beginning. I'm not ashamed. I've purposely never slept with anyone—I wanted to give my virginity to the man I'd fall in love with and marry.

I've always believed in love stories. To me, they're like whispered promises in a world that sometimes feels too chaotic. And God knows, being the daughter of an important figure in the mob is no easy feat. I needed something to cling to.

I know that love isn't always perfect, but my mother told me it was worth fighting for. So, I grew up thinking I'd find my own happily ever-after. That I would find a man to love me, cherish me, and who'd want to spend the rest of his life by my side.

That's until my dreams got shattered by my father.

Playing with the ends of my hair, I meet Dion's gaze. "I'm a virgin," I repeat.

"What the fuck, Aria? Couldn't you have said so before I stuck my dick inside you? No wonder you're so goddamn tight," he argues, though it's not anger lacing his tone but apprehension. "I don't want to hurt you."

My heart flutters, his concern catching me off guard. No one takes the time to ask about my well-being anymore. Dion cares enough to worry about me, which reaffirms that I made the right decision.

"I didn't know how to tell you," I say, honestly.

Dion scoffs, voice rising. "Why the fuck would you let me do this, Aria?"

"Don't yell at me," I snap, but I can't hide the hint of hurt in my tone.

He runs a hand through his short, brown hair. "*Gamoto, Signómi*. I just can't believe you'd let me take your virginity," he says, as if it's a terrible thing, and my vulnerability makes way to anger.

"Is the thought of fucking a virgin that bad?" I spit. "Would you have said no if I told you?"

"That's what you took from what I said?" A wave of hysterical laughter overtakes him, his eyes wide with disbelief. "Come on, Aria. We could've at least had a conversation about it."

"I didn't want to talk about it, Dion. It's my decision." *How dare he...*

He braces his arms on each side of my body and leans down, a menacing look on his face. "No, little liar. It's *our* decision. As much as I fucking *love* the idea of taking your virginity, it would've been fair for me to have known at least."

"What about *my* virginity makes it *our* decision, Dion?" I grit out. "My body, my choice."

"It's not about that, Aria. Fuck, take a second to understand. I don't want you to *regret* this," he says, sounding exasperated. I pause. Something about his demeanor strikes me as sincere.

He looks into my eyes, and I hold his steady gaze. It's devoid of any pretense.

Everything with Dion feels real and unfiltered, and it scares the shit out of me.

As I observe him, still lying underneath him, practically naked, I feel nothing close to uncomfortable. Through this whole conversation, Dion hasn't pulled out, his dick still hard. It's *throbbing* inside me, and I've never wanted someone to fuck me so badly.

Dion is still wearing his suit, the top of his shirt unbuttoned, showing a hint of his broad chest. A lock of hair falls across his forehead, and I can't help but imagine gripping onto it with my fingers and he drives into me.

My breath catches as I take in the sight of him.

I never knew having sex could be like this and we haven't even *had* sex.

I wiggle my body under him, and a moan slips out of my mouth. I close my eyes.

"Aria," Dion scolds. "Stop moving."

"Or what?" I taunt. "You're going to fuck me? That's what I want." I bite my bottom lip. I realize having sex with a stranger isn't the wisest choice, but there's something about Dion I can't shake. An inexplicable tug at my heart.

You're getting engaged, I remind myself. Any notion I had that any of *this* could become something disappears, dissolving into nothing. But I won't let it deter me from the moment.

Dion growls, the sound going straight to my center.

"Please," I beg, shifting my body under him once more.

His resolve breaks, and he starts to move. "We're going to talk about this when we're done, Aria. But I can't stand being inside you without fucking you for another second."

I nod, tingles exploding over my entire body. Dion pulls his dick out slowly and shoves it back in enough times for my pussy to lubricate again. "Fuck, Aria. *My* good girl. Your virgin pussy was made for me." He circles my clit with his thumb, making me squirm. Once his movements become smoother, he begins fucking me at a hard and steady pace.

The feeling is all-consuming, the pain gone.

"How are you doing, baby?" Dion murmurs while pounding into me, his voice strained with pleasure.

"Good. *So good*," I gasp. And it's the truth. Every ridge of his cock against my walls. Every thrust sends a current of electricity through my nerves. It's euphoric.

"Your pussy is sobbing all over my cock, Aria. Fuck."

When he first slid in, I admit it was painful. I almost felt myself rip. But now—I never want it to end.

"Oh—" The words get stuck in my throat when Dion pulls back, plunging back in with the force of a hurricane, stealing the air from my lungs.

"You're taking me so well, *astéri mou*," he grinds out, his words only intensifying this incredible feeling of ecstasy. The sound of my arousal between our bodies echoes through the space. "Do you hear that, baby? You're so fucking wet for me."

Is this what it's like to have sex? What I've been missing out on all this time? No. This is what it's like to have sex with *Dion*.

It's not just the sex, but the person I'm having sex *with*. The way he pays attention to my every move, every sound, every reaction, careful not to hurt me.

I've had my fair share of experiences with guys, but none of them ever went all the way. Nothing ever came close to what I'm experiencing now.

Fuck waiting for the right man. I wasn't going to let my future husband, a man I don't even know, have something so sacred.

It was the last thing I had ownership of. The only thing left I could control. And no one could take that away from me.

Dion fucks me like it's our first and last time, and a pang of sadness hits me when I realize it will be. I will soon be engaged and won't be able to do this again. The thought makes me want to cry. *Dramatic*, I know. But now that I've gotten a taste of Dion, I'm utterly ruined for anyone else.

Sensing my head is elsewhere, Dion grabs my chin and directs my gaze back to him. "Come on, baby. Focus on me."

His emerald-green eyes are scorching with heat, burning like embers in a fire, drawing me in.

He lifts my hips, putting me at a different angle, and thrusts hard, hitting me at a sensitive spot. "Oh, God. Do that again," I moan, the sound desperate.

"You like that, *moró*? I just found your G-spot."

He rams into me again, and my lids shut tight. When I look back at Dion, he's sporting a huge grin. *Smug asshole.*

I roll my eyes.

"What did I tell you earlier, little liar? Roll your eyes at me again, and I'll give you a reason to," he reminds me, and then pulls out all the way, leaving me feeling empty.

"No!" I protest.

Dion grabs me by the waist and flips me onto my knees to face the back of the couch.

Then, I hear his belt slipping out of the loops.

Before I'm able to ask what he's doing, he wraps the leather strap around my neck and fastens the belt buckle. When he squeezes it tight, my eyes grow wide. I try to take a full inhale, but my breath is stunted, my throat constricting.

I grab onto the belt, attempting to loosen it. Dion pulls on it hard and my body almost flies back. I can barely breathe, eyes watering, but my blood has completely rushed to my core.

"Now, the only reason your eyes will roll back is because of the way I'm fucking you unconscious, little liar," Dion says, his voice low and full of lust.

"Hold on to the headrest. You're gonna need it," he adds, before spreading my ass cheeks open and spitting onto me. He puts his thumb right at the entrance of my asshole, the feeling causing me to jolt forward. "One day, I'm going to claim you in each of your holes and make you mine, Aria Kastellanos."

At this moment, I'm glad he can't see my face. He knows I'm getting engaged and that nothing can happen after this, and yet he's still making ridiculous promises.

This is one night, and one night only. That's all it can be.

I jerk forward when Dion mercilessly drives into me, his thrusts drawing out cries, as he tugs on the belt strap at the same time. Each pull takes more and more air from my lungs.

I begin to panic, every breath becoming painful as I desperately crave oxygen.

Just as my vision starts swimming, Dion snaps me back to consciousness by releasing some pressure from my throat.

"I told you." He slaps my ass, and I let out a choked yelp. "Not to." Another slap. "Roll." *Slap.* "Your eyes." *Slap.* "At me." *Slap.*

"Ah, fuck!" I shout, a burning sensation spreading across my ass cheek. My skin is pulsing. *He's fucking* spanking *me.*

Dion lets out a wicked chuckle as he rubs the sensitive flesh with his palm. "Don't cross me, Aria. Take this as a reminder to never roll your eyes at me, unless you want to get punished."

No one has ever treated me like this before and the mixed emotions dancing within me are leaving me confused. *Do I like it?*

I'm unexpectedly even more turned on than I was, as if the lack of air and slaps have awakened something in me. The line between pain and pleasure blurred as Dion hit and choked me, sending adrenaline through me and heightening my senses.

He continues to fuck me, and I feel my climax budding to the surface.

All the while, the pressure on my neck continues to vacuum air from my lungs. White spots start floating in my vision. I can barely keep my eyes open anymore.

Dion brings his face close to my ear, his hot breath on my

skin. "You're almost there, baby. Stay with me. Who's my good girl?"

"Fuck—" I croak, and he doesn't let up.

"Say it. Who's my good fucking girl, Aria?"

"M-me. I am," I manage to mutter.

"That's right. And good girls get to come. Come all over my cock like my perfect little slut."

As if on command, I let go.

My orgasm ripples through me, and it's an out-of-body experience. Waves of pleasure wash over me, and Dion rides them out with me, blurting out a string of curse words as his orgasm tears through him. Every sensation is amplified beyond anything I've ever experienced.

Dion quickly loosens the belt around my neck and rubs at my sore skin. His touch is warm. "You did so well. So good," he praises.

He turns me around, pulls me in for a kiss, and it's charged with a new intensity. *We just had sex. I'm no longer a virgin. Holy shit.*

The thoughts disappear when my body surrenders to his embrace. Our kiss is more than just the meeting of our lips. Right now, nothing else matters. I might never get to experience Dion again, but I'll bask in the moment for as long as I can.

When we finally pull apart, I feel intoxicated.

Dion jumps up, then walks inside the house.

He reemerges with two wet towels and places one of them on my neck, the cold feeling good on my sore skin. "Keep that there," he instructs as he uses the second cloth to wipe between my legs.

I lean all the way back and stare at the starry sky, suddenly too embarrassed to look him in the face. Heat rises to my cheeks. I've never been this tended to, and it makes me feel as happy as it makes me feel nervous.

"Don't be shy, baby. This is part of the package," Dion says with a grin and *a lot* of satisfaction in his eyes.

I groan but can't contain my smile. "Okay."

Even though whatever this is with Dion is temporary and can't go past tonight, I can truly say that I have no regrets.

Dion lifts his head from where he's cleaning me up, his tousled hair making him look as edible as ever. "Shall we do that again?"

DION

I'm *so* fucked.

ARIA

My eyelids flutter open to soft morning light filtering through the curtains. As I stretch out beneath the covers—my body a little sore and an unfamiliar ache in between my legs—I remember that I'm in Dion's guest room.

With a yawn, I swing my legs over the bed and pad over to the window. Peeking through the blinds, I see a quaint garden bathed in early sunlight. Birds chirp in the distance, and a gentle breeze rustles the leaves of a nearby tree. *Did I wake up in a fucking fairytale?* Everything about this house is so charming, it makes me want to gag rainbows. *I love it.*

The events of last night trickle back into my mind.

After our heartfelt moment—and the sex—Dion and I stayed up late chatting in his kitchen.

When it was time to finally go to bed, he offered to give me a change of clothes: one of his oversized t-shirts which I'm still wearing now. I laughed when he first gave it to me, because it has the face of Post Malone smoking a cigarette printed on it.

"I didn't expect you to be a Posty fan," I say, staring down at the tee.

He shrugs. "I'm full of surprises, especially when it comes to the range in my taste of music."

"Is that so? Give me an example," I taunt.

"Well, it goes from classical Chopin to Papa Roach."

My eyes widen. "Papa Roach?"

A chuckle escapes his lips, and I can't help but smile back, cheeks heating. The sound of his laughter is infectious. He's cute as hell.

"Yes. Are you not a fan?" he asks, his eyes sparkling in amusement.

"Our taste in music might be the only thing we have in common," I joke, and at that moment, I am reminded of the effortless connection we seem to be forming.

Again, he lets out an unrestrained chuckle.

I can't stop staring at him. Despite the warmth I feel from his cheerfulness, I can't allow myself to fully embrace it. I ignore the fluttering in my chest and close myself off.

"Well, thank you for the shirt. I should get to bed," I say, awkwardly shifting on my feet.

He gives me a small bow. "Goodnight, Aria."

"Goodnight, Dion."

I'm glad he had the decency not to suggest sleeping in the same room or having sex again. Not sure I would've said no.

I step into the adjoining bathroom and catch sight of my reflection in the mirror. "Oh, my God." I look terrible: makeup smudged; skin blotchy. I can't go out there like this.

Scrambling for anything to clean my face with, I'm happy to find a container of wipes in the bottom cabinet. There's a whole basket of bathroom essentials and skincare. *Thank God.*

I wipe the makeup off my face, then cleanse it with some face wash.

Feeling like myself again, I turn around to get a good look at the bathroom.

It's huge, with a massive walk-in shower and a big whirlpool tub to the left.

I should probably take a quick shower to wash off the remnants of last night. Maybe it'll help distract me from the flashbacks I've been getting of Dion's face between my legs since I woke up.

My body feels different. I can still remember the nervous excitement that hung in the air as we explored each other for the first time.

The moment was filled with uncertainty, on my part, but I was determined to see it through. I couldn't ignore the undeniable need to let Dion inside me. I felt raw, exposed, vulnerable—yet exhilarated.

He didn't ask about birth control, and I didn't even care to ask him about protection.

In that moment, nothing else mattered. We blindly trusted each other.

I touch the skin at my neck, thinking back to how it felt to be choked by him.

Come all over my cock like my perfect little slut.

The memory of his filthy words and the *spankings* sends a pang of arousal down to the pit of my stomach. *Am I always going to be this horny now that I've had sex?*

Deciding it's best to rinse off, I look for a towel, finding a collection of them in a side closet sitting on warmers.

I'm used to luxury, given I live in a mansion with way too many rooms and amenities, but being in Dion's cozy and charming house is different.

I grab a large bath towel and strip out of his shirt. Bringing it to my nose, I inhale, smelling a mixture of my perfume and his scent. Gosh, I'm being such a creep.

Stepping under the hot water, I grab a bottle of body wash and squeeze some onto a brand-new loofa. Rubbing the soap on my skin, I'm once again assaulted by memories of Dion's hands traveling all over my curves.

He could be right next door, and I'm thinking of him doing the dirtiest things to me. I should feel ashamed.

When I'm done soaping up my body, I grab the shower head and rinse.

The hot jet lingers a second too long on my breasts, causing my nipples to harden. Immediately, a tingle starts at my center. The more I let the water hit my nipples, the more the ache between my legs grows.

What if I just...? No. He could hear me, and that would be mortifying. Dion is a stranger, and I wouldn't want him to know that I'm touching myself in his house.

*But I could make it quick...*no. It's not a good idea.

I huff. Ignoring the two arguing sides of my brain, I bring the shower head to my mound, right over my clit, and a jolt of pleasure shoots up my spine. I close my eyes.

Fuck it. It'll only take a minute.

I'm so turned on; it won't take long before I come.

My head springs back, a throaty moan escaping my lips. My eyes fling open. *Oh my God.* Was that loud? Fuck.

I stop moving for a few seconds. I didn't lock any of the doors, so Dion could barge in here at any moment. Not that he should. That would be a major invasion of privacy.

Hearing nothing, I continue to assault my clit with the water, small moans passing my lips. I can't help it.

Just as I thought, my climax quickly builds in my core. I'm close.

Upping the speed, I move my hips to meet the spray, my orgasm rising to the surface. "Yes," I hiss under my breath. "God, yes," I moan. Then, waves of pleasure hit me hard and quick.

I brace myself with one hand on the shower wall, breathing heavily.

Now that I've gotten rid of the ache, I feel ready to face the day. *Sort of.*

When I step out of the bathroom, I notice a pair of jogging pants and a new t-shirt on the bed. *Did Dion come in while I was showering?*

Just then, a noise comes from the walk-in closet, so I step toward it, expecting to see Dion rummaging in there. But a short, middle-aged woman appears in the doorway.

"Oh my God!" I yelp, grasping onto my chest, almost dropping the towel around me.

The woman also jumps, before smiling at me. "I'm so sorry, Miss Kastellanos. I didn't mean to scare you. Dion told me to bring these to you," she says, pointing to the clothes on the bed.

I breathe out. "No worries, uh..." I stop mid-sentence, realizing I don't know the woman's name.

"It's Helen, dear." *Of course.* Dion's housekeeper. He briefly mentioned her last night when he offered me a snack that I refused. I didn't have much of an appetite once I remembered how I'm never going to see him again after this. Helen must be the one keeping everything tidy and fully stocked.

"Thank you, Helen. Please, call me Aria."

She nods and smiles. "I'll let you get changed. When you're ready, join us downstairs for breakfast."

When she shuts the door behind her, I sit on the edge of the bed and run a hand over the clothes.

I unfold the pants and put them on, pulling the drawstring tight. Then, I slip on the t-shirt. Another band tee. Again, I'm surprised that a man like Dion would have clothes this casual when he looked so good in a suit last night. Like suits were made especially for him.

The aroma of freshly brewed coffee hits me, so I let my nose lead me down to the kitchen.

Dion is at the counter, making himself a shot of espresso that he pounds back like a shooter.

My heart quickens. His hair is tousled, and a fine sheen of

sweat glistens on his forehead, highlighting the sharp angles of his face.

"Rough night?" I call out, my voice getting caught in my throat.

He turns around, his smile beaming as he takes me in. I try to act nonchalant despite the butterflies fluttering in my stomach under his gaze.

"Something like that. A certain someone kept me up all night," he says, wiggling his brows.

I laugh. "If it makes you feel any better, I feel like I got hit by a freight train."

"Not used to staying up late, huh, sleepyhead?" he asks, grabbing a bottle of water from the fridge. "I just got back from a run."

He takes a large swig, and I watch his Adam's apple bob as he gulps down the water, finding it increasingly difficult to focus on our conversation. I'm clearly not well.

My gaze wanders to the way his chest rises and falls with each breath, the beads of sweat trickling down his neck. I shake my head.

"Not really, and I think I'm hungover," I say, rubbing my temples. Suddenly, I feel a headache creeping in.

"Here, drink this." Dion grabs another bottle from the fridge, sliding it across the counter to me.

"Thank you."

After downing half of the contents, I look around the space awkwardly. "I should get going." *I need to get out of here.*

Dion's gaze bores into me like he's trying to figure me out. A flush spreads across my cheeks, and my heart beats faster. *Does he feel this too?*

I thought I'd be able to sleep off this insane attraction I have for him, but after a couple hours of sleep, a shower, and even a self-induced orgasm, I still feel everything we did last night. I swallow hard, trying to seem normal. Deep down, I'm freaking out.

"I'll take you home. I have to go into the city, anyway. You're on my way."

"How do you know where I live?" I ask, surprised.

Dion laughs. "I know everything, *astéri mou*," he says, walking out of the kitchen. "Grab something to eat before we leave. I'll ask Helen to make you a coffee to go. Meet me out front in thirty minutes."

In a daze, I stay in place. Is it possible to have a reaction this visceral to someone you just met?

I spot a plate of baked goods on the breakfast nook, so I grab a muffin and small pastry, taking bites of each as I head back upstairs to get my stuff.

I didn't get the chance to explore the second floor yesterday, so when I pass the room right next to mine, I'm surprised to find Dion inside. He's now shirtless, every muscle of his back glistening from the sweat.

He was only a wall away when I was in the shower, touching myself to the thought of him. Now, I'm *truly* mortified.

I hide by the slight opening of his bedroom door and watch him through the narrow gap as he drops his shorts, then briefs, exposing his round ass. My breath hitches in my chest. He is beautiful. Built like a Greek God, every muscle defined and sculpted to perfection. His strong back is broad and powerful. His tanned skin glows, sun-kissed, highlighting every contour and dip of his body. Covering his entire back is a striking Phoenix tattoo, its intricate details making it seem almost alive.

I gulp to moisten my throat.

He stops moving. *Shit.* I freeze for a few seconds, my heart skipping a beat.

Holding my breath, I quickly step away from the door as quietly as possible. Relief washes over me when I hear the shower start in his bathroom. *That was close.*

Letting out a breath of relief, I continue to the guest room, grab my things and head back downstairs to where Helen is now in the kitchen, preparing a travel mug of coffee.

"Is that for me?"

She turns around and smiles. There's something about her presence that feels reassuring. "Yes, here. Have some while you wait for Dion."

I thank her and take a sip, letting the caffeine flow through me like a small surge of energy.

We stay in a comfortable silence for a bit while Helen works, but something urges me to make the most of this opportunity.

"Have you worked for Dion long?"

"It's been a while," Helen nods, glancing over at me. "I met him and Evander many years ago when they were teenage boys. Their uncle employed me. Now, I work for them."

"Are they cousins?"

She shakes her head and lets out a little chuckle. "More like brothers."

"I didn't realize that Dion and Evander were related," I mumble with a frown.

"Family isn't always about blood. It's about who's willing to be there when you need it the most. True family is not always defined by biological ties."

She makes a good point. I consider Angelica and Gianis my siblings, even though we have no blood relation.

"Oh," I say simply, not wanting to pry further.

Helen puts down the dish she was washing and wipes her hand with the towel slung over her shoulder, probably sensing my curiosity. "It's not my story to tell, but Evander and Dion had very traumatic childhoods. They both lost their parents at a very young age and were taken in by Evander's uncle. They grew up together."

My heart squeezes as I'm reminded of the conversation Dion and I had last night.

I ponder her words, lost in thought.

"He's grown into such a good man. Evander, too. I know the business they carry might not be ethical, and what they went through affected how they show their feelings and their relationships with others," Helen continues, sorrow flashing across her face, "but they are unwavering in their loyalty to each other."

Curiosity gets the best of me.

"Why is Dion single?" I cringe, regretting it instantly. *It doesn't matter why he's single, Aria. It's not like anything can happen between us, anyway.*

"I wonder the same thing all the time. He never brings women home, either." Helen looks at me intently.

My heart jolts. "Never?"

She smirks. "Never."

Although none of this should matter, knowing that I'm the only woman he's brought home makes me feel special.

Right as I'm about to ask her another question, Dion pops into view. "Ready?"

I nod quickly and stand up. "Thanks, Helen. It was great meeting you."

"Likewise, dear. Hopefully, I'll see you again soon," she replies with a wink.

I smile back, but a twinge of sadness washes over me.

When I step outside, the sun is bright and warm on my face, almost blinding me. I look around but there's no sign of Dion. He's not in the car we used yesterday.

I walk around the side of the house and stumble upon a four-car garage. I hadn't seen this last night.

"Dion?" I call out.

I enter the garage and I'm shocked by how big the space is. A fleet of cars and four motorcycles line the back wall.

Dion pops out of what seems to be a storage space, making me jump. "Shit! You startled me."

He chuckles. "My bad. I wasn't trying to scare you. Let's take the G-Wagon." He unlocks the doors, and I climb in.

"Do you mind taking me to Angelica's? I'll ask my driver to pick me up from there." I wouldn't mind getting a ride home, but I'm sure I'll get questions once the guards tell my parents that a man dropped me off.

From the corner of my eye, I catch Dion's amused smirk. "How old are you again? Please tell me you're legal. I'm starting to question it."

"Don't be a smartass," I argue. "I realize how this sounds, but you know how arranged engagements work in our world. If I'm seen coming home the morning after a night out with another man, it won't bode well for me."

"You're not the confrontational type, huh?" he says, his tone slightly mocking. "From how you were at the club last night, I assumed you would take no shit from anyone, whereas you're letting your family control your life."

My blood curdles. "More like I know how to pick my battles," I snap, crossing my arms at my chest and looking out the window. Fuck him. I don't know why what Dion just said made me so angry. *Maybe because it's true.*

"Someone is groggy this morning."

"And you're way too fucking chipper," I spit.

He laughs as we pull out of the gates.

"Could you please stop fucking doing that?" I turn to glare at him.

"Doing what?" he replies, confused.

"Laugh. It's irritating."

Dion looks at me, dumbfounded. "Could you please stop fucking doing *that*?"

"Doing what?"

"Acting like a bitch."

I gasp. "Excuse me?" Did he just call me a *bitch*?

"You heard me."

"Let me out of the car."

"No."

"Let me out of the car, Dion," I repeat, reaching for the belt buckle.

Dion slams on the brakes, bringing the car to an abrupt halt in the middle of the street. His hand grips the steering wheel tightly, his jaw locked.

"What the hell are you doing?" I yell, as the cars behind us swerve, annoyed horns blaring in protest.

"I swear to everything that is almighty, Aria. If you dare get out of this car, chaos *will* ensue," he seethes, putting his hand on top of mine to stop me from unbuckling my seatbelt. I stare at him. It's the first time since we met that I'm almost...*intimidated* by him. Even last night when he told me not to run to Angelica at the club, he wasn't this stern.

This behavior is doing the opposite of that it should do.

Instead of feeling threatened, I'm...*turned on*. Something is *seriously* wrong with me.

But my brattiness gets the best of me. "Or what, Dion? You're going to chase me out in the street in the middle of your neighborhood?"

"Do you want to bet, little liar? You don't know what I'm capable of." His hand is still on top of mine, preventing me from moving. "If you want to fuck around and find out, go for it," he adds, a devious smile plastered on his face. Then, he lets go.

Part of me wants to get out of the car and see if he'll chase me, but the other doesn't want to run down the middle of the street in broad daylight, wearing heels, in my walk-of-shame outfit.

Regardless, my core is pulsating with a need so intense it's almost impossible to ignore.

I fold my hands over my thighs. "Just take me home." If he wants to judge me for being too careful with my parents, I'll show him I'm not afraid to face them.

Satisfied with my response, Dion resumes driving.

We spend the rest of the journey in silence until we reach my area in Old Cebrene. As soon as we pass the gates to my family's estate, Dion breaks the quiet.

"We have to talk about last night."

I exhale and nod, and suddenly our little spat seems so silly. I feel a mix of emotions about giving Dion my virginity. On one hand, I'm satisfied to have chosen him as my first. However, it's also a bit terrifying to open yourself up in a new way, to be vulnerable, especially to someone you don't know.

"To preface, I had a good time," Dion says, and I can hear the tentative smile in his voice.

The corners of my mouth lift, but I don't look at him. "Me too."

"I still think you should've told me *before* I stuck my dick inside you," he teases.

I chuckle and any tension between us from before dissipates. "You're right. I'm sorry. I was so focused on deciding for myself that I almost forgot there was another person involved."

"How do you feel about it now?"

I turn to look at him. His expression is uncertain, even concerned.

"I wanted it to be special and it was," I reassure him. "But now, I'm feeling a little overwhelmed. I gave you something I can never give to anyone else again."

"I understand. It's a big deal. I'm honored that you chose me." His soft words send warmth through my chest.

I give him a small smile. "I'm glad I made that decision."

Truly, I am. Even though I might feel a tad guilty for having to lie to my future husband about my virginity, I'm happy I spent last night with Dion.

"But it can't happen again." I reluctantly pull the door handle, feeling a twinge of hesitation as I prepare to get out of the car. "And Dion?"

"Yes." He holds my gaze, and a shiver runs up my spine.

"I don't regret it. Not for a second."

His lips curve into a bittersweet smile. "Friends?"

I nod. "Just friends."

I get out and walk to my front door, trying my hardest not to steal a look at him over my shoulder.

My hand hovers over the doorknob, and I take a deep breath, trying to rid myself of the uneasiness that has settled in my chest. I hear the G-wagon back out of the driveway, so I tempt a final glance back at the car, now a fading silhouette.

Just like last night, the lingering sense of being watched returns. I look around the grounds, past the gate.

There's no one there.

I shake my head before turning the doorknob and going inside.

When I step into the foyer, I'm met by my mother's piercing gaze. Her arms are crossed, and she taps her foot impatiently.

"Aria. Where were you? I was worried sick!" she almost shrieks.

I put my purse down on the marble floor and slip off my heels. "*Mama*, I was out. I told you."

"It's eight in the morning of the *next* day, Aria. You're lucky your father's been too busy to notice." I wince, ignoring my disappointment. My *baba*'s been a lot less present lately.

My mother catches my reaction and sighs. "I know it's been *different* around here, and we all miss your father, but that doesn't change the fact that I don't believe for a second you were out with your friends until now."

I open my mouth to protest, but she cuts me off. "And you'd better be careful about being seen with another man when you're already promised to someone else."

My heart races, though I keep my face neutral, willing myself to stay calm. "I wasn't with another man."

Mama gives me a pointed look but doesn't push further and turns away. I take a deep breath and head upstairs. *You're already promised to someone else.*

The mere thought of it makes me want to scream, but I force myself to remain composed.

After dressing, I make my way back downstairs to join my family for brunch. My brother and father are already there, seated in their usual spots in the breakfast nook. The familiar setting feels different today, some unspoken tension thick in the air.

Dimitri gives me a weary look and subtly points his head toward our father. I understand it: *Baba* isn't in a great mood. I let out a breath.

I take my seat, trying to ignore the way my mother's eyes linger on me.

Magdalena, our housekeeper, fills the table with a variety of foods that I start piling onto my plate.

We sit in silence, the only sound the clinking of cutlery and the occasional rustle of *Baba*'s newspaper. My father finally breaks the quiet, his voice steady but with an edge I can't quite place.

"I spoke to your soon-to-be fiancé," he says, looking directly at me.

I freeze, my fork halfway to my mouth. The room seems to shrink around me as I meet his gaze, heart pounding in my chest.

I swallow down my food. "What did he say?" I ask, trying to keep my voice calm and even.

He takes a sip of his coffee. "We're making arrangements for you to meet soon."

My throat constricts. I pick up my glass of orange juice and take a large gulp.

My father sets his newspaper down, folding it neatly before placing it beside his plate. "I'm concerned."

I force myself to maintain eye contact. To my side, Dimitri shifts in his seat, sensing impending chaos, and picks up his phone as a distraction.

The urge to get up and run out of the kitchen—out of the house, far away from here—is strong.

"Concerned about what?"

"About your *commitment*, Aria," *Baba* replies, his tone leaving no room for misunderstanding. *Does he suspect that I was with another man, too?* Shit. I hope my mother didn't say anything.

I feel her stare on me, her earlier suspicions hanging in the air.

"I'm committed," I reply with as much conviction as I can muster.

My father leans back in his chair, studying me with a critical eye. "I hope so." He picks up his coffee again, taking another measured sip before setting it down. "This marriage is important, Aria. We've worked hard to build what we have, and this alliance will secure our place for generations." What the hell does he mean by *we*? Last time I checked, I was not involved in this arrangement.

A surge of frustration and defiance rises within me. "But what about what *I* want? Don't I get a say in my own life?"

His eyes flash with irritation. "You need to understand the bigger picture. We have responsibilities and traditions."

I lean forward. "But it's my life. I should get to choose who I spend it with."

He sets his cup down with a loud clatter, his jaw tightening. "You think I don't understand that? You think I haven't made sacrifices for this family? We all have to make choices we don't like. That's part of growing up." I look away, blinking back tears as he continues. "Happiness isn't always about getting what you want. Sometimes it's about doing what's *right*."

I exhale. "Fine," I relent. I love my father, and I want to make him proud, despite the tight leash around my neck.

Silence falls over us again, heavier than before. I look down at my plate, my appetite gone.

Dimitri clears his throat, trying to lighten the mood. "So, Riri, any plans for today?"

I glance at him, grateful for the distraction. "I thought I'd spend some time in the studio," I say, forcing a smile. "I have a few projects I want to work on."

"That sounds good," my mother says, her tone a bit warmer than before. "Just make sure you're back for dinner."

"I will," I promise, pushing my food around my plate. My father picks up his newspaper again, his fingers smoothing the pages as if nothing happened. Dimitri tries to engage our mother in small talk, but the tension remains.

As soon as I can, I excuse myself from the table and retreat to my studio, seeking solace in my work. The familiar smells of plants and flowers are comforting, and I lose myself in the creative process, trying to forget the storm brewing outside these walls.

9

FIANCÉ

An hour earlier

I watch my soon-to-be fiancée step out of the G-Wagon and my annoyance intensifies.

Every time I think of what I saw last night, my chest tightens in frustration. There's too much on the line for this not to go my way. She will *not* fuck this up for me.

I followed Aria to Academia, wanting to get a closer look at her life and the people she hangs around. We're not technically engaged yet, but the arrangement I made with her father is of utmost importance.

I blended into the club's crowd with ease, keeping a close eye on her.

At the beginning, there was nothing out of the ordinary. She drank, danced, and declined advances from every guy that dared to approach her.

But then, *he* appeared.

Their exchange didn't raise any alarms   at first. But as soon as she slid into the seat next to him, I sensed the tension radiating from her body. She was affected by him, that much was clear. And I needed to know why. *Do they have history? Is there a boyfriend Philip didn't tell me about?*

I watched as she fiddled with her dress, evidently nervous. As he whispered in her ear with an air of cockiness. Their connection was obvious.

Even though I have no say in who she interacts with—yet—I wanted to punch him in the face for touching her.

When the club was abruptly shut down, I left to avoid suspicion. I stayed in my car, waiting for her to emerge. People trickled out, but Aria never appeared. Minutes ticked by and turned into hours. *Did I miss her leaving*? There's no way.

I resisted the urge to burst through the doors to see what she was up to. I had a gnawing feeling that she was still with *him*.

My virgin wife-to-be was inside a club with another man. My fists clench at my sides. Her virginity is fucking mine to take. It's owed to *me*.

When she finally appeared, she looked sober, content—*too* content.

Poutána.

It was a risk to follow them, but one I had to take. I had to get to the bottom of their relationship.

I kept a close eye on them as we wound through the quiet streets of Cebrene.

When we ventured deeper into an unfamiliar neighborhood, I couldn't help but feel a twinge of apprehension. This wasn't a part of town I knew well.

Tension gripped my jaw as I watched them disappear into a house together. It wasn't because of jealousy or anger, but rather inconvenience. Another guy to deal with, another situation to navigate until I get what I want. I felt frustrated at the thought of having to address a potential rival for her attention. That's not what I signed up for.

I sat outside in my car for an hour, my patience wearing thin.

With a heavy sigh, I gave up and pulled away, vowing to return in the morning, determined to find out if she'd stayed the night.

The next day, I drove by the house again. It looked empty, shutters closed and no sign of life. As I started to head back to the Kastellanos estate, my phone rang, jolting me from my thoughts. It was one of Philip's guards.

"Yes?"

"Mr. Galanis," the guard's voice crackled through the line. "I wanted to let you know that Miss Aria made it home."

"Thanks," I replied, already halfway to her place.

He hesitated for a moment, stopping me from hanging up. "She's with a man."

I gritted my teeth. I needed to know who that fucking man is.

As I finally approached the grand gates of the estate, I parked the car far enough not to be seen.

I took a picture of the guy's license plate and sent it to one of my associates who works for the CPD, the Cebrene Police Department. Within a few minutes, I got a name to match the face.

Dion Loukas. Apparently, he's part of the Vasilakis family. *Motherfucker.*

I watched as she looked around, sensing eyes on her, before she shook her head and stepped into her house.

I need to get rid of this Loukas asshole. Aria Kastellanos is mine.

10

DION

The rumble of my Ducati sends a surge of adrenaline through my body as I pull out of my garage. The concrete beneath my wheels rushes past as I lean into a sharp turn.

Navigating through the familiar streets of my neighborhood, I head toward our main warehouse in the Lower District of Old Cebrene.

The engine growls with each twist of the throttle, propelling me forward into the cool evening air. Yet, amidst the exhilaration, my mind keeps drifting back to smooth, blonde hair, soft moans in my ears, and a laugh I can't get out of my head.

Ahead, the lights of the warehouse flicker into view, casting a glow against the darkening sky and bringing me back to the present.

As I approach the building, I slow down, pulling up to the entrance. The gates open with a metallic groan, allowing me access into the maze of shipping containers. The industrial surroundings are a stark contrast to the softness of Aria's presence in my memories. I have to get the fuck over her. But how can I?

She left a mark on me. I took her *virginity*. She gave me a sacred part of herself, and the still fresh memory of her legs wrapped around my waist makes me want to punch a hole through a wall. I even found out where she does hot yoga and waited for her outside of the studio a few days ago. I had to see her. I *needed* to see her.

I park my bike in a secluded corner and remove my helmet, running a hand through my short hair.

When I make my way inside, I'm greeted by Leon, cigarette in hand.

"*Kalispéra, afentikó.*"

"*Ti nea echís?*"

"The crates arrived about an hour ago. The guys picked them up from the port earlier today. There are a couple missing."

For fuck's sake. We've been dealing with a slew of our containers going AWOL lately. It's been driving me and Evander nuts trying to figure out who's been stealing from us.

"I think you should see this," Leon adds, pulling out a piece of paper from his pocket.

When he hands it to me, I unfold it and find a message scribbled in red ink.

I KNOW WHO YOU ARE. GO NEAR HER AGAIN AND
YOU'LL GET WHAT'S COMING TO YOU.

Ti sto diáolo?

I stare at the piece of paper clenched tightly in my hand. It's the second time in the past two weeks that I've received a threatening note. The first one made me raise a brow. It said: You think you're untouchable, but everyone has a weakness.

I'd crumpled it up and tossed it aside, thinking it was just some petty gang shit. There's always drama in the metropolis, and I've never been one to get involved.

But now, this one. Anger simmers beneath my skin as I reread the words scrawled across the paper.

"We found it in an empty crate. It was addressed to you," Leon explains.

Who could this be? I assume the 'her' the message refers to is Aria.

I clench my jaw, fists tightening around the note until it crumples in my grip. Has someone been following me? Who the fuck has the nerve to threaten me like this?

Enough is enough. It's time to find out who's behind these notes and put an end to it once and for all.

I stuff it in my pocket. "Don't tell a fucking soul about this, Leon," I threaten, and he lifts his hands up.

"I didn't see a thing."

"Good. Gather as much information as you can regarding the missing crates and reach out to our contact at the port. I'll talk to Xan."

I turn on my heels and head to the office. When I walk in, Xander is sitting at the desk, staring at the computer. He nods in my direction.

"What are you up to?" I ask, sitting in the seat in front of him.

"I'm looking into the cameras at the port. I believe the perpetrators were able to steal from us right before we got there for pick-up."

Xander is our in-house hacker. He works with a team, but when we need to get something done quickly, he's the man for the job. He's also been my best friend ever since we met twenty-one years ago.

I was twelve when he stumbled upon our door, beaten and bloody. Ignatius had been warned by the guards that a young boy was trying to get through the gates, and when they let him in, we were shocked to find him in terrible shape. His face was swollen with a black eye and a busted lip, and his legs were covered in scrapes.

Turns out, his father had beaten him up so badly in a drunken stupor that he ran away, not stopping until he found help. He cut through the woods and came across Ignatius's estate in the middle of the night.

The only thing I vividly remember was his smell. It was foul.

As he was running through the forest, he'd gotten sprayed by a skunk. Evan and I have never stopped giving him shit about that.

Ignatius had ushered him into the house and asked Helen to clean him up. She had bathed him in a mixture of dish soap, baking soda, and hydrogen peroxide.

Evander was fast asleep at the time, and when he woke up the next morning, he almost beat the shit out of Xander when he found him sleeping on the couch. The memory still makes us laugh.

Xander finally looks up at me from the monitor and must notice my unease. "What's going on?"

I pull the note out of my pocket and throw it at him. "Someone addressed this to me in one of the crates."

He quickly peruses it. "Do you have any idea who could be targeting you?"

I shrug my shoulders. "My only guess would be Philip Kastellanos."

Aria's father is a known enemy of ours. Given his relation to Peter Kouvalakis, he's on our shit list. They're both involved in some shady shit that we're trying to uncover, and I expect he wouldn't be too happy if his daughter started seeing someone like me.

When I dropped Aria off the morning after our little encounter, I hadn't noticed anyone watching us from the house.

Then again, he has guards and cameras all over the property, so I'm sure if he was, he hastily figured out my identity.

"Is this the first time you've received a threat?" Xander asks. He's aware of what happened with Aria that night.

I bring my attention back to him and shake my head. "This is the second one."

Xander's eyes widen in shock, his usually easygoing demeanor replaced by concern and frustration. "Why the fuck didn't you say anything before?"

I shrug again. "I didn't want to worry you unnecessarily."

"Could it be her fiancé?"

I debate my answer. "Not sure. But I haven't looked into the fucker yet. I don't even know his name."

Xander takes another look at the note and throws it back to me. "I'll investigate. We'll get to the bottom of this. If someone left something in one of the crates, I'm bound to find footage."

I let him type away for several minutes, watching him get completely engrossed in the task, and then he speaks up. "I found something. Come look."

He really is the best hacker in the city.

A spark of stress ignites inside me as I walk over to him and face the monitors. His finger hovers over the play button, and anticipation tingles through my veins like a live wire as we watch the grainy footage.

The silhouette of a man moves stealthily across the dock, shrouded in darkness. His movements are calculated as he skirts around the edge of the cargo ship.

The man's form disappears briefly behind a stack of crates, only to reemerge moments later, clutching a piece of paper. He slips between two containers, his figure illuminated momentarily by the dim glow of a nearby light. I lean closer to the monitor, my eyes straining to catch any distinguishing features.

"Pause the video," I say, and Xander freezes the footage with a quick flick of his fingers. The image stutters to a halt as the man hunches over a crate.

I squint, zooming in, desperate for even the faintest glimpse of his face. But his features are obscured by shadows cast by the surrounding cargo.

Frustration gnaws at me as I rewind and play back the footage. "I can't fucking see a thing," I complain, pounding my fist on the desk. I want to find this motherfucker and pay him a little visit for threatening me. Xander releases the pause button, allowing the scene to continue.

The perpetrator pries open a seam and tucks the note inside.

As he retreats into the shadows once more, my mind races with questions. Who is he? It can't be Philip himself, so who did he send to do his dirty work? And if it's not Philip's doing, who else could it be?

"There's one thing we know for sure," Xander says, breaking the quiet of the room. "This isn't linked to the thefts, since they were done at different times."

"Call Evan and tell him about the missing crates. But don't mention the note."

Xander nods.

I hate keeping secrets from my brother. We've always shared everything. But this time, telling him about the situation I'm in will only serve as a distraction, pulling his attention from what's truly important.

Avenging Ignatius.

PART TWO
Two Months Later

11

DION

"P *outánas yos!*" Evander yells as I pummel him to the floor.

He quickly recovers and stands across from me, the sound of our heavy breaths surrounding us.

We circle each other at the center of the mat, and Evan looks at me with something resembling concern. "What the fuck is up with you? You're fighting me like I'm one of our enemies."

"You *are* technically my enemy on the mat, E."

"Don't be a smartass. Why the fuck are you using me as a punching bag?" he asks, grunting from exertion.

"We're fucking boxing, Evan. What do you expect?" I retort.

But what I really want to say is: it's because I'm sexually frustrated and have been losing my mind for the past two months because a woman I met for only a few hours has ruined me for anyone else.

And trust me, I've tried.

A couple weeks after our one night, I decided it was time to wash all memories of Aria's sweet pussy out of my mind the only way I knew how. balls deep in another woman.

But when I was sitting down in the booth at Academia with

a rather attractive woman, the only thing I could see was Aria's face.

Everything about that chick was wrong: her look, her demeanor, her smell, her voice.

My dick was inverted, like a turtle hiding in its shell that didn't want to come out to play.

If that had happened to me in any other circumstance, I would've taken it as a hit to my ego. I would've thought that something was wrong with my dick. But I knew exactly why I was experiencing erectile dysfunction.

Aria fucking Kastellanos. That's why.

So, I haven't tried to fuck another woman again.

A rush of adrenaline shoots through me as I throw a punch —a quick jab aimed at Evander's chest. He sidesteps smoothly, countering with a swift kick toward my gut. I block him just in time, the impact reverberating through my arms. *Holy hell*. He's not making this easy tonight.

Evan is a fighter, and every time I train with him, he pushes me to my limit.

There's a rhythm to our fights born from years of training side by side. He knows my moves as well as I know his.

Evander grunts again and gives me a menacing look. "Drop this bullshit act. I've known you almost my entire life, D. I know when something is wrong."

"Fuck off. I'm fine," I pant. With every strike, my breath becomes more labored, and I'm forced to inhale deeply to maintain my stamina. I manage to land a solid punch to Evan's shoulder, causing him to stagger a bit, but he recovers, retaliating with a series of rapid strikes. I weave and dodge his moves. As the spar continues, our movements become more aggressive.

Evan shoves at my chest, causing me to fly back on the mat, and I almost trip on my own feet.

"What the fuck was that for?" I grit out.

Evander charges at me again, but this time, I'm ready, so I lift my arms in front of my face. He unleashes a combination of punches aimed at my head, and I manage to block most of them.

He throws a jab, and I dodge it. He throws another and it grazes my left cheek. "Ow! Fuck."

I counter with a spinning kick, which he narrowly avoids, ducking under it.

Going for a takedown, Evander closes the distance, grappling me by my arms and using his momentum to flip me over. We both hit the mat hard, rolling apart.

"I'm going to fucking beat the truth out of you. So, if you'd rather avoid the pain, I'd suggest telling me what the fuck is wrong," he says, anger lacing his tone.

Evander is the only person who knows exactly what I'm feeling when I'm feeling it. As kids, we developed a way of communicating with each other without having to say a word. He'd know when I was sad, upset, or angry, even before I did. He would notice the smallest shifts in my behavior and call me out. I couldn't hide shit from him then, and I can't hide shit from him now.

But I refuse to tell him that the reason I've been beside myself is because of a woman I only met once. I'm fucking embarrassed just thinking about it. When did I grow so soft?

I'm not a man attuned to his feelings. I don't *feel*.

Stripped from any emotion as a child when my parents died.

I still relive those moments.

Two separate occasions when my heart was ripped out of my chest, leaving me with nothing. The only people I care about are my brothers.

One of those said brothers punches me in the gut, hard, snapping me out of my haze.

"Speak, motherfucker," he growls, still on the mat next to me.

I look up at the ceiling and exhale. "It's *her*."

Evan lets out a low chuckle. "I knew it."

My head snaps toward him, and I narrow my eyes. "Then why the fuck did you just beat the hell out of me to find out?"

This time, he laughs even harder. "Because I needed you to man up, *Dionaki*."

I groan loudly. "You're fucking annoying, man," I say, putting my head back down on the mat. I fold my hands above my chest.

I can't seem to shake the memory of Aria. Two months of longing, replaying our brief encounter in my mind.

It's fucking foolish. She's unattainable, yet I can't help but hope we cross paths again.

"I still can't believe you spent the night with her," Evander says. I scoff in response, saying nothing else.

What Evan doesn't know is that for a while, I was watching Aria.

We mutually agreed to not see each other again, a decision meant to protect us both. Yet, I couldn't stop thinking about her, wondering what she's doing, who she's with. I still can't. So, I kept tabs on her from afar, feeding my need to see her even though I knew I shouldn't.

I tried to rationalize it, telling myself that it was harmless, that I was just looking out for her. But deep down, it's more than that.

The same morning, after I'd dropped Aria back at her parents' estate, Evander had called me.

That's when I had told him she was getting married to one of her father's business associates. Just like I knew he would, Evander warned me to keep my interactions with her to a minimum, given she's Angelica's best friend. He didn't want our identities to be uncovered in case our revenge plan got out.

With everything happening in Cebrene, and the death of Ignatius, Evander had a one-track mind: revenge. I wanted it, too.

I'd lost every parent figure who ever cared for me. Other than Evan, I had no one.

So, the least I can do is not fuck this up.

But I still couldn't stop thinking about Aria. How different she is from other women. I couldn't stay away.

I grimace as thoughts of those notes flood back. I watch the ceiling fan whir above us. *Have I fucked up the revenge plan already?*

"There's something I have to tell you."

Evander turns his head to look at me, eyes narrowed. "What is it?"

I wipe my brow with the back of my glove. "A little while ago, I received two threatening notes. I still don't know who they're from, but—"

He sits up abruptly. "What? Why the hell didn't you tell me before?"

I hold up my hands to calm him down. "Xander took care of it. He's been monitoring the warehouses extra closely. I haven't received anything in a couple months."

Evander's anger doesn't dissipate entirely. "Do you think it was because of Aria?

I pause. "I don't know. Maybe."

His gaze hardens. "Like I said before, you better not fuck up our plan. You need to make sure Aria didn't tell anyone about us, especially Angelica."

I'm almost certain that Aria hasn't said a word, given her predicament, but Evander is right. This entire situation is risky. "I know. I'll make sure of it."

Evan's voice is filled with hesitation. "We'll have to go to her engagement party. And find out who her fiancé is, or if anyone is onto us. Are you going to be able to handle it?"

I scoff. "I'm not fucking in love with the woman, Evan. Of course I can *handle* it."

Evan throws his hands in the air. "Just asking, Brother. I'll need you to be on your A-game."

I roll over and spring to my feet, sweat dripping down my forehead, blurring my vision. For some reason, this conversation is starting to piss me off. Why is he acting like I can't fucking take care of myself? I'm a grown man, and Aria is just a girl I fucked.

At least that's what I'm trying to convince myself of.

I need to snap out of this lust-filled craze.

And I need to get in the shower and get the fuck out of here.

"I'll be fine," I spit, turning to walk away, but Evander gets up and stops me, putting his hand on my shoulders.

"*Adelfé*," he begins, his voice low but firm. "I need you now more than ever. Our plan to take down Peter Kouvalakis is well underway, but we have to up the ante."

"I know, Evander. I've been keeping up with everything."

"This means you'll need to take on more responsibility. This is what Ignatius prepared us for."

I hold his gaze. "I'm in. You know I am. But I was never meant to be in this role."

He sighs, nodding as he crosses his arms. "I get it, D. I really do. But Ignatius always said we were destined for something greater, and now that he's dead, it's our duty to see it through. He wanted us to uncover the Sisterhood. That's why he left those breadcrumbs."

My heart tightens.

I grit my teeth, memories of my childhood flashing through my mind. "Just because my father wanted different things for me, doesn't mean I'm not grateful for where I'm at today. I wouldn't change it for anything," I argue.

Evander's face softens, and he uncrosses his arms. "I know.

Life's a bitch and dealt you a shitty hand, but you've done well for yourself, man."

I nod, the weight of his words settling on my shoulders.

Evander claps me on the back. "Let's finish what Ignatius started. Together."

THIRTY MINUTES LATER, I GRAB MY BURNER PHONE FROM MY gym bag.

Stepping outside, I perch onto my bike and turn on the engine, the vibrations creating a familiar sense of calm.

I dial a number and put it to my ear. The ringing on the other end seems to stretch on forever.

Then, finally, the line clicks, and a voice fills the silence.

"Hello?"

The sound is a melody—soft, familiar.

"Aria."

There's a hint of surprise in her tone when she responds. "*Dion?*"

12

ARIA

My heart stutters when I hear Dion's voice on the other end of the line.

The last person I expected to call me was him.

I lift my glasses over my head as if it'll help me focus and shut the book I was reading. Sitting up on my bed, I try to gather my thoughts.

I haven't heard from Dion since the night we spent together two months ago. We never exchanged numbers, so I never thought I'd speak to him again.

However, I'm not surprised that he found my contact information.

"*Dion?*"

"Yes, it's me, *astéri mou.*"

My heartbeat slows at the sound of my nickname. "I..Wha..." I stammer, not really knowing what to say, so I'm thankful when he continues to speak.

"We need to talk." I hear a gate opening behind him.

"What's wrong?" I ask, nervously fiddling with my pajama shirt.

"Nothing. I just need to ask you some questions."

"Uh, okay...Shoot."

"In person."

I pull the phone away from my ear to check the time. It's 11:45 p.m.

"It's almost midnight. Can it not wait until tomorrow?"

Honestly, I'm tired, but that's not the real reason why I don't want to see Dion in person. I'm just not ready to face him.

I've been grappling with this inner conflict for what feels like an eternity now, and the mere thought of seeing him sends shivers down my spine. Not from excitement, but dread.

I've spent our time apart in a tug-of-war between longing for the connection we shared and trying to move on with my life. Trying to erase all fantasies of us being together from my mind. I'm afraid that seeing him again will ruin all my progress. Not that there has been much of that.

Though we only spent a few hours together, I've never had that type of attachment to anyone before.

I thought it was just because I gave him my virginity, making me feel as if we had a special type of bond. But it wasn't about the sex.

It was about *him*.

"No. It has to be now," Dion replies, no room for discussion.

What could be so urgent?

"How am I supposed to sneak out?"

Dion chuckles into the phone. "I'm sure you've done it before, little liar. Figure it out. Meet me at the edge of the forest beyond the trees of your property in twenty." He hangs up.

He's not wrong. I've snuck out of my room many times before, but it was to go out with Angie or one of my other girl-friends. Not to meet a boy while I technically have a fiancé. If I get caught, I'll never hear the end of it.

But I guess I'm going. I'm not wearing anything appropriate, so I decide to change into something more *incognito*.

I slip on a pair of black jogging pants and a black sweater, pulling the hood over my head and tucking my blonde strands inside.

After putting on my running shoes, I open my window and let the cool night air kiss my skin.

My room faces the backyard. At this time of night, there are no guards walking behind the house, so it should be relatively easy for me to run into the forest unnoticed.

As I step onto the windowsill, a familiar thrill races up my spine. I grip the edges of the frame and lean out, assessing the descent.

I lower myself down, my muscles responding instinctively. My feet find purchase on the uneven surface of the wall, between the nooks and crannies, with precision honed through countless climbs.

Just then, I hear the flicker of a lighter.

Who the hell could be out here smoking at this hour?

Not wanting to fall, I continue going down, as slowly and quietly as possible. When I reach the bottom and my feet touch solid ground, I release the breath I didn't realize I was holding.

Standing beneath the window, I try to locate where the sound came from, but I can't see anyone. It must've been my imagination.

I turn to walk toward the woods when a voice scares the living crap out of me.

"Where do you think you're going?" *Shit.* Dimitri.

I whip back around and squint in the dark. He's sitting on a stone bench near the rose bushes.

It's not like Dimo has never caught me sneaking out. He's also guilty for doing the same. But this is the first time I'll have to come up with an excuse. I can't even say I'm going clubbing as usual, seeing as I'm in sweatpants and a hoodie.

"For a walk." I shrug, trying to sound as casual as possible.

His brows crease. "Really, Aria? At midnight?"

I turn to fully face him and shrug again. *Real* casual. "I couldn't sleep."

"So, you decided to venture into the forest? *Alone*? Bullshit, Ri." He takes a large inhale of his cigarette. "Where are you going?"

Wait a second. I cross my arms over my chest. "First of all, I'm your big sister, so you can't question me. Second, since when do you smoke?"

He laughs at my attempt to switch the topic. "You might be older, but I still have a duty to protect you. And I've been smoking since *Baba* decided to start showing me the ropes."

Ah, yes. Now that my brother is eighteen, our father has begun teaching him about the business. Training him on how the mob works for when he'll have to take over for him.

As a legal adult, and the male heir, he's obligated to begin working for the clan. But Dimitri was never interested in following in my father's footsteps. He's creative, an artist. He has such unique quirks and sense of humor and spends a good chunk of his days playing video games. The mob life is not for him.

"Shit. How's that going?"

He shifts and raises his cigarette into the air. "What do you think?"

"That bad, huh?"

"Yup."

"Have you tried telling *Baba* again that you don't want any part of the clan?"

"Yes, and it didn't go well. He yelled at me about the importance of continuing the family's legacy and went on about having a "big break" soon. Whatever the fuck that means."

I ponder that for a moment. Lately, my father has been more invested in work than ever. I thought it was because of arranging my upcoming engagement. But now, I feel like there might be more to it.

I remember that I'm meeting Dion in a few minutes. I have to get going.

"Well, I'm here for you, Dimo," I tell my brother, and he nods, a soft smile at his lips. "I'm going to meet a friend for a bit. I'll be back soon. Please don't tell our parents," I plead, hoping he won't ask any more questions.

He pretends to zip his mouth shut just as he blows out the remaining smoke from his cigarette before crushing it under his foot.

"Thank you!" I exclaim, running to give him a peck on the cheek. He chuckles and pretends to push me away.

At the edge of the forest, I take a deep breath in. *All you're going to do is talk. Nothing more.*

When I've finally convinced myself—or barely—I step onto the mossy floor.

Darkness presses in around me like a heavy blanket. The only light comes from the faint glow of the moon filtering through the trees. I rarely wander through these woods anymore, but when I was younger, they used to be my playing grounds. Other than planting flowers and gardening, this used to be my sanctuary. I'd hide here when life *out there* felt too overwhelming.

Each step I take seems to echo through the silence. Suddenly, a rustling sounds nearby. I freeze.

This might not have been a good idea after all.

I try to determine the source of the noise, but my own heartbeat thuds in my ears. *It has to be an animal of some sort.*

Then, I hear it a faint crunching of leaves, followed by the unmistakable sound of footsteps.

Panic grips me as I realize I'm not alone. I'm still far away from where I'm supposed to meet Dion, so it can't be him. *Right?*

My breath quickens, palms growing clammy with sweat. I

didn't bring my phone in case I somehow got tracked into the forest. I'm now regretting my decision.

Every instinct screams at me to *go*, to get out of here as fast as I can.

I break into a frantic run, my steps loud and erratic. The shadows seem to twist around me, playing tricks on my mind. I try to rid myself of my imagination. But the snap of a twig sends me into a frenzy.

My chest tightens with each passing moment, my lungs urging for air as I push myself to go faster. I can see the end of the treeline.

As I continue my distraught dash through the forest, I catch a glimpse of movement out of the corner of my eye. Out of instinct, I turn my head—and there, illuminated by a shaft of moonlight, is a figure clad in dark clothing, a motorcycle helmet obscuring the face.

My pulse quickens. It's undoubtedly a man. And there's something about the way the helmet fits snugly on his head, accentuating his rugged features. It's *hot*.

The figure lifts the visor, and for a moment, time seems to stand still as our eyes lock in a silent, tense standoff. *Dion?* What is he doing?

I blink, heart pounding in my chest, and try to make sense of what's happening. But before I can react, he darts behind a nearby tree, disappearing into the shadows.

"Dion?" I call out. No response. I turn in circles, looking for his large frame, but there's no one in sight.

Out of nowhere, I hear a whisper, soft and insidious, right beside my ear. "Run, little liar."

My heart lurches and I whip around. There's no one there. Just the stillness of the forest, broken only by the sound of my own ragged breaths.

"Dion, come out. This isn't fucking funny," I spit, irritated.

Why is he playing games? He was supposed to wait for me *outside* of the forest.

The rational part of my mind tells me to run. But curiosity and fear keep me rooted to the spot, unable to tear my gaze away from where his figure vanished.

Every nerve in my body is on edge, every sense heightened as I strain to catch any sign of movement. But the forest remains silent and still, as if holding its breath, waiting for me to make the next move.

I start running again, and the sound of footsteps reappears, this time closer and faster. He is moving at lightning speed, and I have nowhere else to go.

Adrenaline surges through my veins when Dion lunges out from behind a tree, and the real chase begins.

With a strangled cry, I pivot on my heels and tear through the undergrowth, branches whipping at my face and limbs as I push myself forward. When I look back, I see he's getting nearer. Fear grips me in its icy embrace. But beneath it all, there's something else—a rush of exhilaration that courses through me like a wildfire.

Am I actually getting turned on *by this?*

The pounding of my heart fills my ears, drowning out all the other sounds as I race through the darkness. Dion's heavy footfalls get louder.

I run faster, now a willing player in his game.

Dion notices my boost of energy and lets out a loud and deep maniacal laugh, slightly muffled by the helmet. "Oh, little liar. I'm going to catch you. And when I do, you're going to wish you outran me."

His threat only builds the arousal within me, leaving me breathless with anticipation.

I can feel his body closing in, his presence hot on my neck as he gains ground with every stride. And then, with a suddenness that steals the air from my lungs, his strong arms wrap around me in a vice-like grip.

Our bodies collide, his chest pressing against my back, and he steadies us. In that instant, fear and arousal blur into one.

His touch is rough, yet strangely intoxicating, his hands roaming over my body with a possessiveness that sends shivers down my spine.

"Stop," I mutter, sounding unconvincing even to my own ears. "We're just supposed to talk."

"I changed my mind, little liar. Having you this close makes me want to fuck you against that tree."

His helmet brushes against my ear, sending a thrill of anticipation through me. I should be fighting, struggling to break free from his grasp, but instead, I find myself leaning into his touch, my body responding to him with a hunger I can't deny.

"We shouldn't," I moan.

"Your body is betraying your words, *astéri mou.*"

I shouldn't want this. I know that.

Dion presses my face against the rough bark of the tree. Every rational part of me screams to push him away, to resist his advances, while my body responds eagerly to his touch.

His hands explore my skin with a gentleness that contradicts the urgency of our arousal, and the warmth of his touch leaves me paralyzed, making me crave more despite myself.

A moan escapes my lips when he reaches under my hoodie and grabs onto my breasts. He squeezes them hard, and I jolt.

His fingers travel down my stomach, reaching the waistband of my pants. I try to summon the willpower to resist, to stop him before things go too far, but his proximity overwhelms my senses, clouding my judgment.

Dion caresses the delicate skin above my pants and sticks his hand between my legs. He presses me harder against the tree, his other hand trailing a path of fire along my neck, and I surrender to the forbidden longing, knowing full well the consequences of succumbing to him.

"Fuck me, please," I beg, and he emits a raw, guttural noise.

Dion unbuckles his pants right before pushing down my joggers with force, eliciting a gasp out of me.

He grabs onto my wrists and arches my back, pinning my chest to the tree. Then, I hear him spit and it only intensifies the wetness between my legs.

"Fuck, Aria. You're soaking. Is that all for me, little liar?"

A flush heats my cheeks and I nod.

"This pussy is mine. You know that, right? I took it, claimed it, fucked it, so it's mine," he growls.

I nod again and he pulls on the neckline of my hoodie, causing my head to fly back. "Say it, Aria."

"This pussy is yours," I choke out.

He grunts in approval and kicks my legs open right before angling his cock at my entrance. With one sudden movement, he slams inside of me. I scream.

I immediately regret it when I remember that we are still in the forest, not far from my house, which means that anyone in proximity could hear us.

"Are you trying to get us caught, baby?" Dion teases. "Be a good girl and stay quiet for me while I pound into your perfect cunt."

Fuck. Me.

I've been fantasizing about feeling Dion inside me again, but nothing could've prepared me for this primal, raw reality. He's still wearing his helmet, and it makes this even hotter.

"I missed this tight little cunt."

His presence envelops me, and I get closer to the edge, losing all sense of time and space.

"Touch yourself, baby," he orders, and I bring my fingers to my mouth, moistening them, before placing my hand between my legs, flicking my clit while Dion fills me from behind.

He holds onto my hips with a vice-like grip, nails digging into my skin. Each thrust carrying the force of a lightning strike, sparking all my nerve endings and leaving me breathless.

"Who's inside you? Spell out my name and tell me who's inside your pussy."

"D-Dion," I mutter. "D." *Thrust.* "I. Ahhh," I moan, feeling him in every crevice of my body. "O." *Thrust.* "N." An overwhelming tide of sensations invades me.

"Atta girl. It's *me*. Remember my fucking name as I let you come all over my cock."

I surrender to Dion, getting lost in the ecstasy of my orgasm.

"Yes! Don't stop. Don't stop," I chant, ripples of pleasure cascading through me.

Dion's moves grow frantic as he releases inside me.

We're both left breathless.

After several labored inhales, he finally pulls out of me, and I stand against the tree, longing for more, yet fulfilled at the same time.

"Keep your legs parted," he orders again.

After a few seconds, something leaks out of me.

I turn my head just as Dion reaches up, slowly removing his helmet. He shakes his head, his hair falling over his eyes, framing that beautiful, chiseled face. His tanned skin glistens with a slight sheen of sweat, highlighting the sharp angles of his jaw and the intensity in his eyes. His gaze is piercing, yet calm, as if the chase has only improved his focus.

Then, he kneels and places himself in between my legs, letting his tongue swipe up my inner thighs to lick up the mess.

My heart races and heat creeps up my cheeks. A gasp gets caught in my throat as I look down at him, my knees almost giving out.

When he stands back up, his stare locks onto mine. Squeezing my cheeks, he forces my lips apart and spits our combined juices into my mouth, his penetrating gaze consuming me. "Taste that, Riri baby?" Dion grabs my wrist, yanking me close. I gasp, my breath hitching as his grip tightens. "You need to understand something, Aria. You're mine. No one else's. And no one will take you away from me. Not even your fiancé."

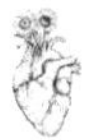

Dion

My heart races, thundering against my chest as I struggle to catch my breath. My body is fucking electrified after our chase. I feel so alive.

Aria turns around and closes her eyes, leaning against the tree for support, and trying to steady her trembling limbs.

"Here," I say, helping her slip her jogging pants on, before buckling myself back up in my jeans.

She looks at me, and I gaze into her beautiful gray eyes, sparkling brighter than the moon and stars combined.

"What did you want to talk about?" she asks, a slight tremor in her voice. Her gaze darts around, suddenly nervous, avoiding direct eye contact. The conversation I had with Evan plays over in my mind—I need to find out if our plan has somehow been compromised.

I grab onto her hand and rub circles over her soft skin. Immediately, she relaxes with my touch.

"Did you tell anyone about us?"

"No," she responds quickly.

"Not even Angelica?"

She shakes her head. "I trust her, but I don't want to risk it. If this makes way to my *baba*, it'll cause a huge issue."

I nod in agreement. "Did your father ask you about that night?"

I remember when I offered to drive her home, she had initially refused, worried that she might be seen with me. At the time, my ego hadn't allowed me to comprehend the implications. It might've been a smarter idea to drop her off at her best friend's house.

"No. I'm sure he didn't see us, but I can't confirm if the guards told him. I'm assuming they didn't think to notify him."

I'd be surprised if his men didn't tell him that his daughter was dropped off by a guy. Especially when she has no need to take a rideshare as she has a driver. Something's not adding up.

"Why?" Aria asks, her gaze focused on me, searching for an answer.

I reach into my pocket and pull out the notes I received, handing them to her. She opens the pieces of paper and reads the messages.

Her eyes dart back up to me. "*Oo theé mou.* Are they talking about me?"

I nod. "I think so. My guess is that it's your father trying to scare me away. Us being together poses a threat to whatever arrangement he has."

She quiets, seemingly processing the information.

"I'm meeting my fiancé for the first time tomorrow. My *baba* will be there, too. I'll try to pick up on anything."

Jealousy grips me like a vise, an intense wave sweeping over me. The thought of her and her fiancé stirs something inside me. I drop Aria's hand and clench my fist.

What the hell is happening to me? I should be pushing her away, keeping my distance.

I can't let myself get too close. I can't let myself *fall*. Because once you fall, there's no going back. And I'm not ready for that. Not now. Not ever.

"Dion," she says, faintly, reaching for my hand again, but the green-eyed monster has taken hold. It's too late to stop my whirring mind.

What perplexes me most is why Aria has such a powerful effect on me. It's a question I can't answer, no matter how hard I try to rationalize it. All I know is that the potential of her being happy with someone else ignites a fire within me that I can't extinguish.

"I have no choice," she murmurs.

"I fucking know that, Aria," I spit.

Her eyes widen at my outburst, flashing with anger, and I instantly regret taking out my fury on her.

"What, Dion? What do you expect me to do?" She throws her hands up in frustration. "Do you think I want this?"

My chest tightens, and I struggle to find the right words. "I don't know what you want, but thinking about you with *him*, whoever he is—"

"You have no right to be jealous," she interrupts, her voice trembling. "What is it that we're doing, anyway? We know this can't go anywhere."

I take a step back, raking a hand through my hair. "I don't fucking know!" I shout. "But I can't stop it. Whatever this is, we have to see it through. I'm not letting you marry him."

Aria shakes her head, tears now filling her eyes. "Dion, we don't even know each other. This could just be the remnants of lust from that one night."

I push her back against the tree, bringing my face to the crook of her neck. "Have you thought about me in the past two months?" I demand, my breath leaving goosebumps on her skin. "Because I haven't been able to get you off my mind no matter how hard I've fucking tried."

She looks away, biting her lip. My heart pounds in my chest.

"Tell me the truth, Aria," I say, my voice raw. "Have you thought about me?"

She finally looks back at me, her jaw locked. "Every single day. But that doesn't change anything."

My hand reaches out to cup her face.

She doesn't pull away, but I can feel the tension in her body, see the conflict in her eyes.

"It changes everything," My voice is barely more than a breath. "Because it means this isn't just in my head. It's fucking real."

Aria's tears spill over. "I'm scared," she admits, leaning into my touch, her eyes closing for a moment. "I'm scared of what this means."

I pull her closer, my forehead resting against hers. "I know. But I'd rather face whatever comes our way than keep pretending this doesn't matter."

We stand there in the darkness, the forest around us silent.

"Then what do we do?" she asks in a whisper.

I take a deep breath, my fingers gently wiping away her tears. "Tell me who he is, and I'll figure it out."

"Andrew Galanis," she responds, not hesitating.

His last name sparks a flicker of recognition in my mind. Have I heard it before? I quickly rack my brain, trying to recall any previous encounters with that family, but I can't quite put a finger on it. This is a job for Xander.

"I'll handle it from here, *astéri mou*. But if you notice something tomorrow, text me."

"I don't have your number," she says, pulling away from me.

"Give me your phone, then."

"I don't have it," she replies with a guilty smile.

I hand her mine. "Put in your number and text yourself." She does, then gives the phone back to me. "Now, go back home before you're caught."

I kiss her again, savoring her soft lips, before releasing her.

As I watch Aria weave through the forest, a mix of emotions, a concoction that my damaged heart struggles to comprehend, stirs within me.

My heart is scarred and wounded, but perhaps it is still capable of feeling *something*.

What I feel for Aria can't be love—it's too fast, too soon. Love requires a certain vulnerability, a willingness to open up and connect on a level that I just haven't been able to reach in years.

But there's something else inside me, undefined, something my mangled soul can't quite grasp. And it's pulling me toward her.

13

DION

The next morning, I wake up sprawled out on my couch.

I blink, groaning as I become aware of my surroundings, and rubbing my eyes to clear the sleep from them. Memories of last night start to trickle back into my mind. I let out a sigh, running a hand through my disheveled hair.

Yesterday didn't go exactly as planned, but I have no regrets when I think back to Aria pressed up against the tree while I watched my hard cock slide in and out of her.

I called with the purpose of asking her about the note, but when I got to the edge of the forest, the impulse to stake my claim on her again was uncontrollable. I was consumed by a burning need to mark my territory.

And I'm so fucking glad I did.

When Aria first saw me, I could practically smell the fear on her. When she understood the game I was playing, it was exhilarating to watch her embrace it and join in.

She was my prey, and I was the predator.

She's mine. There's no way in hell I'm letting her marry her fiancé.

I need to call Xander and have him find out who Andrew Galanis is.

I fish out my phone from my pocket, my body protesting the movement. I was so exhausted when I got home, I didn't even make it to the bedroom. But now, as my muscles scream at me for sleeping on the couch in a less-than-ergonomic position all night, I regret my laziness.

Xander picks up on the third ring, his voice groggy.

"Are you fucking serious, man? It's five a.m.," he yawns.

"I got a name."

I hear an exasperated sigh and some shuffling in the background, then the sound of clacking on a keyboard.

"What is it?" he grunts.

"Andrew Galanis."

Xander types on the computer, and I wait. "I got nothing. I'll have to dive."

"Nothing at all?"

"Nope. He's definitely not from a high-ranking family. At least not in the last fifteen years."

"Then why the fuck would Philip want his daughter to marry him of all people?"

"That's a good question. We'll have to find out what Andrew has to offer," Xander replies.

"And we could use that as leverage against him to get Aria out of the marriage."

Xander chuckles.

"What's so funny, *maláka*?" I grit out.

"You're down *bad* for that chick."

He's not wrong, but he can fuck off with the jokes. "Fuck you," I say, pursing my lips.

"Chill, man. It's cute."

"*Cute*? Am I fucking five years old?"

Xander's laughter booms through the speaker. "Calm down, *vlakas*. It's not a bad thing. Anyway, this could be useful to find out more information about Philip's doings. I've been looking into his involvement with Peter Kouvalakis and the Sisterhood."

After Ignatius was killed, Evander found a file on his computer titled 'The Sisterhood.' After digging into it, he found a dark web forum with multiple users asking how to get access. From what Evan could gather at the time, it seems like some sort of secret society that only allows access by referral.

He'd found pages and pages of girl names and their information. Something shady was going on there.

We discovered that it was an organization that kidnapped girls from Greece and reformed them into child brides and sexual slaves for the rich, led by nuns. *Fucking disgusting.*

Evander thinks that Angelica's father has something to do with this establishment, so naturally, Philip must be involved too. I can't wait for these pieces of shit to get what's coming for them.

I sigh into the phone. "See what Marco can find and let me know. Get some sleep.'

"I'm wide awake now, asshole. I'll call you later."

We hang up, and I push myself off the couch with another yawn, stretching out the kinks in my back as I make my way toward the kitchen. It's time to brew some strong coffee and face the day.

Several minutes later, I hear the front door open.

"*Kaliméra, Heleni,*" I shout.

Helen pops into view with a large smile. "*Kaliméra, agóri mou.* You look...well," she says, after a moment of hesitation, and I snicker.

Helen has been like a mother to me. The only woman, other than my *mama*, that I've ever gotten close to. She's always been there for me, offering advice and support when I needed it the most. I can't imagine my life without her in it. Especially without her playfulness. Though, I've been careful not to let myself get too attached. I refuse to get hurt again.

"Thank you. I got a whopping three hours of sleep on my very comfortable couch." I grin.

She rolls her eyes. "You're more chipper than usual today."

"What do you mean?" I ask, taking a sip of my black coffee.

"You've been a sad mess for two months. Ever since that girl came over and left, I've watched you mope around every day."

"I don't know what you're talking about," I say, feigning ignorance.

"Did you see *her* last night?"

I stifle a smirk. "Maybe."

"That's what I thought."

"Whatever."

Leaving Helen in the kitchen, I head upstairs to take a shower. I usually start my days with a workout, but I'm too tired.

My phone vibrates in my pocket.

Little liar: Hi.

Instantly, a smile tugs at the corners of my lips. *Little liar.* That's how Aria saved her number in my contacts.

My phone buzzes a second time before I get the chance to respond.

Little liar: Did you steal my underwear again?

I almost spit out my coffee.

Reaching into the back pocket of my jeans, I pull out Aria's ripped, blue thong. I forgot that I'd snatched it off her last night.

I bring the flimsy piece of fabric to my nose and inhale.

Fuck. Her scent drives me wild. My cock strains in my jeans as I'm assaulted with the memory of her pussy around it.

Me: Sniffing it as we speak.

Little liar: You're disgusting.

Me: There's nothing disgusting about your pussy, baby.

I watch as the three dots appear and disappear in our chat.

Little liar: It's too early for this.

I laugh, placing my coffee down on my nightstand and lying on my bed.

Me: You're the one who texted me at 6 a.m. asking about your thong.

Little liar: Good point.

Me: Are you still in bed?

I shift on my mattress, slipping off my jeans to get more comfortable.

Little liar: Yes...

Me: What are you wearing?

Her response comes in at lightning speed.

Little liar: Nothing.

My dick stands at attention, and I groan. I'm picturing Aria, naked and tangled in her blanket...and I'm now *jealous* of her fucking bedsheets.

Me: Nothing?

Little liar: Uh huh. I stripped out of my clothes and jumped straight into bed after I got back last night.

Me: Show me.

It takes a minute for her response to come in. As the image appears on my screen, I bite my bottom lip hard enough to draw blood.

Fuck me.

Her perfect tits are on full display, one pebbled nipple pinched between her fingers. Her smooth and supple stomach and her grabbable hips are *begging* to be manhandled.

Finally, my eyes reach her mound, and I salivate at the view of her bare pussy. I'm fucking dying to stick my tongue in it.

I throw my head back, not able to take the torture any longer. I have to relieve the ache. I quickly pull my briefs down, freeing my hard cock.

Me: Touch yourself.

Again, the text bubble appears and disappears.

Little liar: No, Dion.

Me: Why the fuck not?

Lying in bed, thinking about Aria touching herself while talking to me is already driving me wild. And her pushback only makes me want her more. I crave her lips around my dick.

If she wants to play hard to get, I'm ready to break her.

> Me: I know you can still feel me inside you, little liar.

I grab the base of my dick and squeeze it tight, causing the blood to rush to the head. I let out a groan. This feels good.

> Me: I'm stroking my cock thinking of your tight pussy as we speak.

Little liar: Oh God.

I wrap Aria's torn thong around my shaft and use it to stroke the length, picturing her tight cunt swallowing me whole.

> Me: Stick a finger inside, baby, and show me how wet you are.

I press send and wait for her reply. If a photo comes through, I'll know I have her right where I want her.

A few minutes go by. I get a notification and open the attachment: a picture of her glistening fingers.

> Me: Fuck, Aria. I'm gonna come.

Little liar: Me too. I'm so close already.

Little liar: Se thélo.

> Me: I need to fuck you again.

I'm nearing the edge of ecstasy, feeling a tingle originate from my sack. I can barely hold on any longer. It has been a mere few hours since I was balls deep in Aria, and I already can't wait to make her feel good again.

I click on the camera app and press record.

With one hand holding her thong around my throbbing cock, I stroke myself, starting from the base. I spit on the tip to lubricate it, then use my fingers to spread my saliva around.

"Fuck, baby. I'm going to explode just thinking about fucking you. The things I'd do to be buried deep inside your cunt again," I grunt into the camera, my voice raw.

I rub my cock a few more times until I feel a slight prickling sensation in my nuts, then stop filming and send the video to Aria. A few moments later, I receive her response.

> Little liar: Fuck. I'm coming.

> Me: Let it go, moró mou. I'm right there with you.

As if on command, my orgasm overtakes me, and I release my cum into Aria's thong. A thick coating that drips onto my abdomen. Holy fuck.

I'm sixteen again, feeling the excitement of sexting a girl for the first time.

I snap a picture of Aria's soiled panties and send it to her.

> Little liar: You're a freak.

> Little liar: I kinda like it…

I let out a deep, hearty laugh that reverberates through the room.

> Me: I know you do, astéri mou.

> Little liar: Don't be so cocky.

A moment later, she sends another text that makes my heart sink.

> Little liar: And I thought about it…this can't keep happening, especially after today.

What the fuck?

I call her. She picks up on the first ring.

"I thought we had this convo yesterday," I grit out.

She sighs into the phone. "Dion, I'm meeting Andrew in a few hours."

"Don't say his fucking name," I bark. Hearing that fucker's name so soon after coming is ruining my fucking mood.

She scoffs. "Fine. My *fiancé*," she drawls, and that makes me even angrier.

"That's fucking worse."

Aria lets out a growl of frustration. "What do you want from me, Dion? You can't have it both ways. You want me for yourself, but you know that's not possible right now. Unless I miraculously find a way out of this predicament, I'm pretty much already engaged, so you'll have to accept—."

"I'll never accept you being someone else's, Aria," I seethe, cutting her off.

She exhales, her voice softening. "Trust me. I don't want this either, but what am I supposed to do?"

"I'll take care of it."

She sneers. "Is that your response for everything?"

"Trust me. I *will* take care of it," I argue, and hang up.

My hand trembles as I swipe it through my hair, my heart pounding against my chest relentlessly.

Aria is right. We technically shouldn't keep doing this.

I want her, but at what cost? How far am I willing to go? Anything I do might risk compromising what Evan and I have been working toward.

Regardless, a rush of determination fills my chest.

I'm ready to do anything to make her mine.

14

ANDREW

I throw myself back on the chair in front of my computer, fists almost digging holes on the edge of my desk. Dion and Aria were just *sexting*. Disgust churns in my stomach.

I thought sending Dion threats would be enough to scare him off, keep him away from her. It worked for a little while.

After discovering them together for the first time, I sent Dion a threatening note, but it didn't seem to have the desired effect. As I kept a close eye on Aria, I realized that Dion was also lurking in the shadows, keeping tabs on her. It infuriated me that he had blatantly ignored my warning.

Determined to protect what was mine, I penned another even more menacing note, warning him to stay away. This time, I made it crystal clear that there would be dire consequences if he didn't back off.

And he did—for almost two months.

But now, they're back together. My threats were fucking useless.

Their connection seems to go deeper than I imagined.

Around midnight I got a call from one of Aria's guards, informing me that she'd left the house.

The footage he sent me doesn't cover the entire back property, so he wasn't able to confirm where she went. I tapped into her phone to check her location, but it pinged at her house. *Weird.* I had to give up, hoping she'd only gone for a walk in her massive garden.

But when I logged into her phone this morning, I saw the text messages appearing on my screen in real time. They met last night, and he *fucked* her.

This is a fucking slap in the face.

The night before we're supposed to meet for the first time, she fucks her lover boy, then sexts him mere hours before seeing me. She's supposed to be a virgin and now, she's sullied. *Whore.*

Aria will need to be told who she belongs to.

Once my ring is on her finger, my plans will be set into motion, and I can solidify my role in her family and in her life.

It's time Aria meets her new fiancé once and for all.

15

ARIA

"Are you ready to meet your future husband?" *Mama* asks as she fidgets with the zipper of my dress. I'm wearing a modest, light-pink one-shoulder cocktail gown for the occasion. My long hair is pulled back into a sleek bun, and my makeup is light with bold lips. Exactly how my mother wanted it.

The idea of meeting the stranger I'll be tied to for the rest of my life is terrifying, especially since I had no say in the person chosen. My father warned me again not long ago to behave, claiming that it's what's "best for the family."

But what's best for the family isn't what's best for *me*.

I've imagined this moment countless times—what Andrew might be like, how we'll connect, and the life we'll build together. But now that it's happening, I'm consumed with anxiety.

I suck in a breath so that my mother can zip up my dress.

"Of course," I lie, and my *mama* smiles.

"Good. Andrew will be here soon. I'll send Magdalena to get you when he arrives." She moves toward the door. "You look beautiful, *Arioula*," she adds, right before leaving the room.

I look at my reflection in the mirror and smooth the fabric of my dress, taking deep breaths to calm the butterflies in my stomach, but the sense of uncertainty persists. What if we don't click? What if I don't make a good impression? Even worse, what if he's a dick?

These questions and more echo relentlessly in my mind, amplifying my anxiety. The weight of this encounter feels immense—my future happiness hinges on this singular meeting.

But each time I close my eyes, I'm transported back to that moment in the forest, where time stood still, and my world collided with Dion's once again. His touch lingers on my skin, every sensation still vivid and electric.

And his words...those he spoke with such determination, cutting through the darkness of the night. *I'm not letting you marry him.* They reverberate in my mind, each syllable etched into my memory with lasting ink. The intensity in his voice, the sincerity in his eyes.

Now, as I face the day ahead, a facade of normalcy is expected of me. The weight of expectation presses down on me, urging me to wear a mask of happiness, to carry on as if nothing has changed. But how can I pretend that everything is fine?

I step into my bathroom and open the cabinet under the sink, reaching behind the baskets. I need something to calm my nerves.

"There you are," I say, finally finding what I was looking for, worried for a moment that Magda had found my stash and thrown it.

I pull out a small, half-empty bottle of tequila. Removing the lid, the scent of the liquor hits me immediately. I bring it to my mouth and take a quick swig.

The tequila washes over my tongue, fiery and potent.

Warmth spreads down my throat, a comforting heat that soothes my nerves almost instantly.

I exhale slowly and set the bottle back in its hiding place, feeling a tad more composed than before.

Right then, there's a soft knock on my door. *"Arioula."* Magda's voice travels through my room.

"Coming!" I call out.

Grabbing the bottle of mouthwash on the counter, I swish some around my mouth to get rid of the stench and taste of the alcohol.

Rushing to the door, I take another deep breath, then swing it open, plastering a fake smile on my face. "I'm ready."

As I head down the stairs, I hear my parents' voices talking to our guests. Andrew should be here with his mother.

On the last step, I remind myself that it's okay to feel anxious. "You got this," I whisper, pushing aside the doubts and fears that gnaw at my insides. Magda squeezes my shoulder and shuffles away.

When I turn the corner, I see him. Actually, I hear him first: a deep, unfamiliar laugh erupts in response to something my father said.

The sound of my heels clicking on the floor gathers everyone's attention, and they all turn.

Baba greets me first. *"Kóri mou."* He extends his arm to me, and I walk toward him with a coy smile. "This is Andrew Galanis." He points to the man standing next to him.

"Nice to meet you, Mr. Galanis." I extend a hand, and he surprises me when he places a kiss on the top. My palms feel a tad clammy, and a slight blush creeps up my cheeks.

"Likewise, Miss Kastellanos," Andrew replies with a soft smile.

A sigh of relief slips out of my mouth. He's nothing like I expected.

When my father told me I'd be marrying one of his

associates, I thought he would be an unattractive, old man. But Andrew is young, very tall, and quite handsome, with light-brown hair and a strong jawline. At least he'll be good to look at and won't disgust me every time he wants to have sex.

Sex. My stomach churns, my mind drifting back to Dion. His deep, steady gaze that holds me captivated, his touch that ignites a fire within me. Warmth shoots down to my center.

I close my eyes, and I can still feel the patterns he traced on my skin. It's like a fever dream that slipped through my fingers too soon.

Reality is cruel.

My father's voice interrupts my daze. "Aria, did you hear me?" he asks from the other end of the hallway. They've all started heading toward the dining room, and I'm still frozen in place, assaulted by images of Dion between my legs.

What the fuck, Aria? Your fiancé is standing right *there.*

When I look up at Andrew, I notice a subtle shift in his expression—a hint of suspicion flickering in his eyes. *Fuck.* Does he know I've been seeing someone else? Surely not. The mere idea sends a shiver down my spine.

A wave of guilt washes over me. I've been too careless, too reckless in my interactions with Dion.

I shake my head to clear my thoughts. "Yes, sorry," I say, hurrying to join them.

Sat across from Andrew, I watch him interact with my family. He's polite and well-mannered, engaging in small talk with everyone at the table. He even gets Dimitri chatting, and my brother hates these kinds of dinner parties.

My *baba* leans closer to him, and they start talking, their voices low. Andrew's expression becomes guarded, thoughtful. I strain my ears, desperate to catch any hint of their conversation. I have to find out if they are responsible for the notes that Dion received.

But amidst the chatter in the dining room, I only hear snippets of meaningless phrases that offer no insight into what they're discussing.

Frustration knots in my stomach.

Andrew looks up at me, catching my stare, and I try to smile, even though deep discomfort gnaws at me. The entire situation is surreal, like I've stumbled into someone else's life.

I bite my lip, torn between relief and disappointment as their conversation continues without revealing anything. *Perhaps it's for the best*, I tell myself, trying to quell the rising doubts.

"Aria, your mother tells me you're a florist," Andrew's mother says, snapping me out of my haze. I turn my head toward her. *My future mother-in-law. Mama* introduced us before dinner, but I've been in such a trance that I forgot her name.

I fiddle with my napkin, my fingers tracing the delicate embroidery as I struggle to find my footing. "Something like that," I reply with a smile.

"Don't be so humble, Aria," my mother quips. "She's amazing. She created the beautiful arrangements on the table tonight. And she turned the guest house into a floral haven."

My cheeks heat. "Thanks, *Mama*."

I really love working with flowers. Whenever I'm surrounded by fresh blooms and the sweet scent of petals, an immediate sense of calm washes over me. The process of arranging flowers is meditative, like therapy. And right now, I wish I could hide away and do exactly that, because I'm anxious as all hell.

Andrew's voice cuts into our conversation. "I'd love to see it, if you don't mind."

I steal a glance at him. "The workshop?" I ask, trying to decipher his tone.

"Yes. These flowers are beautiful. I'm interested in seeing

your workspace," he responds, his expression polite and masked with a practiced charm.

"Sure. I'll show you sometime," I reply with a nod.

Dessert arrives, and I yearn for a chance to retreat and collect my thoughts. As soon as the table is cleared, I rush to the lounge area to grab a strong drink from the bar.

Everyone moves into the room while I stand by the window, looking out to the night sky, deep in thought. One arm tucked under my chest; I swirl my drink in my other hand.

"Gin," a voice says from behind me. It takes me a second to recognize who it is.

Without turning to meet his gaze, I reply, "Good guess."

"I didn't take you as a gin type of person," Andrew says.

I let out a small scoff, turning to meet his intense gaze. My eyes narrow slightly. "Enlighten me, then. What type of person would you have taken me for?"

He chuckles. "You look like more of a dark liquor girl. Rum or whiskey."

"I enjoy those, too. Can't I be an *all* types of alcohol person?" I retort, raising a brow.

He smirks, looking down at his glass. Right before taking a sip, he says, "I guess you can."

I glance at his drink, and I can tell what it is just by its potent smell.

"*Ouzo.* Surprise, surprise. Greek men are so predictable." I roll my eyes, a grin pulling at my lips. I don't know why I feel comfortable enough to engage in this type of banter with him, considering how uncomfortable I was moments ago, but I can't deny that Andrew seems quite pleasant. I guess I should be thankful that he's not an asshole. Yet.

Things could easily change once we're married. I won't think about that now.

This time, Andrew laughs out loud, grabbing the attention

of our parents. I look at them, and my mother smiles at me. She's probably happy that we're getting along.

"Not my first choice, but your father offered me a glass. I couldn't refuse."

"Uh huh," I say, with a little wink.

I turn and look outside again. I can see the soft glow of the guest house in the distance. Andrew follows my gaze.

"Is that where the magic happens?"

His question catches me by surprise until I realize what he's referring to. The flowers.

"Yes. Yes, um, that's my makeshift studio."

"*Thélis na figis apó edó?*" he asks.

Do I want to get out of there? With him? I glance over at our families. My brother's face is buried into his phone. My father looks half asleep on the lounge chair, and our mothers are in deep conversation, probably already planning the engagement party and wedding.

I have nothing better to do.

I shrug. "Sure."

We manage to sneak out of the room, topped-up drinks in hand, and I lead Andrew to the back patio doors. Once we step outside, the cool air hits my face, instantly calming me.

We walk down the path in silence, passing through my backyard garden. The moonlight casts a glow over the tangle of plants, where fireflies twinkle like tiny lanterns. The scent of herbs reaches my nostrils, and I'm grateful for this moment of tranquility.

When we reach the entrance, I input the code. The door unlocks, and I step inside, Andrew a safe distance behind me.

Just then, I realize that I'm alone in a small space with a stranger. *He won't do anything crazy, right?* I mean, our parents aren't that far away. *Please, God, don't make him a rapist.*

Awkwardly, I walk deeper into the studio. Andrew doesn't follow me, and I'm relieved.

"Wow," he whispers. "How much time do you spend here?"

I check on my peace lily plants, dipping my fingers into the soil to check the moisture. "A lot, I guess." I shrug. "I don't work, so this is what I spend my days doing. I'm a certified botanist and plant mom," I say proudly.

Andrew walks through the studio, looking at every flower on his way and stopping right in front of me. "Does that mean I'll have to build you one of these?" He smiles, pointing around the space.

A niggling feeling of skepticism creeps up on me. It's not that I don't appreciate kindness, but it feels...a bit too good to be true. We've only just met, after all.

Part of me wants to believe it's genuine, that maybe I've been lucky enough to be tied to a man who will be caring and attentive. But a small, cynical voice in the back of my mind whispers doubts.

I can't help but wonder, is this all an act? I sure know I'm playing a part.

As much as I should be flattered by his offer, I feel nothing.

"Why are you being so nice to me?" I blurt out.

Andrew's brow creases. "Why wouldn't I? We're going to be married."

"Yes, but you don't know me."

He crosses his arms. "So, you'd rather be treated like shit because we're strangers? It's just common decency, Aria."

It's the first time I've heard him say my name. And again, it does nothing to me.

I keep expecting a familiar flutter in my chest, a rush of excitement. But as I stand here, there's no inexplicable spark.

It's not like how I feel with Dion, and it leaves me with a sense of disappointment. Will I ever have a connection like that again?

The corners of my mouth curl down. "I guess not. Sorry, I'm just having a hard time with all of this."

He lets out a sigh. "I understand. This isn't my ideal scenario, either. But I have to protect my family." Andrew's gaze seems a little more distant now. I wonder what his story is. From what I've heard through the grapevines, his father passed away when he was young. He has no other siblings. It's just been him and his mother for most of his life.

"Was the marriage your idea?"

He shakes his head. "Your father made me a proposition I couldn't refuse," he responds, not giving away too much. I decide to pry anyway.

I place my drink on a side table and pull out two stools. I sit on one of them, gesturing for Andrew to do the same.

"What could my father possibly offer you? It can't be his estate or business, given he already has a male heir."

"It has nothing to do with your family." He takes a sip from his glass, staring out toward the rows of plants and flowers in front of us.

"So, what is it? My father won't tell me anything and I have the right to know. There shouldn't be any secrets between husband and wife," I say pointedly.

Andrew smiles. "You're a cheeky one, aren't you?" I grin back at him. This isn't so bad. There might not be any love between us, but if there's friendship, I think I could do this.

And who knows? Maybe love could grow. Andrew is an attractive, pleasant man.

"He promised financial stability for my mother."

I furrow my brow. "I thought your family had generational wealth?"

"We do. But if I leave this earth, my mother will be left with nothing. I'm the last of the Galanis name and we're not from a prominent family." Something flashes across his face but disappears before I can make it out.

"And he promised you that how?"

"That's what I can't tell you," he responds in a playful tone, meeting my gaze with a smirk.

I let out a dramatic sigh. "Fine. I'll get you to crack eventually."

Andrew winks at me. "Game on."

We keep chatting for a while until we hear a knock at the door.

"Come in!" I holler.

The door beeps open and my mother's head pokes through the door, covering her eyes. I laugh. What did she think we were doing? "The coast is clear, *Mama*." I roll my eyes.

"We didn't want to interrupt, but Cora is getting tired." *Cora, that's it. Mrs. Galanis waves sleepily behind my mother.*

I look at my phone and notice it's way past midnight. Andrew and I have been talking for well over two hours.

"Sorry, *Mama*. I didn't see the time pass," he says, throwing another wink at me, and I feel my cheeks heat. Maybe, *just maybe*, this attraction could grow into something more. A pang of guilt hits me as Dion's face appears in my thoughts, but I try to stifle it. "Let's take you home," Andrew adds to his mother.

He turns back to me and holds my hand. "Aria, it was a pleasure." He places a soft kiss on my knuckles. "Thank you for having us over," he tells my mother.

Then, Andrew stops suddenly, as if just remembering something, and reaches into the interior pocket of his suit jacket.

"I forgot to give you this."

In his hand is a small velvet box. My heart falters.

Inside, rests a ring, simple and elegant. My *engagement* ring.

I force a smile, trying to mask my unease, though my mind is already racing ahead.

As I gaze at it, I can't shake off the worry of how he'll react.

I thank Andrew, giving him a small, uneasy smile.

"May I?" he asks, pointing to the ring, and I nod.

He takes it out of the holder and slips it onto my finger.

My mother smiles at Andrew and gives Cora a quick embrace. "We'll be in touch for the engagement party preparations."

As soon as they leave the estate, I don't waste any time climbing up the stairs to my room. Once inside, I grab my phone to text my best friends. Gianis, Angelica and I have been inseparable since childhood. They are my anchor, my confidants, the ones who know me better than anyone else. Gianis may spend most of his time rolling his eyes at our antics, but he's always there when it matters.

> Me: Andrew just left.

A few moments later, a message comes in.

> Angie: So??? Is he hot?

I chuckle out loud. Of course that's the first thing Angelica would ask me.

> Me: Yes, he is...

I think back to Andrew's face as I was seated across from him.

> Angie: Describe him!!!

> Gianis: Why am I here for this?

> Me: He's tall and handsome. At least 6'3, dark hair, and stark blue eyes.

> Angie: Sounds yummy! Did you get along?

> Gianis: Oh, for fuck's sake. I'm leaving.

Me: We did, actually. I was surprised. I thought he'd be old and wrinkly.

Gianis: I mean it.

Angie: Phew! At least you'll be married to eye candy.

I smile at my phone. I know exactly what Angelica is trying to do. She knows how much I've been dreading this arrangement.

Gianis has left the chat

Angie: LOL. What got up G's ass?

Me: Maybe it's because you rejected him…

Angie: Shut up.

Me: Love you, too!

Putting my phone down on my nightstand, I roll over in bed and lay my head on my pillow.

For a first meeting, it didn't go badly at all. However, a part of me believes that Andrew is hiding something behind his charming demeanor.

It's frustrating, really. I *want* to trust him.

But it's hard to do so in this world. I've seen people get fucked over by family, friends and associates more times than I can count.

And I got screwed over by my own father.

If I can't trust my own parents, who can I count on?

My phone vibrates, and I pick it up, thinking it's another message from Angie.

Unknown: It was nice finally meeting you,
future wife.

I clutch the device in my hand and close my eyes. I have no idea how to feel right now.

Maybe one day, when this is all said and done and I'm happily married to Andrew, I'll understand the reasoning behind my father's decision without feeling like I've been taken advantage of.

Until then, I'll tread carefully and guard my heart.

16

DION

I't's been a week since I've spoken to Aria.

Seven days since I last saw her, felt her, was inside her.

She didn't text me after meeting her fiancé, and I can't help but wonder why she's gone radio silent.

I asked her to let me know if she overheard something between her father and Andrew, but I'm guessing there was nothing out of the norm.

It's also been a week of watching the footage of that man sneaking onto the ship to drop off the note.

I pick up the crumpled piece of paper, turning it over in my hands as if expecting answers to reveal themselves.

I lean back in my chair, frustration mounting as I realize I'm no closer to unraveling the mystery. Every angle I explore leads to more questions.

Andrew's file is open in front of me, and I flip through each sheet obsessively, my eyes scanning every word, every line, searching for anything, any tiny detail that I could use against him. I know there must be something in here, some weakness I can exploit.

Xander has been looking into Andrew, but he keeps reaching dead ends. It's like his family never existed.

All he was able to find was that his father is dead, leaving Andrew and his mother the sole survivors of his family lineage.

He's the last of the Galanis name, which is probably why he's so interested in getting married. Most likely in the hopes of having a son who will inherit Aria's family's business.

I pause for a moment, and stare at the photo of Andrew paper-clipped to the top of the file. His face stares back at me, calm and composed. He's younger and more attractive than I thought he'd be, and I don't know if that makes me feel better. The desire to punch that smug expression is strong. I imagine the satisfaction of feeling my knuckles connect with his jaw, releasing this pent-up rage.

The very thought of Aria marrying someone else and creating a family...I clench my fists, trying to contain the rage that threatens to consume me whole. But it's futile.

I should be the one filling her with *my* children.

Patience. I can't act on impulse, no matter how strong the urge. I need to find something concrete, something to bring him down. So, I force myself to return to the file, to keep searching, to keep digging. I won't stop until I find what I'm looking for. Andrew won't know what hit him.

My phone rings, distracting me from the firestorm brewing inside me.

"Yes," I bark.

"*Christé mou.* Who pissed in your coffee this morning?" Xander snaps back.

I rub my temples. I really need to get my fucking temper in check. But when it comes to Aria, I can't control it.

I sigh. "What is it?" I ask in a calmer tone, listening as he gives me an update.

My heart pounds like a drum in my chest. "What the fuck?"

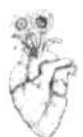

As I weave through the streets on my motorcycle, I can't shake the feeling of urgency eating away at me.

Aria does hot yoga a couple times a week at a studio in the town square, right next to Black Bean café, a quaint coffee bar. It's customary for her to stop in after a session. But she fucking went with *Andrew* today? I asked Xander to start monitoring her again the day after our forest meet-up.

After only a week of being engaged, they're already doing normal couple activities. *Fuck that.*

Realization hits me like a ton of bricks—I've become completely obsessed with Aria. Every move she makes, every word she says. Having her tracked like some kind of stalker. Still, I don't give a damn, and I won't apologize for it.

When I pull up to the shop, I park my bike in front of the door, quickly dismounting and striding toward the entrance.

If Aria thinks she can replace me, she has another thing coming. I'll make sure to be a constant presence in her life, in her thoughts. She'll never get rid of me. I refuse to fade into the background of her life. Every fiber of my being is determined to make sure she doesn't forget me.

As I push open the door to the café, the scent of freshly brewed coffee hits me, distracting me. My eyes scan the room, searching for a familiar face—and there she is, engrossed in conversation with *him*, the sound of her laughter somehow reaching me. Seeing her so content should make me happy. Instead, it just stokes the flames of jealousy burning inside me.

Andrew leans into whisper something in her ear, and her smile widens. That's when I notice the glint of the ring on her finger. It feels like a punch to the gut, and I struggle to contain the rage threatening to spill over. I can't let my anger ruin the illusion of normalcy in public.

I take a deep breath, trying to compose myself before I approach the counter to order. I plaster on a fake smile and greet Anna, the barista.

"Hey, you," she says with a smile. "Long time no see!"

I haven't come to this side of town in a while. Ever since Ignatius died, I believe. We've been too preoccupied.

"I know. It's good to see you again, Anna. How's your son?"

"He's great. He joined the Little League, so I've been busy!"

After a few short minutes of conversation, Anna hands me my coffee. I turn around, just as Aria's eyes meet mine.

Her expression shifts from delight to shock in an instant, like she's seen a ghost. Her fiancé follows her gaze, his brows furrowed in confusion.

Aria's mouth opens and closes, though no words come out. Her eyes dart between me and Andrew, guilt and discomfort written all over her face.

I turn away without acknowledging her and seat myself at a table across the room.

From the corner of my eye, I see Aria continue to sneak glances at me. Andrew shoots her a puzzled look before turning his attention back to me. I'm picturing pulling out my gun and shooting him right between the eyes, his bloodied body slumping on the table.

Aria's eyes widen as if reading my mind, and casts Andrew a quick, panicked glance before composing herself.

He murmurs something, but I can't catch even a snippet of their hushed conversation, the ambient noise of the café drowning out their words.

If he suspects anything, he doesn't show it. And it's better that way because it's taking every ounce of effort in me to not march over there, kill him, then drag Aria out over my shoulder.

I pull out my phone and send her a text.

> Me: Tell him to leave or I'm crashing your little date.

Her gaze flickers toward her phone, and I can sense her hesitation to check her messages, perhaps not wanting to seem suspicious in front of Andrew.

When she finally unlocks her screen, her brows knit together, and discomfort crosses her features. I can almost feel the tension radiating from her as she quickly puts down her phone, pretending like nothing happened.

There's a subtle shift in her demeanor as she continues her conversation. She's a bit more guarded now, a bit less at ease.

I text her again.

> Me: I'm giving you 30 seconds, Aria.

I've been trying to keep calm. But right now, anger bubbles up inside me, threatening to overflow.

Aria reads my message, her eyes widening. Without hesitation, she springs up from the table, a sense of determination in her movements. She exchanges a few quick words with Andrew, their expressions serious, before they both head toward the door.

As Aria rushes out, her phone clutched tightly in her hand, I seize the opportunity to send another message.

> Me. Go your separate ways and meet me in the back alley.

I can't help the pang of jealousy as I observe Andrew bending down to give Aria a tender kiss on the cheek. She smiles at him. Then, he leaves, crossing the street and disappearing into the distance as Aria continues down the sidewalk.

After a few moments, I decide it's time to follow suit. I leave the café, my anticipation growing as I make my way to the back alley. I lean against the brick wall, my eyes scanning the area, eagerly awaiting Aria's arrival.

The sound of footsteps echoing against the pavement signals her approach. My heart quickens when I catch sight of her.

She finally reaches the spot where I stand, a mixture of confusion and anger in her eyes.

"I got your message, loud and clear," she spits. "What the fuck is wrong with you? How did you even know I was here?"

"I've told you once before, I know everything."

"Are you *stalking* me?"

"No. I'm just keeping an eye on you."

Aria's expression shifts to one of shock, her mouth opening. "That's the same fucking thing, Dion. How dare you?"

"Someone might be following you. Given the threats I received, I'm trying to be vigilant."

She scoffs. "So, you thought showing up to the coffee shop where I was with my fiancé was being *vigilant*?"

"I'm trying to protect you. And what the fuck is this?" I seethe, grabbing her left hand and gesturing at her engagement ring.

Aria jerks her hand back and crosses her arms. "Andrew has been nothing but nice to me."

"So, being *nice* is enough for you?"

She grits her teeth in frustration. "That's not the fucking point!"

"Then, what is it? Just a week ago, I was buried inside this." I reach over and palm her pussy. She tries to push me away. "And now you're playing the doting fiancé? Come on, Aria."

We might be out in broad daylight, but this back alley is hidden and secluded.

My chest heaves as I stare into her eyes. I want to kiss her so fucking badly.

Aria laughs. "Are you fucking jealous?" she asks, in a mocking tone.

"Well, it sure looked like you were cozy and comfortable in there," I spit, closing the distance between us, and I push her against the brick wall. I reach for the handle of my handgun and pull it out of my belt. Aria gasps, her gaze meeting mine.

With a swift motion, I press the muzzle against her throat, the pressure of the barrel making her gulp.

"If you think you can get rid of me that easily, try again, little liar," I murmur into her ear.

Her breath catches in her throat, and I wrap my palm around it, squeezing until she struggles to inhale. I pin her further against the wall, lifting her off the ground. She scratches at my hands to let her go, but instead, I lean in and crash my lips against hers.

I place the gun back in my waistband and reach between her legs, shoving her panties to the side with two fingers, connecting with her warmth. She lets out a strangled moan. Pushing past her wet folds, I press my digits into her pussy. Her entire body freezes at the intrusion.

My grasp on her neck is still strong, her gurgles mixing with her whimpers.

"I hope you choke as I'm fucking you with my fingers, *astéri mou*. The air you breathe is mine," I begin, my voice low. "Your every inhale and exhale are bound to me," I add, shoving my digits deeper into her warm hole, eliciting a cry from her. "Your oxygen, your life—it *all* belongs to me."

My grip tightens slightly around Aria's throat, and I feel her struggle beneath me. Panic flickers in her eyes as she's losing too much air. Her movements become frantic, her attempts to pry my fingers away grow desperate.

But I can't stop.

Something dark within me drives me forward, a primal urge that drowns out reason.

A sickening thrill I can't deny myself.

Her body grows weaker, and I let her go, still pinning her to the wall.

She gasps for air, finally able to take in a full breath. Her eyes widen in fear, but there's something else there too —arousal.

My fingers keep up with the ministrations until her legs start to shake, her entire body withering in my grasp.

Aria shouts, her eyes rolling back, and I don't care if anyone hears. I can't tear my gaze from the sight.

When she finally comes down from the orgasm, I kiss her hard, nipping at her bottom lip, and she squeals. A droplet of blood forms, and I lick it clean.

Aria shudders, and I press myself between her legs, letting her feel my hardened cock.

"You're fucking mine, Aria. Never forget that. No matter how hard you try to play house with your fiancé, you'll always belong to me."

I put her down, and she takes several breaths to compose herself.

I trail kisses down her neck, inhaling after every peck, getting high on her scent. "Do you know how badly I wanted to blow his brains out in that café and fuck you over the table in his blood?" Her breath hitches. Bending to my knees, I slip my hands up her skirt and grab handfuls of her plump ass.

I'm transfixed by the sight of Aria's long, slender legs. They seem to stretch on for miles, and I just want them wrapped around my waist as I drill into her perfect pussy.

She gasps for air when my mouth connects with her mound over her panties.

"Fuck, *astéri mou*. You look like a little slut in this skirt. You shouldn't wear clothes like this around me. It makes me feral." I let out a growl. "I've been hungry for your cunt ever since I first tasted you," I say, placing kisses along her inner thighs. "I want to devour you."

Aria shoves my head away and closes her legs. "Fuck! We can't keep doing this," she hisses in a panic. "Especially not here in broad daylight. Anyone could see us."

"Isn't that part of the fun?" I tease.

The hint of a scowl forms on her brow. "Stop."

"Please." Pushing her wet panties to the side again, I let my nose trail her clit, and her knees buckle. "I'm begging you, baby. Let me have the honor of tasting you again."

I don't know who I am anymore. *Begging*?

A moan escapes her lips and her fingers tangle in my hair, a half-assed attempt to push me away and pull me closer.

"I'm dying here, Riri baby," I breathe against her pussy, her skin erupting in goosebumps.

Her resolve begins to crack, the lines of tension on her face softening. Though Aria is strong-willed, determined to stand her ground against me, I know she can't resist this thing—this *pull*—between us.

Her shoulders surrender, the hesitation in her gaze dissipating as she meets mine.

She pushes her hips toward me, giving me the go-ahead to bury my face in her folds. And I do just that. I lap my tongue around her clit, hitting where she's most sensitive with every circle.

Aria bucks to meet my mouth, moaning in ecstasy as I eat her pussy like it's the most delectable dessert.

Flattening my tongue, I lick from her entrance all the way up her mound and her body quivers.

"Yes, baby," she moans, and I lose it. Hearing her call me *baby* unleashes something within me.

I pull out my dick from its confines and tug on it at an assaulting pace. I can't stand the pressure anymore. My own limbs tingle, responding to every pull.

I'm completely lost in the moment, consumed by Aria's taste and smell.

I suck on her clit until she begins to cry out, and it sends a shiver down my spine.

"Ah, fuck!" she shouts as she rides my face, and I feel myself losing control along with her.

We both climax, surrendering to the blissful chaos. I release onto the brick wall and asphalt as Aria comes in my mouth.

I keep lapping at her folds for a few moments and then stand up, grab Aria by the nape and pull her into me, letting her taste herself on my lips.

Eventually, we pull away, our foreheads pressed together as we breathe into each other.

"What are we going to do?" Aria mutters, her voice trembling with emotion. Her usual vibrant energy is replaced by a hollow emptiness, her eyes dulled and distant.

I exhale heavily.

"What we've been doing all this time, *astéri mou.*"

"But for how long?" Her despair is palpable, hanging in the air like a dark cloud.

"Not much longer," I reply, burying her in my arms.

And I mean it.

17

ANDREW

The engine hums softly as I sit in the shadows of my car, frustration scratching at me like a persistent itch. Aria and I parted ways mere moments ago, but something isn't sitting right.

Call it intuition or maybe just years of being underestimated, but I can't shake the feeling that she is up to something.

There was a weird tension in the air when we said goodbye that wasn't there before.

I watch as she reaches the corner where she'll turn left toward her house, but instead, she pauses, her eyes darting around as if searching for something—or someone. My heartbeat picks up.

Did she think she could deceive me? That I'm some naive *prick?*

I felt the change in atmosphere as soon as that man walked into the coffee shop—saw it, tasted it.

I noticed him immediately, a hint of familiarity that made my senses prickle with unease. I hadn't seen his entire face yet, but Aria's reaction was unmistakable.

She froze.

Her smile faltered, eyes widening in recognition. It was almost imperceptible, but I caught it.

When I asked if something was wrong, she said it was "nothing," and that he was just an old "friend of a friend."

Then, I saw his face. *Dion Loukas.*

She's a fucking liar.

Were the text messages she received from *him*?

My grip tightens on the steering wheel, my jaw clenched.

Without warning, she pivots on her heel and retraces her steps. A flicker of guilt flashes across her face before she swiftly changes direction, disappearing into the shadows of the alley behind the café we were just at.

Is she meeting with him now? After being with me?

I glance around to make sure no one is watching and slip out of the car. I need to get a better look without drawing attention. I edge forward, sticking close to the wall of the building, my eyes trained on Aria as she moves deeper into the alley where Loukas waits for her.

Fucking whore.

I need to get rid of him. Make him stop messing with what's mine, with my future.

Ever since the Vasilakis clan inherited a new Godfather, things have been hostile. He's one of the main people my future father-in-law, Philip, told me to stay away from.

The hierarchies have changed in the past decades. I haven't been part of the families since my father died.

We were respected, influential, and our name carried weight. But that all changed when my father's life was taken away too soon. With his death, it felt like the very essence of our importance dissolved into thin air.

With no family left other than me and my mother, the five families voted us out.

I was a little boy at the time, so I couldn't take over for my father, and my poor mother was defenseless.

She told me the truth when I was old enough to understand. I was so angry. Angry that they belittled our family. Angry that they left my mother powerless. Angry that they stripped my title when I was too young to claim it.

I vowed to find a way back into the ranks.

In the years that followed, I attempted to reclaim some semblance of our former glory, but it felt like grasping at shadows. The world had moved on, and so had our place in it.

And now, the key to my re-introduction into the world is standing in an alley, getting finger fucked by an enemy.

My blood is boiling, disgust washing over me in a wave.

I swallow it down, forcing myself to remain composed, to keep my emotions in check. It's not the time or place for a confrontation. Not yet.

I walk back to my car, barely able to grasp the handle in my furious haze.

Teeth grinding, I start the car and pull away from the curb.

People always underestimate me. But when I'll have power again, I won't be taken advantage of anymore.

And no one, not even Aria, will get in my way.

18

ARIA

Andrew Galanis is my fiancé, and I will be loyal to him.
Andrew Galanis is my fiancé, and I will be loyal to him.
Andrew Galanis is my fiancé, and I will be loyal to him.
Andrew Galanis is my fiancé, and I will be loyal to him.
Andrew Galanis is my fiancé, and I will be loyal to him.
Andrew Galanis is my fiancé, and I will be loyal to him.
Andrew Galanis is my fiancé, and I will be loyal to him.
Andrew Galanis is my fiancé, and I will be loyal to him.
Andrew Galanis is my fiancé, and I will be loyal to him.
Andrew Galanis is my fiancé, and I will be loyal to him.

19

ANDREW

A day earlier

I pull up to the Kastellanos estate in my black sedan, gravel crunching beneath the tires as I come to a stop. Philip is expecting me here to discuss business.

I pass security at the gates and nod at the guards, my mind wandering back to Aria.

Before I met her, I thought she'd be innocent and sweet. For a moment, I had a good feeling. I thought maybe we could actually build something real.

That was until I caught her with another man's fingers up her cunt.

So, to put her at ease about the marriage, I've been keeping up an act, even asking about her flowers and studio that I don't give a fuck about.

The memory serves as a reminder that, as of today, there will be no more lies. No more deception.

I push the thought aside, focusing my attention fully on the matter at hand.

When I step up to the heavy wooden doors, I'm greeted by Philip's housemaid.

Maggie...Madeline?

"Magdalena," I say, finally remembering her name.

The woman nods politely. "He's down the hall in his office."

I walk down the corridor and hear the faint sound of people speaking. Peter Kouvalakis must already be here.

From what Philip has told me, he will do anything to keep his business and partnerships alive. The biggest one being with Peter, the Godfather he works for as second-in-command. Together, we'll ensure that the plans they've put in motion will remain untouched.

My main goal is to reinstate my family among Cebrene's elite. It's what's owed to us. Philip is merely a means to an end. By marrying Aria, I get direct access to the Kastellanos name and clan and to the Cebrene families. And Philip gets an heir who's willing to do anything to maintain power and social stature.

Given that Dimitri has no idea what his father is planning, Philip has begun to show him the ropes, making him believe that he's being taught to one day take over. But it's all for show, and when the time comes, *I* will be head of the family.

At that point, Dimitri won't be able to fight his father's decision.

Philip isn't planning on stepping down anytime soon. But that doesn't matter. Because, in the meantime, I'll be fucking his daughter every night so I can produce a son that will continue my family's legacy. The Galanis legacy.

I gently knock on the office door and step in.

Philip sees me first and greets me with a smile. "My boy," he says, walking over to me to clap me on the shoulder. "This is Peter, Godfather of the Kouvalakis clan."

I shake the other man's hand. "Nice to meet you, Godfather."

Peter nods, the faintest smirk appearing on his lips. "I've heard a lot about you, Andrew."

"All good things, I hope," I joke, and the men laugh.

"You wouldn't be here if they weren't," Peter says with a greedy grin.

We exchange pleasantries for a couple minutes before settling into the plush armchairs.

"I wanted you to officially meet before the engagement party," Philip says, gesturing between me and his boss. "Andrew here is a fine young man, and I'm glad to have him in the family. He's going to be an asset to us."

The atmosphere is professional but tense, hints of underlying power dynamics swirling around us. Philip leans back in his chair, a confident smirk playing on his lips, while Peter's expression is unreadable.

"Good to hear. We're working on big things, Mr. Galanis. Things that could put your father's name back on the map," he says.

The mere thought of being welcomed back into the fold of the five important families ignites a fire within me to prove myself even more.

Every step I've taken, every decision I've made, has led me to this moment.

"However, there's something you don't know," Peter adds.

I lean forward slightly, resting my elbows on my knees.

"The reason we're counting on your cooperation is because your late father was our associate when Philip and I first started our business. He was a third of the group that created the Sisterhood. With you—with your father's name—we can extend our project."

"What is the Sisterhood?" I ask, confusion and curiosity filling me. Neither my father nor my mother ever mentioned a partnership with the Kouvalakis and Kastellanos leaders.

Peter raises a hand to dismiss the question, shaking his

head. "It's not important for now." I lean back, attempting to appear calm, though my mind races with annoyance.

"All you need to know is that it's a private society, membership only."

My gaze narrows. "But why was my father involved? Why haven't I heard about this before?" I force myself to maintain eye contact with Peter.

"Your father was a vital part of our early days. He believed in our vision and helped us build the foundation of what we have now. But there are details that are...sensitive. For now, it's best if some things remain undisclosed," Philip replies instead.

"I believe I should know every detail for this partnership to work," I grit out, my voice still somehow sounding smooth and calm.

Something flashes in Peter's eyes as he reaches into his jacket to retrieve something. "And I suggest you tread carefully and do as you're told," he says in a warning tone. He places a sleek, metallic object on the table between us. An unspoken threat hangs heavy in the air. My gaze flickers between Peter and the gun.

I nod, jaw clenching, and the conversation continues.

Finally, after what feels like an eternity, we reach a pause in the discussion, and I stand to leave, thanking them for their time. Philip nods, his eyes glinting with a hint of amusement. He thinks this whole power play is funny. Prick.

Once I step outside the office, I come face to face with Aria's mother.

"*Yassas*, Elena," I say, greeting her with a kiss on each cheek. "*Ti kánis?*"

"*Kalá, efkharistó*," she replies with a warm smile.

"Where is Aria?" I ask.

"She's in her studio working on some arrangements. I'm sure she'd be happy to see you."

I thank her and navigate through the hallways and out into

the garden to get to the guest house. My steps quicken as I approach the door, and I push it open.

Aria looks up from arranging a bouquet, her eyebrows arching when she sees me standing there.

"Andrew, what are you doing here?" She drops my gaze and goes back to the flowers.

I stride toward her and lean against the counter she's working on, hands in my pockets. "I'm here to see my girl," I say, nonchalantly.

A flash of unease crosses her face as her lips curl into a smile. But it doesn't quite reach her eyes. She's trying to mask her discomfort. *Good, because what I'm about to tell her isn't going to make it any better.*

"Oh, that's nice," she says, still averting her gaze.

I decide to cut to the chase. "We need to talk."

She sets down the bouquet, eyes darting around nervously. "About what?"

I wait until she meets my eyes. "About Dion Loukas. Your *friend* from the café."

Aria takes a step back. "What about him?" Despite her attempt to maintain her composure, there's a subtle tremor in her voice.

"Don't give me that bullshit, Aria," I snap. "I know what's been going on between you two," I say, my voice a barely contained growl. "And I'm here to make sure it stops."

Aria's breath catches in her throat. "I don't know what you're talking about," she stammers.

I take a step forward, caging her in between me and the counter. "Don't lie to me. I know you've been seeing him behind my back." My anger is simmering just below the surface, ready to boil over. "I've seen you with him. More recently in the back alley of Black Bean."

Aria swallows hard, her eyes now wide with fear.

"Andrew, please—"

"Please *what*, Aria?" I cut her off with a sharp wave of my hand that makes her flinch. "Save it. I'm not interested in your fucking excuses. I'm here to deliver a message."

I lean in close, my breath hot against her ear. "You don't know who I am. And you especially don't know the lengths I will go to make sure you don't mess up my plans." I pull back briefly. "I couldn't care less about who you love or who you let touch your body. What I *do* care about is my motherfucking reputation," I seethe, each word coming out with more force than the last. "If anyone sees you with him, or any other man for that matter, *I* will be the one they talk about."

Her hands are now shaking at her side, her body quaking with fear.

"If I catch you anywhere near Dion again, if I so much as hear his name pass your lips, I won't hesitate to make you regret it," I hiss.

Aria's breath comes out in shallow gasps.

"And if you even think about crossing me again, I won't hesitate to go after Dimitri or your mother." I pause for a moment to allow the weight of my words to sink in, and I watch as her chest rises and falls rapidly with each shaky inhale. "Consider yourself warned. Do you understand?"

Aria's eyes brim with tears as she nods frantically. "Yes," she whispers, her voice barely audible.

I reach out and grab her by the neck, fingers closing around her throat, and a strangled gasp escapes her lips.

I'm in control. I have the power.

She's trapped, helpless against my strength. I can feel the fear pulsing through her veins, mingling with the adrenaline coursing through mine.

"Now, repeat after me," I instruct.

"Andrew Galanis is my fiancé, and I will be loyal to him," she chokes out.

"Again."

"Andrew Galanis is my fiancé, and I will be loyal to him."

Aria repeats the sentence over and over until the tears that were threatening to fall from her eyes drench my hand.

I let her go, and she gasps for air, clutching her throat.

"You'd better remember that."

I give her one last hard look before turning on my heel and striding out of the studio.

PART THREE
The Engagement

ARIA

A week before the engagement party

I wake to the sound of my door bursting open.

Before I can fully grasp what's happening, Angelica strides into the room, and I bolt upright in bed, heart pounding. The intrusion slices through my drowsiness like a knife.

"*Christé mou*, Angelica. You scared the shit out of me!" I cry out, rubbing my eyes as I try to shake off the fog of sleep.

The merciless throb in my head reminds me of my hangover. I drank way too much tequila in bed last night.

I press a hand to my forehead, hoping to quell the persistent ache, but my entire body conspires against me.

My best friend stands in the doorway, arms crossed, a frown plastered on her face.

"Glad to see you're alive," she says, dryly. Though I can see the concern hiding behind her joking tone.

I glare at her, the remnants of sleep still clinging to my mind like cobwebs. "Couldn't you have just knocked, like a normal person?" I mutter, pushing the tousled strands of hair out of my face. With a groan, I cover myself with my blanket. "What are you doing here?"

"Saving you from yourself, apparently. What's going on, Ari? You've been avoiding me."

It's been a while since I last saw her, or anyone else for that matter.

With a resigned sigh, I throw myself back on the mattress, my gaze pointed at the ceiling. "I don't know, Ang. I'm lost. My whole life is being taken away from me."

A pang of guilt pricks at me. I haven't told Angelica about Dion yet, nor about what Andrew did to me, and it's been eating away at me. She's my best friend. I always tell her everything. The weight of the unspoken secrets presses down on me, though a part of me hesitates, a part that fears the consequences of letting the truth slip.

I know Angelica wouldn't say a word to anyone. However, there are eyes and ears everywhere, and I worry it'll somehow get out. That my father will find out. That Andrew's reputation will be ruined, and he'll make good on his threat.

Angie lies down next to me and grabs my hand, intertwining our fingers. "I can't begin to imagine how you feel about the engagement, but staying locked up in your room isn't going to help, *Arioula*." She studies me for a moment, then adds, "You know you don't have to deal with this alone, right?"

I swallow hard, the truth threatening to spill out. I bite my lip, silencing the words before they escape. I can't risk it—not when rumors spread like wildfire in Cebrene. And I don't want to worry her by telling her about Andrew. She has enough on her plate.

Tears well in my eyes, and the lump in my throat makes it difficult to speak.

"I don't want to get married to him, Ang. I'll have to live with him, sleep in the same bed, have *sex* with him."

Angelica's expression softens, her eyes filled with sorrow

and understanding. "We have to find a way out of it," she replies.

"How, Ang? My engagement party is next week." I want to tell her about Dion, how I feel about him, how he promised he'd find a way out of my arranged marriage.

And Andrew...when we first met, he was charming and funny. But now, in such a short time, he's changed into someone unrecognizable. Truth is, I'm terrified. Terrified of what lies ahead if I can't get out of the engagement, of the future that's been mapped out for me before I even had a chance to choose.

Angelica whips her head around to look at me, stunned. "How? Your engagement was just announced. What's the rush?"

I struggle to find my voice, to form coherent words amidst the frustration rising. "That's what I said! But our families want us married by the end of the year."

When I'd asked my father why so quickly, he simply said there was no reason to wait. And with the wedding being only a few months away, Dion will have even less time to put whatever plan he has up his sleeve in motion. *If he even has a plan...*

"That's six months from now, Aria!" Angelica exclaims.

My heart thuds in my chest, and I raise a hand to my forehead, pushing back my hair as if I can physically push away the turmoil that's threatening to overwhelm me. Angelica pulls me into a tight embrace, and I settle into her body, relieved that I don't have to face this alone right now.

"We'll find a way to stop this. We just have to," she repeats.

We hold each other for several minutes, while I let out all the tears—the frustration, the anger, the fear—I've been holding in for weeks. As we sit in silence, I vow to tell Angelica the truth soon. But for now, I'll bury the secret deep within me.

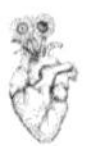

A few hours later—Angelica having just only left—I decide to venture outside my room.

I push myself off the bed, wincing slightly at the bright light streaming through the window. I clutch onto my head, squeezing my eyes shut for a moment to relieve the pain.

Before stepping out, I pull on a sweater and socks. Comfort is the goal for today.

As I make my way downstairs, I run into Magda in the hallway, her arms full of laundry. I rush over to help. She looks at me with that knowing gaze of hers.

"*Yassou, liákada mou, pós eísai?*" Her voice is gentle but probing.

I manage a weak smile at her nickname: sunshine. "I'm okay," I reply, but I know she can see right through me.

She raises an eyebrow, not buying it for a second. "You can't hide your true feelings for long, Aria. I know you well enough."

I sigh, shoulders slumping. "I don't see any other way but to keep quiet and see how things play out. You know I can't argue with *Baba*."

Magda places a comforting hand on my arm. "You're strong, Aria. Remember that. You have a voice. Never dim it."

Her words give me a small measure of comfort, and I nod. Though that's easier said than done.

I continue downstairs. When I step into the kitchen, I spot Dimitri. He's wearing a sharp suit, looking every bit the serious mafia man—except for the oversized headphones clamped over his ears. He's engrossed in something on his phone while biting on a sandwich. The juxtaposition makes me chuckle softly.

He sees me and pulls one headphone off his ear. "What's up?"

"You look ridiculous, you know that, right? All suited up with those huge things on," I say, approaching the fridge.

He smirks and looks back down at his phone. "A man needs his distractions. Keeps me sane."

I shake my head, unable to hide my amusement.

He then notices my appearance. "Oh, shit. You look terrible."

I grab a bottle of water and a muffin. "Gee, thanks." I'd rather not tell him that I was crying, so I quickly change the subject. "What are you even doing dressed like that?"

Dimitri grins mischievously. "Wouldn't you like to know."

I roll my eyes. "Fine, keep your secrets." I take a bite of the baked goods and another sip of water. "How's it going with *Baba* now that you're working with him?"

Dimitri shrugs, his expression shifting from amused to resigned. "I don't like it, but I'm trying to embrace it for the time being." He pauses, taking off his headphones and setting them aside. "I've come to realize he won't let it go. He's so focused on his work now, it's everything that matters to him, it seems, and I have no interest in arguing with him anymore."

I nod thoughtfully, taking another bite of my muffin. "Do you find it weird that he's so secretive now? He wasn't like this before."

Dimitri leans back against the counter, crossing his arms. "Yeah, it's strange. It's like he's hiding something."

I sigh. "I wonder what happened to make him change so much."

Dimitri's eyes narrow as he thinks. "Whatever it is, he's not going to share it easily. We'll have to keep our eyes and ears open if we want to find out."

I nod in agreement. "We'll figure it out."

He smiles at me, a softness in his eyes. "Now, please get something more to eat. You look like you could use it."

"Fuck you," I say with a laugh, appreciating the normalcy of the moment. Something that I've been lacking as of late. Despite the chaos around us, at least we have each other.

Then, my chest clenches as I think of what Andrew said: that he'd hurt my brother if I stepped out of line.

Dimitri chuckles and puts his headphones back on, diving back into whatever video has captured his attention, not noticing my change in mood.

After scrounging the kitchen for more food, I decide to go upstairs to find my father. I need to talk to him—maybe he'll listen to me. *Mama* is out for the day, so I figure it's a good time to pop into his office.

I approach his door, taking a deep breath before knocking, my knuckles tapping against the wood.

"Come in," his voice calls from the other side.

I push the door open and step inside, finding my *baba* buried in paperwork at his large mahogany desk. The room smells faintly of leather and his favorite cologne. He doesn't look up, his pen scratching against the paper with a sense of urgency.

I try to ignore my nerves; all my conversations with him in these last months have felt different, calculated. Ever since he told me he'd be arranging my marriage, our easygoing father-daughter relationship has morphed into something more businesslike. It's as if my existence now is only important because of the arrangement. The thought saddens me.

"Do you need anything?" he asks, his tone brisk, eyes flicking up to meet mine before returning to his work.

I shift awkwardly from one foot to the other. "No, I just wanted to talk."

He pauses, his eyes softening for a moment as he sets his pen down and leans back in his chair. "I don't really have time to talk right now, *Arioula*." His words are accompanied by a weary sigh.

The pang in my chest intensifies. I step closer, wrapping my arms around myself as if to ward off the growing distance between us. "Are you mad at me?" I ask, my voice coming out unsteady, as if I'm five again, and I've just broken a precious vase.

He looks puzzled. "Why would you think that?"

"Because of me not wanting to marry Andrew."

My father sighs again, shaking his head. "No, I'm not mad at you. But it is your duty, your responsibility toward your family." He leans forward, resting his elbows on the desk.

My stomach sinks, even though I expected the response, the same one he's given me every time we've spoken about this. But I can feel there's something else he's not telling me. Something more to all this.

"I can't do this, *Baba*. Andrew is not a good man. He—" I cut myself off, unsure of the consequences if I tell him the truth. "I can't swallow the thought of marrying a stranger."

His brows furrow, the lines etched deep into his forehead. "Andrew is an exceptional man and will be an asset to this family, Aria. The faster you realize it, the easier this will become."

Tears swell up in my eyes as frustration washes over me. How can he not care about my wishes? How can he stand by and watch his own daughter drown in unhappiness?

I just then glimpse a side of my father I have never seen before—stubborn, uncompromising, and seemingly indifferent to my feelings. A sharp reminder of the power he holds over my life.

I can't believe it. Growing up, I was undeniably a daddy's girl. He was my hero, the one I turned to for comfort and guidance. But all of that seems to have vanished into thin air. He's treating me as if I was just another business transaction, nothing more. The coldness in his eyes, the detachment in his voice—it all feels so foreign, so harsh.

I want to tell him what Andrew did, of his threats, but before I can respond, *Baba* picks up his pen again and gestures toward the door. "I have a lot of work to do now, Aria. We'll talk later."

I nod, my throat tight with unspoken words. "Okay."

Leaving his office, I feel even shittier than when I entered, and I can't help but wonder if we'll ever bridge the gap that has grown between us.

21

DION

"Tell me everything you know," I snarl at the man in front of me, his arms and legs bound on a chair.

The air is thick with the tang of dampness and the acrid stench of fear. Dim, flickering lights cast shadows against the cold concrete walls. The sound of dripping water echoes through the space.

"Please. I don't know anything," he cries, and I slap him across the face with my Glock.

Before me, lies a canvas of suffering, a broken soul, eyes wide with terror, body trembling with anticipation of the horrors to come. The man is still slowly emerging from the depths of his sedation but is awake enough to realize it's not looking good for him.

I decided it was time to up my game. If I couldn't find any valuable information about Philip and Andrew's plan using technology, then I'd resort to the old-fashioned way: getting my hands on one of Philip's men.

It was no easy feat, but I was able to follow him to a seedy sex club just an hour ago.

I was careful to stay hidden as I snuck in behind him into the dingy building.

There was a lady smoking a cigarette behind a counter that was a little too high for her height.

"Name," she demanded, not even lifting her eyes past the rim of her glasses.

"Marcus Stavros," I lied, using a name Xander had given me from their visitor's list.

She handed me a key card, still not looking up. "You may go."

Then, I slipped through when I heard the buzzing of the door unlocking.

Inside, the air was thick with the mingling scents of sweat and sex. The stench was foul enough for my breath to catch. I navigated through the dimly lit corridors, catching glimpses of intimate encounters in shadowed corners.

I'm no stranger to sex clubs, but I'd never been to a place so sleazy.

Finally, I spotted him walking into a private room, being guided by a woman wearing nothing but a negligee and high heels. Anger simmered beneath my skin as I watched him.

He'd done nothing to me personally, but the thought of him being an accomplice to anything orchestrated by Philip made me want to string his neck.

Slipping on my black ski mask, I closed the distance between us, weaseling through the crack of the door before it could shut. My hand reached for the cloth tucked in my pocket, my grip tightening on the fabric.

The fucking idiot was so engrossed in his little rendezvous, he didn't even notice me until it was too late.

In one swift motion, I pressed the cloth over his mouth and nose, cutting off his muffled protests. His eyes widened in shock before rolling back, consciousness slipping away as the sedative took effect.

The woman recoiled in terror, a yelp escaping her lips before she hastily covered her mouth with a trembling hand. I spared her only a glance before focusing on the man again.

I hoisted his limp body over my shoulder and made for the back exit, the woman's terrified gaze following me until I vanished out the door. No one paid me any notice as I carried him through the club and outside, where my men waited in a van.

And now we're here, in the basement of our main warehouse near Cebrene Harbor, and he still hasn't answered my question. "Oh, Alexis. You have no idea how much fun I'll have torturing you. It'll make my job a lot easier if you simply cooperated. And a lot *cleaner*," I say, looking down at my already soiled clothing. There are splatters of his blood on my trousers, from giving him a punch to the nose too many. That sure woke him the fuck up.

I reach over and grab the nail bat. It's not the most sophisticated torture tool, but I had a lot of fun making it, and I fucking love baseball.

I stand by, swinging the bat around, watching him as his eyelids flutter, fighting both the remnant effects of the sedative and his fear.

I let out a sigh. "Fine. We'll play, then," I relent, pulling the bat back and swinging it onto his left knee. Blood splatters all over my clothes. *My dry cleaners are going to have their work cut out for them.*

His screams pierce the silence, his anguish reverberating through the very foundation of the warehouse above. Gasping for air, his face contorts with pain.

I observe him with detached curiosity. I should feel bad for him. Really, I don't even know if he's done anything wrong. Though he must've if he associates with men as corrupted as Philip.

Instead, I'm filled with an intoxicating rush, a perverse

harmony that speaks to the depths of my depravity. I am not a good man right now. Perhaps I never have been.

Finally, after a series of sobs and desperate pleas, Alexis speaks.

"Philip is planning on giving his estate to Galanis instead of his son," he blubbers.

I absorb the news, somehow both surprised and expectant. Philip passing his estate and clan to Andrew when he already has an heir?

Now we know the reason why Andrew is marrying Aria. I ignore the pang in my chest, my jaw locking. But it still doesn't explain why *Andrew* of all people, when the piece of shit has nothing to offer Philip.

I bend over and shove my thumb into one of the open gashes in Alexis's knee, He howls in pain.

"What does Andrew give in return?"

He stammers, struggling to reply between each bated breath. "His unwavering loyalty." So, essentially, Philip got himself a little bitch. For what? I need answers, and I need them now.

I crouch down. "What else does Philip have planned?" I ask, my voice low and tight with barely restrained anger.

He swallows hard, his eyes darting around nervously. "I—I don't know," he stammers, his words tumbling out in a panic. "He didn't tell me much."

I lean in closer, searching his face for any sign of deceit. "You're lying."

Alexis shifts, wincing as the ropes dig into his wrists. Then, a flicker of memory seems to cross his face. "He mentioned something," he says, his voice trembling. "S-something about a secret society."

I straighten up, the pieces suddenly clicking into place. "The Sisterhood," I mutter under my breath. Alexis nods frantically. Of course. I need to find out what Andrew's involvement is in that establishment.

I pull my finger away from his fucked-up knee, rubbing the blood all over his cheek to clean it off, before slapping him. "Attaboy. Wasn't so hard, right?"

Alexis chokes on an inhale. "Are you going to kill me?" His voice trails after me as I stride away.

With my back to him, I let out a laugh. "No. But if you think about telling anyone about what just happened, I'm going to kill your family, and I'll make sure that Philip finds out you betrayed him. I'm sure he won't be as merciful."

My footsteps echo against the concrete floor as I ascend the worn staircase leading to the upper level of the warehouse.

I pull out my phone and dial Xander's number, my thumb tapping against the screen impatiently.

"Xan." I try to keep my tone steady despite the urgency prickling at the edges of my words. "I need you to arrange a meeting for me, but it has to be discreet."

I PULL UP TO THE UNDERPASS OF THE BRIDGE IN OLD CEBRENE, the rhythmic rumble of my motorcycle fading into the background. It's a quiet spot, a perfect meeting point.

Xander rode by my side. Behind us, two cars roll to a stop, our men staying inside while scanning the surroundings with practiced vigilance.

I lean against my bike, gaze fixed on the road ahead, waiting for the person we've come to meet. The minutes stretch on, each second feeling like an eternity, and I let impatience creep in.

"What time did he say he'd be here?" I huff.

Xander looks at the time on his watch. "3:30. It's 3:29, chill."

I shoot him a disapproving glance. "We told him not to be late."

"He's fucking eighteen years old. Give him a little grace," he argues.

"Exactly, he's a man now. He needs to learn the concept of punctuality. And you know how much I hate being stood up, so he better show."

Xan chuckles. "Oh, yeah. I forgot. Abandonment issues. Dead parents."

My face twists in utter disbelief. I ought to kill the motherfucker.

"That's rich coming from a guy who was born to a junkie and an alcoholic father."

Xander brings his hand to his chest. "Ouch. You hurt me, Loukas."

I roll my eyes at him.

"Consider yourself lucky you don't have a bullet in your fucking ball sack. You're the only person I'd ever let say that kind of shit to me." *Evander, too. I should shoot both the insolent bastards.*

Xander full-on belly laughs. "You're fucking twisted, dude." *Guilty.*

Just then, a not-so-distant hum breaks through the stillness. The sound of an approaching vehicle.

My muscles tense in anticipation. I really fucking hope this doesn't turn into an ambush.

I exchange a glance with Xander, and he nods, putting his hand on the back of his waistband where his gun is hidden. I pull mine out and place it on the seat of my bike.

The sleek car comes to a stop beside us, and a tall, young man steps out.

Relief washes over me when I realize he's alone.

"To what do I owe this pleasure?" Dimitri Kastellanos, Aria's brother, smirks, though his body language is a little guarded.

I peek at the bulge poking out behind his shirt. *Good boy. He came strapped.*

"I need to talk to you about something important. Something pertaining to you."

He crosses his arms. "I took a huge risk in coming here to meet you—this better be good."

I stifle my smirk. For a kid who just got roped into the mob, he sure has some balls. I'm impressed.

"It'll be worth your while. Just know that I'm only looking out for you."

Dimitri furrows his brow. "Why?"

"We have a *common* interest," I say, not wanting to mention Aria's name out loud.

After a moment, his eyes light up in realization, a smile tugging at the corner of his lips. "Ah. So, *you're* the friend she went to see the other night."

I don't deny it. "Your father is planning on giving his estate and control of your family's clan to your sister's fiancé."

Dimitri stills, and I observe him as he processes the information. "*Poutánas yos,*" he swears and starts to pace back and forth, muttering under his breath. "How sure are you?"

"One hundred and ten percent." I open the small compartment in my bike and pull out a manila folder, slapping it down on the seat. "We have your father's will to prove it."

"Fuck!" Dimitri shouts, his fists clenching.

He turns and punches the back window of his car. It cracks. *Wow. He's strong as fuck for an eighteen-year-old.*

"That motherfucker has been playing me. He's been forcing me into the business, even though I explicitly said I wasn't interested. All of this to keep up appearances when he's going to abandon me as his heir," he seethes.

I can empathize with his frustration.

"That's probably why he found a replacement. He knows you want nothing to do with the clan, so he can't count on you to do his bidding when he steps down," I explain. "Do you have any idea what he's up to?"

"No, and I want to keep it that way. The less I know, the better."

I agree. "But we still can't let him give your family over to Andrew."

Dimitri nods. "So, what's the plan?"

DIMITRI IS A GOOD KID.

And even though he says he wants nothing to do with mob life, it suits him. He's got the attributes, the drive, and now, the motivation.

We spend the next hour talking about his upbringing, until our conversation becomes filled with gaming jargon and inside jokes that only we understand.

Xander rolls his eyes for the umpteenth time. He doesn't get it and doesn't share our enthusiasm. Xander is the only hacker I know who doesn't like video games. *Weirdo*. I catch his eye for a moment, and he smirks, shaking his head. "You guys and your games," he mutters, half-amused, half-exasperated.

We steer back to the matter at hand, Dimitri explaining how Philip always had plans for him, ever since he was a kid. The typical "you turn eighteen and get initiated into the mafia" plans.

Despite having other goals in life, Dimitri decided to follow in his father's footsteps, for the time being, just to get him off his back. He never wanted to take over for the Kastellanos clan, especially given that they aren't a prominent family with a Godfather. But now, things have changed.

"I'll do it," Dimitri says. "I'll have the initiation." The last task he must do to become a valuable member of his clan. Once blood is shed, he will be *made.*

"Are you sure?" I ask him.

He nods. "Philip won't take me seriously unless I do. And if he doesn't believe that I'm serious and have had a change of heart, he won't trust me with the business and any information. And I won't let a stranger oversee my family."

He's right. Until Dimitri murders a man in cold blood, he won't be regarded with respect.

I was also eighteen when I killed my first target.

I remember the night vividly. The dark alley, the weight of the pistol heavy in my hand. My heart pounded so hard I could hear it in my ears, my palms slick with sweat. I had always wondered about this moment, imagined how I would feel, but nothing could prepare me for the reality. I didn't want to do it. Every fiber of my being screamed to run, to throw the gun away. But I couldn't. Ignatius was watching, and I wanted his respect more than anything. I wanted to be a part of his family.

I glanced at him, his eyes piercing through the darkness, urging me on silently. He believed in me and had *chosen* me for this. I wanted to show him I was worthy. Evander had done it a year before, and he hadn't changed much. At least, not on the surface. But Evan *was* different. He was being groomed to be a Godfather, destined for greatness.

I was just trying to survive, to prove my worth.

The man in front of me trembles, his eyes wide with fear and pleading for mercy. I hesitate, finger hovering over the trigger. My heart pounding in my chest.

Ignatius's gaze burns into my back, a reminder of what the consequences will be if I fail. I close my eyes, take a deep breath...and pull.

The sound is deafening, and the recoil jolts my arm. I open my eyes and see the man crumple to the ground. My stomach churns and

I fight the urge to vomit. I feel numb, detached from my body, as if I'm watching someone else kill a man.

Ignatius steps forward and places a hand on my shoulder. His grip is firm, reassuring.

"You did well," he says, his voice calm and steady.

I nod, unable to speak, my throat tight.

I did it. I made him proud.

But as we walk away, the reality of what I've done begins to sink in. The image of the man's lifeless body is seared into my mind. I wonder if I will ever be able to forget it, if I will ever be the same. Evander seems fine, but maybe he is just better at hiding it. Maybe this is what it takes to survive, to earn respect.

My life changed forever that night. I crossed a line, but I don't regret it. Not anymore.

I clasp Dimitri on the shoulder. "There's no going back if you initiate."

"I know. But it has to be done. To save my family. To help Aria," he replies, sounding so sure of himself despite the nerves clear on his face. He's ready.

I see a lot of myself in Dimitri.

He's got that same fire, that same drive to prove himself, and maybe a bit of the same stubbornness I had at his age. I recognize the struggles he's facing, the doubts he's trying to hide, and the determination to help his family that keeps him going despite it all.

I remember how it felt to be in his shoes. He needs someone who understands, someone who can see past the bravado and help him channel his energy in the right direction.

"Here's what we'll do. Xander and I will keep digging for info on the Galanis family. If your father is giving his estate and control over to Andrew, he must've involved his lawyer, so we'll look for him too. Once we find him, we'll pay the fucker a little visit and make sure he annuls those documents and reinstates you as the heir."

Dimitri nods, his jaw set.

"In the meantime, you keep doing what you're told and what's expected of you and try to pick up on as much information as you can from your meetings," I add, now pumped that we have a direction.

"What about Aria?" Dimitri asks, and my heart skips a beat at the mention of her name.

"I'll tell her our plan at the engagement party. If we reverse Philip's scheme, his plan becomes null and void, and she won't have to get married."

Dimitri goes to say something before his brows furrow, as if remembering something. "We might have a small problem." I pause, waiting for him to continue. He looks up, meeting my gaze. "The agreement was sealed in blood."

My stomach sinks.

Gamoto.

A bond forged in blood. An old tradition in the mob where a contract can't be breached unless both parties die or back out.

We're never going to get Andrew and Philip to retract their deal.

I lean my head back, casting my eyes up to the sky.

"Then, we'll have to convince them."

"How?" Dimitri questions.

"The best way I know how. With violence."

22

———

DION

I t's Aria's engagement party today, and even though I tried to convince myself that I'd be able to handle it, I don't trust myself not to lose my shit.

But there's no way I'm telling Evan that he might've been right. *I can* handle it.

I've been so preoccupied with coming up with a reason to justify our presence at the party, completely forgetting that I'm going to come face to face with Andrew and Aria.

Aria, who hasn't spoken to me since I asked her to meet me the other night. She never responded.

Sitting in the confines of my car, my fingers tap anxiously on my phone screen as I stare at the thread of messages I sent to her.

> Me: I know where to find you, little liar.

> Me: Please give me a sign of life.

I've tried giving her space, respecting the boundaries she might need, especially with the engagement looming over us. But something doesn't feel right.

The only reason I haven't been pressing her is that I got Xander to virtually plant a tracker on her phone. It gives me some peace of mind knowing she's safe, though it doesn't ease the ache in my chest or the questions swirling in my mind. Tonight, I'll tell her about the plan we've set in motion and about the talk with Dimitri.

Despite the uncertainty, one thing remains clear: I miss her. I miss her presence, her warmth, her light that brightens up even the darkest corners of my mind.

I hop out of my car outside Evan's building, the Saintville, and throw my keys at the attendant.

Angelica will also be there. She and Evander have been getting closer, but she still has no idea who he truly is.

So, in the hopes of not uncovering his revenge plan, we had to come up with an excuse as to why we were attending Aria's engagement party. Realistically, all Godfathers are to be present, but Angelica doesn't know that Evan is head of the Vasilakis clan.

We've thought of nothing.

Like a pair of bumbling fools, we're stuck in this situation because we couldn't think on our feet, and we've become the poster children of incompetence. The real Dumb and Dumber.

I walk inside and nod to the concierge. The elevator doors open with a chime, and I step inside, pressing the button for Evan's penthouse, perched high above the city.

When the doors slide open, I go straight to his living room and pull out a bottle of ouzo from the bar cart.

Evander pops out from the hallway and snickers when he sees me. "I didn't know it was *that* kind of night."

Unamused, I pull two shot glasses from the cabinet and pour our drinks.

"I've spent the whole day trying to figure out how to avoid tonight, and the best I could come up with is to get drunk and pretend I was never there," I say glumly, passing him a shot glass.

We clink the glasses together and shoot the ouzo back, the burn down our throats making us grimace. I grab the bottle and pour some more.

After our second shot, we decide it's time to go.

When we hop in the elevator, Evan leans against the mirrored walls, his reflection staring back at him with an unreadable expression. I can sense his unease—it matches my own.

"You sure you want to do this?" I ask, breaking the silence.

He nods with a forced smile. "Yeah, let's just get it over with."

As the driver navigates through traffic, I try to relax, despite the nervous energy buzzing through me. Our conversation drifts from business to lighter topics, providing a welcome distraction.

When we finally arrive, Evander's driver maneuvers the car up the driveway of the Kastellanos estate. He turns off the ignition and turns to us. "Here we are, gentlemen."

Stepping out of the car, I straighten my suit jacket. I look to my side and see Evan doing the same. We make a fucking striking pair. Evan in a classic black tux, me in midnight blue.

As I step into the grand foyer of the mansion, my senses are immediately on high alert. *Holy fuck there are a lot of people here.*

Among the sea of guests, my gaze scans the crowd almost automatically, seeking out a familiar face. *Aria.* She must be here somewhere.

My chest tightens. This isn't my scene. It never has been.

Each voice, each movement, is an intrusion into my bubble. When I'm in a crowd, I feel exposed, vulnerable. And I fucking hate it.

So, I've never tried to force myself to blend in, always kept myself more on the sidelines of business.

I wasn't always like this. Once upon a time, I used to be the kid who never shut up and talked to everyone. I thrived on chaos and noise, feeding off the energy of those around me.

But when my parents died, everything changed. Suddenly, the world felt colder, lonelier. And though Evander and Ignatius were there to pick up the pieces, I could never quite shake the emptiness that settled in my chest. We leaned on each other, and silence became our companion.

I weave through the crowd, my breaths shallow as I try to find a sliver of space. I decide to slip outside, the cool night air a welcome relief against my skin. My hand trembles when I reach for my pack of cigarettes, fingers fumbling as I light one up.

The smoke curls around my head and a semblance of calm washes over me.

As I turn the corner of the patio, I catch a glimpse of someone standing in the shadows.

My heart stumbles. Even from a distance, I recognize her silhouette.

I pause, my gaze fixed on Aria.

Her gown looks as if it's made of black liquid velvet, the fabric shimmering with every blow of the wind. The back of the dress dips into a deep V, showcasing her gorgeous, blonde hair cascading along her slender back.

She's *breathtaking*.

Aria stands there, looking out into the garden and lost in her own thoughts, unaware of my presence. A surge of peace overtakes me at the sight of her.

I take a drag from my cigarette and walk over.

Aria finally turns, and our eyes meet. A flicker of something, shock maybe—or is that *fear*?—flashes in her expression. *What the fuck?*

But, as quickly as those emotions appeared, her face softens, a charged moment passing between us.

Every time I see Aria, everything else fades into the background and my heart swells with an emotion I can't place. I want to drink her in and ask for seconds, thirds.

"*Eísai ómorfi, astéri mou*," I murmur, before moving closer and burying my face in her hair. She smells like flowers, as if I'm standing in the middle of a blooming garden. A blush rises to her cheeks, but she doesn't say anything.

"I sent you some messages a few days ago. Why aren't you talking to me?"

Aria stammers. "You shouldn't be here."

"What do you mean?" I'm confused. I understand that if someone sees her alone with another man, it'll look suspicious, but the way she's acting is…different, not in her usual character. A sense of dread tightens my stomach.

I turn her face to me. "Aria, what's wrong?"

She backs away from me, her eyes full of sorrow. "Please go."

"Did something happen?" I ask, now worried.

There's a split-second pause before Aria scowls. "Look at where I am, Dion. At my fucking *engagement* party! It's too late."

Frustration makes me snap.

"If you hadn't spent the last week ignoring me, you'd know that I've been working on a plan," I spit. "There's a way out of this. I spoke to—"

"Stop," she hisses and retreats a few more steps, her shoulders slumping. "I can't do this anymore, Dion. I mean it," she murmurs, suddenly sounding defeated, looking up to the sky to keep her tears at bay. "It's over. Whatever you're doing—just stop."

I throw my cigarette over the balcony and grab her by the shoulders. "Don't give up on me now, *astéri mou*. I have a way out. You have to trust me," I tell her, almost begging her to listen, my voice filled with desperation.

Aria looks at me, and her expression says what a thousand words couldn't. I'm losing her.

She looks away, her gaze far off in the distance. "No, Dion. I don't want this anymore. I–I don't want *you* anymore. It's over."

I stand there, stunned, as her words sink in. "What are you saying?" I don't believe my eyes and ears. She's said in the past that we couldn't do this anymore, but she never *meant* it. I knew it in my heart. But now...

Her eyes brim with tears, her lips trembling ever so slightly. "I don't want to be with you. I'm marrying Andrew."

My chest clenches as if I've been stabbed, but beneath it, anger courses through me. "The fuck you are, little liar," I shout, and Aria recoils, her gaze darting around to make sure no one else has heard. "You don't love him."

She locks her jaw before meeting my gaze with something like *pity* in her eyes. And right then, I feel like a complete, utter fool. "Yeah, well. I don't love you either, Dion. I made a promise to my father, and I'm going to keep it."

My heart splits in two. I don't fully understand this emotion, but I know that without Aria, I'll never come close to experiencing anything like this again.

I brace my hands on the balcony railing and let my head hang between my shoulders. "I'm not letting you marry him, Aria."

I'm not *letting her marry him.* Fuck this.

I turn around and hike up Aria's leg around my waist, pulling her dress up to her hips. She yelps in surprise but doesn't push me away. My fingers dig into the flesh of her bare ass, bringing her closer as I smash my lips onto hers in a feverish kiss. Her lips are soft and warm, responding to me with an intensity that sends shivers down my spine.

Mine.

I slip my index through the fabric of her thong and rip it off. Aria gasps into my mouth, wrapping her arm around my shoulders, her fingers grasping onto the nape, pulling me closer.

But then, she pushes me away, her hands firm against my chest. "Dion, stop," she whispers urgently, glancing nervously over her shoulder. "My fiancé is just behind those doors."

"Fuck your fiancé. You're mine," I growl, trying to pull her back into my arms. My heart is pounding, the taste of her still lingering on my lips.

"No, Dion," she pleads. "I have to go. Please, let me go." Her eyes are wide, filled with regret and an emotion so strong it takes my breath away.

I feel her slipping away, the warmth of her body retreating. My hands drop to my sides, clenching into fists.

"It's over," she repeats once more.

The cool night air chills the spot where she was pressed against mine. My chest tightens, a hollow ache settling in.

I look deep into her eyes. "Go on. Pretend that you're happy alongside your fiancé in front of all those people. But just remember, I know who you think about at night when you're alone. The sounds you make when you're desperate to come."

Aria's breath hitches in her throat as I close the distance once more and weave my hand up her dress, shoving my middle and ring fingers up her entrance.

My thumb circles over her clit as I move my digits inside her tight walls. Aria clenches around me when I curl them upward, beginning beckoning movements. It doesn't take long for her legs to shake and moans to escape her pouty lips.

In a matter of seconds, Aria's inhales come in short bursts as she struggles to contain her moans.

"That's it, little liar. Let everyone hear how fucking eager you are to come all over my hand while your fiancé is right behind those doors."

"Oh, fuck," she whimpers, her release dripping all over my fingers.

"What a filthy fucking girl."

I pull my digits out of her to smear her lips with her wetness.

"I know who your heart belongs to, and it's not. Fucking. *Him.*"

With that, I move away. "Oh, and good luck trying to convince him you're a virgin. I took that, too."

I disappear back into the party.

My heart is still racing from the confrontation, Aria's words echoing in my mind like a relentless drumbeat, too caught up in my emotions to even care about the crowd around me. I make my way to the bar and order a stiff drink. "Bourbon, please."

Evander appears behind me. "What's gotten up your ass?"

I scoff. "I just saw Aria," I mutter, chugging down the glass of liquor. I need more if I want to wash away the memories of her words.

"Another one," I ask the bartender.

"What happened?" Evan asks impatiently.

Not wanting to rehash the details of our conversation and feel her rejection for a second time, I simply say, "She told me it's over. And she seemed to mean it."

"Dion, I know you. When you want something, you don't give up easily. I have no doubt you'll get the girl if you really want her."

My brother knows me well, and he's right about this. I'm not a quitter.

When I set my mind on something, I don't stop until I get it. I'm relentless.

Nothing can stand between me and what I want. Not even Aria herself.

She might think she wants to be with Andrew to fulfill her family obligation or whatever it is that's made her change her mind, but I know her feelings lie with me. She can deny it all she wants. I'll keep pushing until I succeed.

"I really do, bro."

Evander clasps me on the shoulder and gives it a squeeze. Then, we grab another drink.

I lean against the bar, staring at the amber liquid swirling in my glass. Maybe if I get tipsy enough, I can forget that I'm even here, forget the congratulations, forget the smiles, forget everything. Just for tonight.

I lift the bourbon to my lips, letting the burn of the liquor wash over me, momentarily numbing the pain. The clinking of glasses and the murmur of voices fade away.

The alcohol starts to do its work, coursing through my veins and clouding my senses, and soon, I don't care that I'm surrounded by people anymore. I barely even notice them.

It's just noise, insignificant against the backdrop of my own turmoil. I'm here, but not really. And for now, that's all I need.

I haven't seen signs of the happy couple or their families, yet, but right now, it doesn't matter.

Soon after, we're ushered into the dining hall for the celebrations to commence.

I catch a whiff of food, and my stomach rumbles loudly. Drinking always makes me fucking hungry.

Then, the doors swing open again. And there she is.

Like a vision, she appears in the breathtaking gown I saw her in not long ago. Accompanied by her mother, she walks in, commanding attention and admiration from all around.

I drink in the sight of her, and despite—or maybe because of— the haze of alcohol, something blooms in my chest.

What the hell is wrong with me? I've never had feelings of this kind for anyone before. It's like my heart deemed itself irreparable, closed off to any semblance of emotion.

Now, everything's different.

Aria makes her way to the head table, where her fiancé

awaits, but for a moment, time slows, the world narrowing to just the two of us. Our eyes lock, and she takes a shaky breath, her steps faltering just slightly.

I mouth the word, "Mine." A silent claim, a declaration only for her.

Aria's eyes widen and a delicate blush spreads across her cheeks.

She doesn't look at me again as she takes her seat, but the message has been received. I can see it in the way she glances down, her teeth nibbling on her lower lip.

She can tell me it's over all she wants, that she doesn't want to be with me, but I know the truth.

Aria makes me feel all these things I can't quite understand.

Now fate is fucking mocking me, dangling something I can't reach right in front of my eyes.

Is this fucking hell?

Yet, despite how beautiful she looks, I'm consumed by a bite of jealousy.

Aria's not wearing that gown for me. She's not here for me. She's not getting engaged *to me*.

I try to distract myself during the dinner, the food and steady flow of wine helping ease some of the tension in my shoulders.

The clinking of a glass pierces through the air, drawing all eyes toward the head of the table. Philip Kastellanos rises to his feet with a commanding presence.

"Welcome, everyone. And thank you for joining us on this joyful occasion to mark the engagement of my beautiful daughter, Aria, and Andrew Galanis."

Poutánas yos. This is all *his* fault.

Andrew leans over and murmurs something in Aria's ear, causing her to smile, even though it looks strained. He then wraps his arm around her shoulders, and she leans into him. Intense rage courses through me like a wildfire. That's *my* girl.

Suddenly, the room seems to grow hotter.

I push my chair back from the table, the wood scraping against the floor. A few people at our table startle, looking over at me. Evander gives me a warning glare to sit back down, but I can't think of anything over the pounding of my heart in my ears. Rage is boiling inside me. I get off my seat and run across the dance floor, fists clenched, to where Philip is standing.

There are some shocked yells before I start releasing a torrent of blows at his face, each strike landing on his nose. The cracking of his bones reverberates in the air.

Hands grab at me, attempting to pull me back, but I refuse to stop.

Voices blur into background noise, drowned out by the thundering of blood in my ears.

"Dion."

Aria's screams pierce through the chaos, a desperate plea for reason, but it's as if her words are lost in the storm raging within me. "Dion."

My vision narrows to a tunnel, oblivious to anything else around me.

"*Dion*," the voice is louder now, and the chaotic scene dissipates like smoke in the wind.

I blink, disoriented, and turn round.

"What the fuck, bro?" Evander hisses, staring at me with concern and confusion. "It looked like you were about to have a seizure."

The violent confrontation was all in my head. I blink a few more times, trying to dispel the lingering remnants of the vivid illusion. It was just a fantasy, a dark figment of my imagination.

"Holy fuck. I'm so drunk," is all I manage to say, words slurring.

"Dion, come on, man." Evan's voice is gentle but firm, as he helps me to my feet. "Let's get you home."

I sway unsteadily, the alcohol still in my system, but I nod in agreement. "Yeah, okay."

Evan wraps an arm around my waist, supporting me as we make our way out of the crowded room. The stares of the onlookers feel like daggers, piercing through the haze with judgment and pity.

As I stumble down the hall, my vision blurred, I see Dimitri at the other end. Our eyes meet, and I can tell he's waiting for some sign from me. I shake my head, signaling that the plan with Aria didn't work out. He understands immediately, his face falling. His shoulders slump, mirroring my own disappointment. I turn away.

Bringing my attention back to Evan, I mutter, "I'm sorry." I know the last thing Evan wanted was to take care of my drunken ass.

"Don't worry about it," Evan replies. "We all have our moments."

I nod, though the motion makes my head spin.

Evan guides me out into the cool night air, the darkness offering a welcome break from the chaos in my head.

ANDREW

I storm out of the engagement party, the cool night air hitting my face like a slap.

My pulse pounds in my ears, drowning out the laughter and music that drift from inside the Kastellanos estate. I clench my fists at my sides, the muscles in my arms tightening painfully as I try to control my breathing. Each step I take is heavy, as if I'm restraining myself from turning back and causing a scene.

What happened on the patio flashes in my mind, clear as day. Aria, standing *too* close to Dion. My teeth grind together. Dion's smug face as he leaned in to whisper something that made her breath catch. I stop in my tracks, hands trembling with rage. I told her to *never* speak to him again. But she didn't listen. She defied me.

My vision blurs at the edges as anger surges through me. If it weren't for the fact that I need Aria to solidify my position within the clans, I'd kill her right now. The thought of it is tempting, *so* tempting. My fingers itch to wrap around her throat, to squeeze until she understands the price of her betrayal.

But without her, my plans crumble. My grip on power weakens.

I resume walking. There's only one other option. Dion must die. Even though killing him could have repercussions, I don't care anymore. I can't stand being played for a fool. The thought of his blood spilling, his life ending, is the only thing that cools the fire inside me.

Reaching my car, I yank the door open with such force that the metal groans under my grip. I slam it shut behind me, the sound echoing in the quiet night. As I sit in the driver's seat, my breath comes out in harsh, uneven gasps. My hands grip the steering wheel so tight that my knuckles turn white.

I make my decision.

I pick up my phone and dial my friend from the CPD. The ringing seems to stretch on forever until finally, he answers.

"We need to escalate things. It's time to make a move."

There's a pause on the other end. "What do you have in mind?"

"Dion Loukas has been a thorn in my side for too long, and we can't afford to let this slide anymore. We need to act now."

Another pause. "Alright. Let's do it."

"One more thing," I add quickly. "Don't say anything to anyone. I don't want Philip to find out what we're doing. Things have been rocky between Peter and the clans. We can't risk any leaks."

"Got it. I'll start working on it right away."

I take a deep breath, filling my lungs with anticipation.

Aria will learn what happens when you cross me.

THE NEXT DAY, I'M IN MY HOME OFFICE, SITTING AT MY DESK.

I'm trying to focus, but my mind keeps wandering back to

what I saw yesterday between Dion and Aria. The anger blinding me.

My phone buzzes, jolting me out of my thoughts. I pick it up, recognizing the number immediately. I've been waiting for this call all day.

"Yes," I answer, my voice steady despite the adrenaline starting to pump through my veins.

"It's done," the voice on the other end says. "We set a bomb under Dion's Ducati. It was parked behind the Vasilakis warehouse near Cebrene Harbor. It went up in flames as soon as he touched it."

I lean back in my chair, letting out a slow breath.

"Good. Any witnesses? Any complications?"

"None. It went off clean. No one saw anything, and there's nothing to trace it back to us."

"Perfect," I say, grim satisfaction settling in. "Keep it that way. Remember, not a word to anyone. Especially to Philip."

"Understood."

I set the phone down and stare at the ceiling for a moment. It's fucking done. The move has been made.

Dion Loukas is no longer a problem.

24

DION

I'm halfway through my morning run when my phone buzzes in my pocket, interrupting the steady rhythm of my breathing. I slow to a jog, pulling it out. It's a video call from Evander and Xander. Strange. I swipe to answer and come to a stop, my pulse still racing from the exertion.

"Thank fucking God," Evander's face fills the screen, looking unusually alarmed. "Are you okay?"

I wipe the sweat from my forehead, feeling a prickle of anxiety. "Yeah, why wouldn't I be?"

"There was an explosion at one of our warehouses," Xander says, his voice tense. "Leon called us. Said it was pretty bad."

My heart drops. "What? Which warehouse?"

"The one at the Port."

I'm already turning on my heels, sprinting back home. "I'm heading there now."

"We're on our way too."

I end the call, adrenaline pumping through my veins, pushing me to run faster. The distance back to my house blurs and before I know it, I've grabbed my keys and I'm in my car, speeding toward the warehouse. The drive feels interminable, even though I'm well over the speed limit.

When I arrive, it's as if a fist is squeezing my chest when I see the smoldering remains of my Ducati. It's been blown to pieces. The smell of burnt rubber and metal fills the air. I'm momentarily frozen, staring at the scorched ground.

Then, I notice something even worse—a body being pulled from the wreckage. Was someone targeting *me*?

"Dion!" Leon rushes over.

I snap out of my stupor. "What happened? Who is it?" I mumble.

"Luca." Fuck. The kid was only nineteen.

I march toward the warehouse. "Did anyone see anything? Anyone suspicious?"

He shakes his head. "Not yet. We're still trying to get everyone accounted for." Leon looks around, lowering his voice. "We're not sure, but it could be a rival clan...though it seemed more personal. *Your* bike, specifically."

I clench my fists, trying to keep my cool and storm inside, finding everyone already gathered in a huddle. "Alright, listen up," I bark. "Did anyone see anything or anyone out of the ordinary before the explosion?"

Silence. Nervous glances exchanged. I grit my teeth. "Speak the fuck up!"

A timid voice finally pipes up, "I saw a man last night. He was hanging around the parking lot, but I didn't think much of it. He had a cap pulled low over his face."

I'm about to press for more details when Xander and Evander burst in.

"We need to check the cameras," Xander says, not wasting a second as he heads to the office.

We rush to the security room. Xander rewinds the footage from last night, eyes glued to the screen.

Then we see him: a shadowy figure slipping onto the property, moving with deliberate purpose. He approaches my bike, fiddles around with it, and a few minutes later, he's gone. Shortly after, Luca, unaware of the danger, lights up a cigarette and leans against the bike. Moments later, the explosion rocks the camera.

The man's silhouette was painfully familiar. My mind races back to the footage of the man leaving me the threatening notes on the ship.

It all clicks in my mind.

"It's Andrew Galanis," I say, my voice cold and certain. "He's been trying to get rid of me."

Xander looks at me, understanding dawning in his eyes. "You sure?"

"Positive." I pull out my phone, hands shaking with rage, and dial a number I've been avoiding for a long time. The line connects. "Andrew."

There's a moment of silence on the other end. "Dion. You're supposed to be dead."

I can practically taste the shock in his voice. "Not dead, Andrew. Far from it. But this ends now."

He chuckles, a sinister edge to the sound. "Are you threatening me, Dion?"

My grip tightens on the phone. "Yes, Andrew. I swear to God I will fucking *end* you."

"Do you really think so? You and I both know you won't do anything to risk *her*."

My blood runs cold. "Don't you dare touch a hair on Aria's head."

"Oh, soon the whore will be mine to do whatever I want with."

"You have no idea what I'm capable of, Andrew," I growl. "If I see you around, I won't hesitate. You'd better watch your back, because I'll fucking slice your head off and revel in every drop of your blood, you worthless cunt."

I hang up, fuming, seeing red. The office is a blur as I start trashing everything in sight, overturning chairs, sweeping papers off desks.

"Dion, stop!" Evander's voice cuts through my rage. He grabs my shoulders, forcing me to look at him. "We have to be smart about this. We're still working on our own plan. We need to keep the chaos at a minimum for now. You can't go and just kill him."

I take a deep breath, trying to rein in my fury. "He's going to get what's coming to him."

Evander nods. "He will. But we have to be strategic. Trust me."

I exhale slowly, hands still shaking with rage. "Alright. But when the time comes, I want to be the one to take him down."

25

ARIA

A few months later

The bass thumps through my chest, reverberating through every fiber of my being as I dance in the dimly lit club, surrounded by swirling lights and the scent of sweat and alcohol.

We crossed the border over to Antium City—The Big A—to go to the Watertower Bar.

Cassie, a longtime friend looks back at me, her cheeks flushed, her eyes glossy. She looks so carefree, so uninhibited. And I'm…jealous.

I'm definitely drunk. Just not the happy-go-lucky drunk like her.

She leans in close to yell over the loud music. "I'm going to the bar to get another drink. Want anything?"

I smile and shake my head, raising my glass. I'm still drinking my tequila on the rocks.

She gives me a kiss on the cheek before bouncing away, and I chug the remainder of the liquid, adding to my drunken haze.

As soon as Cassie's out of sight, a man appears in front of me.

"Hey there, beautiful. You seem a little lonely. Mind if I join you?"

Burp.

God. I shouldn't have drunk that tequila so fast.

I'm too far gone to refuse. With a tipsy giggle, I sway closer to him, letting his arms wrap around my waist as we move in sync.

When he brings his face closer to mine, his breath hot on my lips, reality crashes back in, a slow, almost sobering wave that pulls me back to the present. I can't be seen like this, not with another man, not in public. Antium City may be across the pond from Cebrene, but the risk is still there. What would Andrew do if he found out?

I'm such an idiot.

I push the man away, stumbling slightly as I regain my balance. "I can't," I mumble, my words slurred.

"Come on, gorgeous. You look like you could a distraction." He leans in closer, his breath hot against my ear. "And if you want to have some real fun, follow me." His gaze flickers to a nearby table where a group of girls dance with abandon. One girl with long, tousled hair twirls around, her arms outstretched, eyes closed. Another, with vibrant tattoos tracing intricate patterns across her skin, moves with such raw sensuality that it pulls me in.

They look like they're having the time of their lives, as if their every worry in the world has melted away, leaving behind only the beautiful, radiant version of themselves.

Everything I'm not. Not anymore.

A third girl, a redhead, catches my gaze and grins, gesturing for me to join them.

I hesitate only a moment before I follow the guy, drawn to the promise of escape. But as I approach the table, a sinking feeling settles in the pit of my stomach. One of the girls is snorting something off the glassy surface, her eyes glazed with a euphoria that sends warning bells ringing through my head.

I look away, planning to go back to the dance floor and find Cassie, when I catch a glimpse of the ring on my finger, glinting in the flashy club lights. My upcoming wedding, a presence looming over me like a shadow.

Lately, Andrew's been coming around more, giving me gifts, making plans for our future as if talking about the weather, as if nothing happened, as if he didn't put his hands on me, threaten my family. His existence is felt in every corner of my life, a reminder of who he is, of whom I'm supposed to be. *His wife.*

The girl kneeling in front of the table offers me some.

I'm not letting you marry him.

Dion's words come back to haunt me. A promise he couldn't keep, not until it was too late. *It's better like this, so you can protect both him and your family.* My heart sinks just as my head spins, the alcohol getting to me even more.

I lean forward, inhaling sharply as the powder enters my system, a rush of warmth spreading through my veins.

I push all thoughts of my life aside, burying them beneath the haze of alcohol and drugs and losing myself in the moment as the world spins around me.

A FEW HOURS LATER, I STUMBLE INTO THE FOYER OF MY HOME, the scent of alcohol clinging to my clothes like a suffocating cloud.

I wasn't intoxicated enough to black out, *unfortunately*, but the night is a haze.

My steps falter as I climb up the stairs to reach my bedroom. Everything seems so big, and my head keeps spinning. The tequila sits heavily in my stomach, but the warmth of it is fleeting, leaving me colder and emptier than before.

When I reach my room, I collapse onto my mattress, sweat coating my skin. My high crashed like a tidal wave, the remains of the cocaine still lingering in my veins, leaving a bitter taste on my tongue.

In the last few weeks, I've found that, when intoxicated, the edges of my shitty reality blur into a comforting fog. I no longer think about my family, my fiancé. *Or him.*

For a brief while, I'm able to forget everything. The forthcoming wedding, the shattered remnants of my heart, the expectations pressing down on me like a suffocating weight.

But when the alcohol-induced euphoria began to fade a few hours ago, the guilt and shame set in with a vengeance. The bitter taste of self-loathing rose in my throat, a visceral reminder of my own weakness. I'd never tried cocaine before. How could I succumb to such impulses?

I try to push away the feelings of disgust and stand in front of the mirror, staring at the reflection that no longer feels like mine.

I've been withdrawing from myself, becoming a mere shell of the person I once was.

Who am I becoming? Aria, the dutiful daughter? Aria, the obedient fiancée?

Tears well in my eyes, silent and unrelenting.

I wipe them away. Maybe, just maybe, this pain is a necessary evil, a storm through which I must pass to emerge stronger on the other side.

Dion's face, his voice, echo again in the recesses of my mind, like they have been doing every day.

But that's done. He was a casualty of circumstances beyond our control, and I have to accept our fate.

A part of me still hopes that he'll genuinely be able to find a way out of this, no matter Andrew's threats. I've tried to mourn the loss of what could have been, but beneath the facade of composure, I can feel the cracks beginning to form. How much longer can I keep up this pretense without breaking? How much more of myself will I have to sacrifice on the altar of societal expectations?

I stumble out of my room, thoughts spinning. The walls seem to close in, suffocating me. I need air, something to ground me. The woods, my sanctuary, call to me.

Swaying slightly, I navigate through the house. Each step is slow, careful—I don't want to wake anyone. My hand brushes against the wall for support as I reach the patio door.

The cool night air greets me when I step outside, filling my lungs with a refreshing chill. I pause, inhaling deeply, savoring the moment, then make my way toward the forest.

The night is dark and eerily quiet. I pass my garden, the familiar scents barely registering. As I reach the treeline, a faint rustle breaks the silence. I freeze, my heart pounding. Last time, it was Dion who cornered me here. I haven't seen him in months. Could it be him?

I scan the shadows but see nothing.

With a deep breath, I continue into the forest. The darkness envelops me, the silence almost deafening. Suddenly, I see a figure in the distance heading toward the street on the other side of the woods. It looks like a man. Fear grips me, rooting me in place. He turns, sensing he's not alone, and our gazes lock. The moon casts a pale glow on his face, making his eyes shine. I try to discern their color, but it's impossible in this light. He's too far for me to make out his features, but I'm too scared to speak, to move. My hands are trembling, a cold sweat forming on my brow.

We stare at each other in silence, the moment stretching on. Then, he disappears into the darkness. I remain frozen, my body refusing to move until he's out of sight. My legs finally obey, and I scurry back to the house, heart racing.

Adrenaline courses through me, making my head spin even more.

I'm not sure if what I saw was real. It must be the alcohol or the coke. Shaking, I make my way back to my room and collapse onto the bed, ignoring the sweat and the aches throughout my body.

Exhaustion washes over me, and I close my eyes, hoping for sleep to take me away from this nightmare.

I drift into a fitful sleep, but the image of the man lingers.

PART FOUR

One Year Later

26

ARIA

A year.

So much has changed.

I sit on the edge of my bed, absently running my fingers over the soft quilt. A letter from Andrew sits on the nightstand. He postponed the wedding. There was no explanation given, only a vague hint of "unforeseen circumstances" and "difficult decisions." I can't help but assume that the escalated tension in Cebrene between the Godfathers and the recent revelations about the Sisterhood have something to do with it. It's as if everything is in a state of uneasy balance, and Andrew's abrupt departure only adds to the mystery.

He left town for "business," not even bothering to mention when he'd be back. Honestly, it's a relief. And the thought of him potentially never returning almost gives me hope. The quiet is more welcome than I'd ever anticipated.

This past year has been a whirlwind. I haven't seen or spoken to Dion in all this time. The emptiness inside me aches every day, and I miss him more than words can express. But I know staying apart is for the best, to protect my family and myself. And to protect him.

If only I could tell him why I had to end things between us, why it had to be this way.

Dion's messaged me since the engagement party. And each time breaks my heart anew, but I can't risk responding. I have this gnawing feeling that Andrew's watching my every move. He probably has my phone tapped, waiting for any slip-up.

So, I keep my silence, no matter how much it hurts.

I've spent most of my time traveling between Cebrene and Antium with Gianis to be with Angelica. After her relationship with Evander fell apart, she needed all the support.

He kept so many truths hidden, betraying her trust in ways that left deep scars. To gather her thoughts and heal, Angelica moved back to Antium.

But the biggest revelation was about her father, Peter. Learning about his involvement in the Sisterhood was a shock. The secret society that kidnapped young girls, grooming them to be sold as prostitutes or child brides, and some, deemed unfit, even ending up as nuns to keep up the establishment's appearance. It was unthinkable, horrifying.

Angelica asked me to help find more information, suspecting that our fathers were partners in this dark enterprise. So, I've been waiting for the perfect moment, when both my parents would be out.

With my heart pounding, I sneak through the house and into my father's office. Immediately, I'm filled with a sense of unease.

The room is lit by a single lamp on the mahogany desk beside neatly stacked papers and a few framed photographs. The air is heavy with the scent of old leather and paper, mingling with a faint hint of my father's cologne. It's a smell that brings back memories of my childhood, but today, it feels oppressive. Last time I was here was just over a year ago, when I begged *Baba* to stop the wedding.

Shelves line the walls, filled with books that look like they haven't been touched in years. The rich, burgundy area rug muffles my footsteps as I walk further inside, adding to the eerie silence.

I feel like an intruder, as if the walls themselves are watching me, ready to reveal my presence to my father at any moment. A cold sweat forms on my brow as I glance around, trying to steady my nerves. Every corner of this room holds a piece of my *baba*'s life that I never fully understood, and today, I might uncover secrets that will change everything.

I approach the desk first, opening drawers with trembling hands. Papers rustle softly as I sift through them, but there's nothing out of the ordinary. I move to the cabinets, pulling them open one by one, only to find more mundane office supplies and documents. The sense of dread grows with each passing second, and I have to force myself to keep going.

I search the library next, fingers tracing the spines of the books, hoping to find a hidden compartment or a clue. But it's just endless volumes of law books and literature.

I search every nook and cranny. Nothing.

Just as I'm about to give up, my foot hits a loose floorboard. The sound it makes is different, hollow. My pulse quickens as I step on it again, testing it, and it gives slightly under my weight. I crouch down, hands shaking, and try to lift it. It doesn't budge.

But then, for some reason, my eyes are drawn to a framed picture on the wall—a photograph of our family. I move toward it, feeling a strange mix of nostalgia and apprehension. When I pick up the frame, I discover a lever hidden behind it. My heart skips a beat as I pull it, and the sound of a hidden door sliding open fills the room. *Holy shit.*

The secret closet behind the wall is filled with boxes on various shelves, and I immediately catch sight of one labeled "Sisterhood." I pull it out and set it on the floor, my hands now steady, no longer trembling. Inside, I find a stack of files.

I scroll through them and find one with a boy's name on it.

Confusion ripples through me. *What would a boy be doing there? I thought it was an all-girl school.*

With a shaking breath, I pull out my phone and text Angelica.

My best friend calls me right away.

"Hi, Ang. I don't have much time. I'm in my *baba's* office, and I found something I think could be useful to you," I whisper, barely able to get the words out for fear of being overheard.

My eyes dart around the room, checking the door to ensure it's still closed.

"Oh my God. Get out of there before you get caught."

"I will, but I can't take these files with me. He'll know someone was in here. I'll take photos of everything, but have you ever heard of someone named Atlas?"

"No. Who is it?"

"I don't know, but apparently he was raised at the Sisterhood during the time you were there."

"It's an all-girl institution. I doubt they had a boy enrolled there," Angelica states, her confusion evident.

"Well, there's a full file on him, but some of the information has been blacked out—his birth parents, last name, and location of birth. The only personal detail I have is that, if he's still alive, he'll be twenty-eight years old now."

As I'm scanning the contents of the file, I land on a photo of a little boy. A chill runs down my spine and I go silent. I feel like I've seen him before, but I can't quite place where or when.

"Aria, what's wrong?"

"Oh. Sorry, I just saw his picture and he is...strikingly familiar," I murmur, unease in my tone.

"Have you seen him before?"

"I haven't, but he looks like someone I know—he has the craziest eyes."

"We don't have time to go over his appearance. You need to

get out of there!" Angelica exclaims. She's right. I need to leave before I'm caught.

"I'll send you a picture of his file in a few seconds," I say, and we hang up.

My fingers linger on the photo for a moment before slipping it back into the folder. With one last glance at the box, I place it back on the shelf, making sure everything looks undisturbed. Then, I make my way to the door.

I slip out into the quiet hallway, my heart still racing as I walk away, the enormity of what I've found sinking in.

The discovery of the boy's presence at the school adds another layer of mystery to this already tangled web. And my father's involvement seems to go deeper than I expected.

I desperately hope that whatever I found is just a misunderstanding. That *Baba* is still a good person.

But the nagging doubt remains, making me wonder what my father has up his sleeve.

27

ARIA

I sit across from Gianis in Black Bean, the hum of conversations and clinking cups surrounding us. Freshly brewed coffee fills the air, blending with the scent of pastries.

Gianis looks tired as he sips his espresso. I stir my latte, the creamy swirl mesmerizing for a moment before I look up at him. It's nice to see him again, especially with everything going on. And I know he's been through a lot, too.

"So," I begin, my voice light but curious. "How do you feel about Angie now? I know it's been hard..." Gianis has had feelings for Ang for years. Once Evan came into the picture, he confessed how he felt to her, but she didn't reciprocate. Safe to say, he and Evan aren't each other's biggest fans.

Gianis sets his cup down, exhaling softly. "It's complicated. I still care about her a lot, but I've come to terms with it all. Seeing her happy is more important to me than anything else. And she seems in a better place now, especially with us visiting her in Antium."

"I'm glad you're handling it well. It's not easy to let go of someone you love."

"No, it's not." He chuckles, a hint of sadness in his eyes. "But we have to move on, right? What about you? How are you holding up with everything?"

I take a deep breath, feeling the weight of his question. "Honestly, it's been a lot. The forced engagement, dealing with Andrew...It's— I don't even know where to begin."

Gianis's gaze sharpens. "I'm worried about you. You don't have to go into detail, though, know that I'm here if you need to talk."

His words catch me off guard, a lump forming in my throat, and for a moment I debate telling him what happened. But I can't. "Thank you for being there for me. It means a lot."

He reaches across the table, squeezing my hand gently. "Anytime." Though I can tell, he won't let it go easily.

"Ri, I don't know what's going on, but I can sense something isn't right."

I glance away, my heart pounding. "It's nothing I can talk about right now."

Gianis nods, not pressing further, and he reluctantly switches to a different topic.

We chat for a while before falling into a comfortable silence, both lost in our thoughts as we finish our coffees.

When we head outside, the bright sunlight momentarily blinds me.

As my vision adjusts, I spot Andrew leaning against his car, his eyes fixed on me. My stomach churns, anxiety creeping in. Gianis notices him and turns to give me a reassuring smile, before squeezing me against his chest.

"Take care, Aria. And remember, I'm here if you need anything."

I offer a weak smile in return. "Thanks, G. I'll see you around."

The cool breeze hits me as I make my way along the sidewalk toward Andrew.

My heart skips a beat—in an "I want to throw up" kind of way—as I meet his gaze again, but I try to maintain my composure.

Ever since his threat, Andrew's been going away for long periods at a time, popping up unexpectedly like this, lurking in the shadows like a predator. I know he's always watching me, though I refuse to give him the satisfaction of acknowledging it. The only time I'm confident he's not keeping tabs on me is when I'm home. Though, I'm almost positive he has the guards reporting to him. I haven't seen him in a few weeks, and he seems oddly on edge, his gaze shifting around us, as if he's looking for someone.

Andrew's erratic behavior has given me whiplash over the past year. One second, he's playing nice, acting like the perfect fiancé with his charming smile and considerate gestures. The next, he reverts to a pompous asshole who doesn't give a shit about anything but himself.

It's as if I'm constantly walking on eggshells, never knowing when he'll snap.

"Hello, Aria," he drawls, his voice dripping with false charm. "Fancy meeting you here."

I force a tight-lipped smile, fists clenching at my sides. "What do you want?" I ask, trying to keep my voice steady.

He pushes himself off the car, glancing over his shoulder, as if looking for someone. Tension radiates off him, making me uneasy. "Oh, just checking in on my favorite girl," he says, eyes glinting with something dark and unsettling.

"I'm not your girl," I retort, my voice coming out sharper than intended. *I really need him to stop calling me that.*

He chuckles, a sound that sends shivers down my spine. "Oh, but you are, Aria. You belong to me, whether you like it or not."

I swallow hard, trying to suppress the fear bubbling up inside me. "I belong to no one."

His smile widens, a wolfish gleam in his eyes. "We'll see about that," he says, reaching out to brush a strand of hair from my face.

Andrew has this uncanny ability to make me feel so small, so insignificant. When I'm around him, my usual fire flickers out. It's like he has this power over me that I can't shake off.

He has broken me.

I used to be strong, level-headed, a force to be reckoned with. Now, there's only a fraction of myself left, clinging desperately to that sliver of sanity so I don't lose myself completely.

But I decide to fight back a little.

I flinch away from his touch, skin crawling. "Don't touch me," I snap, taking another step back.

He laughs again, his amusement making my hairs stand on end. "Feisty as ever, I see," he says, his tone mocking. "I like that in a woman."

I resist the urge to roll my eyes, clenching my jaw. This isn't the first time he's said that. He may say he *likes* the rare times I answer back, but I know I need to get away from him before he decides I've overstepped. I also know he won't make it easy.

"I want to take you for a little drive. Maybe get some dinner at my place."

My pulse quickens. I've only been to his house a few times, with our families. I managed to avoid being alone with him there...until now. I know that it'll eventually be my place too, but I'd rather not set foot there until I have to.

I yield, not wanting to argue with him or ruin his apparently good mood and hop into his car.

When we pull up to his house, I glance out at it. It's just as I remember it. The exterior is neat but uninviting, lacking the warmth and charm I've grown up accustomed to. The facade is plain, with minimal landscaping and a monotone color scheme that fails to hold my attention.

Andrew opens my car door, and I step out, feeling a sense of unease. I feel chilly, even though it's not particularly cold outside.

I follow him up the pathway to the front door, my footsteps echoing in the silence of the evening.

As we enter the house, I can't help but notice again the contrast between Andrew's home and Dion's. It is stark and immediate, the interior cold and impersonal, with muted colors and sparse furnishings. There's a lack of life, a sense of emptiness that weighs heavily on my heart. *How am I supposed to ever feel comfortable here?*

I can't help but feel yet another wave of despair. This is not a place I can imagine myself ever calling home. It's too...clinical, too devoid of personality. Just like the thought of Dion, it leaves me with a hollowness inside.

I crave the warmth and comfort of Dion's home more, a place where I felt truly welcome and at peace.

Andrew snaps me out of my thoughts. "Are you hungry?"

I want to say no, but my stomach growls loud enough to alert the fucking neighbors. "I guess I am," I say sheepishly. I'd rather not eat with him, though I can't avoid it now.

As Andrew puts the *moussaka* in the oven, an awkward silence settles between us. I try to fill it with small talk, anything to break the tension.

"So, how was your day?" I ask, fiddling with the hem of my shirt.

He shrugs. "Oh, you know, the usual. Busy."

I nod, even though I have no idea what his *usual* day entails. "Right, right. Work stuff."

The oven timer beeps, signaling that dinner is ready. Andrew takes out the steaming dish and places it on the table. "Help yourself."

I nod again, forcing a smile as I serve myself a generous

portion. The *moussaka* looks delicious, and it's a relief to finally have something to distract me from the discomfort of the situation.

"It's really good," I say between bites, hoping to fill the silence with some semblance of normalcy.

Andrew mumbles something in response, but I can barely hear him over the sound of my own chewing. I take another bite, trying to focus on the taste of the food rather than the tension in the air.

My mind keeps drifting back to the small packet in my purse, the promise of relief it holds. I've become more dependent on drugs over the past year. It feels like I'm losing control, and every day it gets harder to resist. What started as a way to cope for a short while, has turned into a necessity, and I'm scared of where this path is leading me. I fidget with my clothing, the urge to leave growing stronger and stronger.

I force myself to finish my meal, making polite conversation with Andrew as best as I can.

When I'm finally done, I excuse myself and go to the bathroom, ignoring his eyes on my back.

My heart is pounding in my chest. The white tile floor seems to sway beneath me as I lock the door behind me. I reach into my purse, fingers trembling as they fumble for the baggy. *Just one line*, I tell myself, *just to take the edge off.*

I lean over the sink, my reflection distorted in the mirror. With a shaky hand, I prepare the line and inhale sharply. The familiar rush floods my senses, momentarily drowning out the guilt and anguish clawing at me. I don't know how much time passes while I let myself float in the euphoria, a moment when everything is okay, everything is bearable and good.

But it fades so quickly, and I crash hard. The emptiness and shame rush in with a vengeance, worse than before. My highs don't last as long as they used to, leaving me chasing bliss more desperately each time.

What am I doing? I can't keep doing this to myself. I think of Andrew, out there, waiting for me. I can't face him like this.

Panic hits me, and I flush the baggy down the toilet, a futile attempt to erase the evidence of my weakness. I open the door of the bathroom, and there he is, leaning against the opposite wall with that infuriating smirk on his face.

I freeze before trying to brush past him, but he blocks my path, eyes narrowing as they take in my dilated pupils.

"What were you doing in there?"

"Nothing," I lie, my throat dry and constricted.

His lips widen into a knowing grin, and before I can react, he pins me against the wall, body pressing into mine.

"You're lying," he hisses, his breath hot against my ear. "I can see it in your eyes."

Fear wells up inside me, and I push against him, desperate to break free, but he only tightens his grip.

"Let me go," I plead, my voice cracking.

He just laughs, the sound echoing in the small space, mocking and cruel.

My vision blurs, thoughts scattering like leaves in the wind. I'm trapped. Trapped between the wall and Andrew, between guilt and the drugs.

I writhe against him, my movements frantic as I try to break free from his grasp. But Andrew's hold only tightens, his fingers digging into my arms like claws.

"You're a druggy, aren't you? Do you think I haven't noticed what you've become," he sneers, his words like venom in my ear.

I shake my head, tears pricking at the corners of my eyes. "No, Andrew, please."

He doesn't listen. Instead, he leans in closer, his breath hot against my skin as he tries to kiss me. I turn my head away, my stomach churning with revulsion.

"Stop it," I whimper.

He ignores me, hands roaming over my body, greedy and possessive. "I've had enough of waiting. And it's your duty to give me an heir."

I fight against him, nails scratching at his skin as he slides his hands under my shirt, and I thank myself for not wearing something easily accessible.

"So, you like it when that fucker Dion chokes you and fucks you against an alley wall, but you can't do the same for your fiancé?"

My blood runs cold, and a wave of nausea washes over me.

"Oh, Aria," he chuckles, the sound harsh and grating. "You're a little *poutána* for everyone except me."

I close my eyes, trying to block out the memory of that day behind the café, of Dion's hands on my skin, his lips on mine. It was a mistake, a moment of weakness I've been trying to forget. But now, with Andrew's words hanging in the air between us, I realize that it's not something I can just erase.

I struggle to break free, to escape the suffocating grip of his hold. It's becoming harder and harder to breathe.

Andrew has tried to come onto me before, but never like this. It's never been this intense or aggressive. Usually, it doesn't go beyond a few suggestive comments or lingering looks. But this time is different. The change in him is crazy. Ever since he found out about me and Dion, it's like he's a completely different person, and it's unsettling.

Tears well up in my eyes, and with a surge of adrenaline, I summon all my strength and manage to free one arm. In a swift motion, I swing my hand toward him, the force of my slap echoing in the air. He staggers back, a shocked expression flashing across his face as he rubs his cheek.

A cruel smile twists his lips then as he glares at me, his eyes cold and calculating. He dabs at his lips and finds a smear of blood, his sneer deepening.

"You shouldn't have done that," he growls.

Before I can react, he reaches into his waistband and pulls out a knife, the blade glinting in the dim light of the hallway. I gasp as he presses it against my throat, the cold metal sending shivers down my spine.

"If you put your hands on me again," he hisses. "I'm going to give you a reason to cry, bitch."

I swallow hard, the lump in my throat threatening to choke me as I stare into his eyes. He shoves me away, and I fall to the ground with a loud thump.

I stay on the floor, crying and shaking, for God knows how long. With trembling hands, I reach for my purse beside me and rummage through it until my fingers wrap around the familiar shape of my phone. Relief floods through me as I unlock the screen.

I quickly navigate to my messages, fingers tapping out a text to the one person who always manages to make me feel safe, even when I know I shouldn't turn to him. It's a risky move, reaching out to someone who stirs up emotions I've tried to bury, but in this moment of vulnerability, he's the only one I can think of.

I type and delete over and over, unsure what to say, but eventually settle on a *hey*, simple yet loaded with unspoken words. It's a silent plea for comfort, for reassurance, even though I know deep down that it's a dangerous game.

I hit send and wait, heart thudding in my chest. Minutes pass, and still, there's no reply. Sadness creeps into my chest, mingling with the mess of emotions already present.

I understand, though. I've been there, on the other side of the screen, ignoring messages from him for a year. I can't blame him for not responding, not after the way I shut him out. It's a bitter pill to swallow—I'm reaping what I sowed.

With a heavy sigh, I text the next best person. My brother.

As I finally push myself off the floor, I tentatively start to wander around the house. There's a strange stillness in the air, and I can't help but wonder if Andrew has left me here alone.

I make my way through the hallway and, just as I reach the door to Andrew's office, I catch a faint murmur.

"As soon as we're married, I'll set the plan in motion."

Panic grips me. What plan?

Just then, my phone vibrates, and I quickly back away from the door.

Dimo: I'm on my way.

Relief fills me. I need to get out of here as soon as possible.

Everything about Andrew feels off, but one thing is clear: he won't let anyone get in his way.

I quietly step into the kitchen to grab my things. As I bend down to put on my shoes, Andrew's voice startles me.

"Where are you going?"

My hand flies to my chest. "Home. Dimitri is on his way."

He crosses his arms with a skeptical look on his face. "That seems unnecessary. I could've taken you."

And get in the car with you after you sexually assaulted me? No, thanks.

"It's fine. He was already out, anyway," I lie, and I pray that my brother is close, because every second I spend in Andrew's presence is a second too long.

Sweat runs down my forehead and I already feel the urge to take the edge off again, but the rest of my stash is at home.

As if summoned, my brother texts me that he's arrived.

I wiggle my phone in front of Andrew, avoiding his gaze. "Well, that's me. I'm going to head out."

As I'm about to leave, he grabs onto my bicep, hard. I let out a hiss.

"I'd suggest you keep our business private, Aria," he warns, venom lacing his tone. "Husband-wife confidentiality, you know?" he adds with a wink, and I want to spit in his face for using the line I said the first day we met. At that time, he seemed like a decent human being, and I had faith that we'd be friends, at least. I chuckle inwardly at the thought. *Joke's on me.*

I jerk my arm away. "Then, I'd suggest you keep your hands off me, Andrew."

"We're going to have so much fun," he says with a devious smirk.

"Fuck you," I spit, before running down the driveway to my brother's car.

When I hop in, Dimitri eyes me with concern. "What the fuck happened?" He quickly pulls out of the driveway, passing the two guards at the gate. "Those fuckers almost didn't let me through."

"I hate him, Dimo. I fucking hate him," I stammer, tears pooling in my eyes.

"I know. We'll find a way out of this, Riri."

I scoff in annoyance. "That's what everyone fucking said a year ago, yet I'm still in the same situation. I don't know what to do anymore."

Dimitri is silent for a few moments. "I spoke to Dion," he then says.

My heart stutters in my chest.

"What? When?"

"Well, we've been keeping in touch for the past year."

I'm flabbergasted. I had no idea that my brother was even acquainted with Dion, let alone on talking terms. I knew they'd probably cross paths at some point now that my brother is involved in the clan, though I didn't expect this.

"He reached out to me over a year ago."

"Why didn't you tell me?" I growl, angry that he'd keep

something like this from me for so long. "I thought we told each other everything."

"I didn't want to worry you unnecessarily, Ri," he replies, giving me a once over. I scoff.

"Turns out, he found out our father's actual plan with Andrew," he explains as he weaves through the traffic.

"What plan?" I ask, now remembering what Andrew said on the phone. Could he have been speaking to my father?

"Philip is planning on giving Andrew our clan and business when he steps down."

I notice how Dimitri has started calling him Philip instead of *Baba*.

I'm shocked, but at this point, I shouldn't be surprised anymore. Everyone has a hidden agenda these days.

"What do you mean? You're the rightful heir. How can he just bypass that?"

Dimitri shrugs his shoulders. "He can do whatever he wants with his estate. But giving it to a stranger? The *malaká* thought he could pass a fast one on me," he grits through his teeth.

"What did Dion say?"

"He's the one who told me the truth. I've been working with him ever since to stop it."

A glimmer of hope shines in my chest, but I squash it down, remembering Andrew's threat to harm Dimitri and my mother.

"Is this what you want, though?" It's clear that Dimo was never made for mob life, but I can't deny that I've noticed a shift in his behavior over the past year. He's become tougher.

"It's not what I initially planned for myself, but I have to take care of you and *Mama*."

I nod, understanding his need to protect us. Dimitri might be the baby of the family, but he's always been protective of us.

I glance out the window, the hum of the engine filling the silence.

"So, are you going to tell me what happened between you

and Dion?" he asks, and I can hear the smidge of a smirk in his voice.

I fidget with the edge of my shirt, suddenly feeling exposed. How do I even begin to explain the way my stomach still somersaults and my cheeks flush whenever his name is mentioned?

"I...um." I struggle to find the right words. How do I put into words the intensity of feelings I can barely comprehend myself? "It's...complicated," I finally mumble, hoping that vague answer will suffice.

But my brother isn't one to be easily deterred. His brow furrows. "Complicated how?" he presses.

I swallow hard. I can't tell him the whole truth, especially the bit where Andrew threatened to hurt him, but I'm tired of keeping it in.

"I really like him, Dimo. But we can't be together."

He squints. "Why not?"

I laugh. "Seriously?" I retort, lifting my left hand in the air to show off my engagement ring.

Dimitri lets out a puff of air. "That's just a technicality, Riri."

"A really fucking big one. How the hell am I supposed to be with another man when I'm getting married to someone else?"

"Dion had a plan," Dimo says, in a serious tone.

"Here we go again with all these *plans*," I utter with a heavy exhale.

"If you would've heard him out at your engagement party, you'd know what I'm talking about," he argues.

I whip my head around. How the hell does he know about that?

Calling his bluff, I ask, "What is it, then?"

"Ah! That's not for me to tell, Aria."

We pull up to our estate, my mind still reeling with questions.

Had Dion actually found a way out, and I abandoned him without giving him a chance?

I remember the look in his eyes when I rejected him, the hurt and confusion. He tried to speak, and I shut him down before he could utter a single word.

Now, I can't help but wonder what he was trying to tell me. If it would've changed anything.

28

DION

The sun peeks through the curtains, casting funny shapes on the carpet.

I'm hiding behind the chair, tracing patterns on the rug with my finger. I was playing with my toy cars and got bored, but Mama didn't want me to play outside. She seems worried and tired, as if she hasn't slept. She keeps trying to call Baba, but he isn't picking up the phone.

I look out the window. Kids are playing, but inside, everything feels strange and quiet. I want to be out there with them.

I don't know why I'm hiding, but something is wrong. The doorbell rings, and I hear footsteps as Mama goes to open the door. There's a man I don't know, his face serious. I crawl a little closer to hear their conversation, careful not to make any noise.

I try to listen, though they're talking very quietly. I hear the man say something about my baba. It doesn't make sense. Then, something about him being...gone.

My mom starts crying, and I want to run to her. She looks so sad like she is falling apart. The man tries to help her, but she doesn't want it.

"Ma'am, I'm so sorry for your loss," the man says gently, his voice full of sympathy.

She shakes her head, tears falling freely. "How...how could this happen? He...he was just...he was supposed to come home..."

"I know. It's a terrible tragedy. But you're not alone. We're here to help you through this."

Now, everything is different. My mom is different. She moves around like a robot, like she isn't really there.

Days pass, and things don't get better. Then one morning, I find her in bed, not moving, empty bottles everywhere.

I attempt to wake her up, but she won't. I'm scared. Why won't she wake up?

"Mama?" I whisper, shaking her gently. "Mama, wake up, please."

There's a note in her hand.

My son,
I'm sorry I couldn't be stronger for you.
You will always be my guiding light, and one day, we'll
find each other again among the stars.
Until then, always remember that I love you more than all
the galaxies in the sky.
Mama

Why did she leave me?
I cry and cry until I fall asleep next to her.
Later, a man gently touches my shoulder.
"Come on, kid. Let's get out of here."
I don't want to go, but I don't have a choice. I take his hand and, together, we leave the only home I've ever known.

"TELL ME ABOUT THE LAST TIME YOU HAD ONE OF THOSE nightmares, Dion," my therapist prompts, her voice echoing in the quiet space.

I hesitate for a moment, gathering my thoughts. "It was a few nights ago," I begin, the memories still fresh in my mind. "It was about my childhood. Again. But this time, it felt different. More vivid, more real." My heart races as I recall the images.

Her brows furrow slightly as she leans forward. "And do you think there's a reason for that?"

I pause, searching for the words, feeling uneasy. "This is really fucking uncomfortable for me," I grit out. "Sorry. Language."

Dr. Goode nods, a gentle smile on her face.

I don't even know why I'm here. *Fuck.* I should just leave. This is stupid.

I had the bright idea to go to therapy. You know, to unravel the tangled mess of memories that keep assaulting me, especially the ones of my parents' deaths. It seemed like the logical step, the pathway to peace. So, I mustered up the courage, made the appointment, and now I'm here, five sessions later, and I feel like a little bitch.

As if she can read my mind, she interrupts my thoughts. "It's okay, Dion. Remember, this space is for you to explore and express yourself without judgment. Take your time."

I exhale slowly. "Since I met...*her*, things have been...different," I admit. "It's like she managed to uncover things within me I've been ignoring for so long."

It's been a year since I last saw Aria. And as each day crawls by, I'm dragged further into the suffocating grip of my anguish.

Since our last conversation at her engagement party, I've been haunted by nightmares of my past, as if the wound of her rejection opened the floodgates. They claw at the edges of my consciousness, threatening to consume me. I believed then that she didn't mean any of it, that something had made her push me away. I was still going to fight for us. But after months of her ignoring all my messages and calls, I started to think that maybe she really had changed her mind.

My therapist nods thoughtfully. "She opened you up to vulnerability," Dr. Goode explains. "Now that you're more in touch with those feelings, that's why your dreams are becoming more intense. You're allowing yourself to feel what you hadn't for years."

The weight of her words settles over me, a realization dawning in the silence of the room. "It's overwhelming some-times," I confess, my vulnerability laid bare before her.

Her gaze softens. "It's understandable," she acknowledges. "But confronting these feelings is the first step toward healing. We'll navigate through it together." Her words, somehow, are a guiding light in the darkness of my mind.

The gentle hum of the air conditioning fills the silence as I shift in my seat.

"It's hard to face the past when I've suppressed it for so long. When Ignatius found me in my mother's room that day, I didn't realize the magnitude of the situation. That I was an orphan," I say, the words heavy on my tongue.

"Do you think you grasp it now?"

I run a hand through my hair then brace my elbows on my knees as I think about my response. "I don't know. I guess I never took the time to fully comprehend it. I was too young to ask questions, and Ignatius did his best to build a new life for me. One where I could forget what happened."

As I sit here, thoughts of Ignatius flood my mind. It's hard to accept that he's gone, too. I owe him so much—he offered me a home and opportunities that shaped the very course of my life.

When I was old enough to understand what had truly happened, Ignatius told me who my father had been to him. They were childhood best friends who grew up together in life and in business. When my father died, Ignatius was the first to be notified, and he immediately came to my house to deliver the news.

My mother succumbed to the unbearable weight of heartbreak. She couldn't bear the pain, not even for her son.

It's a truth I still struggle to accept.

She sought solace in pills, hoping to dull the ache, to silence the relentless pounding of grief in her chest. But in the end, it was an overdose that claimed her.

"What are you thinking about?" Dr. Goode asks me.

"Why are the people who mean the most to us the ones who are taken too soon?"

She leans forward slightly, and her lips press together, holding back a small smile.

"What's so funny?" I frown.

"Nothing at all. I'm just so proud of your progress. The first three sessions, we spent in silence. The fourth one, you told me a bit about your past. And now, you're opening up. My efforts are paying off."

I roll my eyes and sit back. "Don't get too cocky, Dr. Goode."

She chuckles and sets her notebook down.

"Look. It's hard to put into words, but sometimes there's no rational explanation for why the people we cherish the most are snatched away from us so soon. Or why they leave." Her voice is full of sorrow. "It's a cruel twist of fate, I know. We search for meaning, for some grand design that might offer comfort, but often, we're left grappling with the incomprehensible," she continues, and my gaze drifts down to the floor. "Life itself is unpredictable, indifferent to our deepest bonds and affections. All we can do is cherish the time we had, hold on to the love they left behind, and find a way to carry on amidst the ache of their absence."

I nod slowly, a silent acknowledgement of the harsh truth.

Her eyes hold mine with a depth of understanding. "Dion," she continues, her voice tender yet firm. "Part of this journey is also about accepting your feelings, even those that might be difficult."

"What if they are for someone I can't have but don't want to forget?"

Her lips curve into a compassionate smile. "Acceptance doesn't mean erasing those emotions. It means acknowledging them for what they are—a part of your experience, but not defining your entire reality."

A knot forms in my stomach as her words sink in.

"Tell me more about *her*," she adds.

My jaw clenches. Aria has shunned me for a year, cast me aside like a shadow. And it's left me feeling abandoned—again. *And I hate feeling abandoned.*

She chose *him*. She decided to trap herself in a role she never wanted to play yet felt obligated to fulfill. She's not my problem anymore.

Though I haven't fully given up on her, I've lost momentum. I need to find that spark again, the drive to push forward, because deep down, I know she's worth it.

But it still doesn't take away the anger and hurt.

"There's nothing to talk about," I snap. "I liked her, gave her a way out, and she chose him. Plain and simple."

"You said *liked*. Does that mean you don't anymore?" Dr. Goode asks, her head tilted to the side.

I exhale a breath. "I could never not like her."

"Do you love her?"

I hesitate, the image of her, her laughter, her sass, the sound of her moans, all flashing in my mind. "I don't know."

"When we develop strong emotions for someone, it often means we're opening ourselves up on a deeper level. Allowing them the power to hurt us. Those feelings can be uncomfortable or even painful, especially for someone who may have buried or suppressed their emotions over the course of their life."

My knuckles whiten as I grip the armrest, an attempt to hold myself together. *Uncomfortable is a fucking understatement.*

"The moment you start feeling something intense, it's like stepping into uncharted territory. Like entering a room you've kept locked up for years."

My gaze flickers away momentarily.

"Now, add to that mix the fact that these feelings are directed toward someone who doesn't reciprocate them. It's a tough pill to swallow, isn't it? You've poured your heart out, after years of not doing so, only to realize that the person on the receiving end doesn't feel the same way. But rejection from someone else doesn't determine our worth; it doesn't make us unlovable."

I let out a nervous laugh and put my hand to my chest. "I feel attacked, doctor," I say, raising an eyebrow in mock indignation. A weak attempt at trying to diffuse the discomfort.

My attempt at humor is met with a knowing smile from the doctor, her eyes crinkling at the corners. "That's what you're paying me the big bucks for, Mr. Loukas," she winks.

I laugh, and she continues.

"That's why it hurts. It's a reminder of the walls you've built around yourself, and it stings, because it confirms everything you've believed about emotional avoidance."

"How am I supposed to handle these emotions? I'm losing my fucking mind, doctor," I growl out. I've hit a dead end, with no clear path forward.

"Just remember. While it may hurt now, this pain is not in vain. It's a part of your emotional journey. This vulnerability can trigger memories, especially ones buried or suppressed— which may explain your vivid memories and dreams. Facing these demons head-on isn't easy, but it's essential for growth and healing."

I nod, acknowledging the challenges ahead, ready to confront them.

Aria. Her name echoes in my mind like a mantra, a prayer, a curse. The fire she ignited within me still burns bright, refusing to be extinguished by the passage of time or the distance between us.

I can't deny the anger that simmers within me, knowing she chose *him* over me. But strangely, it doesn't diminish my desire for her.

If anything, it intensifies it.

Talking to Dr. Goode only served to reaffirm what I already knew deep down.

I'm not ready to let her go. Not yet.

Maybe not ever.

29

DION

It's Angelica and Evander's courthouse wedding today, and I've been called to be a witness.

Evander somehow convinced Angelica to marry him despite having betrayed her a year ago. Turns out, Angelica and Evander have a common goal, and getting married is the best way to attain it. Apparently, it's just for "mutual convenience."

But I'm no fool. I know my brother. Evander is using this opportunity to lock down the love of his life by any means necessary.

He definitely gets an A for effort.

I know I'm going to see Aria today. It's inevitable and makes me nervous as fuck. I don't know if I should try to talk to her or not. Part of me wants to tell her that I miss her and want her back, whatever getting her back means, and another part wants to curse at her for abandoning me.

My footsteps echo off the pavement as I approach the courthouse. The building is imposing, its facade lined with columns and heavy wooden doors. Angelica and Evander meet me at the front, under the archway. Angelica is in a simple black dress, looking both radiant and tense, while Evander is in a sharp suit that somehow emphasizes his imposing form.

"Hey, you two," I force out a smile.

"Dion," Evander nods, his arm possessively around Angelica's waist. "Thanks for coming."

"Wouldn't miss it," I reply, my eyes flicking to Angelica. "Where's your friend?"

She gives me a look, one eyebrow slightly raised, lips pressed into a thin line. The suspicion is clear in her eyes.

Last time I'd asked Aria if she had told Angelica about us, she said no. But that was months ago. A lot has happened since then. I shift my weight from one foot to the other, my hands finding their way into my pockets.

Angelica tilts her head slightly, studying me. I can't help but feel a flicker of annoyance. At this point, I don't even care if she knows, especially since Evan fucked up and had to reveal everything.

"She should be here any second now," she finally replies.

As if on cue, a black town car pulls up next to the sidewalk.

Aria steps out, draped in a somber black dress, her eyes hidden behind dark sunglasses, a stark contrast to the brightness of the day. A lump forms in my throat and my hands clench involuntarily. She's just as beautiful as the last time I saw her.

My heart skips, but it's not with joy. I feel fucking sick.

Even from a distance, I can sense the weight of her unhappiness, the strain in the smile she's trying to maintain. Even the light hair cascading over her shoulders seems duller, less bright.

Seeing her like this tears at something inside me. I want to reach out, talk to her—but I stay back.

Evander lets out a loud breath. "Jesus. You'd think someone fucking died."

Aria lifts her sunglasses and her gray eyes shine in the sun, catching me completely off guard. It's like seeing a ghost from my past, and for a moment, I can't breathe. I used to get lost in those eyes.

But now, they seem guarded, distant.

"You think you'd be used to all the black by now with the amount of death you surround yourself with," Aria snaps back at Evan, and it makes me smile. It's a small crack in her cool exterior, a glimpse of the real her. Of the Aria I know—the one who wouldn't take crap from anyone, not even Evander. It's comforting, somehow, to see that fiery spirit still alive beneath the surface.

Evander raises an eyebrow but says nothing. Angelica looks between them, not surprised by their exchange at all.

My stare lingers on Aria, until Evander shoves me with his elbow. "Get a grip, *vlakas*."

The ceremony is a quick affair after which we head to Xander's family restaurant to celebrate the union with a small crowd, mainly composed of Cebrene's Godfathers. Another political move on Evan's part.

Despite the tense atmosphere, my eyes scan the room.

I spot Aria sitting near the head of the table, her posture relaxed, yet her eyes are distant as she sips her wine. Without thinking, I make my way through the crowd and slide into the chair next to her. She stiffens immediately, fingers tightening around the stem of her glass.

Aria glances at me, her gray eyes narrowing for a moment before she looks away. It's oddly satisfying. I still have an effect on her, even after everything that happened. Even after all this time.

We sit in silence for a while, the air between us thick with unspoken words. The rest of the table is lively, filled with laughter and animated conversations, but here, in our little corner, there's a charged stillness. I savor simply being near her again, not needing to say anything.

When the newlyweds arrive and are finally seated, dinner is served.

The entire time, I watch Aria, noting the way her fingers drum lightly against the table, a sign of her nervousness. The tension between us is palpable like a live wire crackling just beneath the surface.

Aria takes a deep breath, her shoulders rising and falling as she tries to steady herself. The silence of our bubble stretches on, despite the noise of celebration around us.

Eventually, I stand up and clink my glass to make a toast. The table quiets as people look over at me.

Aria also turns to me, her eyes cautious yet curious. Evan smirks, his arm along the back of Angelica's chair.

"*Adelfé*, today is a special day. We finally see two families unite, not only in power—but in love." Aria shifts uncomfortably in her seat. "When I look at you and your new wife, I see devotion. This marriage maybe didn't happen in the most *conventional* of ways or reasons." I wink at the couple and light laughter fills the room.

I raise my glass higher, eyes now fixed on Aria's. "But nothing easy is worth fighting for."

Aria bites her lip, fingers toying with the edge of her napkin, and I can tell my words have hit close to home.

"To the bride and groom," I toast before downing my drink. The room erupts in applause and cheers, glasses clinking together in celebration. I sit back down, heart pounding. Aria is still looking at me, her eyes shimmering with unshed tears. She quickly blinks them away and takes a sip of her wine to compose herself.

Nicholas Matsoukas clears his throat, lifting his own glass. "I'd like to congratulate the couple. I see bigger and better things in all our futures because of your union." Evander nods at him. "I'm sorry for bringing up business on such a joyous occasion, but we must discuss our next moves."

"You're right. Other than to celebrate, we invited you all here today to inform you of our plan," Evander says, placing his hand on Angelica's thigh. "Now that Angelica and I are married, our families have united. But there's one problem: Peter has disappeared."

Damon Petrakis, another Godfather, confirms that Peter must be in hiding since they've not met for business in some time. He and Evander exchange heated words, their argument escalating quickly. Angelica steps in, trying to calm Evan, while I notice Aria is watching the scene unfold with a worried expression. Her eyes meet mine.

Things begin to simmer down, just as the doors to the restaurant swing open with such force to draw everyone's attention. The room falls silent, and all eyes turn to the entrance.

In walks Philip Kastellanos...with Andrew. My insides boil. That *motherfucker*. I told him to not show his face around here anymore. If we weren't at Evan and Angie's reception, I'd tackle the piece of shit straight to the ground and feed him a bullet.

"*Baba*," Aria stands, and I follow suit, her body going rigid beside me. I instinctively move a little closer, my protectiveness kicking in.

ARIA

What is my father doing here? Even more, what the *fuck* is Andrew doing here with him?

"I think someone forgot my invite to the happy celebration," my *baba* says with a smirk.

I want to make sense of it all, but the only thing I can focus on is Dion's possessive frame next to me.

I haven't seen him in a year, and my feelings haven't changed. I'm still consumed by him.

His toast during dinner made my heart leap into my throat. I knew he was talking to me through his speech, his words carefully chosen, each syllable resonating with unspoken emotions.

But I can't do anything about it. I'm stuck. Stuck in this hell hole. Stuck in my engagement.

I glance up at Andrew. He's staring at me with a vicious smile.

Then it clicks. Shit. *Dion*. He's right next to me.

My heart starts fluttering erratically. My chest heaves. Andrew is going to think that I'm engaging with Dion when I haven't even uttered a word to him. *Oh my God*. I'm going to pay for this.

Andrew has tried over and over for a year to catch me still talking to Dion. To no avail.

I subtly glance over at Dion and he looks like a kettle about to explode. His fists are clenched so tight his knuckles have gone white, and the strength of his death stare directed at Andrew is almost palpable. The two men are locked in a silent battle, and I'm caught in their path, a pawn in their twisted game.

The room is stifling. I can barely breathe. My hands are trembling behind my back, hidden from view.

I'm snapped back to reality when my father speaks again.

"Enjoying your little party, are we?" His voice cuts through the thick tension. The Godfathers all reach for their weapons, without drawing them.

My father pulls out a chair at the other end of the table. "It seems like my invitation got lost in the mail."

"Tell me what you want and get the fuck out," Evander seethes.

"Isn't that a little rude, *Diávolos*?" my father sneers. "Congratulations, by the way," he says, pouring himself a glass of ouzo. "If you thought we wouldn't find out about your little celebration, you're not as smart as you appear to be."

"If you know anything, it's because I *let* you find out. Do you really think you just stumbled across that information?" Evander retorts.

"Whatever," my father dismisses. "I want to know why Peter and I weren't invited to this dinner, considering his beloved daughter was getting married, and my own daughter is one of the guests." He looks over to me and I stiffen. From the corner of my eye, I notice Dion leaning into me, like a bodyguard ready to shield me from my father.

"Don't be stupid, Kastellanos. You know very well that your boss has gone into hiding. And I have no doubt he sent you here to do his bidding. You and Peter no longer have the right to sit among us," Evander says.

"I beg to differ!" my *baba* suddenly shouts, slamming his glass down on the table. "We deserve to know what you're plotting. Especially if it involves our business!"

Evander's gaze narrows on my father. "I must say I'm very disappointed at your sheer audacity to grace us tonight. You no longer have any right to be here, even more so considering you're not a Godfather. What makes the situation even worse is your unapologetic association with the Sisterhood."

A chill runs down my spine at the mention of the Sisterhood. At how deeply entrenched my father was in it.

Not only were his traces all over the establishment, but he was also an *active* participant, running underground bordellos, using girls from the institution. He and his men preyed on those young girls, kidnapped them, trained them to be sex slaves, child brides, prostitutes.

My stomach clenches tightly at the thought.

I haven't been able to look my father in the eyes since Angelica told me all about what she and Evan discovered.

"To have the nerve to walk into a room full of your enemies speaks volumes about your obliviousness and lack of respect for the delicate balance that holds our partnerships together," Evan continues. "So, I suggest you reconsider your decision and get the fuck out, Philip."

My father looks around the table, realizing he has no support. "This isn't the end of this, Evander." He takes a last swig of his drink. "And *you*." He points to me with a snarl, and I wince. "We're going to have a talk when you get home." His tone is stern, disapproving.

Dion nearly growls at him, moving in front of me, creating a barrier with his body.

Andrew is the last to leave the restaurant, nodding toward the doors and giving me a knowing smile as he walks out. His eyes are cold, calculating. My stomach churns with dread. I know what's coming.

I fall back down on my chair, trying to calm my breaths.

Dion hasn't moved. His hand reaches out, a hesitant, almost imperceptible gesture. My fingers itch to reach back, to feel his touch, to draw strength from him. But I can't. I pull my hand away, placing it firmly on my lap.

"I'm sorry," I whisper. That's all I can manage. Dion's jaw tightens. He looks away, the pain in his posture mirroring my own. This is our reality.

"Take care, Aria," he says softly. His voice is strained, holding back so much. I nod, and he walks off, back straight, his strides purposeful. My heart breaks a little more with each step he takes away from me.

I quickly hug Angelica goodbye and head out, where Andrew is waiting for me by his car. I force myself to move, to walk toward him. Each step is a betrayal of my heart, a reminder of the prison I'm in.

His face is a storm as he towers over me, his voice a low, controlled growl. "Why the fuck were you sitting next to Dion at the party, Aria?" His anger sends a shiver down my spine.

"I didn't mean to," I stammer. "He sat next to me on his own. I didn't even say a word to him."

Andrew's eyes narrow, and he steps closer. "Bullshit," he spits. "You looked *cozy* enough. Have you been in contact with him?" His tone is sharp, accusatory.

"No," I whisper, shaking my head. "I swear I haven't." My heart races, hands trembling at my sides.

Without warning, Andrew's hand shoots out, grabbing me by the neck. He slams me against the car, the metal biting into my back. Pain shoots through me, but I can't make a sound, my breath caught in my throat.

"Don't lie to me, Aria," he hisses, his grip tightening. "You remember what I said would happen if you crossed me, the threat I made against your family, don't you?"

I nod frantically, tears welling in my eyes. "I remember," I croak.

Andrew's grip loosens just enough for me to gasp for air, but his hand remains firmly around my throat. "Good," he says, his voice dangerously calm. "Because if I find out you're lying, if I find out you've been in contact with Dion, you know what will happen."

I nod again, my head swimming with fear. "I won't," I manage to say.

He releases me suddenly, and I collapse against the car, coughing and rubbing my sore neck. Andrew steps back, his eyes still locked onto me, as if daring me to defy him.

"See that you don't," he says coldly, turning away and leaving me trembling and breathless.

He straightens out his jacket. "Ready to go, darling?" His voice is smooth, sickeningly sweet. A stark contrast from his behavior a minute ago. I force a smile, playing the part.

I slip into the car, the weight of the night settling over me.

As we drive away, I steal one last glance at the restaurant.

Dion is standing outside, smoking a cigarette as he watches us leave. *Did he see what just happened?* Our eyes meet for a brief, agonizing moment.

Then, he's gone.

31

DION

S o, how's it been going, Dion?" Dr. Goode asks.

I sit in the familiar, slightly worn leather chair in my therapist's office, fingers tracing the stitching on the armrest.

"I saw her at my friend's wedding the other day. We barely spoke. And she'd texted me a few days before that," I say, bouncing my leg up and down, a nervous tic I can't seem to control now.

"What did the text say?"

"Hey."

"That's it?"

I nod. My throat feels tight like there's a lump I can't swallow.

"Did you reply?"

I take a deep breath, but it gets stuck somewhere in my chest. "No."

"And why's that?"

"I don't know. A mixture of not knowing what to say and a little resentment."

"Why do you resent her?"

I clasp my hands together, knuckles turning white as I squeeze them.

"She's been ignoring me for an entire year, Dr. Goode."

My therapist looks at me with that familiar, gentle expression.

"Ah, yes. Abandonment issues."

"What's with everyone making fun of my abandonment issues?"

She laughs. "I'm not making fun of you. That would be very unprofessional of me. Why do you feel she abandoned you?"

I run my tongue over my lips, trying to find the right words. I want to talk, to let it all out, but the words are tangled up. Dr. Goode nods slightly, encouraging me to take my time.

"Every woman in my life has."

She leans forward slightly, her hands resting lightly on her notepad, not writing anything yet. "Do you think you're not good enough for people to stay?"

I shrug my shoulders. "Maybe. That would explain why I feel unworthy."

"You're worthy of love, Dion."

"She doesn't love me. My mother didn't either, or else she wouldn't have left me."

Dr. Goode sighs. "I can empathize with how you're feeling. It's okay to be hurt."

My throat tightens again, but I know she's right. "Yeah," I murmur. "Since my mom left, there's always been this...hole, you know?"

She nods, her eyes softening with understanding. "That kind of sense of abandonment can leave deep scars, and also affect your sense of worth and trust in others."

I take a breath, the tightness in my chest still present.

"When you've been hurt so deeply, it's natural to worry about being hurt again. But it's important to recognize that she is not your mother. She's a different person with her own way of caring for you," Dr. Goode adds.

"But she rejected me. She's no better than my mother. Granted, she didn't leave earth, but she still left me hanging."

She leans in. "She must've had her reasons."

"Bullshit," I spit. "She could've at least heard me out."

"And did you take the time to hear *her* out?" she retorts. I settle deeper into the seat, clasping my hands behind my head, looking up to the ceiling.

I never asked Aria her reason.

I ARRIVE AT THE WAREHOUSE A COUPLE OF HOURS LATER, THE roar of my motorbike cutting through the quiet night. I pull up to the side of the building and kill the engine. Evander is letting me use our main warehouse to bring our guest for questioning.

I stare at the burnt spot on the asphalt where my Ducati was found charred, and where Luca's lifeless body was lying nearby. My fists clench, anger simmering at the thought of what Andrew did.

Aside from Evan and Angie's dinner, I hadn't seen him since the day I told him to get the hell out of the city and vanish if he valued his life. But I know he's still around. He's been careful, keeping a low profile, avoiding places where he might run into me or anyone who might report back.

He's been smart about it; I'll give him that. No sightings, no traces—just the occasional whisper or rumor, enough to remind me that he's still pulling strings.

I can't wait to fucking kill him.

He thinks he can evade me, but he's wrong. No one can stay hidden forever.

For now, though, I'm going to focus on ruining Philip's plan.

With Dimitri's help, Xander was able to locate Philip's lawyer. It took a while, but we convinced him to meet us for a "friendly" talk. Though the knife and gun tucked into my waistband may say otherwise.

I shrug off my jacket, taking off my gloves to shove them in my back pocket.

When I step through the entrance, I nod at Elias, the manager from Academia who now leads our foot soldiers. When Evander abruptly left Cebrene on his love quest to win back Angelica in Antium a year ago, I assigned Elias to oversee our men, given I had to fill in for Evander.

As I push open the heavy metal door to the warehouse, my shoulders slump slightly, the weight of everything I've been carrying hitting me all at once. I've been running on fumes, covering for Evander on top of dealing with my own mess. Don't get me wrong, I'm happy to do it—I'd do anything for my brother—but, damn, it's a lot to deal with. I take a deep breath, feeling the tension knotting my shoulders and back.

We waited all these months before making a move on Philip's lawyer to ensure it was the right moment. We wanted Dimitri to earn the trust of his father and establish himself within the clan.

I became a sort of mentor to Dimitri until we both felt confident to proceed with the plan. That time is now.

But my attention wasn't solely on Dimitri. I was consumed by Evander's revenge plan, making sure that every step was meticulously mapped out.

We've made huge strides lately. Uncovering the Sisterhood was a massive breakthrough. It's taken months of effort, but we finally know who's been stealing from our ship—Angelica's father, of course. He's responsible for all of it.

As I approach the room where Xander and Dimitri are waiting, my pulse quickens. This meeting with the lawyer is crucial. Everything we've planned is riding on these next steps.

I pause for a moment at the door, running a hand through my hair and rolling my shoulders back. Time to get my game face on. I've handled worse than this, and I'll be damned if I let Aria down now. With a final, steadying breath, I open the door and step inside.

"Hey, fellas," I say, greeting Xan and Dimitri.

They both nod at me, and my eyes narrow on our guest.

"Haris Georgiou," I say, letting his name roll off my tongue.

I sit across from him in our office, Xander and Dimitri standing behind me.

Xander passes me a laptop that I slide in front of Haris, who looks like he's about to shit himself.

I lean forward as I begin to speak, pointing at the screen.

"We need to discuss Philip's will. There are some...changes that need to be made."

He swallows hard, his fingers trembling as he fidgets in his seat.

"What do you mean, changes? The will is already finalized."

I exchange a glance with Xander, who now stands imposingly by the door, arms crossed, his broad frame casting a long shadow across the room. Xander's presence alone is enough to intimidate, but I know we need to apply more pressure.

I pull out the knife from my waistband and twirl it around my fingers, feeling the sharp blade nip at my skin. "I have no time to argue, Mr. Georgiou. I know many other ways I could convince you, so like I said, we need Philip's will to name Dimitri as the primary heir again. You make those changes now, in front of us," I command, my tone brooking no argument.

Haris's eyes widen, and he shakes his head. "I can't just change it like that. Philip will kill me."

Dimitri steps forward, his expression dark. He grabs Haris by the collar, lifting him off his chair. "You're going to do what

Dion says, *Haris*, or you'll have bigger problems than my father," Dimitri growls.

The lawyer gasps, hands scrabbling at Dimitri's grip. "Please, please! I'll do it, I'll do it!" he cries, his face turning pale.

"Good," I say, nodding to Dimitri. "Put him down. Let him work."

Dimitri releases Haris, who falls back into his chair, panting and shaking. He quickly turns to the computer, fingers flying over the keyboard. His face is slick with sweat, his breath coming in short, panicked bursts.

Xander steps closer, watching his every move with a steely gaze. "Make sure you get everything right. No mistakes," he warns.

"Yes, yes, I understand," the lawyer mutters. He types the new clauses, naming Dimitri as the sole heir, his eyes darting nervously between the screen and us.

When he finishes, he prints the document, hands shaking so badly that the papers flutter as he sets them on the desk. "Here, it's done."

I pick them up, scanning them quickly. Everything looks in order. I nod, satisfied. "Good. Now, sign," I instruct, placing a pen in front of him.

Haris hesitates for a split second before his survival instincts kick in. He takes the pen and scrawls his signature at the bottom. He then looks up at us, a plea for mercy in his eyes.

Dimitri steps forward again, this time gripping onto Haris's shoulder in a mockery of reassurance. "See, that wasn't so hard, was it?" he says, his tone deceptively gentle.

"No, no, it wasn't. Please, just let me go now," Haris begs.

I nod to Dimitri, and he places the lawyer's hand flat on the desk.

"Please," he screeches. "I did everything you asked. The will is changed. Please, I've done everything."

"We're aware, Mr. Georgiou. But there's still the matter of ensuring your silence."

His eyes widen further. "I-I won't say anything. I swear it."

I pick up my knife and he recoils, pressing back into his chair. "No, please! There's no need for that. I swear I'll keep my mouth shut!"

Dimitri steps forward, grabbing Haris's right hand and slamming it back onto the desk. Haris cries out, struggling in vain to free himself from Dimitri's iron grip.

In one swift motion, I bring the knife down, plunging it through his hand and into the wooden table beneath it. The blade pierces flesh and bone, eliciting a scream of agony from the man. Blood wells up around the knife, spilling onto the desk.

His shouts echo in the small office, his face contorted in pain and tears stream down his cheeks.

I lean in close, my face inches from his. "Remember this pain, Haris. If you breathe a word of what happened here, if you even think about betraying us, this will be a pleasant memory compared to what comes next."

I yank the knife free, and he collapses onto the desk, cradling his injured hand, sobbing uncontrollably. Xander and Dimitri step back.

"Let's go," I say, turning to leave. "We've made our point. One of our men will come in to clean up the mess and get rid of him."

I wipe the blade clean and slide it into my jacket, grim satisfaction settling over me.

Step one is complete: Philip's estate belongs to Dimitri again.

Next step: get my girl back.

32

ARIA

I feel *alive*. Everything is like a gentle embrace.

The bass thumping in my chest. The thick air, a medley of sweat and smoke. The neon colors dancing around me, blurring the lines between reality and euphoria.

It's like a wave, slowly enveloping me in its clutch, yet simultaneously hitting me with a rush.

It's as if I'm experiencing it for the first time.

But it's been many, many times. *Too* many times.

I've lost count how often I've felt this intoxicating sensation, where my worries melt away, and all that exists is *me*. Utterly and completely *alive*.

I weave through the pulsating crowd and head to the bar to get some water. If there's one thing I've learned, it's to stay hydrated.

I struggle to fish my wallet out of my clutch and pay for the water, swaying along with the music and sweaty bodies around me. After chugging almost the entire bottle, I turn around to find my friends.

And by friends, I mean the group of people I party with.

When I'm with them, it's like slipping into a different skin.

They see the version of me that's always smiling, always ready with a joke or a laugh. But it's a mask, a shield against the reality of my true self.

They don't know the real me, and in a way, that's a blessing. Because the real me is messy, full of doubts and insecurities— unhappy. I don't want to burden them with my struggles or bring down the mood. So, I play the part, pretending to be care-free and problem-free.

It's the same crew I met at the club when I snorted coke for the first time.

They're not the kind of people you take home to meet your parents. They live for the moment, unapologetically reckless, and utterly irresistible in their own chaotic way. They're the ones who make me forget, if only for a moment, the ache in my heart.

In their company, I can be someone lighter, someone who doesn't carry the weight of the world on their shoulders.

But deep down, these girls shouldn't be the ones I turn to. I've secluded myself from the people who really love me. The thought of my real friends and family seeing me, *truly* seeing me, paralyzes me. I've become a stranger to myself, unable to face my own reflection. So, what will they think of me?

These new friends are also leading me further away from the path I know I should be on.

That path definitely doesn't include drinking every night and doing hard drugs. My life has taken a sharp turn for the worse. Every day seems to blend into the next, a haze of bad decisions and numbing escapes. I find myself using almost daily now, chasing a high that feels like it's just out of reach. The nights are even worse; I drown my sorrows in alcohol, hoping to silence the chaos in my mind, if only for a little while. With each drink I get a small reprieve, a momentary silence to the constant noise. Every choice I make just pulls me further down this spiral, and I don't know how to stop.

My trusted bottle of tequila stashed under my sink has turned into a mini bar. And there are bags of pills and coke scattered around my room in various hiding places.

I stand under the pulsating lights, looking for my *friends* somewhere in this sea of faces.

My heart sinks when I don't see them, the isolation closing in around me like a vice. It's a strange feeling, being surrounded by so many people yet feeling utterly alone.

My phone buzzes in my pocket and I pull it out, my eyes blurring.

Dimo: Where are you?

My dear brother.

He's taken protectiveness to a whole new level, checking in more often, making sure I'm okay. He doesn't say it, but I know he's afraid of losing me. But sometimes his concern can be suffocating.

Dimo: I know you're at the club, Ri.

Fuck. I forgot he has my location.

Me: Then why'd you ask?

Dimo: So that I wouldn't have to check your location.

Me: Stop tracking me.

Dimo: Not until you stop hanging out with those girls.

There's this unspoken understanding between us. He knows I've been struggling, though he doesn't pry. And I don't tell him about the drugs. It's like an invisible barrier between us, this secret I'm keeping. I know he's not stupid—he probably has suspicions.

Suddenly, my head spins. The room feels too bright, too loud, every sound reverberating painfully in my ears.

I clutch at my stomach, the queasiness rising with each passing moment. I need to find a bathroom.

I run until I reach a narrow hallway and stumble into the restroom, bracing myself on the sink. My breath comes in ragged gasps, each inhale a battle against the stifling weight tightening my chest.

In this moment, I couldn't be more thankful to be alone.

I collapse against the wall, sliding down to the floor in a trembling heap.

My body feels like it's been wrung out and left to dry. Every muscle aches.

Panic coils around me, squeezing tighter with every frantic beat of my heart. I press my palms against my temples, trying to steady the relentless pounding in my head. Hot tears sting my eyes, blurring the edges of my vision.

I'm trapped in this bathroom, trapped in my own mind. I want to scream.

I'm weak and drained, as if all my energy has been sapped. I know this will pass, but right now my body is betraying me, punishing me.

My hand shakes as I reach into my purse, fingers fumbling over the baggy inside. I tear it open and hastily scoop up a line. In one swift motion, I bring it to my nose, inhaling deeply, the burn searing through my sinuses.

For a moment, the panic recedes, replaced by a blissful numbness. And for a short while everything is okay. I'm okay.

Then, regret sinks in and the panic returns and I drown into the darkness.

I'm a disgusting human. I'm shameful.

I need to get out of here.

I reach for my phone again.

My eyes land on Dion's name in my contacts as I look for Dimo's. A name that both soothes and hurts me in equal measure.

I know it's a bad idea, but my fingers still fumble over the screen.

Me: I need you.

I close my eyes and wait. At the same time, someone pushes the door open. I'm still seated on the gross floor of the bathroom, high off my ass. A very proud moment.

The woman who walks in barely offers me a glance before heading into one of the stalls.

Seconds later, my phone vibrates. I blink a couple times to focus.

Dion: Are you okay?

I squeeze my eyes shut again, the alcohol and cocaine making my brain tremble in my skull. There's a ringing in my ears, a constant, high-pitched noise that adds to the assault.

My phone buzzes. He's calling me.

I pick up.

"Hello," I say, voice cracking.

"Aria," Dion breathes out, and hearing his voice, under these circumstances, causes me to break. I start to sob into the phone.

"Baby, it's okay. Don't cry. Please tell me you're safe," he murmurs.

I sniffle and swallow a big gulp. "I'm sorry. I'm so sorry," is all I'm able to say. "I-I fucked up. I need you."

I hear commotion on the other end of the line and a door shutting. "I'm coming. Stay put."

I don't know how long passes, but I stay in the bathroom, head in between my knees, fighting the tremors that rack my body, skin sticky with sweat, until I hear a deep voice on the other side of the door, followed by a knock.

"Aria, are you in there?"

I lift my head, wiping the tears off my face. "Yes," I croak.

The door opens—and Dion is here, his tall figure towering over me.

He kneels. "*Astéri mou.* What have you done?" His tone is soft. It's not reprimanding or judging. He's worried, concerned. My heart swells.

I allow myself to truly absorb him. The sight of him gives me an overwhelming sense of peace, and an equally immense feeling of sadness.

At Evander and Angelica's courthouse wedding, I didn't allow myself to *really* look at him, not able to face the pain of being without him just yet. The realization of how much I have missed him sweeps over me like a current.

Without another word, Dion swoops me into his arms and carries me out.

Instead of walking through the crowd, he takes me through a back door that leads to a parking lot where his car sits idle, his driver waiting for us.

He gently sets me down in the back seat and hops in after me.

I curl into a ball next to him. He caresses my hair, though I sense his hesitation when he speaks.

"What did you take?"

"How do you know I took anything?"

"Your eyes. They're red and glossy, and your pupils are dilated."

I release a trembling sigh. "Coke," I reply, heart racing.

He lets out a breath. "Is it the first time?"

I shake my head.

"*Why*, Aria?"

A knot forms in my stomach. I contemplate telling him the truth. But what if he sees me differently?

I sit up, moving away from him, and my head spins again, causing me to sway. Suddenly, I begin to sweat, at the same time shivering from the cold. Dion grabs onto my arms to steady me.

"Do you need some air?"

I nod.

He tells his driver to pull over and helps me out of the car.

I have no idea where we are, but I sit down on the edge of the sidewalk, clutching my head. I need to sober up. Dion sits next to me.

"Who knows about this?"

He pulls out a pack of smokes, tapping one out to hand to me. "You look like you could use this," he says softly. I take the cigarette with a shaky hand, and he lights the tip for me. I try to give him a small smile.

"No one knows," I finally respond. It's terrifying to think about exposing my shameful secret to someone right now. Especially to Dion.

I take a drag, smoke curling around my fingers, and exhale slowly, my shoulders relaxing just a bit.

Dion nods. I can't read him, and it scares the hell out of me. He's so cool and composed. I can't tell if he's sad, angry, or disappointed.

I chance a glance at his profile. His gaze is on something distant.

"It's been a year since we've properly spoken."

"I know," I say with a sniffle.

He takes a deep breath as if to steel himself. "You rejected me."

My breath hitches. I know I should muster up the courage

to tell him the real reason I refused him that night, but I can't risk Andrew finding out.

"I had no choice," I mumble.

His eyes flash with frustration as he meets my gaze. "You always have a choice, Aria."

"Believe me, I weighed every option, considered every angle. I didn't want to hurt you," I say, hoping to diffuse the growing tension.

"What are you even talking about? You didn't even give me the chance to tell you my plan." His jaw tightens, a muscle ticking in his cheek as he struggles to contain his emotions.

I look down, grabbing onto my dress to play with the hem. "It wouldn't have mattered. I know you're upset—"

He cuts me off. "You don't know shit, Aria," he snaps. His harsh words sting. But I deserve them. "I've spent 365 days wondering *why*. Why would you lie and make me believe you wanted a way out of your engagement?" His breathing grows heavier.

"I didn't lie," I whisper, trying to keep my tone steady. "I truly wanted a way out."

Dion laughs, but it's not a joyful sound. "Bullshit."

"This is bigger than you and me, Dion. You don't understand."

His smile doesn't reach his eyes. "I wouldn't know, Ari. You haven't talked to me in a year. You wouldn't even respond to my texts. And the first time you message me after an entire year is to have me come save you from a dingy club fucking high off coke."

Dion's sharp words pierce through me. But I understand his frustration. I shunned him, turned my back on him. It's a bitter pill to swallow, knowing that I've caused him such pain.

I wish I could explain to him why I acted the way I did.

I want him to know that I regret my actions, that I want to make things right.

But I can't—because of my brother.

"*Signómi*," I mutter simply, but the words seem inadequate.

Dion expels a deep sigh, then gets up and extends a hand to me. "Let's get you home."

As soon as we're back in the car, he tells his driver to take me to my estate. I don't even care enough right now to avoid being seen. I hope it doesn't bite me in the ass.

The entire drive is quiet, and our silence feels heavy.

When we pass the gates and the car has come to a stop, Dion turns to me. "I know your life is in shambles right now, so I'm not judging you—in any way. But you have people who care about you deeply, Aria. Your mother, your brother, Angelica... And me," he says, his tone comforting. "You don't need the drugs and alcohol to cope."

I scoff half-heartedly, a rare burst of emotion rising within me. A flicker of what I used to be. "I don't need you or anyone else telling me what I can or cannot do, Dion. I'm not a child, and I don't need to be rescued." My words come out sharp and defensive. Hurt flashes in Dion's eyes. I know it's not fair. I know it's the guilt talking, making me lash out because I can't stand to face what I've done. I'm projecting all my anger and disappointment onto him, and it only makes me feel worse.

"Then why the fuck did you text me then?" he retorts, his voice rising as frustration boils over. He has every right to be mad.

I stay silent and look down at my hands that are once again fidgeting with my clothes. Dion's eyes dart to my short dress and uncovered legs. His heated gaze intensifies the butterflies fluttering inside me.

"I had no one else," I murmur.

How do I tell him that he's the only one I ever want to call? That he's the only person I think of when anything happens to me, good or bad. How do I tell him these things without feeling the guilt of laying my emotions everywhere except with my future husband?

"Don't lie to me, Aria," Dion adds, softer this time, as if he can see the swirling thoughts in my head. I feel the weight of his eyes on me, the scrutiny suffocating. It's as though I'm under a microscope, my every flaw magnified for him to see.

I turn my body to face him, finally meeting his gaze, and what I find, a mix of anger and despair—longing—makes my breath hitch.

"I needed *you*, Dion. Not anybody else," A knot tightens in my stomach, my palms growing clammy. *I could say more, so much more.*

"When do you need me, Aria? It seems like you only called me because you needed saving."

I can see the urgency in his eyes, sense the blazing fire inside his body. My heart races and heat creeps up my neck.

I always need you, Dion. I open my mouth to say the words out loud, but the ringing of my phone interrupts the moment.

We look at each other, realization dawning on Dion's face. His lips form a straight line as his jaw tenses.

We both know exactly who is calling me.

Ring. Ring. Ring.

The tension in the car thickens and Dion looks like a kettle ready to explode.

We still don't take our eyes off each other as the phone continues to ring in my clutch.

My breathing goes ragged as Dion's gaze pierces into me, and I find myself wishing for the ground to swallow me whole.

"Answer it."

"No," I reply breathlessly.

"Answer it, Aria," Dion repeats in a no-bullshit tone. I can *feel* the fire burning within him.

My phone is still ringing.

The sound is deafening, but I can't hear anything other than the tension bubbling inside me.

I want to take my phone and throw it out the window, but I can't move, my body frozen from Dion's penetrating gaze.

My hands go back to my hem. I breathe in and out, my rib cage expanding with each breath, and I notice Dion glancing at my chest before forcing himself to look away. He's not going to let this go, and if I don't answer the call, I'm going to pay for it later. *Fuck.*

I swallow the nervous lump in my throat and shut my eyes tight, trying to temporarily sober up.

"Hello."

"Aria." The hairs at the back of my neck rise. "Where are you?" Andrew's voice is low, but I don't miss the underlying anger in his tone.

"I'm home," I say hesitantly.

Just then, Dion slides over to my side in one swift movement, his thigh grazing my bare leg, and I'm not sure if it's to offer me comfort or to torture me. My body stills when he brings his nose to my ear.

A deep breath sounds through the speaker. "I've been calling you all night."

I bite my bottom lip, hard enough to hurt. Anything to sober the fuck up before this conversation turns to shit. "I'm sorry. I was watching a movie, and my phone was on silent."

I can feel and hear Dion's warm and heavy breathing in my ear. Goosebumps erupt all over my body.

If Andrew doesn't believe my bullshit, he doesn't make it known.

"Text me in the morning." He hangs up.

I exhale a pent-up breath, the tension slowly leaving my body. *That was close.*

Dion grabs my left hand in his and runs his thumb over my

engagement ring. It feels like a prison, confining me to a destiny I didn't write, binding me by a chain.

"Now, answer me, Aria. When do you need me, if not just when you need saving?" he asks again, right into my ear.

"Always," I whisper.

His lips are now touching my earlobe as he inhales sharply. "Say it again," he demands.

"I always need *you*, Dion," I mumble.

His hand travels up my thigh, fingers trailing over my skin, all the way up to my chest, before he puts his palm flat over my heart.

"This heart beats for me," he states.

It isn't a question, but I nod, letting out a breathless *yes*.

"In spite of everything, I've only ever had one want," he continues. "My need for you goes beyond anything that can be put into words. *It's madness*, Aria. To have the burning desire to be with a woman I can't have. Take me out of my misery, I beg you."

My heart skips two beats at his plea, his words striking me right in the depths of my soul. *I can't take this anymore.*

I want to tell him I picture his face every time I look into my fiancé's eyes. I want him to hear how much I yearn to be with him.

I want to end his suffering. *And mine.*

I open my mouth to say something, but Dion stops me by removing his hand from my chest and bringing his fingers to my lips, closing them gently.

He doesn't want to hear my rejection.

I close my eyes and squeeze them shut, tears threatening to fall.

Dion brings his face down to my neck and buries it in the curve, inhaling long and hard, soaking up every ounce of my scent.

A pool of wetness gathers in between my legs at his feral

gesture, and I suddenly want to open myself up to him, body, and soul. My body begs to be touched by him. Every ache is screaming his name.

He senses the shift in my body language and bites down on my neck, gently sucking and swirling his tongue along my skin.

I close my legs, but it does nothing to relieve the pressure now concentrated right at my throbbing clit.

He removes his mouth from my neck and puts his hand down my dress, cups my right breast in his hand and pinches my nipple, sending ripples down my body.

"We shouldn't do this here, Dion," I manage to say.

"No, we shouldn't," he confirms. "But it doesn't change the fact that I want to."

I try to find the courage to speak. To thank him for saving me and leave.

Instead, I do something I might come to regret tomorrow morning.

I slide over to Dion and lean in, heart almost beating out of my chest, and press my lips to his. His warmth sends a surge of electricity through my veins, as if every nerve in my body has suddenly awakened at his touch.

And it's as if a floodgate has been opened.

His lips start to move against mine, matching my rhythm before he grabs me by the back of the head and deepens the kiss. I moan into his mouth.

A rush of need flows through me, and I want more.

Our kiss becomes frantic, as if we're going to wake up from a beautiful dream and realize this was only our imagination.

Dion nips at my bottom lip. My exhales turn rugged, hard, desperate. I climb on top of him, my dress rising up my legs. He squeezes my thighs, not once letting go of my lips, and pulls me closer to his crotch, his dick hard through his trousers.

"Fuck, Aria," he breathes as I start to rock myself against him, pleasure hitting me right away. I'm already on the edge. It's not only that I haven't done anything sexual in over a year—since being with him—it's the effect that *he* has on me. No one else ever could.

I hold on to his shoulders, letting the friction bring me closer to my orgasm. I need this so badly.

Dion moves his mouth to my neck and inhales deeply before continuing to kiss and lick my skin. I erupt in goosebumps.

"Ah, yes. Fuck," I moan into his ear, and he grunts.

"You're going to make me come in my fucking pants," he grits out, sounding frustrated. But I know it's because he's just as drunk on this as I am.

We shouldn't be doing this. Not now, not *here*, in front of my house, the guards only several feet away. But I can't help it.

He reaches down my dress and pinches my nipple between his fingers, and I yelp. "Oh, God," I pant. "I'm so close."

I'm lost in the moment, lost in *us*.

With a few more humps against his leg, I ride the wave toward my orgasm.

Dion whispers in my ear. "I've missed you, *astéri mou*."

And I come undone.

I cry as I reach my climax, tears flowing freely. Dion wipes the wetness off my cheeks while stifling his own grunts.

I can't bring myself to say it, to admit that I miss him too. But I really do.

My heart weighs heavily with the knowledge that I have to go back to real life. This moment, this slip-up, cannot last, as much as I want it to.

I'm not crying because it feels good.

I'm sobbing because nothing will ever feel *as* good as being with him. No amount of alcohol or drugs will ever alleviate the heaviness in my chest.

So, I mourn the inevitable end, wishing for more time with Dion in this blissful bubble of ours.

33

DION

The feel of my phone incessantly buzzing in my pocket wakes me up from my slumber.

Eyes half open, my head throbs, consciousness reluctantly seeping in. The room spins.

I look at my watch. It's four o'clock in the morning. Fuck. I must've passed out on the couch when I got home, too tired to take myself to bed. This seems to be a recurring habit.

A sour taste lingers in my mouth, a bitter reminder of last night's indulgence.

When I got back after rescuing Aria, I drank my fucking weight in alcohol. It was midnight, but I was wired. The thought of her hollow eyes and the lingering scent of her on my clothes were enough to keep me far away from slumber.

When I caught sight of her on that bathroom floor, my heart stopped.

A sinking feeling settled in my chest when I wrapped my arms around her frail body to carry her out of the club. Aria looked different, changed in a way I hadn't anticipated. Granted, my men told me she had stopped doing yoga and barely left the house as of late, but I didn't realize she had gotten to this point.

Her eyes were dull. She looked fucked up, and I could tell it wasn't from alcohol.

Turns out, she's been getting high off her mind.

The phone keeps ringing. "Okay, okay, damn," I grumble. *Who would try to contact me at this godforsaken hour?*

I sit up just as the buzzing finally stops.

Disoriented and disheveled, I pat myself to find the device, locating it in my back pocket. I groan as I reach for it.

I put the phone up to my face, rubbing my eyes, and squint against the unwelcome intrusion of light. Forty-eight missed calls from...*Angelica*?

"Holy shit!" I jump off the couch. My body feels heavy, limbs uncooperative.

Panic sets in. Did something happen after I left Aria? Is Evan okay?

Angelica calls me again, and I pick up before the first ring is even over.

"Ang, is everything okay? Are you hurt? Where's Evander?" I ask, going a mile a second.

Angelica's voice trembles. "We're fine, D." The knot in my stomach loosens. "It's Aria." Just as quickly, the weight I thought was lifted crashes back down, heavier than before, and my muscles tense up again.

But I swallow, my mouth and throat dry, trying to keep my cool. "What is it?" I was just with her a few hours ago, what could have happened?

"We can't find her. Dimitri called, asking if I knew where she was. Turns out, she snuck past her guards last night and still hasn't returned home," she explains, her tone filled with sorrow. "She texted me last night, telling me she was going out for a drink. I thought nothing of it, that she was meeting up with one of her friends or something. But it's four a.m. and her phone is off and they can't find her anywhere," she cries, her panic escalating, and I hear Evan in the back trying to comfort her.

"I'll find out where she is," I reply. "Don't tell anyone that I'm looking for her. They might not like what they find." Angelica agrees through a sob. We hang up.

I clench my fists, hard, searing pain traveling through my head. "Fuck, fuck, fuck. FUCK. Why, Aria?"

I hurl my phone across the room, and it crashes against the wall with a sharp impact.

I pace back and forth, each step matching the racing of my thoughts. I run my hands through my hair, a futile attempt to release the tension.

I can't keep doing this. What I feel for Aria is a bittersweet ache, both beautiful and excruciatingly painful. It's all-consuming, leaving me feeling so powerless and empty. Every memory of her is a reminder of what I want but can't grasp. Yet I'm always the one at her beck and call. Her knight in shining armor. Her protector. *The Sotíras.*

It's like watching my heart slowly crumble into dust, knowing that each piece I offer her takes a part of my soul with it.

After her rejection, I tried to bury these feelings, push them down, but they kept resurfacing, stronger than before. It's like an unquenchable thirst, an insatiable desire that consumes my thoughts.

The room feels too small, too confining, as if it's closing in on me, so I head to my bedroom. I sink onto the edge of the bed, clutching my head in my hands.

The more I try to distance myself from Aria, the more I realize how deeply I've fallen for her.

Lifting myself, I head to my office and sit at my desk. As soon as my computer hums to life, I quickly type in my password and navigate to the tracking software.

My fingers fly over the keyboard as I enter Aria's phone number. The screen refreshes, but instead of seeing her location, I'm greeted with a message: "Device Offline."

I slam my fist on the desk, making a few papers flutter to the ground. "Where is she?" I mutter under my breath. I run a hand through my hair, trying to think. "She must've destroyed her cell...But why?"

I grab a new phone from the drawer, input my SIM card, then scroll through my contacts, tapping on Dimitri's name. The phone rings, and I drum my fingers impatiently on the desk, waiting for him to pick up.

"Dion," he says as if expecting my call.

"Did you look for her around the property?" I bark.

"Of course I did, *vlakas*. She's nowhere to be found on the estate, and I can't track her anymore."

"You've been tracking her?" I ask, surprised.

"Yes. Ever since she started hanging out with those degenerates." I'm assuming he means the friends she was with at the club.

I rub the back of my neck. "I was just with her a few hours ago. I dropped her home." I feel like such an idiot. I should've checked if she got inside safely, but I was so focused on leaving the property before anyone noticed me. "What?" Dimitri purses his lips. "Are you *trying* to get killed, Loukas?"

I'm about to answer when it hits me. I exhale, the sound rough and shaky. I know where Aria is—and I'm fucking terrified of what I might find.

"I'll call you back," I say, hanging up before Dimitri can utter a response.

Aria

My head is pounding, a relentless throb that drowns out any coherent thought. Every sound is muffled, distant, as if underwater. *Where am I?*

I crack my eyes open, my vision swimming in and out of focus. Everything is hazy. It takes me a moment to realize I'm not indoors.

It's not light out, but it's not fully dark either—everything is bathed in an eerie glow.

I try to move, but a sharp pain stabs through me. Every muscle, every bone, every fiber of my being protests. My body feels heavy and sluggish, like I'm moving through thick, sticky mud.

I grit my teeth, a groan escaping my lips.

I close my eyes again, just for a moment, trying to gather my strength.

Cold sweat slicks my skin, and I shiver uncontrollably. Nausea rolls through me in waves, threatening to spill over at any moment. My mouth is dry, but the thought of drinking anything turns my stomach. Each breath is a conscious effort, as if I have to remind myself to keep breathing.

Fear grips me, a tight, unyielding band around my chest. My heart hammers wildly, and I'm terrified it might just stop. I can't think straight, can't grasp onto any sense of normalcy or control.

I lie down, curling into myself, hoping to find a position that offers a hint of comfort. I can no longer hold on to any single worry; it all slips away into the darkness that envelops me.

Dion

I head to my garage, chest tightening as I slide into the driver's seat of one of my cars.

I speed out of my driveway, not caring about the loud screeching sounds I leave in my wake.

My heart races as I tear through the street, every passing second feeling like an eternity. I can still see Aria's face, the worry etched into her features as I left her just hours ago. I told myself she'd be safe at home, but now doubt claws at my mind.

What if I'm too late? What if something's happened to her? The mere thought sends a surge of panic through me, driving me to push my limits even further.

The city lights streak by, but all I can focus on is Aria.

When I finally arrive at my destination, I jump out of the car and make a beeline for the forest behind Aria's family estate.

As I was racking my brain, trying to figure out where she could be, a brief snippet of a conversation we had many months ago popped into my head.

Aria told me she would find comfort in these woods as a young girl.

That whenever things got too overwhelming, she'd escape into the forest, exploring every nook and cranny until she felt calm again. I remember the nostalgic smile on her face, the way her fingers traced patterns on her knee as she spoke.

I can't imagine her being anywhere else but these woods if she didn't leave through the estate gates. It's so obvious now, yet I feel like an idiot for not seeing it immediately. My chest constricts with guilt. I left her alone when she was in that state —fragile, on the edge.

I knew she was a ticking time bomb, and I let her slip out of my sight. My throat is dry and my heart pounds harder. I should've taken her to my place, should have watched over her better.

I push that thought away and plunge into the dense forest.

The last time I was here, I told Aria that I wouldn't let her marry Andrew, and I still haven't been able to make good on my promise. *What a fucking joke.*

It's still quite dark, but a hint of light pokes through the expansive trees. The sun will make its appearance soon.

The further in I go, the darker it becomes under the thick trees, and the more difficult it is to see past my arms. There's a heavy cloud of fog floating in the air, but I push through it.

"Aria!" I shout.

Not hearing anything except my footsteps on the mossy floor and the twigs breaking underneath my shoes, I call again. "*Aria.*"

My breath comes in ragged gasps as I dart between trunks, eyes darting frantically side to side, searching for any sign of her.

"*Aria!*" I yell for the third time, my voice breaking. The only response is the echo of my own desperate plea, mocking me in the stillness of the forest.

I have to find her.

Branches whip against my skin, the forest floor uneven beneath my pounding footsteps. But I press on, driven by a primal instinct to protect her at all costs. She's out here somewhere, waiting for me to find her, and I won't let her down. I can't.

Just when I feel like all hope is lost, I see something beneath the trees: a streak of blonde hair. I sprint toward Aria.

My heart lurches in my chest as I reach her side, breath catching in my throat at the sight before me. Aria lies unconscious by a tree; her usually vibrant face now pale and still. *Too pale.* I drop to my knees beside her, my shaky fingers brushing against her clammy skin.

"No, no, no," I murmur, the words barely more than a whisper as I frantically check for signs of life.

Relief floods through me when I feel the faint thud of her pulse beneath my fingertips, but it's quickly replaced by a gnawing fear as I take in the scene around her.

Baggies of pills litter the ground, their contents spilled everywhere.

My stomach twists when I realize what must have happened. What the fuck could have driven her to this? I stifle a sob, bringing my fist to my mouth.

I gather her limp form into my arms, cradling her against my chest as if my embrace alone could chase away the darkness that threatens to engulf her. Her body is unresponsive, her face still and ashen. But even in her unconscious state, there's something in her expression—a vulnerability, a fear, a plea for help that tugs at my heartstrings.

The forest floor is cold and damp beneath us, the smell of pine and earth mingling. I shake her gently, but she doesn't respond.

"Baby, please. Wake up," I whisper, caressing her face.

My hands are trembling as I brush her hair away from her forehead.

A memory surges up. I'm a kid again, standing in my mother's bedroom doorway. She's sprawled on the bed, an empty pill bottle clutched in her hand. I remember the stillness of her body. My throat tightens. I try to push the memory away, but it's relentless.

"Aria, *please*."

Just then, she stirs in my arms and groans. Something in my chest flips.

"That's it, *astéri mou*. Come back to me. Show me your light."

Her eyes flutter open. "Dion?" She tries to move, but I hold her down.

"Shhh, baby. Relax," I coo.

"Where am I?" she croaks, squeezing her eyes shut.

"In the forest behind your property. Do you remember coming here?"

She shakes her head.

"Speak to me. Tell me what you last remember."

She licks her dry lips. "I-I-," she stutters, and then notices the pills around her as if for the first time. Her eyes widen and she doesn't meet my gaze, as if scared to reveal the truth.

Every fiber of my being screams with rage, yet I force myself to stay calm. She's so fragile right now, and I don't want my anger to cause more harm than good. I want to tell her how stupid she is. How reckless she's been. How selfish she's become.

I swallow down the fiery words that threaten to escape my lips.

Instead, I focus all my energy on trying to understand her perspective.

"Aria, you could've overdosed. You could've *died*."

She lets out a weak laugh, but it's strained. "Would that be the worst thing?" she chokes out, and a rush of anger courses through me. I can feel my face getting hot, my jaw tightening as I struggle to keep my voice steady. "I almost lost you!" I shout, my gaze locking onto hers. "Do you have any idea what that feels like? Do you?"

She looks at me with those wide eyes, hurt and confused, but the words keep pouring out of me.

"Do you know what it's like to think you might never see someone you care about again? To be that close to losing *everything*?"

Aria's shoulders slump, her gaze dropping to the floor. "I-I'm sorry. I just...I don't know. It's like nothing I do matters. Like I'm just existing, not really living."

"Don't fucking say that. It matters. It fucking matters, Aria," I spit.

"None of it feels real, Dion. I'm stuck in this endless cycle of disappointment and failure," she murmurs, tears trickling down her cheeks.

I grab her trembling hands in mine. "Do you really think your life is fucking worthless? Trust me, you are so worthy."

She scoffs. "Worth being used."

"You're much more than that and you know it, *astéri mou*. But you have to fight for yourself, too. You are loved by so many people."

She shakes her head, her face crumpling. "And what if I don't love myself?"

"Then I will keep telling you until you do."

Aria looks up at me again, something flashing across her gaze, and my hands reach out to her face.

"I need you to understand how much you mean to me. I need you to be more careful. Because if I lose you, I don't think I'd survive it."

"Dion—" I put my finger on her lips to silence her.

"Don't. Come here," I say, tapping my chest, and she brings her head down to the crook of my neck.

And I know it now. I love her. I fucking *love* her. And it's so liberating to finally accept it.

I never thought I'd fall in love. It seemed like a distant, abstract concept, something reserved for others but not for me. My heart was guarded, surrounded by walls I thought impenetrable. It was a foreign language.

Then, Aria came into my life like a chaotic storm, and she effortlessly tore down my walls. Even though I didn't want to admit it, she unlocked a part of myself I never knew existed.

I've learned to embrace vulnerability, to savor the beauty in the chaos of emotions.

Now, as I look into her eyes, I realize that I've opened my heart in ways I didn't think possible.

Her breathing steadies as she relaxes into my hold, our heartbeats joined. Even if Aria doesn't love me back, it's okay, as long as I get to hold her like this a little while longer.

34

ARIA

I wake up, feeling groggy, mouth dry as sandpaper. The room is dim, and it takes me a moment to recognize where I am.

Dion's guest room. I haven't been here in a year, but the familiar sight brings back memories.

I look down at my clothes; I'm wearing one of his oversized band tees. *Nirvana.* I smile.

Just then, a figure hovers over me, and I blink to clear my vision. A man with kind eyes and graying hair is checking my pulse.

"Good, you're awake." He smiles. "I'm Dr. Grant."

I try to sit up, but a wave of nausea crashes over me, and I sink back into the pillows. "What happened?" My voice is barely a croak.

"You had quite a cocktail," Dr. Grant explains, pulling up a chair beside the bed. "Alcohol, cocaine, and painkillers. A very dangerous combination. You passed out, and Mr. Loukas called me. We had to flush your stomach while you were unconscious."

I shudder at the thought, my body still heavy and sluggish. "Am I going to be okay?"

"You'll be fine," he assures me. "But the effects will linger for a bit. You might feel weak and disoriented for the next few days."

I close my eyes, a tear slipping down my cheek. "I didn't mean for this to happen."

"I'm sure," he says softly. "But you need to be careful. Mixing substances like that is incredibly dangerous."

I nod, feeling a deep sense of shame. "Thank you, Dr. Grant. And...Dion, he—"

"He's just outside. I'll let him know you're awake."

As Dr. Grant stands up, I catch a glimpse of concern in his eyes. "Try to rest," he advises, before stepping out of the room.

I lie back, staring at the ceiling. The last time I was here, things were different. *I* was different. The thought hits me hard, and I take a deep, shuddering breath.

The door cracks open again, and Dion stands in the frame.

Suddenly, deep realization dawns on me. I'm at *Dion's*. I sit up fast, the movement causing a jolt of pain through my brain. I hiss.

"Are you okay?" Dion asks, coming to the edge of the bed.

I rub my temples. "Andrew," I manage to croak, wetting my parched lips with my tongue. "Andrew," I repeat, my tone growing more frantic.

He can't know that I'm here or he'll lash out at me. Even worse, hurt my family.

I'm so stupid. I texted Dion from my phone in my intoxicated haze, not thinking of the consequences.

I'm two seconds away from freaking out.

Dion reaches toward the nightstand and hands me a bottle of water, taking off the lid first. "Drink this," he orders, and I chug almost the entire thing.

"Don't worry about him," he grits his teeth. "He won't know

you're here."

"If he finds out, he'll—"

"He'll what, Aria?" Dion challenges, cutting me off. His eyes are fixed on mine, searching, probing, seeing more than I want him to. I look away.

My fingers fidget with the hem of the blanket, unable to meet Dion's gaze again.

I can tell he's trying hard to stay calm.

I swallow hard, forcing a tight smile that doesn't reach my eyes. "Never mind. It's nothing. Really."

His eyes narrow, not buying my weak attempt at deflection. He reaches out, placing a hand over mine, stilling my restless fingers.

"Aria," Dion murmurs. "I won't sit here and force you to tell me exactly what he did, but don't mistake me for a fool."

The warmth of his touch sends a shiver down my spine, and I can feel my resolve crumbling. But there's nothing that can be done, not if I want my family to be safe. My fiancé might be aggressive, but it's nothing I can't handle.

I peer out the window, searching for something to change the subject, and my eyes land on Dion's manicured lawn.

"You planted more flowers."

Dion sighs, catching on to my plan, though gives in with a small smile. "I want to show you something. Are you up for it?" I nod, ignoring my aching body.

"Stay put," he orders when I start to move. He lifts me off the bed, cradling me in his arms.

"Dion, it's okay. I can walk," I protest, but he shushes me.

"Let me take care of you. Please."

I relent, burying my face in his neck to inhale his vanilla and cedar scent. I love the way he smells.

Dion carries me downstairs and to the back of his estate, his arms strong and secure around me. I then notice a new structure in the distance. As we get closer, I realize it's a greenhouse, something that wasn't here last time. I blink rapidly, trying to make sure my eyes aren't deceiving me.

"What is that?" I mumble, my voice weak yet filled with curiosity.

Dion glances down at me, a soft smile playing on his lips. "You'll see."

We reach the greenhouse, and Dion pushes the door open with his foot, careful not to jostle me too much. The smell of plants and flowers immediately fills my nose, a sweet and earthy aroma that's both invigorating and calming.

He sets me down gently on the ground, and I wobble slightly. Dion keeps a hand on my arm until I find my balance. I look around, taking in everything. *It's beautiful.* Sunlight filters through the glass, while rows of vibrant flowers and lush greenery surround us, creating a little oasis of life and color.

"I can't believe you did this," I murmur.

Dion smiles, but I can see a hint of sadness in his eyes.

"I needed something to distract myself with while we were apart," he explains. "When you told me how much you loved gardening and growing flowers and plants, I decided I needed to add more to the property."

He takes a deep breath. "That's when I planted the new flowers at the front." My hands instinctively reach out to brush against the soft petals of a nearby flower. The sensation is grounding.

"But it wasn't enough. It wasn't enough to mend the hole that had formed in my chest. So, I planted more and more. Eventually, I had this structure built," he adds, gesturing around the space filled with greenery.

"I needed something to keep me going. To give me hope that one day, you'd come back to me, and you'd have a place where you could feel at peace."

I swallow hard, my throat tight with unshed tears. "It's gorgeous, Dion."

He looks down at me, his eyes searching mine. "Just know that I'm here for you, Aria. Always."

I nod, unable to find the right words. The greenhouse, this moment, it's all too much—and yet not enough. I rest my head on his shoulder, letting the silence speak for us.

"Come on," Dion says softly, guiding me further into the greenhouse. "Let me show you around."

We walk slowly, his arm still supporting me. He points out different flowers, telling me their names and a little about each one.

"Here are the orchids." He gestures to a row of delicate blooms in shades of purple and white. "Those fuckers are a bit temperamental but worth the effort." He grimaces, and I chuckle.

I reach out to touch a petal. "They're stunning. You've done a great job." I look to the right. "Except for the petunias. They look a little feeble, which is surprising given that they're fuss-free flowers," I tease with a wink.

Dion gasps, hand to his chest, feigning indignation at the harmless jab.

I smile as he leads me to the next section. "And here are roses. Not just any roses. Heirloom varieties. They have a stronger fragrance than the ones you usually find in the wild."

"Someone did his homework," I joke, and he laughs. *God*, I haven't heard that sound in forever.

I lean in, inhaling the rich, sweet smell of the roses in front of me. It's intoxicating. "I love them."

Dion nods, pleased, and continues the tour. "Over here, we have some lavender." The air is fragrant with its calming scent, and I can already feel some tension easing from my shoulders.

We move onto a section filled with vibrant, cheerful sunflowers. "These are my favorite," Dion admits, sheepishly. "They're just so...happy."

I smile, genuine warmth spreading through me. "They suit

you," I respond, nudging his shoulder.

"Don't make fun of me," he mock scowls.

I throw my arms up in the air. "I'm not. Scout's honor."

We finish the tour at a small sitting area in the center of the greenhouse. Dion helps me sit down on a cushioned bench.

Suddenly, the sound of rushing water fills the room as the sprinklers go off, dousing us both.

"*Ti sto diáolo?*" Dion exclaims, jumping up from his seat as water cascades onto us.

"Did you forget you'd set them?" I shout over the noise with a laugh, trying to shield myself from the spray. I probably already look like a mess, and my makeup must be running down my face.

"No. They must've malfunctioned." Dion rushes to the control board, fingers flying over the buttons in a frantic attempt to stop the flood. "Damn it, it's not working." He gives up and turns back to me.

Now, we're both soaked. My clothes cling to my body, the chill setting in, making me shiver.

I notice Dion's gaze lingering on me and his eyes land on my breasts, my nipples poking out of the fabric of my wet top. My cheeks heat.

Heat sparks in his eyes, igniting something in me. Is it arousal or the aftereffects from the drugs? I can't quite tell, but the pull between us demands release.

Dion closes the distance between us, his eyes never straying from mine. Droplets of water cascade down his face, and I can't help but admire his beauty. Those fucking green eyes.

My chest rises and falls at a rapid pace, mirroring the erratic beat of my heart.

The tension thickens as he moves closer.

And then, in that charged moment, Dion's hand reaches for my face. My breath hitches, and I see the moment his willpower breaks, just before his lips meet mine in a feverish kiss, shattering the invisible barriers that have kept us apart for so long. The sensation is electrifying, desire rushing through my body. Our breaths mingle, becoming ragged as we lose ourselves in each other.

My fingers tangle in his wet hair, pulling him closer, desperate for more of him. Dion responds with equal fervor, his hands roaming over my drenched clothes, his touch setting my skin ablaze.

His hand lands on one of my breasts, and he squeezes it hard, letting his thumb caress my hardened nipple over the fabric.

I let out a small moan, which only makes him kiss me harder. His tongue explores my mouth, sending tingles straight down to my center.

Despite the intensity of the moment, a chuckle escapes my lips.

Dion pauses, forehead resting against mine as he looks into my eyes.

"What's so funny?" he breathes out, a hint of amusement in his voice.

"I can't believe this is happening," I reply between giggles, looking up toward the sprinklers. The absurdity of the situation is hitting me.

Dion smiles. "I love your laugh," he says softly, his gaze holding mine. "It might be the thing I've missed the most in this time we've been apart."

My heart swells at his words, and I realize just how much I've missed him too. And I don't want to be scared to say how I feel anymore.

"I've missed yours, too," I say, and Dion grins, kissing me again, not hesitating to then pull up my top and expose my tits. He bends down to take one into his mouth.

This time, I moan loudly and throw my head back, enjoying the feeling of his tongue lapping at the tight nipples.

My body reacts instinctively, pressing against him, eager for the closeness we've been denied for so long. Every touch fuels the fire between us, drawing us closer together.

"Fuck," he groans against my breast. "Turn around," he demands.

Once I'm no longer facing him, he pushes me forward so that I'm bent over. I brace my hands on the bench.

I look back at Dion, and hunger has taken over his gaze. He rips my panties off in one swift movement, making me gasp.

Not wasting a second, he spreads my ass cheeks open and spits onto the hole. I startle at the sudden moist feeling, but it quickly mingles with my already wet center.

"I've been dying to taste your pussy for a whole fucking year, Aria," he says, getting on his knees. "Don't ever keep what's mine from me again." His tone filled with sweet venom.

He licks his way from my clit, up to my entrance, and my knees buckle. I'm still not steady on my feet, and the sensation is too much already.

"Go up on all fours, baby," Dion instructs, and I lift my knees onto the bench, now even more open and exposed. But I don't care.

He dips his tongue inside me again, and I moan. "Ahhh, fuck."

Dion eats me out like a man starved. His tongue circles my clit at a steady pace, surprising me with little sucks every now and then. My whole body responds, arching toward him, each of his licks sending spasms through all my nerve endings.

As he continues to devour me, he presses his thumb at my puckered hole, using his saliva and my wetness to moisten the entrance. Slowly, he pushes his finger in, and my body tenses at the intrusion.

"Relax, *moró mou.* It'll feel good," he promises.

I take a large breath in and allow my muscles to loosen, fully trusting him.

Dion eases his thumb in further until it reaches his knuckle, and I yelp. "Ohmigod!" *I feel so full.* He keeps it there, unmoving, and I shift to adjust to the feeling.

After a couple seconds, he buries his face between my legs to continue licking me, gently wiggling his thumb inside me. The combination of both feelings causes an intense, unstoppable wave to grow inside me. I can feel my climax building.

My breath catches as Dion darts his tongue in and out of my entrance, and my body tenses in anticipation. "Fuck, yes. Don't stop!" I chant.

My heart pounds in my chest, a wild, erratic beat that matches the throbbing between my thighs.

Soon, I can't hold back or resist the powerful orgasm overtaking me.

It's too fast, too strong, and finally, it crashes over me, and I'm lost in a torrent of pure ecstasy, moaning and grinding against his face.

When I come down from my orgasm, Dion pops his finger out, and I immediately feel the emptiness.

I turn around and find a devious smirk on his face, the water that's still falling from the sprinklers causing drops to fall from his already glistening lips.

He catches me staring at them, and rolls the bottom lip between his teeth, exposing his pearly whites. "You taste just like I remembered, little liar."

As soon as I hear that nickname, I know his dark, dominant side is about to come out to play.

A shiver races down my spine, excitement curling in my toes.

There's a spark in his eyes, a hint of mischief.

I straighten, my heart thudding.

He stops just inches away from my face, and I can't look away, trapped by the force of his stare. The anticipation is almost too much, my pulse pounding in my ears as I wait for his next move. I can feel the tension coiling tighter, and all I can do is hold my breath and let myself be swept up in his storm.

He reaches above our heads, grabbing onto one of the hanging sprinklers.

It looks like a mini hose, but much thinner, around the size of my pinky finger.

My brows furrow, confused as to what he's planning on doing with it.

"Get back on your knees," he orders, gesturing to the bench with his head.

I don't move. "Why?"

"I need you to trust me," he simply replies.

My curiosity grows stronger. So, I decide to do as he says.

I get on all fours, bent over and exposed in front of Dion once again.

"I told you a year ago that I'd come for this hole," he says, spraying a bit of water on my bare ass. The coldness causes me to jump, and I let out a small shriek.

Dion chuckles. "I want you to be ready for me."

Am I ready for anal? I've never been opposed to trying it, and if I were to do it with anybody, it would be Dion. Plus, he made me come so freaking hard not even five minutes ago, while his thumb was way up there.

"Okay," I mutter, bracing myself for what's to come.

"I'm going to use water to help prep and clean you," he says, reaching out gently to massage the area. My heart beats faster. "I want you to feel as comfortable as possible when I take you with my cock."

Oh, God.

"It won't hurt, and I promise you'll feel much better after."

"Okay," I repeat, my voice low.

He brushes a strand of hair from my face, and whispers right into my ear, "We can take it slow, and if at any point, you want me to stop, say *starlight*."

He slowly pushes in the hose and water sprays inside the muscle. "Oh!" I exclaim, not quite understanding what I'm experiencing. It's not entirely pleasant, but the thought of Dion preparing me for *him* fills me with excitement.

He twists the tube and my body spasms. "*Oh!*" I shout again.

The water pressure is at the perfect level. I feel full, the sensation almost becoming pleasurable.

"You're doing good, *astéri mou*," he praises. "I'm going to take it out now. Okay?"

I nod, and he pulls out the hose, causing my muscles to clench. *Oh, no.*

My cheeks flush with embarrassment as the sudden urge to use the bathroom hits me. I try to maintain a normal expression, but the discomfort is making it hard to focus. My stomach churns, and I shift awkwardly, hoping Dion doesn't notice. But he does. I can't hide anything from him.

He lets out a chuckle. "You're going to feel pressure in your abdomen. That's normal."

I bite my lip. This is mortifying. "Are you sure?"

"Yes," he responds, amusement in his voice.

"I'm glad this is entertaining to you," I retort, rolling my eyes.

"It is." He smirks. "You trust me, right?"

"Unfortunately." I sigh.

"Then you know I wouldn't do anything to hurt you," he says, pinching my chin between his fingers.

He lifts my face and brings his mouth down to mine, temporarily distracting me from my discomfort. While we kiss, he palms the back of my neck, holding me in place until he's done tasting my lips.

When we pull away, the air is still charged with electricity, and Dion lowers my skirt back in place.

"Let's get you inside. I'll draw you a bath."

35

DION

When we get to the house, I lead Aria upstairs.

I grab two towels from the hallway closet and wrap one around her shoulders. She's shivering from being wet.

When she steps inside my bedroom, her gaze lights up, despite the dullness still present in her eyes.

"Wow," she says, taking in the space, her eyes moving slowly over every detail. She hadn't been in my room last time.

She's a little less squirmy than she was in the greenhouse, probably because she's distracted. But soon, she'll have to let all that water *out*.

I don't know what compelled me to use an aeration hose on her, but putting my thumb up her tight hole and feeling the way she writhed around it, mixed with the intensity of her climax, just makes me want to stick my stiff cock so far up her ass, she'll feel me in her bowels for days.

Given that she's never done anal before, I wanted to make sure she was comfortable and prepared. Cleaning isn't necessary, though it felt right. And my little liar enjoyed it.

But I don't want to hop into it right away. Aria's still recovering from her almost overdose, so I need to be certain she's mentally and physically okay.

I watch her as she looks around. She seems intrigued, perhaps even a bit enchanted.

Aria glances back at me, and I can't help my smile at the appreciation on her face. God, she's beautiful.

The way her hair falls over her shoulders, the slight furrow of her brows when she's deep in thought—everything about her captivates me. I want to tell her how I feel, how every moment without her is an eternity. But the words get stuck in my throat, lodged somewhere between my heart and my mouth.

I shift from one foot to the other, hands clenching and unclenching at my sides. My palms are sweaty. I wipe them on my jeans, trying to compose myself. Her eyes meet mine. My breath catches, and I swear my heart skips a beat.

Seeing her in my room makes me feel almost complete. Like she belongs here with me.

I want to tell her I'm in love with her. I *need* to tell her. But how do you tell someone that they mean the world to you without sounding desperate? Without scaring them away?

Aria steps closer, and I can smell her perfume—light and floral, with a hint of something sweet. It makes my head spin. She's so close now, I can feel the warmth radiating from her body. I need to get away from her before I say something stupid.

I can't put that pressure on her. Not now. I can't risk losing her by confessing something she might not be ready to hear.

Her gaze gets caught on one of the shelves lining the wall, and I take the opportunity to leave and fill a bath for her.

I run the water, hopefully at the perfect temperature, and squeeze some soap into the stream. Grabbing a rose from the vase on the counter, I pluck some petals off and throw them in the tub.

Aria pops her head through the door. "Do you mind if I use the bathroom?" she asks, gnawing at her lip.

"Of course not, *moró mou*. Come in. I'll leave you to it," I say with a wink, and she tries to avoid my gaze. She's so fucking cute when she's embarrassed.

A few minutes later, she comes out.

"How do you feel?"

"Empty," she replies, and I laugh deeply.

She shrugs her shoulders. "I guess there's no point in being embarrassed now."

I stand from the armchair I was sitting on and walk up to her, cupping her cheeks with both hands. "That's great. But I mean, how do you feel post-comedown?" I ask, staring into her eyes. I need to make sure she's being honest with me.

"Oh," Aria says, and her cheeks flush a nice shade of pink. "I'm fine, I guess. I don't feel like my head is going to explode anymore. I'm still a little woozy, though."

I nod. "Makes sense. I drew you a bath. May I?" I gesture to her shirt.

It's still clinging onto her for dear life. She's wearing my t-shirt. It's too big for her, but it somehow makes her look even more beautiful. Aria nods, her eyes not leaving mine.

I lead her to the adjoining bathroom where I disrobe her.

I reach for the hem of the t-shirt, my fingers brushing against her thighs as I begin to lift it. She raises her arms, and I pull it over her head, my pulse quickening at the sight of her bare skin.

Her breath hitches slightly. I let the shirt fall to the floor, my hands finding their way to her waist, pulling her closer.

Kneeling on the floor, eyes wandering down her long, slender legs, I kiss my way up her thighs.

My palms land on her bare ass, and I squeeze it, bringing her mound closer to my face.

My nose is right at the perfect level, so I bury it between her pussy and inhale.

Aria gasps for air as I take in her feminine smell. And if it were up to me, I'd spend the entire fucking day eating her cunt to make up for the year we've spent apart.

I get up and palm her small breasts. They fit so perfectly in my hands.

I stand in awe, my breath catching in my throat as I take in the sight before me as if it were the first time. "You're fucking perfect, Aria."

My eyes trace the delicate lines of her collarbone, the gentle rise and fall of her chest with each inhale she takes.

"Get in," I instruct, needing a moment to get over the way my heart somersaults.

I never want to let her leave. I want to chain her to my bed, have my way with her, and keep her all to myself—forever.

Fuck Andrew. Fuck her father. *She's mine.*

Aria steps into the bath and closes her eyes as the water engulfs her. I can still see her naked form, and I drool at the sight. I have the urge to take her right here, right now. But I won't.

"I'll leave you be. Holler if you need me. I'll be right outside."

"Dion." She cracks her lids open. "Stay," she murmurs.

"Are you sure?"

"Yes. Please. I don't want to be alone right now," she admits, and my chest constricts at the vulnerability in her eyes.

"I won't go anywhere, *astéri mou,*" I assure her.

I quickly step out of the room to grab something to sit on and bring back a small ottoman. Once I'm seated next to the tub, I use a cup to wet Aria's hair. She tilts her head back and moans in contentment.

"Tell me about your new friends."

Aria stiffens slightly, and she brings her knees to her chest, hugging them tight.

"They're not really friends," she admits, sinking deeper into the water. "They're more like...distractions. People I use to escape from my real life. I guess we use each other."

I continue pouring water down her back, and she watches the ripples along the water's surface, avoiding my gaze.

"What do you mean?"

She takes a deep breath. "When I'm with them, I feel like I have a different life. A better one, maybe. They don't know anything about me, and I don't know anything about them. It's just how I want it. No strings, no real connections."

She moves her fingers through the water, creating tiny waves that lap against the sides of the tub.

"But—" she pauses, her voice trembling. "Even when I'm surrounded by them, I'm so *alone*. It's like I'm living a double life. One moment I'm trying to be this carefree person with them, almost believing it for a while, and the next, I'm back to feeling trapped and miserable."

"I wish you would've told me instead of shunning me out of your life."

A tear escapes her eye, sliding down her cheek. "I couldn't tell you the reason why I can't allow this to happen." She gestures between us. "And I thought maybe if I just kept pretending, the heartache and pain would go away. But they don't. They never do."

She looks up at me, her eyes filled with tears. "I don't want to live like this anymore."

I cup her face with my hands, wiping away the drops with my thumbs. "Let me help you, Aria. Forget about us," I say, cringing at the words, but her well-being is more important than what I want. "Let me help you find ways to be happy again."

Aria shakes her head. "No. I have to do this on my own," she says, and I can hear the determination in her voice. "I'll get better."

My hand moves to wrap around the back of her head. She leans into my touch, and I lower my head to taste her lips.

"You don't have to face your demons alone, *astéri mou*."

She nods with the faintest of smiles. "I know."

Her face is a mask of calm. The same one she wore earlier when I realized Andrew has been hurting her. The memory of it makes my blood boil. I want to ask her more about what happened, but I don't want to push her; I don't want to make things harder by bringing up something she might not be ready to talk about yet.

But I haven't forgotten. I can't forget.

The thought of Andrew putting his hands on Aria makes me want to rage, to tear him apart for every bruise and every tear he has caused her. I force myself to take a deep breath, to stay calm—for her sake. I promise to myself that when all of this is over, when the wedding is called off and Aria is free from him, I'll make sure he pays. I'll *kill* Andrew for hurting Aria.

But for now, I'll wait, watching her, until she's ready to talk.

We spend a quiet while in the bathroom together. I run my hands through Aria's hair, washing it, the sensation of her silky strands slipping through my fingers soothing. Then, I lather her body, my bare hands gliding over her smooth, wet skin. It sends a jolt through me, straight to my cock, which hardens in my pants, begging to be let out.

Now, as I stand in the doorway, my dick is still rock solid. And watching Aria rise from the bath, water cascading off her skin in glistening beads, makes my heartbeat quicken. Her blonde hair clings to the sides of her face, framing her pouty lips that look even more tempting.

My eyes trail down her body, taking in every perfect detail. Her breasts, round and flawless, shine with the remnants of water droplets. My gaze drops lower, lingering on her bare mound.

A shiver runs down my spine, my mouth suddenly dry despite the sight before me making me salivate. There's a longing in my chest that's almost painful. I can't tear my eyes away from her; she's a vision of pure temptation. Every inch of her screams for my touch.

My mind fills with thoughts of all the dirty things I want to do to her, each more enticing than the last. The desire is almost unbearable, and all I can think about is closing the distance between us and giving in to this primal hunger.

Aria catches me staring. Her eyes widen, and a flush spreads across her cheeks. She quickly glances away and wraps her arms around herself, trying to cover up. But it's too late; the image of her perfect form is seared into my mind. Her shyness only intensifies my desire, making my heart pound even harder.

I walk over to her. Picking up a towel, I hand it to her, our fingers brushing briefly.

I force myself to step back, to give her space, though every part of my being wants to stay close.

"I'll be in the bedroom. Join me when you're ready."

With that, I turn and walk out of the bathroom.

A couple minutes later, Aria joins me, her breathing heavy—expectant.

"Lie down, baby," I tell her. She walks over to the bed and obeys.

I stare at her, my gaze unwavering. "I want you to take control," I say, my voice coming out low and husky.

There's a flicker of confusion on her face. "What do you mean?"

I place my body above hers, bracing my arms on each side of her head on the mattress, and I lean in closer. "I mean I want to show you that you still have a handle on your life," I explain, my words slow and deliberate. "That you're capable of deciding what you want when you want it. You're strong enough to command your life."

"How?" Aria asks as she meets my gaze.

I smile. "Right here. You're going to start in the bedroom," I respond, my hands trailing down her neck. I reach the edge of the bath towel and jerk it open, exposing her naked body. Aria lets out a shaky exhale, her chest expanding rapidly. She's getting turned on, and the way she's almost whimpering under me, when I'm not even touching her yet, makes my cock harden to a painful level.

"Try being dominant here. Show yourself that you're in control," I continue.

She swallows hard. "I don't—I don't know."

"Aria," I say, stopping her from rejecting the idea. I lean in, capturing her lips in a kiss that's both tender and rough. "You can do it. I know you can." I stand up. "Tell me what to do, baby.

Her breath hitches as she bites her lip.

"Do you want me to eat your pussy until your legs shake?" I spread her knees apart and lower myself, blowing air over her mound, causing her skin to erupt in shivers. "Or would you prefer to sit on my face and suffocate me with your perfect cunt?"

"Dion," she whimpers.

"What about tying me up? Do you want me to beg for it?" I say with a devious smirk. "The possibilities are endless, little liar."

I watch as Aria's expression changes from apprehension to intrigue.

She looks around the room, playing with her hands. "Stand against the wall," she says, and I slowly back up.

"Now, take off your clothes," she murmurs, and I can barely hear her.

"Say it louder, baby. Like you mean it."

She clears her throat. "Take off your clothes, but keep your boxers on," she commands, and I smile proudly.

"Atta girl." I do as I'm told and wait for her next instruction.

Her eyes darken with desire, surely mirroring mine as I watch her take control. My heartbeat speeds up.

She sits up at the edge of the bed and opens her legs wide, exposing her wet pussy to me. *Holy fucking Christ.* The urge to say *fuck it* and stick my tongue between her legs, followed by my cock, is unbearable.

Aria—looking a lot more determined—points her finger at me and starts beckoning. "Come here."

I don't hesitate to take a step. She stops me. "No. Crawl to me."

Crawl? Me? But who am I to say no to my star?

Without a word, I drop down to the floor and begin to inch toward her.

With each command she gives, I notice her breathing grow heavier. I can sense her arousal building.

I move closer, slow and deliberate, watching her intently.

When I reach her, I sit up on my knees like a fucking dog—and wait.

"Good boy," she purrs, letting her fingers trail down my jaw, and I feel like I'm about to combust. *Holy fuck.*

I've never been dominated in the bedroom, but this is an experience I'll never forget. I'm so fucking turned on; I could pierce a hole through this mattress with my dick and fuck the shit out of it.

"Eat," she says, pointing to her pussy.

I dive in right away, moaning into her wet cunt as soon as I taste it.

Aria lets out loud whimpers while I lap around her already swollen clit. I suck on the delicate nub with the perfect amount of suction, before circling it with my tongue.

Aria screams. "Oh my God. Fuck, fuck, fuck."

She grabs onto my hair to keep me there, squeezing so tight that I lose air circulation. *If this is how I die, I'll be a happy man.*

When her orgasm starts building, she begins to buck her hips, up and down, using my face to get her to a climax. *I'm in fucking heaven already.*

Aria's moans get louder and louder as she gets closer, and I can't help the groans that come out of my mouth. I'm aching to pull out my cock and tug on it—but she didn't give me permission. *And I'm a good fucking boy.*

Then, her body stills, and she lets out a shout. "Yes, yes, yes. I'm coming," she chants.

I don't slow my movements, and when she finally orgasms, her pussy throbs, squirting her release right into my mouth. *Fuck, I'm gonna come.* I groan as my cum shoots out into my boxers.

The rest of the world fades away as we look into each other's eyes, breathing heavily and just taking each other in. I swallow, savoring the taste of her on my lips. "Aria."

"Dion," she whispers.

As we continue to hold each other's gaze, the tension between us mounts, crackling like electricity in the air.

She taps the bed.

I sit down.

Aria stands and walks over to where I left my pants on the floor, pulling the belt out of the loop. When she returns, she pushes me down so that my back is on the mattress, and then straddles me. The heat from her warm pussy radiates on my skin, making my dick grow hard again. Her tits press against my chest, our breaths mingling.

"Arms up," she orders.

I obey and she wraps the supple leather around my wrists and the headboard. She tightens the belt and leans in close, her lips grazing my ear.

"I'm going to let you fuck me in the ass, just like you want-ed," Aria murmurs, and a breath gets stuck in my throat. "But not before I edge you enough to make you beg for it."

Goddamn. This woman has taken dominating in the bedroom to a whole new level, and I'm not mad at it.

"Understood?" she asks, and I nod, almost too enthusias-tically.

She trails soft kisses down my chest, her lips igniting every nerve along my skin. Slowly, Aria makes her way down my body, and meets my gaze when her face reaches my hard cock. *Hunger.* Pure unadulterated hunger.

She reaches into my briefs and palms it, and I realize that both her hands could comfortably fit the length.

Her mouth hovers at the tip, before slipping it past her lips.

I groan; a jolt of electricity travels through my body, preparing me for the incoming euphoria.

The warmth of her mouth wrapped around my cock is enough to send me into rapture. "*Fuuuuck*, Aria. This is—too good," I mutter. Why did I wait so long for her to suck me off?

She continues bobbing her head over my length rhythmi-cally, letting out the smallest of mewls when I hit the back of her throat, and my eyes roll back. I'm going to burst if she keeps this up.

"I'm not going to last much longer," I grit out, throwing my head backward. She grins around me in response, not stopping her jerking motions.

A feeling stirs within me, a subtle tingle in my balls. With each suck, it intensifies, and my breath quickens in anticipation.

"Oh, fuck, baby," I moan. I'm right there.

Just as I'm about to be consumed by my climax, just before the wave of ecstasy crashes into me, Aria abruptly pops her mouth off my throbbing cock. "Fuck!" I shout, slamming my head back down on the bed.

"Not yet," she teases with a mischievous smile.

With every flick of her tongue, every gentle nibble, she pushes me closer to the edge. My nails dig into my palms, my back arching off the bed as I groan with need.

"Naughty fucking girl," I grunt. "You're reveling in the power you have over me, huh? Knowing that you can bring me to the brink and hold me there, just on the cusp."

Aria flashes a grin and nods. "I'm not going to lie; it feels fucking amazing."

"I knew you were capable, little liar."

She continues to tease and tantalize me until I'm writhing beneath her. I can't take it anymore.

"Please. Fuck. *Riri*. Baby. *Please* let me come," I whimper, my pleas growing louder, more frantic.

Finally, Aria stops, and I release a pent-up breath. If I were ever going to cry, this would be the time.

I need to come. Desperately.

"Go into the drawer," I exhale, nodding toward the small nightstand on the left side of the bed.

Aria pulls out a small bottle of lube.

With a wicked grin, she squirts a large amount into her palm, and massages the liquid onto my length. My cock is painfully hard, in need of release.

She adds more lube onto her hand before rubbing it between her butt cheeks.

I'm salivating just at the thought of being inside her tight ass.

She straddles me again, in a squatted position, and braces one hand on my chest, using the other to angle my cock at her hole. "Slide it in." Our gazes lock, and she slowly lowers herself onto me. A whimper slips out of my mouth. "Oh, fuck. Just like that. Use my cock, baby. You deserve it."

The anticipation makes my heart race, and the tension builds in every nerve of my body.

Aria gasps as I fill her—and it's overwhelming, intoxicating.

My hands are still bound above my head, unable to move. Frustration mounts, the urge to grab her, pull her closer is too intense. I struggle against my restraint, letting out a growl.

Aria's gaze remains on me, mischief dancing in her eyes.

She continues to lower herself on my cock and groans. "Oh, God. It's too much."

"Do you need to stop?"

"No, I'm okay," she half mumbles, half moans while shaking her head. "I'm just so...*full*."

"You can do it, little liar. Show me how good you are at taking me in each of your holes." And that gives her the courage to seat herself fully on my cock.

I grunt at the tightness of her muscles squeezing me.

Aria moans, the sound fucking music to my ears.

"Ride me, *astéri mou*."

Slowly, she lifts herself, hissing in ecstasy, and brings herself back down.

Our eyes remain locked. Every movement, every touch, sends waves of pleasure coursing through me.

I'm dying to feel her. "Baby, please. Let me touch you," I plead, and she finally unbinds my wrists.

My hands grip her hips, guiding her as we move together in perfect sync.

With every thrust, I lose myself more and more in the ecstasy of the moment.

"Can I?" I ask, bringing one of my thumbs to her clit, and she nods. I use the lube to rub circles on the sensitive nub and she nearly loses it. "That's it. Come for me, little liar."

Aria continues to ride me, her movements becoming desperate and frantic. She's close.

I want to come so fucking badly. "Let me come with you. *Please*."

She nods again, finally giving me what I've been yearning for.

I succumb to the intense pleasure, and I fill Aria's ass with my cum, sending her into rapture with me.

Once we both catch our breaths, I collapse back onto the bed, bringing her with me, spent and satisfied.

36

ARIA

I lie beside Dion and stare at the ceiling.

We're both still coming down from our orgasms, and I feel a swirl of emotions in my chest. There's so much on my mind.

When Dion first suggested I take control, I didn't know where to even start. I was about to reject the idea, not wanting to even give it a chance, but I'm glad that he insisted.

My heart pounds with exhilaration and triumph. I'm intoxicated by the rush of empowerment.

I did it.

I took charge, and it felt...incredible.

Dion turns toward me, his eyes reflecting admiration and pride. His words still echo in my mind, and I realize how pivotal his support was.

Without his encouragement and belief in me, I wouldn't have had the guts to step out of my comfort zone.

He was right all along—I need to take charge of my life, not just in the bedroom, but in every aspect. For too long, I've been doubting my own abilities, convinced that I don't have what it takes to stand up for myself. I just proved myself wrong.

He reaches out and takes my hand, giving it a gentle squeeze. "I'm proud of you, *astéri mou.*"

I smile at him. "Thank you for seeing something in me that I hadn't."

He places his palm on my bare chest. "You always had it in you, Aria. When we first met, you had a spark that no one could dim. That was the real you. This isn't. You just needed a reminder."

My smile widens, and I lean over to kiss him softly. As I pull back, I get lost in the warmth in his eyes. *I'm so screwed.* How am I ever going to say goodbye to him again?

Dion's confidence in my ability to assert my dominance gave me the strength to embrace a side of myself I never knew existed. The way he responded to me, his trust and willingness to follow my lead, made all the difference.

I didn't know what to expect for my first time doing anal. I won't deny that it was a little uncomfortable, but Dion made me feel good. He always does.

As our eyes meet, the spark ignites again, the attraction and the delicious tension back like they never left.

"I don't think I'll ever get enough of you," Dion admits.

"Me neither," I respond, dread filling me for what's to come. I don't want to say goodbye, but I can't risk being caught. Not until I figure out what to do with Andrew.

I take a deep, controlled breath. "We can't keep doing this, though," I add, sounding like a broken record. I brace myself for Dion's reaction. I know he won't take it well. Hell, I'm even tired of hearing myself repeat the same thing over and over.

Dion and I are tangled in this web that I keep swearing we won't fall into again.

We find ourselves drawn together, pulled by a force we both pretend to resist but never really do.

Before I know it, our hands and lips are exploring familiar territory.

It's intoxicating and intense, and in those moments, everything else fades away.

However, the aftermath comes with the inevitable weight of reality.

After a few seconds of silence, Dion nods. "I know."

My heart pounds in my chest. *What*?

"You...you agree?" I stammer. My eyes search his face for any hint that he might be bluffing, but all I see is a determined calm.

He nods slowly, his gaze steady. "Yes, I agree. You need to focus on yourself right now, on getting better. You need to learn to cope without the drugs and alcohol, and I don't want to be a distraction."

Cold shock courses through my veins, and I feel my throat tighten. His fingers entwine with mine, warm and reassuring, yet his grip is gentle, as if he's afraid of hurting me.

"I'll always be here for you," Dion murmurs, his voice filled with a quiet intensity. "I'll always need you, and I'll always want to be with you. But I can't get in the way of your well-being."

He cups my cheek; his thumb tracing circles on my skin. "This is something you have to do for yourself. And it's more important than anything."

Even though this is what needs to be done, what's right, I can't help the tears that well in my eyes. I blink them away furiously. He brushes a strand of hair from my face, his touch tender.

I nod slowly in understanding, even though it breaks my heart. "Okay," I murmur, my voice cracking. "Okay." I can't manage any other words, but he doesn't push.

Dion takes a deep breath, his hand slipping from my cheek to rest on the bed between us. "In the meantime," he continues, a hint of steel entering his voice. "I'll focus on Andrew and getting rid of him. I've already started a plan to take him down."

"I know," I admit, my voice shaking. Dion's eyes widen in surprise.

"How do you know?"

"Dimitri told me."

Dion's expression softens, and he lets out a rough sigh. "Of course. Dimitri." He pulls me closer, wrapping his arms around me in a protective embrace. "What did he tell you?"

"He told me about our father's intentions to make Andrew his heir. And that he's been keeping in touch with you for the past year. He didn't give me specifics of the plan, though."

Dion nods. "We will eliminate him one way or another," he promises.

I bury my face in his chest, the sound of his heartbeat soothing my frayed nerves. "I trust you," I whisper, my voice muffled against his skin. "I trust you with everything."

He presses a kiss to the top of my head, his lips lingering there. "When you're ready," he murmurs, "when you feel like you've taken hold of your life again, I'll be there to pick up all the pieces and help you mend yourself back together."

We lie there in silence, the weight of his promise settling between us, binding us together even as we prepare to part.

A COUPLE HOURS AND A FULL STOMACH LATER, I'M SITTING IN THE passenger seat of Dion's car.

I watch the streets blur past the window, a knot tightening in my chest with every mile that takes us closer to my estate. The sun is setting, casting long, golden shadows across the landscape, though the beauty of it is lost on me. I don't want to leave Dion's house. I'm safe there, almost like it's my real home. I never feel that way in my own place anymore, where the air is thick with hostility and my reality presses down on me.

Dion's fingers tighten on the steering wheel as he drives, glancing over at me with concern. I take a deep breath, trying to steady the unease bubbling inside me. "How are you doing?" Dion asks, breaking the silence.

I hesitate, my gaze fixed on the horizon. "Better," I manage to say before looking over at him. "Still a bit out of it, but...better." My head is clearer than it was yesterday—the drugs and alcohol are finally out of my system—but I can still feel the ghost of the hangover clutching at my temples, reminding me of my reckless choices.

He nods, his eyes shadowed, and I can tell he's going over what happened in his head. I can still hear the raw panic in his voice when I came to, the terror as he held me, shaking me, pleading with me to wake up.

"You really scared me, Aria. You almost died in my arms."

A lump forms in my throat, and I struggle to swallow it down. "I'm sorry," I whisper.

He glances at me again, his grip tightening on the wheel. "My *mama*," he begins, and I notice how his voice wavers. "She died of an overdose. I was five. Found her in her bedroom, cold and lifeless."

The pain in his eyes slices through me. "Dion, I—"

"Seeing you like that," he continues, "it was like reliving that nightmare. I can't lose you, Aria. Not like that. Not in the same way I lost her."

Tears sting my eyes, and I blink them back, reaching out to touch his arm. "I never meant to put you through that. I'm sorry. I was just trying to escape...everything. For a while, at least."

He covers my hand with his, squeezing gently. "I get it. But you have to find another way. Please. Not for me. You need to get better for yourself."

The car falls silent, except for the thrum of the engine and the distant sounds of the city drawing nearer. I lean back in the seat, his words settling over me. The thought of leaving him, where I feel sheltered and cared for, fills me with dread. But I know he's right. I can't keep running from my problems this way.

After a moment, I find the courage to ask, "What about your father? What happened to him?"

Dion's face tightens, a shadow crossing his eyes. "He was killed in a drive-by," he says quietly. "Wrong place, wrong time. He was involved in some shady business, as all mob men are, and he was caught in the crossfire when a job took a bad turn."

I nibble on my lip. "That's terrible. I'm so sorry."

He nods, his jaw clenching. "His death was what led my mother to do what she did. She couldn't handle it."

A deep sadness fills me. "I can't imagine how hard that must have been for you. I'm so sorry she couldn't be strong enough for you."

Dion's grip on the wheel loosens slightly, and he looks over at me with a mixture of pain and understanding. "She was broken, Aria. Just like you feel sometimes. But you don't have to give up like she did."

His words hit me hard, and tears brim in my eyes. I can empathize with his mother's feelings, being in a situation where it seems like there's no way out. But hearing Dion's story has made me realize I don't want to give up. I don't want to cause that kind of pain to those who care about me.

We pull up to my estate and Dion parks the car. He turns to me, his expression softening, before reaching toward the back seat and holding out a small package.

"What's this?" I ask, taking it from him.

"Open it," he says quietly.

I tear off the wrapping and find a plain, black phone inside. "A phone?"

"It's a burner," he explains. "Only I have the number. Just in case Andrew is keeping an eye on your texts and calls. If you need anything, use this."

I slip the phone into my pocket, feeling a newfound sense of security. "Okay, I will."

"You can always come back to my place if you need to. You're always welcome there."

I nod, fighting back tears. "Thank you, Dion. For everything."

He leans over and kisses my forehead, his lips warm and comforting against my skin. "Take care of yourself, okay? Promise me."

"I promise," I whisper, hoping that I can find the strength to keep it. "Friends?" I add with a hollow laugh, an acknowledgement to the first day we met.

Dion smiles, but it doesn't reach his eyes. "Just friends."

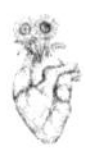

DAYS LATER, I STAND IN FRONT OF A BEIGE-BRICK BUILDING, MY heart racing in my chest. Something coils in my stomach. I've never been here before.

I've been telling myself that this is a good step, a necessary step. But now that I'm here, the enormity of it all overwhelms me.

I clutch onto the pamphlet clenched in the palm of my hand.

This is it. My first Cognitive Behavioral Therapy session with my new therapist.

I glance up at the sign by the door. *Clinical Psychology* is written in neat, black letters that seem to mock my indecision. My feet are glued to the pavement, and I can't bring myself to take that final step inside. What if they judge me? What if I can't open up? What if this doesn't help?

Taking a deep breath, I try to steady myself. I remind myself why I'm here, why I've decided to seek help. The panic attacks, the constant worrying, the nights spent staring at the ceiling with a mind that refuses to quiet down...what led me to take drugs. I can't keep living like this. I need to do this for myself, even if the thought of facing my demons head-on is terrifying.

I take out my phone, check the time, even though I know I'm early. Fifteen minutes. I have fifteen minutes to gather the courage to walk through those doors. Leaning against the cool brick wall, I close my eyes for a moment.

Inhale. Exhale.

Inhale. Exhale.

It's a small comfort, but it helps.

People pass by me, absorbed in their own worlds, probably not even noticing the girl who can't seem to enter a building. I wonder if any of them have felt this way before. If any of them know how hard it is to take the first step toward getting better.

The door suddenly opens, and a woman comes out. She glances at me briefly, offering a polite smile before walking away. For some reason, that small interaction gives me a sliver of hope. Maybe this won't be so bad. Maybe the doctor will be kind, understanding, and patient. Maybe they'll be able to help me untangle the mess inside my head.

I straighten up, adjusting the strap of my bag on my shoulder. The knot in my stomach loosens just a little. I can do this. I *have* to do this. For me. For *Dion*. I made him a promise, and I'm going to see it through.

I take a step forward, then another. Before I know it, I'm pushing the door open and going inside.

After a few minutes in the waiting area, a beautiful, tall woman greets me with a warm smile. "You must be Aria."

I nod, managing a small smile in return.

"I'm Dr. Esther Goode. It's lovely to meet you."

37

ARIA

Three weeks after my first meeting with Dr. Goode, the changes in me are almost palpable. I feel...good. Twenty-one days without a drop of alcohol or a single line of coke—it's a new record for me. I never thought I could make it this far.

My head is clearer, heartbeat steadier, but I still sweat sometimes, shivers overpowering my body, my system working through the last remnants of the poisons I once relied on and the withdrawal from them.

I've even started going to hot yoga again. Today, the instructor, who has become a good friend, asked if I would be her assistant a couple days a week. I signed up immediately. It's great to be back in the studio, this time in a role that is meaningful. Yoga was my sanctuary before everything fell apart, and now it's part of my healing journey.

As I leave class, there's a lightness in my step that I haven't felt in a long time. The warm, damp air of the studio still clings to my skin, but it's comforting.

Working with flowers again has also brought a newfound happiness to my life. I had forgotten how much I love the delicate process of arranging blooms, the explosion of colors and scents. Seeing Dion's greenhouse helped me rediscover a piece of myself that was buried under the weight of my addiction.

Dr. Goode's words from the last session echo in my mind: *quitting drugs and alcohol can seem easy at first, until your brain realizes what's happening and tries to relapse.* I know she's right. The first few weeks are almost like a honeymoon phase, but the real challenge is yet to come.

Even now, the worst part is the cravings. My mind is a broken record, playing the same plea: *just one more hit.* But then, I think about the mistakes I've made, the people I'll hurt if I don't stop, and it motivates me enough to stay strong.

I'm excited about what the future holds, but I'm cautious, too.

I haven't told Dion that I started therapy. Not because I'm embarrassed or shy, but I want my healing process to be something that's only for me. I want to be responsible for my own mistakes. For my path to recovery to be clear.

I replay the events of the last few weeks in my mind. I still can't believe it. Dion saved me from overdosing.

Despite the time and distance, he still came for me. Without hesitation.

Guilt made me want to push him away, tell him to leave, but I couldn't. I needed him.

The truth is, I never stopped needing him, even when I convinced myself otherwise.

I thought staying away from him would make things better, easier somehow. But it didn't. It only made the emptiness inside me grow, like a dark, gaping hole that nothing could fill.

Now, as I'm replaying it all, the shame is unbearable.

I let him see me at my lowest.

And even then, he did everything for me. He lifted me higher than I ever thought possible, reminding me of the power that resides within me.

As I close my eyes, I'm instantly transported back to the way he worshiped my body. Every touch, every kiss, seemed to erase the scars I gained in the past year. His embrace was like an anchor, embracing every part of me—the broken pieces and the ones still shining with resilience.

He made me feel beautiful, sexy, irresistible.

I may not have seen Dion in the past few weeks, but I know he's still around in case I need him. I should be shocked, scared even, that he may know where I am at all times. But in some twisted way, it makes me feel safe. As if he's an angel watching over me.

38

ARIA

Today is Angelica's "real" wedding, and I couldn't be happier for my best friend. The courthouse one was meant to be for convenience, but now, she and Evander have decided to give their marriage a real shot.

Ang has come such a long way since she left Cebrene, for the second time, a year ago. When she first got back, she was a shell of herself. Now, she's taking her life back into her own hands, and she's killing it. *Literally.* And I'm glad she and that shithead of Evan finally realized their true feelings for each other, though I'll still be keeping an eye on him.

I stand at the front of the church, heart pounding in sync with the steady rhythm of the organ music. Sunlight filters through the stained, glass windows, casting a rainbow of colors across the pews. Next to me are Angelica's best friends from Antium, Daniel, Nicole, and Amanda, their smiles bright and contagious. On the other side, are Evander's best men, including Dion.

As we wait, my eyes wander to him, and for a fleeting moment, our gazes lock. My pulse flutters in my chest.

The heavy doors at the back of the church creak open, and I

draw in a deep breath. All heads turn, and we watch as Angelica steps into view, her arm linked with Gianis's instead of her father's. A lump forms in my throat, tears pricking at the corners of my eyes.

My heart swells with pride and gratitude for my best friends, seeing them still this close, even after everything.

Peter Kouvalakis never deserved to witness this moment, this beautiful testament to love and resilience. He was a vile man, one who almost destroyed Angelica's spirit with his cruelty and manipulation. But she found the strength to stand up to him, to fight for her happiness.

I steal another glance at Dion, feeling the weight of my own unresolved issues with my father. Angelica's courage reminds me that I need to find that same strength within myself.

As Angelica and Gianis draw closer, happiness radiates from her face, her eyes shining with love for Evander as he waits at the altar. Gianis looks proud, his face soft with a tender smile. I catch Angelica's eye, and she beams at me. In that moment, I know that everything is as it should be. The past, with all its pain and struggle, has led us to this perfect, beautiful present.

Angelica stands next to me, awaiting the moment when she'll be joined with Evander in holy matrimony. My heart races with joy.

The priest begins the ceremony, and I look across the altar once more. This time, Dion holds my gaze, and the intensity sends shivers down my spine. I can barely handle the heat of his stare as his eyes travel down my body. I see the same longing I'm feeling.

I miss him. I miss him. I miss him.

I find it difficult to focus on the priest's voice. Thoughts of Dion swirl in my mind, distracting me from the sacred rituals unfolding before me. My palms grow clammy, and I clasp them tightly around the bouquet of flowers I'm holding to stop them from shaking.

The ceremony continues without a hitch, regardless of the silent tension unfolding between Dion and me. And as Angelica and Evander exchange vows, I silently pray for the strength to endure, to keep my emotions in check until this day is over.

As the priest's voice echoes through the halls of the church, declaring Evander and Angelica husband and wife, a sudden, loud explosion reverberates in the air. Everyone in the church startles, shrieks ringing out in the space.

For a moment, I'm confused, but then, Angelica and I share a panicked look. We're in fucking trouble.

Chaos erupts around us, time both slowing down and accelerating.

Another explosion rocks the church, a deafening roar that sends me crashing to the floor. Dust and debris fill the air, turning the beautiful sanctuary into a chaotic hellscape. My ears ring, and I struggle to catch my breath, heart pounding like a wild drum.

I lose sight of my best friend, so I turn around, trying to spot her.

"Angelica!" I scream, my voice barely cutting through the noise. I push myself up on trembling arms, glancing around frantically. My vision is hazy from the debris, but I see her white dress, now marred with soot, as she stumbles near the altar. Relief floods through me—she's alive.

Right then, a third deafening bang rips through the air, shattering the windows.

"Angelica?" I shout again, blinded by dust and panic.

I scramble to my feet, trying to stay low, my eyes darting from Angelica to the broken glass and the fallen pews. I have to protect her.

I feel a touch on my shoulder, and I freeze, afraid that it's one of the attackers trying to claim me.

"Aria. You have to take cover," a voice says from behind me. I don't really recognize it, but when I face it, I remember the man from the club. Dion's friend.

He grabs my arm and tries to lead me to the back of the altar, but I tug away. "I can't leave without Ang," I yell through the loud noises. Gunshots are ringing through the air, and I have no idea where they're coming from, but my mind is focused on one thing only.

"Please, Aria. I have to get you all to safety," the man pleads.

"Xander is it?" I ask.

"Yes," he replies.

"I don't know who told you I needed saving, but I don't want your fucking help," I snap, not caring that I'm being a total bitch. I know his intentions are in the right place, but I refuse to be paralyzed by terror and ditch my best friend.

A movement catches my eye at the far end of the hall. *Dion.* He stands there, shrouded in the haze of dust, holding a massive rifle. He looks like a grim reaper, cloaked in darkness. My breath catches in my throat—he's terrifying, and yet, in some twisted way, mesmerizing.

I force myself to move, ignoring the warning shouts from Gianis and the others, and ducking behind an overturned pew. The wood is splintered, rough against my palms as I steady myself. Every instinct screams at me to run, but I can't take my eyes off Dion.

When I finally do, I spot Angelica frantically looking for Evander, calling out his name.

I edge closer to the front of the church, my breath coming in shallow gasps.

My body is tense with fear and adrenaline. I glance back at Dion—he hasn't moved, but his eyes are scanning the hall, predatory and sharp.

Then, everything happens in slow motion.

A masked man points his rifle at Angelica.

My head whips around. *She hasn't noticed him.* I bite my lip, stopping myself from calling out, the taste of blood sharp in my mouth. I have to get to her.

The man raises his weapon further and takes aim. Without hesitation, I propel myself forward. My muscles protest, but I can't stop. My eyes catch Dion and our gazes lock for a split second. A tremor of fear ripples through his frame when he realizes what I'm doing.

I position myself between Angelica and the attacker, my heart beating so hard it feels like it's going to burst.

The shot rings out like a thunderclap, making time feel like a stretch.

The moment the bullet hits me, a searing pain travels through my body, momentarily overridden by adrenaline.

Time seems to slow. Memories flash before my eyes, snippets of my life, regrets, and moments of joy. I think I fall to the ground.

I strain to distinguish the voices calling out to me, urging me to hold on, to *stay* with them. But as darkness creeps in, enveloping me, a strange sense of peace overtakes me, knowing that I may have finally found solace. Perhaps this is the best thing that could happen to me and those around me. I won't be a burden or a nuisance anymore. I won't put my loved ones at risk or feel the shame of my mistakes.

And the last thought before I succumb to darkness is of Dion's beautiful, green eyes.

39

DION

If she dies, I'll die alongside her. Just to find life in her embrace again.

40

ARIA

"Is she going to make it?" I hear a low female voice somewhere in the distance as I cling to consciousness with all the strength I can muster. The urgency in her voice pierces through the fog.

My eyelids flutter, the fluorescent lights overhead harsh against my eyes.

A male responds. I try to focus on his words, but his voice is muted, distant, as if coming from the end of a long tunnel. "Bullet wound to the chest...fractured ribs...significant internal bleeding..." *Holy fuck. How am I alive?*

The words float in and out, and I strain to grasp their meaning, to make sense of it all.

"...Head trauma...concussion...potential memory loss..."

My heart skips a beat, panic clawing at the edges of my mind, threatening to consume me. How much of myself will I lose?

I swim in and out of focus. I just want to sleep so badly.

The woman's voice reappears. I think it's *Mama*. It sounds like she's crying.

"My poor baby," she sobs. Then, I hear another male voice. "She'll be okay, *Mama*. She's tough. You know this." Dimo.

I try to open my eyes and reach out to them, but I can't. Every breath is an effort, a sharp stab of pain radiating from where the bullet pierced my flesh.

Despite the agony, I cling to those voices.

As the doctor continues to drone on, my vision blurs and darkens. My eyelids feel heavy, as if weighed down by chains, and I struggle to stay awake. The throbbing in my head intensifies.

A wave of exhaustion washes over me, dragging me down. I try to fight it, but my grip slips, and I'm pulled under.

"How the fuck did this happen?"

The words buzz in my ears.

"We'll push back the wedding...As soon as she's recovered."

I try to decipher the rest of the conversation, but it slips through my grasp like smoke.

My head is in so much pain. It's pulsing throughout my entire body.

"Philip...dead."

Doesn't matter...still going through with it."

The words strike me like a thunderbolt. My father...*dead*? The realization hits me with a force that steals the breath from my lungs. My *baba* is dead.

In my confusion, my body reacts, causing my heartbeat to skyrocket to dangerous levels.

The monitors around me blare, their shrill cries breaking the stillness that surrounds me. My muscles tense and spasm uncontrollably as my body convulses, each movement sending shards of pain through me.

"Get her sedated, now!"

"We need… heart rate down!"

Through the fog of my panic, I catch shadows of figures and flashing lights as they fight to wrestle me back from the brink of oblivion.

The sedative takes hold, and the world fades to black.

THE WORLD AROUND ME FEELS DISJOINTED—I'M HERE BUT I'm not.

I can't seem to penetrate the dreamlike state I'm in. And my body refuses to let me open my eyes and come back to reality.

A familiar voice breaks through the haze, sounding angry, desperate. "Let me in…"

Another voice filled with concern and perhaps a hint of warning. "You shouldn't be here…if Andrew…I can't help you."

It feels like I'm eavesdropping on a private conversation.

"I don't give a fuck…not scared…I need to see her."

My heartbeat races. *Dion.*

He's here.

A FRAGRANCE ENVELOPS ME.

As I slowly come to, the familiarity of the smells around me floods me with a sense of nostalgia and warmth.

I inhale the soothing scent, and I'm transported back to my studio, surrounded by buckets of blooms.

"How much longer... awake?" My mother's voice trembles. I can clearly tell it's her this time.

How long have I been here?

"Not sure...Any day." The doctor's response is measured, cautious.

I want to reassure her, to tell her that I'm fighting to wake up, that I'm here, somewhere, listening to every word.

But the darkness tugs at me, and I cling to the sound of her voice.

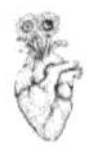

I can't quite open my eyes, but the sweet scent of flowers envelops me once more.

I hear a familiar voice.

"*Astéri mou,* please...wake up."

As I remain suspended between wakefulness and dreams, Dion's soft words become my lifeline, pulling me gently back to reality.

His presence stirs something in my chest. I can feel his touch, warm and reassuring.

Is he the one who brought me flowers?

His fingers brush against my hand, a tender caress that sends ripples of sensation through me.

"I'm scared," he admits, his voice cracking with emotion. "I don't know what...if I lost you..." The haziness returns, and I have a hard time making out all the words.

"I need..." he continues. "You're my... and I can't bear the thought of...Come back to me."

His plea echoes in my mind, and I try to break free from the darkness.

"WE CAN'T TELL HER...NEW BROTHER..."

What the fuck?

"She deserves to know..." Dimitri is speaking to someone on the phone. There's something off about his tone, something I can't quite grasp.

"I'll talk to her...wakes up. She'll want to meet him."

Him?

Dimitri's voice fades into the background.

41

DION

I can't get the image out of my mind.

Two months later, and I can still see Aria lying on the church's floor, blood pooling around her. It was supposed to be a day of celebration. Instead, my heart was ripped out of my chest. After a year without her, she almost lost her life right in front of me. *Twice*.

I've been staying at Evan's penthouse since the incident, not wanting to be alone while Aria is in the hospital. There's something about being in my house that's driving me fucking crazy. I see her everywhere.

Her laughter echoes through the halls, her scent lingers in the air.

I can't bear to stay there, not when every corner, every room, holds a piece of her. It's as if the walls themselves whisper her name, a constant reminder of what I almost lost.

I tried to distract myself, busy my mind with mundane tasks, but nothing worked.

The only respite I found was in the greenhouse, and that only distracted me for a short while.

I had to get the fuck out of there, and Evander was gracious enough to let me stay at his penthouse. *Not like I gave him much of a choice, anyway.*

The sun is just beginning to rise, and I'm already restless. I've barely been able to sleep, just replaying the images in my head repeatedly, thinking what I could've done differently to keep Aria safe. I'm going crazy.

I step outside of Saintville and take a deep breath, letting the cool morning air fill my lungs. Then, I set off on my run, keeping a steady pace. I need this.

When we captured one of the attackers and forced him to tell us who orchestrated the attack, he told us it had been *Philip*—Aria's own fucking father.

A flip had switched, cold fury washing over me, sharper and more deadly than anything I'd felt before.

The first time I saw her in the hospital, I could hardly breathe.

Every day, I visit her and bring flowers, trying to make her feel safe, like she's back in her studio, surrounded by things that make her happy. I wanted to bring her a piece of home, to remind her she's not alone.

I approach a gentle incline and push myself a little harder to distract myself, but it's pointless.

My chest constricts as a flash of her bleeding on the floor hits me again. When we found out they were going to induce Aria into a coma...

"Dion, we have the best doctors," Evander says, trying to calm me down, even though his own pain is clear. Angelica was hurt as well in the attack. "Aria's strong. She will pull through this."

I clench my fists, breathing heavily. "How can you be so sure, Ev? She almost died. She could still die. I can't lose her."

Evan places a hand on my shoulder, his grip firm. "I know, D. I know. But you have to hold it together. For her."

As I crest the hill, each step feels like a release and a torment at the same time. My breathing is ragged, pulse thudding in my ears. The scenery blurs as I push harder, trying to outrun the worry, the what-ifs, the rage toward Philip and Andrew for ruining her life.

Philip had fled the city like a little bitch the instant he heard trouble was looming and then decided to attack us on Evander's *wedding* day, almost killing his daughter in the crossfire. I was already planning on sending him to his grave; that solidified my decision.

We then found out that Peter's will had also been changed: Angelica was no longer the beneficiary of the Kouvalakis estate. Philip was.

The motherfuckers were planning a full takeover.

At first, when Philip had bolted, we hadn't really cared about his whereabouts as we didn't fully know his implication in the entire situation.

We tracked him to an underground lair at the border of Antium where I bombed our way in.

There, we found Angelica *fighting* her way out. It was a sight to behold.

After that, Philip was taken care of, never to be seen again.

Despite Philip's death, Galanis still wants to go through with the wedding, and by law of the blood pact, we can't stop him—unless we kill him. Something I plan to do soon.

Andrew is lucky he hasn't seen me since he showed up at Evan and Angie's first wedding reception. He's been laying low, apparently being away on "business" most of the time.

Finally, I stop, doubling over with my hands on my knees, gasping for breath. But nothing matters right now other than Aria.

I have to protect her.

I straighten up, looking out at Schuylkill River. Right then, my phone vibrates in my back pocket, and I pull it out, seeing Angelica's name on screen.

"Hey," I respond, my voice strained from exertion.

"Dion. She's awake."

Aria

My consciousness gradually returns, and it's like emerging from a deep, murky pool. With effort, I attempt to open my eyes, but they feel glued shut. The light filtering into the room is a glaring spotlight, intensifying the throbbing ache in my head. I groan and shut them again.

"Hey, you're awake." My brother's voice is filled with relief, though tinged with concern.

I hear my mother rush to my side, and softly brush my hair back from my forehead. Her touch against my hand grounds me amid my confusion. "It's okay, *agápi mou.* Take your time," she murmurs.

"Do you need some water?" Dimitri asks.

I try to speak, but my throat feels dry and scratchy, I manage a weak nod, grateful for the offer.

I muster all my strength and try again, coaxing my heavy eyelids to obey. Finally, they relent, revealing the blurry outlines of the hospital room.

As my vision clears, I take in the sterile surroundings—the pristine white walls, the beeping monitors, the faint smell of antiseptic. And the unmistakable fragrance of flowers.

When I look around, what I see takes my breath away.

Throughout the room are vibrant bouquets of flowers, perched on every available surface.

I'm stunned, my mind struggling to reconcile the stark contrast of the hospital with the unexpected burst of color before me. *Mama* notices my surprise and follows my gaze.

"Your *friend* brought them for you," she explains, a knowing smile playing on her lips.

Tears prickle at the corners of my eyes at the beautiful gesture from Dion. But it also stirs up conflicting emotions, as my mind drifts to Andrew.

My mother's keen intuition picks up on my inner panic, and she squeezes my hand, her eyes filled with understanding. "Don't worry, sweetheart," she whispers. "We made sure Andrew wasn't around when Dion visited."

Relief floods through me.

Despite my mother's silence on the matter, I can sense her curiosity simmering beneath the surface. She knows there's something more between Dion and me, something I'm not ready to admit just yet.

With a shaky breath, I manage a faint smile. "Thank you, *Mama*."

My mother returns my smile. "He's a good friend," she says, leaving the unspoken questions hanging in the air between us.

Dimitri hands me a glass of water that I chug down immediately.

"How are you feeling?" he asks, his eyes scanning my face for any signs of discomfort.

"I'm okay," I murmur, my voice coming out faint over the hum of machines. "I'm just glad to see you both."

Seconds later, a doctor enters the room. "Hello, Ms. Kastellanos. Glad to see you're awake."

I recognize him instantly. He's the same doctor who saw me when I almost overdosed. The dreadful night only he and Dion know about. I want to keep it that way—no one else should know. My heart starts beating faster.

The doctor gives me a knowing smile, the kind that says he isn't going to say anything. For a moment, I'm frozen, unsure how to react. Then, I give him a small, grateful nod, trying to appear calm and collected. "Hi."

"How does your body feel?"

"Hurts," I mutter, a grimace crossing my face as pain courses through me.

My mother exchanges a worried glance with my brother, her hand squeezing mine gently. "We'll make sure you're comfortable, *agápi mou*. Dr. Grant will take care of you."

The doctor nods, his eyes filled with understanding. "We'll get you some pain medication right away."

A nurse comes in and begins the examination and my mother leaves to talk to the doctor. As soon as the nurse is done, he also heads out of the room.

Suddenly, all the memories of what I overheard rush back, and I wince at the sharp pain in my head.

My brother notices my distress and furrows his brow. "What's wrong?"

I swallow hard, trying to compose myself before responding. "How long have I been out?"

"Two months," he murmurs.

My breath hitches. "Tell me everything that's happened," I demand, my voice edged with urgency.

"Okay. Well..." He hesitates. "*Baba* was...killed."

Pain slices through my chest, and I let out a rough, shaky exhale. "How? Why?"

"Are you sure this is the right time, Ri? You just woke up."

"Yes, Dimo. I need to know the truth." It might be a hard pill to swallow, but I don't want to stay in the dark any longer.

His eyes flicker, a flash of discomfort crossing his face before he quickly masks it.

"After the wedding, Philip had Angelica kidnapped," he says, his voice trembling with rage. "He was planning to hurt her."

My mind reels. The reality of what's happened crashing into me like a tidal wave.

I lurch forward, and my brother hurries to my bed, putting

a bucket under my mouth. I retch violently, and the acidic taste of bile fills my mouth, my body convulsing with each motion. The room spins around me as I heave, expelling the horror that's lodged itself deep within me.

Dimitri puts a hand on my back and caresses me until the puking stops. The nurse attempts to come back in the room with my mother, but Dimo shoos them away. "Leave us!"

When the waves of nausea finally begin to subside, I lean back against the pillows, drained and shaken. Tears stream down my face as I curl up, the sobs racking my body.

"I'm sorry, Riri," Dimitri says with a solemn expression.

My heart clenches. "Is Angie okay?"

"Yes, she's fine. A little shaken, obviously, but he didn't manage to lay a finger on her. Your friend is a little badass," he says while wiggling his brows, and it manages to make me crack a smile.

"You're an idiot."

My brother chuckles.

I run my hands over my face to wipe my tears. I can't believe all this. I never expected my father, the man I looked up to with unwavering admiration most of my life, to be capable of such heinous acts. He has always been a pillar of strength in our family.

"I never thought..." I stammer, my voice trailing off into a choked whisper. How can I reconcile the image of the loving *Baba* I once knew with the monster he became? And with everything we found out about his role in the Sisterhood...is this how Angelica felt about her own father? My chest squeezes at the thought. I can't wait to hug her and never let go.

My brother's hand tightens on my shoulder, a silent reassurance amid my crumbling reality. "None of us did," he murmurs.

"Why would he want to hurt Angie? It doesn't make sense."

"He was going to use her to get to Evander. Peter was going to leave his estate to our father, not Angelica. But with her marrying a Godfather, father's position was in jeopardy. Evan and Ang could've fought him to regain control."

I feel the blood drain from my face. My father, willing to sacrifice an innocent life for his own selfish gain.

"Evan and Dion went to rescue her—"

"And when they found her, they killed him," I finish for him, and Dimitri confirms with a bob of his head.

Silence hangs heavy in the air.

Cold fury starts to rise within me. "Well, he deserved it," I seethe.

My brother nods, and I can see in his eyes a mirror of my own emotions, unending anger and disgust, mixed with grief and sorrow we can't help but still feel. But there are too many pieces to this puzzle, too many unanswered questions lingering in my brain.

"Is there anything else?"

"Nothing you need to worry yourself with right now, Aria. You have to focus on your recovery," Dimitri replies.

I narrow my eyes, sensing the evasion in his response. I know there's something he's omitting, but I let it go—for now.

There's a gentle knock on the door. Dimitri, my ever-watchful guardian, stands and lets the nurse back in. I can hear their muted voices as they discuss something in hushed tones.

I'm suddenly too tired to concentrate. My body feels like it's been through a war, every muscle protesting with a dull ache.

As the nurse administers the dose of pain meds, a wave of drowsiness crashes over me with unexpected force.

Before I can even utter a word of thanks, my eyelids betray me, fluttering shut.

A LOUD KNOCK JOLTS ME AWAKE.

I rub my eyes and sit up in my hospital bed. "Come in," I groan.

The door cracks open and Andrew stands there, holding a box of chocolates, a strained smile plastered on his face. I grit my teeth and force myself not to call out for my family. I can do this. I can face him.

"Morning, Aria." He places the box on the nightstand, his eyes scanning over the flowers in the room. I wonder if he knows who brought them.

"Just thought I'd bring you a little treat. How's recovery going?"

"Good, thanks," I reply, forcing a cheerful tone. *What do you want, Andrew?*

He takes a deep breath. "I've postponed the wedding...again."

I blink, trying to keep my composure. The promises made to him by my father about the Kastellanos business should be null and void, since Dimitri has no intention of honoring *Baba*'s wishes. My father was going to leave the business and estate to Andrew, but Dimitri and Dion were able to switch the will back in my brother's name. So, how is the wedding still on?

Andrew's mouth turns up in a wicked smile. "You're probably wondering how we're still getting married. Well, *sweetheart,* the arrangement was sealed in blood, so it's my right to carry on with it."

A blood pact? My hands tremble, and I struggle to take a full breath, feeling the panic rise up my throat. "Why, Andrew? You don't love me, and you know I don't love you. My father's dead. Why do you still want this marriage?"

Andrew slams his fist on the table, making me flinch. "It's none of your fucking business," he growls, eyes narrowing.

At this point, it seems like he's playing this twisted game just to get under my skin. He gets a high out of intimidating me. *Sick fuck.*

He grabs me in a bruising grip, pain shooting up my arm.

"This isn't about your father's wishes or Dimitri's power. This is about what *I* want, Aria. What my family deserves. What I'm owed."

"You can't force me into this." Tears well in my eyes, but I try to blink them away, refusing to let him see my fear.

Andrew laughs, a cold, hollow sound. "I can and I will. You belong to me now, and you'll do as I say. Get with it or I'll make your life a living hell."

"It already is!"

His face contorts with anger, his hand crashing across my face, the sting spreading through my cheek like wildfire. I gasp, my vision blurring for a moment as pain explodes in my head.

His expression is cold as he watches me struggle to keep my eyes open.

I raise a trembling hand to my cheek, the warmth of his strike radiating through my skin.

Andrew stares at me for a moment longer, then turns and walks out.

The door closes behind him, and I let out a choked sob.

42

DION

I walk through the hospital doors, Angelica and Evander by my side.

My heart pounds in my chest.

Angelica's steps are hesitant, her eyes darting around as if she's expecting danger at any moment. Evander brushes his hand against hers, and I visibly see her tense shoulders loosen a bit.

We reach the door to Aria's room, and I let Angelica go in with Evan to have a moment with her best friend. This is a reunion that's been a long time coming, and I want to give them space. Angelica hasn't seen Aria in the two long months she's been recovering. Between Angelica's own injuries and the ordeal of being kidnapped by Aria's father, this occasion will surely be monumental for both women.

I pace the hallway, bouquet of sunflowers in hand. This will be the first time I see her conscious and awake.

A few minutes later, Evan emerges from the room.

"How is she?" I ask.

"From first impressions, she looks pretty good. And the little shit is still feisty as ever," he says, shaking his head.

I laugh, the sound rough. Evander smirks when he finally notices the flowers in my hand. "So, you're responsible for the botanical garden in there?"

"Yes. Don't act like you wouldn't have showered Angelica with peonies if it had been you."

He chuckles. "Just get in there already."

I push open the door, and Aria looks up from her bed, eyes widening in surprise.

Once Angelica has left, after giving me a soft, reassuring smile, I step closer.

"Dion," Aria says, her voice still weak. "Hey."

"Hey," I reply with a smile, reaching out to squeeze her hand. "It's good to see you, *astéri mou*. It has felt like an eternity."

She squeezes my hand back. "I'm sorry I put you through this."

"Aria, no. You have nothing to apologize for. *I'm* sorry I couldn't protect you," I insist, shaking my head. "The only thing that matters is that you're here now. You're going to be okay."

She nods. "I missed you." Tears stream down her cheeks. I wipe them away with my thumb.

"I missed you too," I choke out. "So much."

We sit in silence for a few moments, just holding hands.

"Thank you, by the way," she says, pointing to the garden of flowers around us. "I love them. You didn't have to come here every day."

I met Aria's mother when I came to visit her one of the first times, and Elena's been an angel in disguise, making sure that Andrew doesn't catch wind of my visits. Dimitri had my back, too.

They're a solid family—except for her corpse father, of course.

"I couldn't stand not seeing you, Aria."

"What about Andrew?" she asks, glancing nervously at the door.

"Don't worry about him."

She jerks her hand away from mine. "How, Dion? He's been here to see me. He still wants to get married!"

"That won't take him very far. Everyone is dead. He has no back-up, and your brother has things under control," I reply.

"He won't let me go that easily, Dion," she mutters. "Not if the pact was sealed in blood."

"You're right." I remain at the foot of her hospital bed, my gaze turning serious. "But there's something else you should know."

"What is it?" Aria shifts, wincing as pain shoots through her. I stop myself from reaching for her, afraid to make it worse.

"Right after your engagement, someone tried to kill me."

Her fingers grip the thin hospital blanket. "What?"

"My Ducati was rigged with an explosive."

Aria's breath hitches.

"It was Andrew," I continue, my gaze unwavering as I watch her process this. "So, I threatened to kill him if I ever saw him again."

Aria swallows hard. "I wish I'd known."

I let out a sigh, stepping closer to the bed. "I didn't want to worry you, especially with everything else going on. And...we weren't exactly on speaking terms."

Tears well up in her eyes. "I'm sorry, Dion."

I sit next to her and grab her hands, placing a kiss on one of them. "Don't be, *astéri mou*. None of this is your fault. No matter what happens, it's not your fault. I'll take care of everything."

Aria looks up to the ceiling, blinking to clear her tears. "That's why he's been scarce, leaving town for weeks, sometimes months..."

I nod, jaw clenched. "I'd be surprised if he actually does

decide to proceed with the wedding, knowing he has a target on his back."

And if he does, I'll fucking kill him with my bare hands.

43

ARIA

Recovery is not going well.

I mean, physically, I'm making strides. My injuries are on their way to healing. I was allowed to come back home, Dr. Grant satisfied with my progress.

Mentally, though, I'm struggling.

I truly wish my brain would kick rocks. It's like I'm trapped in a nightmare I can't wake up from.

My body feels numb, and the only thing keeping me sane is the pain medication I've been abusing. It blurs reality, making it easier to cope.

For a little while, the ache is bearable.

I know I've made progress, but I still feel the need to take the edge off. I'm scared shitless to feel anything. The grief for my father's death, mixed with my disgust for him. The worry that Andrew may do something awful if I don't show up to the wedding, especially after finding out he tried to get Dion killed.

So, I take more pills, and for a moment, I don't have to think.

I know this is dangerous, especially with my recent history of addiction. Every time I pop another tablet into my mouth,

I'm haunted by the fear of falling back into old habits. It feels like I'm fighting a losing battle.

Like I've taken a step back in my recovery, and it's frustrating. I want to stay strong, and I can't live like this forever. Something has to give, and I don't know if I'm strong enough to face what comes next.

Since my father died, I've had more of a reason to become a recluse.

My mother moves around the house like a hollow version of herself. Her eyes now dulled by sorrow and betrayal. I see it in the way she gazes into the distance sometimes, lost in memories that bring more pain than comfort.

My *baba* was a terrible man, and we never knew. How could we have been so blind?

I've never felt so disgusted in my entire life.

But the loss of my father doesn't only haunt my mother.

I loved him something fierce. We were a tight-knit family— until he surprised me with the engagement news.

Now, I can't un-know the darkness he carried with him. The lies he told, the secrets he kept hidden behind his 'doting husband and father' charade.

I thought I knew him.

I trusted him with my whole heart. But that heart has now been crushed, shattered into a million pieces I can't put back together.

And Dimitri...I'm sure he's hiding something from me. I see it in his eyes, the way he avoids my questions, the way he changes the subject whenever I ask him about the snippets of conversation I overheard while in the hospital. It's driving me insane. What could be so terrible that he can't tell me?

Speaking of the devil, there's a knock on my closed door.

"Hey!" Dimitri yells from the other side. "Can I come in?"

I'm sitting at my vanity, staring at the new scar across my chest.

"Yeah, sure."

He pokes his head in. "Are you decent?"

"Of course, I'm fucking decent, you twat," I retort, throwing a makeup brush at him.

He ducks to dodge it, laughing, and steps inside.

When he notices what I've been doing, he frowns. "Riri, there's no point in covering that up. Be proud. You're officially badass. You're like Scarface now."

I chuckle. Even though Dimitri is now head of the Kastellanos family, he hasn't lost his playfulness, and it makes me happy to still have a sliver of my baby brother, despite the demands of his new role.

"Well, if you put it that way," I say with a smirk.

It's not that I necessarily think the scar is ugly.

I saved Angie's life, and that's something I'll never regret. It just represents so much, everything that happened over the last couple years.

"How are you holding up?" Dimitri asks.

"Better than most in my situation, I guess," I shrug.

He sits on the edge of my bed and taps the mattress for me to join him. When I do, he puts his arm around my shoulders, bringing me in for a hug.

"You're doing amazing, Ri," he says, pride shining in his eyes.

I wrap my arms around his waist and squeeze him back.

"I wanted to talk to you about something," he adds when I pull away. Maybe he's finally decided to divulge the secret he's been keeping from me.

"Go on," I say.

He takes a deep breath. "So, while you were...*asleep*, I found out something really mind-blowing." His eyes lock onto mine. A chill runs down my spine, but I nod for him to continue.

"*What is it*?" I almost shout when he doesn't. My patience is very thin these days.

"Before I tell you, promise you won't get mad that we've kept this from you."

My eyes widen. "We? Who's "we," Dimo?"

He grimaces. "Everyone."

I gape at him, indignation rising within me.

"Aria, you were in a fucking coma. We weren't just going to tell you life-changing information as soon as you woke up."

"Well, you told me about *Baba*," I retort, the pain of his death still very present.

"That's not something we could've really kept hidden. Either way, he wanted to wait until you were better."

"He?"

An exhale. "Our half-brother."

For a moment, I can't process what Dimo said. The words echo in my mind, refusing to make sense. My heart flutters, a wave of confusion and disbelief washing over me. *A half-brother?* Without thinking, I jump off the bed, legs shaking.

"What? How?" I manage to stammer, my voice higher than usual. My mind races, trying to piece together this new information.

I'd overheard Dimitri say something about a brother when I was still unconscious, but I would've never imagined that *we* had another sibling. What. The. Hell?

"I had the same reaction when I found out."

This is fucking jarring.

"His name is Atlas."

"Atlas," I repeat, letting his name linger on my tongue. The name sounds awfully familiar. But my memory has been hazy ever since I woke up from my coma.

"He's a few years older than you. Father's first-born. Bastard."

"He had an affair on *Mama*?" I ask, the word feeling foreign.

He nods. "She didn't know. He hid it well."

I sink back down onto the edge of the bed. "So, all this time, we had a brother, and *Baba* never told anyone?"

"That's correct," he replies.

"Does he know about us?" I ask, my voice faint.

"Yes. He always knew but couldn't contact us. He didn't want to disrupt our lives. Though, now he'd like to meet you, to be a part of your life, if you'll allow it."

I sit in stunned silence, my mind whirling. How could our father cheat on our mother and never once mention another sibling? Where was he hiding him this whole time?

"I don't know what to say," I admit, looking at Dimo with wide eyes.

"Take your time," Dimo rests his hand on my shoulder. "It's a lot to take in."

"How's *Mama*?"

"She surprisingly took it better than I thought. She's met him."

"Wow," I say, nodding slowly to steady my breathing. "I think I want to meet him."

A FEW DAYS LATER, I'M PACING BACK AND FORTH IN MY BEDROOM, the sound of my footsteps muffled by the carpet. My heart is racing, and I can't seem to find a way to calm it down. I keep glancing at the clock on my nightstand.

I could've waited downstairs with Dimo or helped Magda in the kitchen, but they've all but kicked me out of the house because I was being too fidgety.

I catch a glimpse of myself in the mirror as I pass by. My face looks tense, and I try to smooth out the worry lines on my forehead. I take a deep breath, though it doesn't seem to help much.

I stop at my desk, my eyes landing on a picture of our father. I wonder if Atlas has the same eyes or the same smile as *Baba*. The anticipation is almost unbearable. I move to the window, looking out at the driveway, hoping to see a car pull up. Nothing yet.

My burner phone buzzes on the bed, and I jump, nerves on edge.

Dion: Good luck today.

I haven't seen Dion since I came home from the hospital, but he's messaged me every day since.

Though I miss him, we've been sticking to the deal we made to not see each other until I'm better and the entire ordeal with Andrew is over. *If it ever does end…*

I read the message a second time. I never told him I was meeting Atlas today. It must have been my brother.

Me: Are you and Dimo best friends now?

Dion: Something like that.

Dion: Send me an ootd pic.

I laugh out loud.

Me: Ew, Dion. Are we in 2017? If you want to know what I'm wearing, you can just ask.

Dion: Just send me a fucking picture, Aria.

Me: I'm rolling my eyes at you.

Dion: Remember what happened last time you did that?

Within an instant, my heart is hammering, a steady thrum.

The memory of Dion spanking me while penetrating me deeply from behind runs wild in my head.

Warmth spreads through me, starting low in my belly.

Dion: Is my little liar speechless?

My fingers twitch, as if they have a mind of their own, and I bite my lip, trying to focus on my text.

Me: No...

Dion: Then tell me that you're dying to have me inside you again.

I feel a flush rise to my cheeks and my breath quickens, becoming shallower and more rapid.

Holy hell.

The mere thought of his dick inside me still leaves me breathless.

But it's not the time to fall for his charm. I'm meeting my brother in a short while. I don't want to be an aroused mess.

Me: No.

Dion: I didn't realize that was a question, Aria.

I can't help but let out a soft sigh, the sound escaping before I even notice. There's an ache growing inside me, and he's not helping at all.

I give in.

Me: I miss having you inside me.

It's true. I miss the way his touch sets my skin on fire, the way his presence envelops me in a cocoon of warmth. The memory of his fingers tracing patterns along my body sends a shiver down my spine.

He makes me feel *alive*.

Dion: That's my good girl.

Fuck.

Unable to handle the temptation any longer, I throw my phone onto the bed, trying to shake off the memories and refocus on preparing to meet my brother. I take a deep breath.

I move back to the mirror, brushing my hair with deliberate strokes, hoping the mundane task will help ground me. *Think of your grandma, Aria. Or sick puppies. Or hemorrhoids.*

Just as I start to regain some composure, my phone vibrates again. The sound cuts through the quiet, making my heart skip a beat. I glance at the bed, my resolve wavering. Another text from Dion. I can almost feel his presence in the room, his voice echoing in my mind.

With trembling hands, I pick up the phone, my eyes scanning the message.

Dion: I'll be seeing you tonight.

The words send a jolt of excitement through me, reigniting the flames I tried so hard to extinguish.

Then, confusion sets in.

How can we meet tonight? Our deal still stands. On top of that, my brother is coming over soon. I stare at the message.

I type back quickly.

Me: Dion, my brother is coming over tonight. We said we wouldn't do this again...until I'm better and Andrew is out of the picture.

His response comes almost instantly.

Dion: I'll find a way, Aria.

Just then, Magda knocks at my door. I put my phone away and quickly run my hands through my hair, trying to calm my desperate, aroused self.

"*Arioula*, your brother is here."

44

ARIA

With a final glance around my room, I head out into the hallway lit by the soft glow of the afternoon sun filtering through the curtains.

I start walking, my footsteps echoing lightly on the wooden floor. The walls are lined with family photos, each one a frozen moment of time that seems to watch me as I pass. We still haven't taken down the ones with my father in them. We can't bring ourselves to just yet.

It's strange how even when people hurt you, when they hide the truth and betray your trust, love still clings on.

I straighten my shoulders, trying to shake off the nerves. "It's just Dimo and your half-brother," I remind myself. "Just go downstairs and face them."

When I reach the top of the staircase, I grip the banister tightly, the faint sound of a conversation below reaching my ears.

I force myself to continue, stepping carefully down the remaining stairs. The voices become clearer.

The foyer comes into view. The high ceiling and large windows have always made the space feel open and inviting, yet the butterflies in my stomach now flutter more wildly. I take another deep breath, before stepping into the living room with a smile planted on my face. My eyes immediately lock with the blonde man standing by the fireplace, breath catching in my throat.

Recognition hits me like a tidal wave. I've seen him before. He was the boy in the photo from my father's files on the Sisterhood. *How could I forget?*

But that's not the only reason he's familiar. I've seen him somewhere else. Somewhere that feels like a half-forgotten dream. My mind races, sifting through broken memories, until it lands on that night in the forest when I'd first taken drugs.

I had been wandering aimlessly, drunk and high, the world around me a hazy blur. I'd stumbled upon someone I thought was a figment of my imagination.

But now, looking at Atlas, I know it was him. It had to be.

He gives me a knowing look, and I see the confirmation in his gaze. He remembers too. *Holy shit.*

We look almost identical. His blonde hair mirrors mine, our facial structures are the same, and we even share the same nose and lips, with the bottom one just a tad larger than the top. It's like staring at a slightly different version of myself.

There's only one striking difference—*his eyes.*

He has heterochromia, one eye a deep, stormy blue and the other a warm, golden brown. It's the most beautiful thing I've ever seen.

We stand there, staring at each other for what feels like an eternity. My mind races, yet my body feels rooted to the spot. The room falls silent around us, the only sound my own heartbeat pounding in my ears. Finally, I manage to break the silence.

"Hi."

He nods at me, a faint smile tugging at his lips.

"Aria, this is Atlas. Atlas, this is obviously your sister, Aria,"

Dimo says, pointing between us. I'd almost forgotten he was here too.

I extend a hand and Atlas hesitates briefly before grabbing it.

"Nice to meet you."

He nods. *Hmmm. The silent type. Is he a mute?*

"Our mother will be joining us for dinner soon, but I thought you two would like a moment to chat before we sit at the table. Yeah?" Dimo says, looking back at me.

"Yeah. Of course. If that's okay with you, Atlas."

He nods. *Okay...I wonder how this conversation is going to go if I can't get a word out of him.*

As soon as Dimo has left, I blurt out, "It was you, wasn't it? That night in the forest?"

Atlas nods slowly. "I had snuck in to get some info from your father's office. I hadn't expected anyone to be awake."

"I saw a picture of you as a little boy," I begin, my voice trembling slightly. "In his files. I felt like I knew you, but I didn't know why, until now."

His expression grows somber. "That makes sense. After my mother was killed, I was taken to the Sisterhood. The nuns raised me until I was old enough to be on my own. But I was kept underground, where no one could see me or know of my existence."

I shudder at the thought, the horror of it making my skin crawl. How could a father treat his child like that?

Atlas looks away, a hint of pain flickering in his eyes. He seems hesitant to say more, and I can sense the rawness of his emotions. I decide not to push further, dropping the subject for now.

"I'm sorry for what my father did to you, what he put you through all these years. But I'm glad we found each other, even if the circumstances are complicated."

He offers a faint smile, the weight of our shared history pressing down on both of us. "Yeah, me too."

Seated on the large sofa, I avert my gaze to the carpeted floor and fidget with the hem of my shirt. I'm not sure what to say now.

"Anxious?"

My eyes fly up to meet his, and I tilt my head to the side, noticing his tight fists against the arm of the chair. "Yeah. I guess it takes one to know one."

He laughs, and I'm surprised to have elicited such a big reaction. "I guess so."

"What's yours?" Referring to the coping mechanism to relieve stress.

He settles deeper into his seat and extends his arms over the headrest, seeming more relaxed. "Isolation, probably."

My mouth turns downward. "That sounds lonely."

He shrugs his large shoulders. "It's all I know." His gaze seems distant like he's looking right through me. As if he's dissociated from reality. *What really happened to you, Atlas?* I want to know, but I'd rather not press him on our first meeting.

He furrows his brows. "Is that all you do to cope?" he asks, gesturing with his head to my fingers, still playing with the fabric of my top.

I shift in my seat, feeling his scrutiny. "What do you mean?"

"Your eyes," he replies, bringing his elbows to his knees to lean in closer.

My gaze wanders. I blink once, twice, and a single tear rolls down my cheek. I just met him and he's already making me cry.

"I obviously don't know you yet, but I can see the hurt in them. And I can tell you try to mask your pain," he adds, as if he didn't just read me like a damn book. His gaze is piercing, unwavering.

I try to maintain an air of calmness despite the tight knot forming in my stomach.

I swallow hard. "I'm not sure what you mean," I reply, my voice betraying a hint of unease despite my best efforts.

His expression softens. "I can see the toll it's taking on you. It's not healthy, whatever it is you're doing."

A lump rises in my throat, and I avert my gaze.

"Those things that are weighing you down?" Atlas continues. "You need to let them go. It's not worth sacrificing your well-being over. You're stronger than you think, but even the strongest of us need help sometimes."

Tears start to spill over, so I squeeze my eyes shut.

I wipe my face and chuckle. "Such a great first impression, huh?"

He waves me off. "Nah. I recognize your pain because that's all I feel." Raw vulnerability comes through his words. It cuts straight through the tension in the room.

"There's something deeper than words that tells me you need support. And for what it's worth, you have it in me."

There's a flicker of something in his eyes—understanding, perhaps, or maybe even acceptance—and it's enough to break through the walls I've erected around my heart.

"Thank you, Atlas," I whisper, the words coming out in a shaky breath. "I...I think I needed to hear that."

A silent vow forms in my heart—to be stronger, not only for my family, but for myself, too.

Whatever Atlas has endured, whatever battles he fought, if he can still find the strength to carry on, then so can I.

Atlas and I join the others in the dining room, momentarily pushing aside the weight of our earlier conversation.

When I turn the corner, I freeze, my jaw dropping.

Standing with Dimitri is *Dion*.

My mind races, trying to process his unexpected presence.

He stands casually, hands in his pockets, a small smile playing on his lips. My stomach tightens into knots. Why is he here? What if Andrew finds out? When he said he would see me today, I didn't think he meant so soon. Though I can't stop the euphoria of seeing him again, of being so close.

I swallow hard, and my mouth suddenly dries. I clasp my hands together to steady myself. Dion's eyes meet mine, and for a moment, everything else fades away.

We take our seats, and I exchange light banter with Dimitri, our usual dynamic flowing effortlessly as we catch up on each other's day. My mother has also joined us and is chatting away, seemingly in a better mood than she has been in a few weeks.

My attention keeps drifting back to Atlas, seated beside me, his stoic demeanor casting a shadow over the lively atmosphere. He remains withdrawn, lost in his own thoughts.

I steal glances at him throughout the meal, noting the way his eyes linger on his plate, his silence speaking volumes. And then it hits me—Atlas has spoken to me more than anyone else tonight. It's a small realization, but it makes me feel oddly special, like a connection is forming between us, one that goes beyond mere sibling ties.

I look around the table, surrounded by some of the people I love most in the world, and my eyes land again on a pair that always steals the air from my lungs.

Dion's stare on me is like a physical touch, making me want to combust into my chair.

Dinner passes in a blur, my attention divided between polite conversation and the magnetic pull I feel toward Dion.

Though as we gather in the living area afterward, I somehow lose sight of him amidst the chatter and movement. *Did he leave already, without saying anything?* The uncertainty nags at me, fueling my decision to retreat to my room for the night. I murmur my goodbyes to Atlas, promising to keep in touch, before slipping away.

Once inside my bedroom, I remove my clothes and collapse onto the bed, relief flooding through me. But the solitude doesn't bring the calm I crave. I close my eyes briefly, mustering the energy to remove my makeup and shower.

The creak of my door opening jolts me from my thoughts, my heart leaping into my throat. Dion's sudden appearance catches me off guard, and I scramble to my feet.

His gaze travels over me, slowly, deliberately, making my skin tingle everywhere his eyes land. I can feel my heart pounding, each beat echoing in my ears. I instinctively wrap my arms around myself, but it does little to hide the fact that I'm practically naked in front of him.

"Dion!" I manage to gasp. "What are you doing here?" I blurt out, my voice shaky.

Dion steps further into the room, his large figure filling the doorway.

His breath comes in ragged bursts, his chest rising and falling with each inhale.

The air crackles with tension, his presence overwhelming, yet intoxicating. My body reacts, heat rising beneath my skin as I back up, the edge of the bed now pressed against my legs.

He blinks, as if snapping out of a trance, and finally averts his eyes. But not before I see a flicker of something in them— something raw and powerful that makes my heart skip a beat.

His gaze then locks onto the bruise marring my arm. "What is that?"

I swallow hard. *Fuck*. I didn't conceal the mark as I decided to wear a long-sleeved top to dinner.

I still have proof of Andrew's aggression when he visited me in the hospital before I got discharged. I figured it would be barely visible by now, but nothing gets past Dion.

"It's nothing," I mumble, attempting to brush off his concern. But his proximity is suffocating, and I sink onto the edge of the bed.

Dion closes the door behind him. His eyes never leave mine, and I feel a shiver race down my spine.

"It doesn't look like *nothing*," he seethes, his voice low and husky. "Did Andrew do this to you?" he asks, his tone tight with suppressed fury.

I hesitate.

"Tell me," he demands, his words coming out shaky with anger.

I shrink under his intense gaze. As he hovers above me, I struggle to find the words to explain, my pulse thundering in my ears. Instead of responding, my eyes dart away, the silent pause giving it away, and Dion loses it.

"I fucking knew it. I'm going to kill him with my bare hands!" he shouts, his fists clenching at his sides. "He's dead. He's fucking dead."

"Dion, please," I beg, grabbing his arm. "Don't do anything. It's complicated," I stammer. But Dion's gaze remains unwavering.

"Complicated? The only thing *complicated* here is deciding how I'm going to make him pay for every bruise, every moment of fear he's caused you. I had a feeling he'd been hurting you and now he's going to pay tenfold."

"No!" I shout. "He'll hurt us."

Dion's eyes widen in shock. "What the fuck do you mean?"

Summoning all my courage, I reveal Andrew's ultimatum. The air in the room grows thick with tension as I recount the threat he's been hanging over me all this time.

The look of disbelief on Dion's face is heart-wrenching. "Why didn't you tell me?"

Then, understanding dawns in his eyes.

"Is that why you rejected me at the engagement party?"

"Yes," I respond, my voice tinged with sorrow as I watch him connect the dots.

"Has he been hurting you since then?"

I nod silently, but I'm sure my eyes betray the pain I've been hiding.

"I just didn't want to take the chance of him hurting them. I was terrified that he'd see his promise through, and that he'd potentially hurt you, too. And he almost did. I wouldn't have been able to survive it."

"Aria," Dion begins. "Fuck." He starts pacing around my room.

"I almost told you once," I admit.

"When?" he asks, his face snapping toward me.

"A few months ago, before Angelica and Evander's wedding. I had reached out to you. I texted you, but you never replied."

Dion's brow furrows. "Is it the day you texted me 'hey'?"

I nod. His face drops. "What happened?"

Taking a deep breath, I recount the horrifying memory. "We were alone at his house for the first time. He...he tried to come onto me. When I refused, he got aggressive and choked me, then threw me to the floor."

As the words spill from my lips, Dion's expression shifts from shock to anger, then to gut-wrenching guilt.

"FUCK!" he shouts.

He sits next to me, on the edge of my bed, his shoulders slumping. He clutches his head, fingers tangling in his hair as if he's physically trying to grasp onto the gravity of the situation.

"I'm so sorry, Aria," Dion murmurs. "I didn't know."

Tears well in his eyes, and my heart clenches at the sight. "Dion, please." I reach out to touch his arm. "I didn't tell you this to make you feel guilty."

But Dion continues to apologize, his voice cracking with emotion.

"I'm sorry. I'm so sorry."

"Dion," I say, grabbing his face. "It's not your fault."

"I could've replied, Aria. I fucked up. You reached out to me, and because of my pride, I left you with him. How can I ever forgive myself?"

"It's my mistake for keeping the truth from you. I was just so scared. I still am," I admit.

I wrap my arms around him and straddle his lap. We hold each other tightly for a long while.

His apologies, whispered in my ear, gradually transform into gentle kisses trailing down my throat and along my shoulders.

His lips ignite a fire within me, and I can't help but respond, my body reacting to his touch.

I tilt my head, offering him better access, emitting the smallest of mewls as he continues to explore my skin. Dion's groan against my neck gives me goosebumps; he bites me, marking me as his own.

My breath hitches when his lips find the scar along my chest, the reminder of the incident that almost claimed me.

Dion pauses, his mouth hovering over the raised skin. His fingers trace the outline, tender and reverent. "You're so beautiful," he whispers, his breath warm against my scar. "So strong."

His words seep into me, filling spaces I didn't know were empty. As he grazes the mark with his lips, a tear slips down my cheek. I close my eyes, leaning into his touch.

I feel his arms wrap around me, pulling me closer, his kisses turning into slow, deliberate caresses. My skin tingles where his lips have been, my body melting into his embrace. "Thank you," I manage to whisper.

With a swift movement, he twists us around, laying me down on the bed. His expression morphs from sadness and regret to frenzied urgency and desperation. Within a fraction of a second, he pulls me toward the edge of the bed, gets on his knees and spreads my legs open. *Holy fuck.*

My entire body trembles as I prepare to feel his mouth on my center.

I gasp for air when Dion pushes my panties aside and dives in.

"Oh fuck, oh fuck, oh fuck." Somehow, I'm so fucking close already. "Please don't stop, baby," I beg. He doesn't come up for air once.

Pressure builds in my abdomen as Dion flicks his tongue side to side at a fast pace. "I'm right there," I moan. A powerful surge of pleasure releases deep in my core, washing over me in intense waves. My entire body is consumed. "My perfect little liar. You taste better every time," he praises. "Now, I'm going to stick my cock so far up your mouth, you'll feel it down your throat. A warning to never keep anything from me again unless my dick is choking you, preventing you from taking a full breath. Then, I'm going to fuck you and fill you with my cum as a reminder of who owns you. Understood?"

I nod.

His palm wraps around my throat. "Say it out loud."

"Yes," I mutter, tingles rising up my spine.

Using his hand, he pulls me by the neck into a seated position, unbuckling his trousers. "Get on your knees, *astéri mou*."

I scramble to the floor.

"Open wide," he instructs.

I'm not able to take a full breath before Dion shoves his length between my lips, and I choke.

With no mercy, he starts fucking my mouth until saliva runs over my chin and tears travel down my cheeks.

"Fuck, baby. Your tears are going to be my ruin," he grunts, his hand reaching out, fingers gently brushing my skin. "Look at me," he orders.

When my gaze reaches his, he pulls out his phone from his back pocket and takes a picture. My eyes widen; I try to speak, but Dion holds my head in place, giving me a strong thrust that causes me to gag. "Don't worry, Riri baby. It's for my eyes only. I just want a memory of you crying for me."

Then, he suddenly pulls out.

"Get back on the bed on all fours," he demands.

Once I'm bent over in front of him, he whips out his belt and ties it around my ankles. Soft fabric grazes my face as he blindfolds and gags me. My heart threatens to jump out of my chest. *What is he planning?* "Dion, what are you doing?" I ask, my voice muffled.

Cold metal lands on my ass cheek, and I flinch. *Oh, my fucking God.* "Dion..." I mumble.

Deciding to ignore me, he caresses my skin with the object, letting it sweep over my pussy, and I shudder.

He breaks the silence. "No one has the right to hurt you. No one," he growls. "Except *me.*" His low, menacing voice makes my hair stand on end.

His words chill my bones, but it's mixed with excitement. He teases my entrance, and I'm paralyzed, frantic thoughts now consuming my brain. What is he touching me with?

Dion notices the way my body goes rigid, and chuckles, a devious sound. "Don't worry, little liar. It'll feel good. And if it doesn't, I want your pain to become mine." Right before he inserts the object, he adds, "I'm the only one allowed to cause you anguish because I'm the only one who truly understands it. Who truly understands *you.*"

He pushes the tip inside, and I cry out.

"It's about marking your soul in a way that makes you irrevocably mine," he adds, finally pushing the metal all the way in, and I sob against the gag.

Dion slowly inches the object in and out of my opening, sending butterflies all the way down to my toes. Is he going to make me come like this?

"This is the most beautiful sight," he says. "My gun slipping in and out of your tight cunt. You're so fucking wet for me, little liar."

I'm rooted to the spot. There's a loaded gun inside my vagina, and it's turning me on. *Very much so.* And I don't understand it. I don't understand *me.*

My legs try to wriggle against the belt around my ankles, but I can't move. I also can't see, all my other senses enhanced.

"Please, fuck me. I need your cock," I urge. *I need more.*

"Your wish is my command," he replies, pulling out the gun.

But before he proceeds to do so, he wraps my hair around his palm and jerks my head back. My breath gets trapped in my throat.

He tugs off the fabric around my mouth, and something cold and wet presses against my it. "Open up."

I hesitantly do as Dion says, and he nudges the gun into my mouth, my lips quivering around it.

"Look at how turned on you got by me fucking you with my gun. My perfect little *poutána*. How do you taste against the bitter metal, baby?" he taunts.

I moan around the iron, slurping my wetness. I feel so fucking *dirty*.

When he's satisfied with my compliance, he takes the weapon out of my mouth and throws it onto the bed.

Not wasting another moment, he positions his hard dick at my entrance, and pushes himself inside in one go.

"*Fuuuck*," he whimpers.

The feeling of him filling me up causes electric currents to pulsate through my veins.

The sounds of our bodies connecting echoes throughout my bedroom. I struggle to control my volume—I wouldn't want *Mama* or Dimo to hear us.

Dion thrusts in and out of me until I'm a withering mess. He leans over me, putting some of his weight on my back, and pushes my face into the mattress, stunting my breathing again. "Stay with me, baby," he says. "You're about to get really loud."

That said, he increases his speed, his movement becoming frantic. And he's everywhere. Deep in my guts, in every nerve ending, in all my thoughts.

Keeping one hand on my head, he uses the other to grab my

hip, digging his fingers into my skin, and I hiss against the sheet. Fuck. *This. Feels. So. Good.*

Smack. Smack. Smack. The sound of his crotch connecting with my ass is rhythmic.

His grunts and growls turn into desperate whimpers.

He's close, and so am I.

"Come for me, little liar," he encourages.

"Oh, God," I repeat over and over, until I'm devoured by my orgasm.

I close my eyes, fireworks exploding behind my lids.

My climax is powerful—overwhelming.

Dion releases inside me after a few more plunges.

And I cry. I wail. Tears stream down my cheeks uncontrollably. The intensity of the moment, the connection between us, it's all too much.

I can't help but let it all out, my heart laid bare before him.

I love him, I love him, I love him.

I'm in love with Dion. Irrevocably, deeply in love.

It's a truth that settles over me like a warm embrace, comforting yet terrifying.

I've been foolish to think I could just push these feelings away; pretend they didn't exist.

I love him, and nothing can change that. Not the distance, not the silence, not even the fear that Andrew might be watching.

I close my eyes and take a deep breath, my body shaking with sobs.

Dion pulls out and his strong arms wrap around me.

"It's okay, *astéri mou*," he murmurs softly. "I've got you."

45

———

ANDREW

"Fucking bastard!" I shout, pounding my fist on the top of my desk. I run a hand through my hair and exhale a deep breath.

"When was the will changed?" I ask the Kastellanos' lawyer, Haris, over the phone.

"A few months ago," he replies, sounding nervous.

Son of a bitch.

"Philip never told me he changed it." I grind my teeth. Anger simmers beneath my skin.

"It wasn't him," Haris admits.

My head slings back in surprise. I turn around to face the window—I'm this close to throwing my desk through the glass.

"Then who the fuck was it?" I grit out.

I hear Haris gulping. "His son."

Motherfucker.

Philip is now dead—the idiot getting caught in his plan to kidnap Angelica, Evander Vasilakis's wife. I had advised him to steer clear of her, that it was a terrible idea to go after a Godfather's *wife*. But the stubborn old man decided to ignore me. And now he's gone.

I heard through the grapevine that he was killed when his underground safe house got ambushed, but I was spared the details. Not that I didn't want them. There was just no one left to give them. All his men were slaughtered in the crossfire.

Hence why I'm now on the phone with his lawyer.

I was promised control. Promised the clan, the reinstating of my family in the Godfather circle.

Philip had assured me that Dimitri wouldn't be a problem. But he fucking *lied*.

I growl in frustration. "And you didn't think to let me know?"

"I-I couldn't. They threatened my family. They hurt me. I couldn't take the chance," Haris stammers, his voice filled with fear.

"Who the fuck is "they," Haris?" I bark.

"D-Dimitri and his counterpart, Mr. Loukas."

I still. Dion *fucking* Loukas. The thorn in my side.

"So, why are you telling me now? Are they not going to kill you for informing me?"

"N-not if-if they don't find out," he stutters, and he might as well kill himself now before I find him.

"They might not. But that doesn't keep you safe from me, *maláka*," I spit, before hanging up.

I'm going to kill every single one of them.

If it weren't for her use to provide me with an heir, I'd kill that bitch, Aria, too.

We're set to be married in a week, and I have to ensure that nothing and no one will come in our way.

After her joke of a suicide attempt, or whatever it was, she's been even more of a shell of herself. But at least she's been compliant.

You'd think I'd be upset that my fiancée is a druggie and an alcoholic. But I'm not.

As long as she doesn't get in the way of my plans, she can drown herself in a bottle for all I care.

The only time it'll matter is when I fill her with my heir. Then, I'll make sure she doesn't put my child at risk.

Over the past year, my threats to her have been successful. She stayed away from Dion. I guess Aria's soft spot is her family. It's too bad I'll have to kill them now.

If Dimitri genuinely wants to take over for his father, we'll have a big problem.

Fuck what the will says. I'm taking matters into my own hands.

The only way to secure my place in Cebrene is to be in good standing with the Godfathers, and so far, it's not looking great.

Dion is closely linked to Evander and, from what I've been told, he's got a mean pull within the clans. They trust him. And if Dion mentioned anything about me—which I'm sure he did —it's not positive.

But I'm no fool.

I always had a contingency plan in place.

DION

Aria: Dion. Please help.

F*uck*. Not again.

PART FIVE
The Wedding

47

ARIA

Three Days Before the Wedding

A ria?" A voice startles me.

"Uh. Yeah. Sorry."

Angelica looks at me through narrowed lids. "Where did you go?" she asks, eyeing me over the rim of her sunglasses.

We're sitting on the rooftop of her penthouse at the Iris Boutique Hotel, the hotel she owns—courtesy of Evander.

The cute bastard bought it for her and named it after her mother.

I'd love to have my own business one day. A flower shop I can call my own. But given that I'm getting married in a few short days to a controlling asshole, I can officially kiss that dream goodbye. I push the thought away as my heart squeezes.

Angelica has been through so much in her life and seeing her so happy and taken care of fills me with joy, despite my own situation.

My wedding is in three days, and my mother insisted that I do something to "celebrate," even though I'm dreading it. She tried to convince me that it would shift my focus from the negative feelings I have toward it. I don't know why I listened to her.

I didn't see a point in having a bachelorette party, so Angelica suggested we spend a day at her hotel, getting pampered. I wanted to refuse, but I could see how much Angelica wanted to try and distract me.

We spent the morning at the spa, having facials, a massage, and a mani and pedi.

I haven't heard anything from Dion since last night, and unless something changes—or something happens to Andrew—I will soon be *Mrs. Galanis*.

"Earth to Aria," Angelica says, snapping me out of my thoughts.

"Fuck. I'm sorry."

Ever since leaning off the drugs and alcohol, my mind has been a blur, as if clouded in a dense fog. Conversations are more challenging, and I find myself not being able to focus for long. The mess my life is still in doesn't help.

Many months ago, when I decided to quit everything, I was scared, but also relieved. I was ready to not be a prisoner of my own vices anymore.

I stood in my bathroom, staring at the bottles under the sink. There were so many, hidden there like ghosts of the past I wanted to forget. My hands trembled as I reached down, pulling each one out.

I remember the sound they made as they hit the bottom of the trash bag, dull thuds that echoed in the room. The coke and pills went next. I flushed them down the toilet, watching the water swirl and take them away. I felt a strange mix of both empowerment and helplessness. The former because I was taking a step forward, the latter because I knew how hard the road ahead would be.

The physical withdrawal would be a bitch, I knew that, but in that moment, I felt a clarity I hadn't in a long time.

I still go to therapy, even after taking that hiatus to recover from my injury. It's like returning to a familiar place, yet everything is different. There's this new layer now—the thoughts I had before the bullet hit me. The almost disappointment when I woke up and found out I'd lived. They're not just shadows in the corner of my mind anymore; they're front and center in every session.

It's helping, though. I can't deny that. Dr. Goode and I unpack these thoughts, unraveling each one carefully, like defusing a bomb. But it feels like I'm starting from scratch. All the progress I made before, all the hard work, it's like it got wiped clean. I'm rebuilding, step by step, trying to find my footing again, which at times seems impossible with Andrew still in my life.

Some days, it's too much.

"How are you?" Angelica asks, her voice soft.

I look at her. "Scared," I admit.

She smiles, reaching out to take my hand. Her touch is warm, reassuring. I squeeze it, trying to draw strength from her.

Having Angelica by my side during this journey has been a godsend. I remember the day I finally told her about my struggle with substance abuse. I was so scared she would judge me or react harshly, but instead, she cried. She cried for me, cried with me. We held each other for what felt like hours. She shared my pain. Felt it. And in that moment, I felt hers. In a way, it was like we bonded over our traumas, but it went deeper than that. We are sisters, and Angelica promised to be there every step of the way.

Even though she's now five months pregnant, she's been a pillar of strength, at my beck and call anytime I need her.

"You have an army surrounding you, *Arioula*. We'll make sure you're taken care of," she assures me.

I scoff. "Andrew is going to shield me from the world,

Giegie. I probably won't even be able to leave the house." My voice cracks.

Angie squints her brows. "None of the men in your life will allow that. Not your brothers, not Dion—not even Evan," she says with a wink.

I laugh, despite everything. She knows how much Evander and I bicker. Even though he gets on my last damn nerve, I love him. He's family.

My amusement fades quickly. "Then why am I still getting married to him?"

"Stupid traditions. Signed in blood. Blah, blah, blah," she says, rolling her eyes. "You know you can't *technically* get out of it unless Andrew decides to cancel the wedding."

I sigh. So, I have to play the part even if that means getting married to an abusive prick. *Cool.*

"You know your brothers have something up their sleeves. Even if you do get married to him, it surely won't last long."

"Angie. One day married to that waste of a man is a day too long." I exhale again.

Honestly, I'm scared shitless of what Andrew is going to do to me once we're alone again.

But I guess I should have faith in my brothers and Dion.

I get off my chair and lean against the railing, the cool metal grounding me. I take a deep breath.

The doorbell rings.

"Are you expecting anyone?" Angelica asks.

I shake my head.

She walks inside the apartment and, after a few minutes, comes back out, holding a bouquet of sunflowers.

Her grin is contagious when she approaches me. "I wonder who these are from," Ang teases with a wink.

Dion's favorite flowers. Of course, Dion knows how to put a smile on my face when I need it the most.

I take the bunch of flowers out of her hands, unable to stifle my grin, and read the note.

I'M LOOKING FORWARD TO CALLING YOU MY WIFE. -A

My heart lurches into my throat, and cold sweat breaks out on my forehead. I scan the words again. My fingers tremble, and the sunflowers slip from my grasp, falling to the ground as if in slow motion.

"Aria, what's wrong?" Angelica's voice cuts through the thickness of my shock. She steps closer, concern etched across her face.

I can barely breathe, each inhale a struggle. My mind races. "Andrew," I choke out.

"Andrew?" Angelica repeats. She picks up the note and her eyes grow wide. "How could he possibly know that you're here?"

"Dion had said that he might have had my phone tapped." Panic surges through me, my chest tightening.

An image of me and Dion in the alleyway of Black Bean rushes through my mind. "And Andrew has followed me in the past. I guess he still is. He could be watching us right now." My vision blurs with tears, and I start to hyperventilate.

Angelica grabs my shoulders, her touch almost grounding me for a moment. "Aria, breathe. You're safe here. Just take deep breaths."

I try to follow her instructions, but my breaths come out shallow and quick. My knees buckle, and I sink to the floor of the balcony, clutching the note.

The world around me seems to spin.

Angelica kneels beside me, her voice soft but firm. "Look at me, Riri. Focus on my voice. You're going to be okay. You're having a panic attack. We just have to ride through it."

I nod weakly, my eyes locking onto hers. "Sunflowers...

they're Dion's favorite." My voice breaks, tears spilling over. "That's why this is so terrifying. How could Andrew know something so personal?"

Angelica's expression shifts to a mix of anger and shock. "I don't know, but we'll find out," she assures me, brushing a strand of hair away from my face. "Right now, you need to calm down. You're safe here with me."

I cling to her words, attempting to steady my breathing. Slowly, the panic begins to recede.

Angie grabs her phone and calls Evander, telling him what happened.

When she hangs up, she says, "Evan will put the building on a discreet lockdown until they can find if there's someone out there. In the meantime, let's go into my safe room, okay?"

"Okay," I say with trembling lips.

A couple hours later, I'm pacing back and forth in the living room. Evander called an hour ago, saying he caught a suspicious man lurking around the block and we were free to leave the safe room. Angie sits on the couch, eyes darting from the door to me and back again. The tension is thick, and I can't shake the feeling that something terrible is about to happen.

The door bursts open, and Evander strides in. His clothes are splattered with blood, his face grim and hard. I freeze, my heart threatening to burst out of my chest. Angie lets out a small gasp, her hand flying to her mouth.

"Evander," I breathe, "what happened?"

He runs a hand through his hair, smearing more blood across his forehead. "I caught the guy. Had to rough him up a bit to get him to talk." His eyes meet mine, and there's a flash of anger there that makes me shiver.

Angie stands up, her face pale. "Who is he?"

Evander sighs, taking a step closer. "He's been following Aria. Working for Andrew."

I feel the blood drain from my face. "What? Since when?"

"Since you got engaged," Evander says, his voice low. "The guy admitted it. Andrew hired him to keep tabs on you."

Disgust churns in my stomach, and I wrap my arms around myself as if to ward off this new violation. "All this time...he's been watching me?" I had a feeling he was, but getting confirmation makes it feel too real.

Evander nods. "I'm sorry, Aria."

Angie's eyes widen with fury. "That bastard! How could he do this to you?"

I swallow hard, trying to process the information. "I can't believe he would go this far."

Evander steps closer, his bloodstained hand reaching out to touch my shoulder. "We'll figure out what to do next."

I nod, though my mind is spinning. "What happened to the guy you caught?"

Evander's jaw tightens. "I made sure he won't bother you again."

I don't ask for details. I don't want to know. Instead, I sink onto the couch, my legs suddenly too weak to hold me. Angie wraps an arm around my shoulders.

My first thought is to inform my brothers of the situation.

Since meeting Atlas, we've been talking every day through texts. He's a lot more talkative that way.

He and Dimo have been inseparable.

Dimitri offered to transfer the estate and clan to him, since he's technically the rightful heir as the oldest. But Atlas refused.

As I grab my phone with shaky hands, I scroll through my messages.

It's now been almost a day since a word from Dion.

I just assumed he was busy, but with this new revelation that Andrew has been following me, and the sunflowers, something feels off.

Angelica notices me squinting at my phone. "What's up?"

"Have you spoken to Dion recently?" I turn back to Evander.

"We spoke yesterday. He said something about having to go out to take care of something and hung up. Nothing out of the ordinary," he answers.

I tilt my head, fingers absentmindedly tapping against my phone screen.

"Why?" Angelica asks.

"Never mind," I wave a hand, not wanting to make a big deal out of nothing. Maybe it's just my nerves being on edge.

I text my brothers in our group chat to tell them what happened, and we wait until the coast is clear.

So much for my wedding celebrations.

ARIA

I clutch my burner phone tightly in my hand, heart racing faster and faster with each passing second.

Three days.

Three agonizing days since Dion vanished without a trace. It's not like him to disappear like this. Evander's men have been out searching, but there's still no sign of him. My messages and calls remain unanswered. They can't even track his phone. It's maddening.

I scroll through the list of texts I sent Dion since I left Angelica's hotel. What could have happened to him?

I'm in my house, but it feels like a cage. My mother and Magdalena bustle around, preparing for my wedding cere-mony. My hair and makeup are done, though I can hardly focus, my mind consumed by thoughts of Dion.

Magda rushes past me, her words blurring into background noise. My gaze drifts to the window. How can the world outside continue as if nothing's wrong when my entire existence is falling apart?

Dimo's hand on my shoulder startles me, pulling me from my thoughts. "We'll find him," he says, his tone determined.

I nod, grateful for his reassurance, but the knot of anxiety in my chest refuses to loosen. "I hope so," I murmur, my gaze flickering back to my phone—still silent, still empty.

A knock at the door makes me jump again, and I turn to see Evander's grim face framed in the doorway. "No sign of him," he says, his voice heavy with concern. "But we won't stop until we find him."

I nod, trying to swallow the lump in my throat. "Thank you," I manage to choke out.

I sink onto the nearest chair, tears pricking at the corners of my eyes as I realize that I have no choice but to go through with the wedding, to put on a brave face and pretend that everything is fine when my heart is breaking. Dion might be lying somewhere, hurt, and if I don't go to the church, my family might have the same fate.

I head into the foyer where my wedding dress is hanging. I pick it up, and it feels heavier than ever. I glance at the clock for the hundredth time, willing time to move faster, yet dreading the moment I'll have to leave for the ceremony.

And then, the familiar sound of Angelica's voice sounds on the other side of the main doors. She enters, and concern immediately paints her face as she takes in my haunted expression. She ushers me upstairs.

When we reach my bedroom, I take a deep breath, trying to summon some courage.

Angelica helps me into my wedding dress, her hands gentle as she guides the delicate fabric over my trembling frame.

Once the dress is in place, we stand face to face, and for a moment, there's a shared understanding between us. This is not the way I was supposed to get married, and I'll never get a first wedding ever again. I look up to the ceiling to prevent my tears from falling.

Angelica breaks the silence. "I'm sorry, Riri. I wish I could take away all the pain and uncertainty you're feeling right now."

Despite my efforts to hold back the tears, they spill over, tracing paths down my cheeks. Angelica reaches out and gently blots them away, careful not to ruin my makeup.

"Where could he be?" I ask, my voice just a murmur.

She squeezes my shoulder. "I don't know, babe. But he can't be far."

"What if he's hurt?"

Angelica's lips thin. "Even if he is, we'll get him back, and he'll be okay."

I want to believe her, but how can I?

My reflection in the mirror gazes back at me.

The sheer opulence of the dress seems to mock me. It's breathtaking: ivory silk that hugs my curves, lace detailing that sparkles, and a voluminous skirt that swishes with every movement.

It's everything I might have once dreamed of. But as I shift uneasily, the weighty fabric is almost a shackle. The dress represents a cloak of obligation. A cruel reminder of the commitment I'm about to make to Andrew.

I want to be anywhere but here.

A sense of impending doom coils around me like a choking fog.

For the first time in a while, the sneaky voice of temptation creeps back into my head. The thought of using again, of escaping this suffocating reality even just for a moment, is almost overpowering. I clench my fists, nails digging into my palms to anchor myself to the present, to the promise I made to myself. To Dion.

Angelica's voice breaks through the haze, a soft murmur of reassurance that I cling to like a lifeline.

Reluctantly, I tear my gaze away from the mirror just as my mother calls from downstairs. It's time to leave.

With a shaky breath, I straighten my spine.

As our car pulls away from the curb, I steal one last glance at my house.

This is the beginning of the end.

WE STEP OUT OF THE CAR AND APPROACH THE CHURCH, MY EYES darting nervously over the gathering crowd.

I have no idea where Andrew is, so the nervous anticipation is killing me softly.

We stop behind the building, and I follow the others inside, feeling like a puppet being pulled along by invisible strings.

In the bridal suite, Angelica stays with me while the others grab their seats in the church. She hugs me quick, then disappears to join Evander.

Last time we were in a church, we almost died.

Today, I'm in a different church, and I almost *wish* someone would blow it up. *Minus the casualties, of course.*

My mother enters the room, and I give her a small smile as she sits and takes hold of my hands. "I know today is not the outcome you would've wished for. But remember who you are," she says, her voice steady and unwavering. "You are strong, Aria. No matter what happens, you will come out on top."

"Thanks, *Mama*." Though she knows I'm unhappy, she's unaware of how Andrew has really been with me, and I want to keep it that way. We kiss each other on the cheeks goodbye and she, too, leaves.

T-minus thirty minutes until I'm chained to the devil.

49

DION

Three days earlier

W hat the fuck?"
I blink groggily, trying to force my eyes open. I wince as pain shoots through my body with each slight movement. *What the hell happened*?

I try to lift my hands to rub my aching temples, but they're bound tight behind me, the ropes cutting into my wrists.

Taking a deep breath, I finally manage to crack my eyes open. It's dark. The only light comes from a flickering bulb hanging overhead, casting shadows along the damp concrete walls.

The air is thick with the smell of mildew. I must be in some basement, underground.

My ankles are bound too. I strain against the ropes, but they hold firm.

My head pounds harder with every heartbeat, and I can barely think through the haze of pain. Was I drugged? I can't remember anything clearly. The last thing I recall is leaving the house. How did I end up here?

I look down at myself. I'm still wearing the clothes I had on when I left: jeans, a t-shirt, my old leather jacket. That feels like ages ago. How long have I been here? My mind races, trying to piece together the fragments of memory.

Then it hits me—*Aria*. Panic blinds me as I remember the text she sent, asking for help. I was on the phone with Evan, and I'd hung up abruptly. I checked her location: she was at that club—the same one where I'd picked her up before.

When I first saw her message, I immediately thought she'd used again, and disappointment had hit me hard. I thought she was finally on the right path. She has been doing so well lately. What if something else has happened to her?

Fuck, fuck, FUCK.

I struggle violently against the ropes, trying to burst out of the chair. "Aria!" I shout, my voice echoing off the walls.

I doubt she's here, that she can hear me. But I need her to know that I came for her. I didn't abandon her like the first time when she'd reached out and I *ignored* her.

I hear footsteps approaching, the sound ominous, and I stop struggling. The door creaks open, a figure stepping into the dim light.

Andrew.

My jaw tenses. "Son of a bitch," I snap, gritting my teeth.

He stands there, calm and composed, a sinister smile playing on his lips. "Hello, Dion. I see you're finally awake."

"*Ánte gamísou.*" I almost fucking growl at him. "Where is she?"

Andrew chuckles, stepping closer. His face is shadowed, but I can see the cold glint in his eyes. "Aria's fine—for now. It's you we need to worry about."

I buck against my restraints again. I want to free my hands so I can strangle this cunt once and for all. But it's useless. The ropes are too tight.

Andrew's voice cuts through the stale air of the room.

"Seems like those little threats I sent you weren't quite enough to keep you in line. And as for Aria...well, it appears she's become quite stubborn herself. Even the threat against her brother doesn't seem to faze her anymore."

Skatofatsa.

"*Ti thelis*, Galanis?"

"What my family is owed, what *I'm* owed," he replies calmly.

"You're not owed *shit*. Get these fucking restraints off me, *maláka*."

"Tsk tsk." He shakes his head. "I think I like seeing you tied up, Loukas," he says, kneeling in front of me. "What I want from you is to leave Aria alone. She's an integral part of my plan." He grabs my chin roughly, forcing me to look at him. "And *you* have been sticking your nose where it doesn't belong. So, this is just a little reminder to mind your own business."

I jerk my head away and spit in his face. "I'm going to fucking kill you."

Andrew startles and bursts into a fit of laughter, wiping the specks of saliva off his cheek. "It's funny how you think you have the upper hand, Loukas. You're in here," he says, gesturing around the space. "While your dear love is out there," he adds with a smirk, pointing up.

I'm getting tired of his shit. "Tell me why the fuck I'm here, Galanis. What have you done to Aria?" I grit out.

He flashes me a sinister grin. "You really don't know?"

"No," I snarl. "I don't know what the fuck you're talking about."

"You should know already that I've been keeping an eye on you, Loukas," he admits. "Eyes *and* ears. Watching your little escapades with Aria. You two make quite the pair, but I needed it to stop once and for all."

I knew he had been watching her, watching us, but it suddenly dawns on me just how much he has been an eye on her. I should've known that Aria's fiancé, having so much on the line, would make sure that his investment was secure.

I grit my teeth, frustration boiling inside me. But I have to stay calm, to think clearly and find a way out of here. To make sure that Aria is okay.

"Where is she?" I ask again through gritted teeth.

Andrew's smirk widens, and he takes a step back, as if savoring the moment. "She's fine."

"What the fuck do you mean? She texted me for help."

"Well, I did a little thing to her phone called *hacking*," he explains as if talking to a child, chuckling. "I installed a tracker and got into her text messages..."

The realization hits me like a punch to the gut. How did I not realize that Aria texted me from her phone and not the burner? She was never in trouble. It was Andrew who sent the message, manipulating me, using her as bait to lure me into his trap. Anger surges through me, hot and fierce.

My hands clench into fists, the ropes biting into my skin as I struggle against them once more. "You fucking cunt!" I shout.

A wicked grin twists his lips. "Surprised?" Andrew sneers, relishing in my shock. "I must say, you were easier to fool than I expected."

My entire body trembles with fury. "You sick bastard. What have you done?"

Andrew's laughter echoes off the damp walls. "Nothing. Yet."

"You think you can put your hands on her and get away with it?" I growl, my voice low.

He leans casually against the wall. "What are you gonna do about it, Dion? You're tied up in case you forgot."

My muscles scream in protest. "When I get out of these shackles," I say, my breath coming in ragged bursts, "you'd better watch your back."

Andrew steps closer, his eyes gleaming with a twisted pleasure. "Oh? And why's that?"

My jaw clenches. "Because I'm going to kill you, Andrew. You made her suffer, and you're going to pay for it."

He laughs, a cold, heartless sound that echoes around the basement. "Big talk for someone who can't move."

"You think these ropes will hold me forever? Think again. I'll break free, and when I do, you'll wish you never laid a finger on her, you son of a bitch."

His face falters for just a moment, a flicker of doubt in his eyes, before he regains his composure. "You're delusional, Dion. Aria's mine now, in every way that matters. I can do whatever I want with her. In a few short days, she'll be my wife. And you'll be dead."

"She's not yours and never will be," I spit, my words laced with venom. "Either way, you're no longer the heir to the Kastellanos estate."

Andrew's laughter fills the room. "How are you going to stop me? I made a blood pact with her father, and as long as I'm alive, I have the right to claim her as my wife. And when I do, I'll get rid of her fucking brother and take over."

"Not if I stop you first," I growl.

Andrew scoffs. "The reason I brought you down here is to prevent you from doing anything heroic like trying to save that whore from her fate. We are to be married in three days."

Fuck no. I lunge forward in my chair, hands clenched into fists. The ropes strain against my wrists, cutting deeper into my skin, but I barely register the pain. I notice with smug satisfaction his slight flinch, and I smirk.

However, Andrew is quicker than I anticipated.

His fist connects with my jaw with a sickening crack, sending stars exploding across my vision. I taste blood as it floods my mouth, hot and metallic.

"I can't wait to make her mine and enjoy every moment of

it," he smiles. "Starting with fucking the bitch and filling her with my heirs."

The mere thought of Andrew touching Aria, of defiling her in such a way, fills me with a rage so intense it's almost blinding.

He hits me again. I refuse to back down, thrashing in my chair with all the strength I can muster.

Andrew's blows rain down on me like a hailstorm. I feel bones crack beneath his relentless assault, my body convulsing with agony with every strike.

And through the haze of pain and blood, it's Aria who consumes my mind.

I cling to the image of her, safe and unharmed, the only thing keeping me tethered to reality. Despite the darkness closing in around me, her face shines like a star in the night, a small comfort in this nightmare.

ATLAS

I sit in the darkness of my underground sanctuary, clutching my phone tighter, knuckles turning white.

"You really haven't been able to find him?" I ask, trying to keep the frustration out of my voice. I fucking *hate* talking on the phone.

"Not a trace," Evander replies, sounding just as frustrated—but for other reasons. "Even Xander can't track him, and he's my best hacker. It's as if he vanished into thin air."

I sigh, rubbing my temples. "And you came to me because...?"

"We need someone with your skills, Atlas. Dimitri said you're a computer genius. If anyone can find Dion, it's you."

Fucking Dimo. Of course he'd go around calling me a computer "genius." I'm becoming fond of the kid, but he's a pain in my ass.

I glance around my surroundings, feeling the familiar comfort of solitude. Even months after being freed from the chains of my father, from the lies that bound me to him, I can't bring myself to leave this place. Out there, people know the truth about me. Here, in the dark, I don't have to face anyone. I don't have to see their pitying eyes or hear their loud voices. I can just exist, quietly—hidden.

My computer chimes, breaking my reverie. A new message on my dark web IM. I've been chatting with someone named—well, their alias keeps changing, so let's call them Phantom for now. For months, I've tried to figure out who they are, but it's near impossible. It's shocking, really. I've never had this much trouble uncovering anyone before. I even discovered the truth behind the Sisterhood when I was just a kid, and that was no easy feat.

"I'll see what I can do," I grunt, fingers already flying over the keyboard. "No promises."

We hang up, and I turn my full attention to Phantom's latest message. It's another riddle, another challenge. I type out a quick response, my mind already working through the possibilities.

Day blends into night as I sift through every digital trace of Dion's last known moves. Even after talking to Evander's counterparts, Hendrick and Sebastian, in Antium, and having them scour their surveillance network, Dion remains a ghost. Frustration gnaws at me, but I refuse to give up.

Somewhere in this digital maze is the key to finding Dion. And I'm going to find it, no matter how deep I have to go. For Aria.

Then, finally, I get a ping. Dion's last known location was in the Lower District near some shady club. My eyes scan the footage. Nothing. Whoever took him made sure to wipe the footage clean, but they made a small, crucial mistake.

At first, I missed it—a tiny peep of a motorcycle in the corner of the alleyway next to the club. I zoom in, and there it is: Dion's bike. The license plate confirms it. I dive into the footage from a ten-mile radius around the same time his bike was abandoned.

Hours pass in a blur until I see it—a black town car heading east. Bingo. This is it. This is my lead.

I grab my phone and call Evander. "*Ton brika.*"

"*Poú eínai?*"

"Lower District. He was taken from a bar in a black town car heading east. I'll send you the details and footage."

We hang up, and I lean back in my chair, feeling a rare sense of accomplishment.

My computer chimes again—a new message from Phantom. I glance at it, my mind already shifting gears.

But the hunt is on, so Phantom will have to wait.

Tᴀᴇ ɴᴇxᴛ ᴍᴏʀɴɪɴɢ, I ʜᴜᴅᴅʟᴇ ᴡɪᴛʜ Eᴠᴀɴᴅᴇʀ's ᴍᴇɴ, ᴍᴀᴘs spread out before us, as we plan our next move.

I take charge, my thoughts racing through the network of underground passages that crisscross the city. There's a tunnel entrance a mile away from where the Town Car was last spotted. It's our best chance of getting in unnoticed.

"We'll go in through here," I say, tracing the route on the map. "It's off the grid, away from prying eyes. From there, I'll go in alone."

Evander nods. "You sure you don't want back-up?"

"There will probably be soldiers everywhere. We can't risk drawing attention. I'll move faster alone, and no one knows who I am."

With the plan in place, we gear up and head out.

As we approach the entrance, I take a deep breath and pull the black ski mask over my face. With a silent nod to Evander, I slip into the shadows, disappearing into the darkness.

The tunnel is a maze of twisting passages, and I move with determination, my footsteps echoing against the stone walls.

I catch a faint glimmer of light ahead, accompanied by the muffled sound of voices. I slow my pace, pulse quickening with adrenaline. Drawing closer, I strain my ears, trying to decipher the number of men ahead. Three, maybe four voices.

I take a moment to mentally prepare myself, tightening the grip on my rifle. With a steady breath, I step into the room.

Two swift blows from the butt of my rifle send two of the men crashing to the ground, unconscious. But before I can turn around, a third man lunges at me, fists flying. I dodge his punches with ease, countering with strikes of my own. The sound of our grunts and the dull thud of fists against flesh fills the air.

Then, just as I've knocked him down, a fourth man comes out of the shadows.

His gun is leveled at me.

Adrenaline courses through me as I meet his gaze.

"Who are you?" he demands.

I hold his gaze, unflinching, and lower my rifle just slightly. "A ghost."

"Don't fuck with me, who are you?" The man's eyes narrow, his finger twitching on the trigger.

A noise sounds from one of the tunnels, distracting him, and I spring into action. In one quick motion, I bring my rifle up, knock the gun from his hand and swipe my foot behind his legs. He falls with a grunt, and I pin him to the ground with a firm hand on his chest.

He struggles beneath me, his breath coming in ragged gasps as he stares up at me with wide eyes. My gaze is unwavering as I lean in close.

"You picked the wrong fight," I growl.

With a swift blow to the jaw, I render him unconscious, leaving him sprawled out on the ground.

With the threat neutralized, I waste no time. I follow the

faint trail of light. As I draw closer, the sound of a rough, muffled voice grows louder, mingled with the clang of metal.

My grip tightens on my weapon.

Finally, I reach the source of the noise in a dark chamber. I move cautiously, keeping to the side as I scan the room for any sign of Dion.

Then, I see him—a bloody figure in the far corner, bound and gagged.

51

ARIA

Standing by the window in the bridal suite, I reach for my burner phone with the desperate hope to find a message from Dion, but before I can even unlock it, a voice cuts through the air like a blade.

"He won't reply to you." I freeze, fingers hovering over the screen, my heart lurching in my chest. I turn slowly and meet Andrew's smug gaze.

I stare at him, dumbfounded, trying to process his words. "What do you mean?" The quiver in my voice betrays my unease.

"He's made his choice," he replies, his tone dripping with malice, but doesn't say anything else.

"Y-you're not supposed to be here, Andrew," I say, backing up. "You shouldn't see the bride before the wedding."

Andrew laughs and it's a wicked sound. "We both know this isn't a traditional wedding, Aria. I don't give a fuck about what you look like," he spits. "I'm just here to let you know that any flicker of hope you had that your one true love, Dion, would come and rescue you, is a waste of energy."

"What did you do?" I breathe out. My heart is about to leap

out of my chest.

He puts his hands in his pockets. "That's none of your concern. He's no longer a problem."

My fingers instinctively clamp onto my stomach, as if I can physically hold back the sickness rising within me, Andrew's words hitting me like a punch to the gut.

My breath comes in short, ragged gasps. The room feels like it's closing in.

Andrew moves closer, cornering me against the wall. I can't stop myself from shaking, both from fear and revulsion. His breath reeks of alcohol as he leans in, his hands groping me roughly. "You better keep your mouth shut or you'll regret it."

I try to push him away, but his grip tightens, fingers digging into my skin.

"Get off me!" I scream.

That's when I feel his hand move lower, grabbing my crotch with force. In a surge of desperation, I swing my fist with all my might, aiming straight for his stomach. The impact sends him staggering back, but before I can even move away, his hand comes crashing across my face with a sharp crack.

Pain explodes along my cheek, and I stagger backward, tasting blood in my mouth. My vision blurs for a moment as I struggle to stay upright.

Andrew moves toward me again and I yelp, stumbling along the wall.

And then, a sudden presence fills the room.

I look up to find Dion standing in the doorway, his eyes ablaze with rage.

For a moment, time seems to freeze.

"Dion..." I manage to choke out. Here's here. He's *alive*.

His face is marred by bruises and cuts, clothes stained with blood, his nose fractured. The paleness of his skin speaks of sleepless nights and days spent in darkness.

His eyes lock onto mine and he notices the red stains on my

lips.

I look down, and his fingers squeeze around the machete he's holding, its blade glistening with what looks like fresh blood. Yet, there's a sense of power in the way he holds it, a promise of retribution.

Andrew's eyes widen in shock as they flicker from Dion's bloodied figure to the gleaming weapon in his hand. His face pales.

"How—" he stammers, his voice trembling. "How the fuck did you get out?"

Dion's lips curl into a wicked smile as he takes a step forward, slowly closing the distance.

"Nothing in this world could've kept me from Aria today," Dion's voice cuts through the tension like a knife. "I would've sawed off my own feet if it meant putting an end to this wedding."

"Dion, be careful," I whisper, stepping toward him.

But Dion's gaze remains fixed on Andrew, his jaw set with determination. "Move behind me, Aria," he instructs.

I hesitate for a moment, torn between wanting to stay by his side and fearing what might happen if I intervene. I take a step back, swallowing the lump in my throat.

"I've waited long enough to get rid of you, you piece of shit. Soon, I'm going to bury you and dance on your fucking grave," Dion seethes. I've never seen him this angry. Goosebumps rise along my skin.

"First, you hack into Aria's phone and send me a message, making me believe that she was in danger, knowing I'd come for her. 'Cause you weren't man enough to face me alone."

My jaw drops. Andrew did *what*?

Dion takes more steps. "Then, you lure me into a trap and keep me hostage for three *fucking* days."

I gasp, hand flying to my mouth.

Dion's chest is rising and falling at a rapid pace.

"You really thought I'd give up that easily, motherfucker?"

Andrew attempts to mask his fear, scoffing as he straightens. "Really, Dion?" he sneers, though his voice wavers slightly. "You think you can just barge in here and play the hero? I'll have my men kill you."

"What men?" Dion's smile widens, his grip tightening on the bloodied machete. "I'm not playing, Andrew. This ends now."

Andrew's bravado falters. His hand darts to his jacket, and before I can fully process the movement, he pulls out a gun, aiming it at my head. My heart stops as a scream rips from my throat.

Dion's voice cuts through my panic, calm and steady. "Aria, it'll be okay. Trust me," he says softly, never taking his gaze off Andrew. "I've got this."

Dion takes a step forward, his movements slow and deliberate. "You don't want to do this, Galanis. Put the gun down."

Andrew's hand shakes slightly, betraying the confidence he's trying to project. "Stay back. I'm warning you."

Dion's expression remains unwavering, a picture of calm amidst the storm. "If you hurt her, there'll be no going back for you. You know that. My clan is out there, and we won't hesitate to kill you—*very* slowly."

Andrew's grip on the gun doesn't waver, his eyes locked in a dangerous stare with Dion's. In an attempt to distract him, I move toward the door, Andrew's gaze following me. Dion takes the opportunity to charge forward.

The impact sends the gun flying from Andrew's hand, and it skids across the floor.

I lurch for it, my fingers wrapping around the cold metal as I rise and point it at Andrew. My hands are trembling uncontrollably. I've never shot a gun before, but the resolve coursing through me tells me that I will if I have to.

Dion and Andrew clash violently, grunts and the sounds of

fists connecting with flesh filling the room.

Somehow, Dion gains the upper hand, forcing Andrew to his knees.

With a final look, Dion lifts the machete high. "As you take your final breath, never forget that you're *worthless*, and you'll be remembered not for your power or your family name, but for your fucking failures. I hope you rot in fucking hell."

Before Andrew can react, Dion brings the weapon down with a swing.

The blade slices through Andrew's neck, and blood splatters everywhere, reaching my white wedding dress. He gurgles, choking on his own blood, before his body crumples to the floor, lifeless.

Shock paralyzes me, my mind struggling to process what I just saw.

There's *so* much blood.

Dion stands over him, chest heaving with exertion as he ensures Andrew is truly gone.

Then, he turns to me, his eyes softening as he takes in my blood-streaked form. He stands up and gently takes the gun from my trembling hands before pulling me into his arms, holding me tight. I bury my face in his chest and cry.

"It's over," he whispers.

I nod, frantically. *It's over, it's over, it's over.*

I cling to Dion, as the reality of what just happened begins to sink in.

When my sobs subside and the tears finally stop, Dion wipes my face with his rough, bloodstained hands. His touch is tender, a stark contrast to the violence of a few moments ago. He tilts my chin up, and our eyes meet.

Without a word, he leans in and kisses me. It's explosive, a kiss that ignites something deep within me. For the first time, there are no more worries, no fears, no what-ifs. I allow myself to be fully present, to lose myself in the moment—in *him*.

The kiss deepens, growing more frantic with each passing second. Our bodies press together, hands roaming as if trying to memorize every inch of each other. The blood on our faces mingles, a macabre reminder of what we've just survived.

But in this kiss, there's freedom. A release of all the pent-up tension, fear and pain from the past couple of years. It's raw and intense, an expression of everything we've been holding back.

Dion's hands travel up my back, pulling me even closer, and my fingers tangle in his hair. The world around us fades away, and all that exists is this moment, this connection. We say everything we can't put into words—that we're alive, that we're together, and that nothing will ever come between us again.

We melt to the floor, never breaking apart.

Our kiss grows frantic, Dion's hands moving with urgency. He lifts the hem of my bloodstained wedding dress, his touch sending shivers down my spine. My breath hitches as he pulls my panties down, the fabric sliding against my skin.

His fingers find their way to my core, and I tense, a moan escaping my lips.

We're only a couple of feet away from Andrew's lifeless body, but I don't care.

The fear, the violence, the blood—all of it fades away, leaving just the two of us.

Dion's fingers move inside me with an expert touch, eliciting another moan from deep within me. My body responds, arching into his hand.

I can feel my climax building, a powerful rush that threatens to overtake me. Each movement, each stroke, pushes me closer to the edge.

He places his thumb on my clit and begins to circle it.

"Dion," I pant as I cling to him, nails digging into his shoulders. The sensation is almost too much.

His lips find mine again, and I groan into his mouth, the

sound vibrating between us.

The pressure inside me builds, a mounting tension that coils tighter and tighter. My breaths come in ragged gasps, my moans growing louder.

"Dion, I'm...I'm so close," I manage to say, my voice breaking.

He responds by quickening his pace, his fingers working me with a relentless rhythm that drives me wild. Heat pools low in my belly, ready to explode.

And then, with a final, breathtaking surge, I shatter. My climax crashes over me, my body convulsing in his arms. I cry out, the sound muffled by Dion's kiss, every muscle tensing and then releasing in a flood of ecstasy.

"I love you, Aria," Dion whispers against my lips.

My breath hitches.

"You're not spending another day without me," Dion continues. "You're all mine, and I'm *never* letting you go. No matter what storms brew, no matter what pain we face, I'll always love you. You are worth every single moment, every tear, every struggle. I'd cross any darkness just to see your smile, to feel your warmth beside me." He places a hand on my chest. "What I feel for you is like a flame, fueled by the essence of who you are—your kindness, your strength, your beauty, both inside and out."

Dion gazes into my eyes as tears shed down my cheeks. "You're worth every trial, every tribulation, because in the end, it is you. It's always been you."

His words, possessive and devoted, make my heart race. Before I can respond, Dion grabs me and positions me so that I'm straddling him. With one hand, he unbuckles his belt and frees himself.

I feel a surge of desire as I look down at his cock, my body still humming with the aftershocks of my release. Slowly, I lower myself onto him, his thick length filling me. "Oh my

God," I moan. I take him deeper. He grips my hips, guiding me as I begin to move, our bodies finding a rhythm that feels both frantic and tender.

I ride him, hands on his shoulders for support, my eyes fixed on his. His hands travel up my back, pulling me closer, and I lean forward, capturing his lips in a searing kiss.

"Fuck, baby. Your pussy is perfect for me. I never want to fuck anyone else for the rest of my life."

Our movements grow more urgent, driven by a shared need to claim and possess each other fully. The intensity builds again, each thrust of his hips sending sparks of pleasure through my body. We move together until pleasure overtakes us both.

With a final, powerful plunge, we shatter, our cries of release mingling in the air.

Breathless, I collapse against him, our bodies slick with sweat and blood.

Dion holds me tightly, his breath warm against my ear.

After a few moments, I pull back to look into his eyes, and take a deep breath. "I love you, too, Dion. When I'm with you, it feels like the world is a garden in full bloom. You make everything brighter, more beautiful. You make me feel like I can be myself, without fear or hesitation." I reach up, gently touching his face, tracing the lines of his jaw with my fingers. "Your patience, your unwavering support—they've become my anchor, my refuge. With you, I feel seen, cherished, and loved in a way I never thought possible."

Dion's eyes glisten as he leans into my touch.

"I love you so much," I say, my voice filled with all the emotion and certainty I've felt for a while. "I always have, and I always will."

"You have no idea how much that means to me, *astéri mou*," he replies, his voice raw. "You are my light, my inspiration. And I will love you forever."

EPILOGUE

DION

Four months later

I sit on the plush couch in Dr. Goode's office, glancing over at Aria sitting next to me. She's fidgeting with a loose thread on the Post Malone tee I gave her on the first night we met, over two years ago. The sight of her in that shirt brings a rush of nostalgia. It's like a snapshot of our journey together, a reminder of how far we've come.

I reach out and gently touch the sleeve of the shirt, my fingers brushing against the soft fabric. Aria looks up, catching my gaze, and a smile spreads across her face.

When Aria first told me about her therapy sessions, I was completely floored. We had been working in the greenhouse, enjoying a quiet afternoon, when she casually mentioned her therapist's name. I nearly dropped the fucking petunias.

"Wait, did you just say, 'Dr. Goode'?" I ask, my eyes widening in surprise.

Aria frowns, puzzled. "Yeah, Dr. Goode. Why?"

I try to process the coincidence. "That's my therapist."

She stares at me in disbelief. "You're kidding, right?"

I shake my head, a bewildered laugh escaping my lips. "No, I'm serious. I've been seeing her for months."

The initial shock quickly turned into amusement. Of all the therapists in the city, we had both ended up with the same one. It was almost like some cosmic joke.

It somehow made me feel even more connected to her. It was like we had been on parallel paths, not quite meeting for a while. And now those paths had finally converged.

As we shared our experiences, I realized how much we had both grown. Finding out we were seeing the same therapist was a surprise, but it was also a blessing. It brought us closer, made us more open and honest with each other.

Dr. Goode clears her throat, drawing our attention back to her. "It's good to see you both here together. How have things been?"

I reach out to Aria's hand and give it a gentle squeeze. "It's been great."

Aria smiles at me before turning toward Dr. Goode. "It hasn't been without setbacks, but with each passing day, we're learning to build a life together that honors our past while looking into the future."

I stare at my girl in absolute awe. Her strength, resilience and unwavering spirit leave me speechless. I am so deeply in love with her.

"How do you feel about where you are now in your relationship?" Dr. Goode asks.

Aria chuckles softly, and I feel a warmth spread through my chest. "Stronger than ever. We've been communicating better, really listening to each other."

I nod in agreement.

Adjusting to a new normal has been a challenge, but it's one I'm committed to facing head-on. Aria, understandably, was shaken up for weeks—she still is. Her father's sudden death and her brother Dimitri stepping up as the new head were monumental shifts for her. Add to that the discovery of having a half-brother and the lingering trauma from nearly two years of Andrew's abuse, and it's no wonder she's struggling to find her footing.

In the beginning, we had to take things slow. I remember the first few weeks when Aria would wake up from nightmares, drenched in sweat, her body trembling. I would hold her, whispering reassuring words, hoping to provide some comfort. It was a delicate balance between giving her the space she needed and being there for her to lean on.

"We've come a long way," I say, feeling a swell of pride.

Dr. Goode leans forward, her expression warm. "I'm proud of both of you. You've done the hard work, and it's paying off. Keep supporting each other, keep communicating, and you'll continue to grow stronger."

"Thank you, Dr. Goode. For everything."

"Yes, thank you. We couldn't have done it without you," Aria adds, her grin radiant.

"Push!" the nurse says from the other side of the hospital room. She's shouting encouragement, urging Angelica to keep going.

Evander hovers nervously by her side, his eyes never leaving his wife.

Angelica's screams become louder, and I feel myself pale. *Oh, my fucking God.* What am I doing here?

Aria is next to her best friend, holding her hand and passing a damp towel on her head. "You can do this, Giegie! Make your vagina your little bitch and push that baby out!"

I need to fucking leave. I bend down next to her. "I think I'm going to be sick."

Aria shoots me a stern look, her tone not concealing her annoyance. "Seriously, Dion? Don't be rude."

"Why the fuck am I even here in the first place, Aria?" I hiss.

"To support your brother, *vlakas*," she retorts, smacking the side of my head with her free hand. "Now, shoo. You're disturbing us." *Fuck yes.*

I don't hesitate to leave the room, making sure to shut my eyes as I pass Angie's legs. I'm not planning on getting my eyes gouged out by Evan for accidentally seeing his wife naked.

Evander, lost in admiration while watching Angelica, barely registers my discomfort or my exit as he whispers words of encouragement, his gaze unwaveringly fixed on her.

"You're doing amazing, *angeloúdi mou*. Just a little more."

Once in the hallway, I relax on one of the chairs and wait.

A while later, Aria emerges from the delivery room. "The coast is clear. You can come back in now." She rolls her eyes when she sees the relief flooding my face.

When I step back into the room, there, in Angelica's arms, lies their newborn baby, tiny and perfect.

Angelica looks exhausted but radiant, a smile spreading across her face as she meets my gaze.

"Hey, Uncle Dion."

My heart swells.

Evander's eyes are on the tiny bundle cradled in his wife's arms. There's a softness in his expression I haven't seen in years, maybe ever. He looks up, his face breaking into a tired but genuine grin. "Come meet my new baby girl."

I approach the bed. The baby is so small, so fragile, with a mop of dark hair and the beginnings of Angie's soft features. Her tiny fingers curl and uncurl, and I feel a lump rise in my throat.

"Thea Vasilakis," Evan says, his voice thick with emotion. "After my sister."

I nod, swallowing hard. The memory of Evander's late sister

is a tender spot for both of us. Naming his daughter after her is a tribute that strikes deep. I reach out, hesitating for a moment before gently touching Thea's tiny hand. Her skin is impossibly soft, and when her fingers wrap around mine, something inside me shifts.

"She's beautiful," I murmur.

"Do you want to hold her?"

I freeze for a second, then nod. Carefully, I take Thea into my arms, cradling her against my chest. She's warm and light, a reminder that, amidst all the darkness we deal with, there's still innocence and hope in the world.

As I look down at her, I make a silent vow. No matter what comes our way, I'll protect her. I'll make sure she always knows she's loved and cherished, that she's more than just a part of our family legacy. She's the future, and I'll do everything in my power to ensure it's a bright one.

Evan places a hand on my shoulder, his grip firm. "We're going to make sure she's safe."

I meet his gaze. In this moment, we're not just mob men. We're brothers, a father and uncle, and protectors. And Thea Vasilakis is a new beginning for all of us.

Aria comes to stand next to me, tears in her eyes. Her gaze is fixed on the baby, and when she looks up at me, her expression is a mixture of love and pride. She wipes a tear from her cheek and smiles.

"She's perfect," Aria whispers, her voice trembling.

"Can men say their ovaries are tingling? Because this sure feels like it. I think I've caught baby fever." I try to keep a straight face.

Aria snorts, and Evan shakes his head with a laugh.

"You're so stupid, Dion," Angelica says.

I'm sure Aria can see the mischievous glint in my eye as I gently rock Thea in my arms.

"I'm thinking I should start breeding you so we can make a little family of our own."

Aria's eyes widen before bursting into a fit of laughter. "You're impossible."

"Whatever," I retort with a wry smirk. "I guess now I've officially become the best uncle, and I'll spoil her rotten."

Everyone chuckles, but I press on, my grin widening.

"And don't worry, I promise not to teach her how to handle a gun until she's at least—what—five? Maybe six?"

Aria swats her hand at me. "Dion!"

"Just kidding," I add, giving Thea's cheek a gentle nudge with my finger. "She's already got the best defense system —me."

Aria laughs again. "You know, if she ends up with even half of your charm, she'll be unstoppable."

I wink at her. "I'm counting on it."

EPILOGUE II

ARIA

A year later

I step out of my studio, the door closing behind me as the late afternoon sun bathes the town square.

Every morning, I walk this path to my flower shop and feel the same surge of excitement. It's a dream come true.

When Dion first encouraged me to open it, I was hesitant. Women in the mob don't have jobs, don't own businesses. But his unwavering belief in me was something I couldn't ignore. And I took the leap. I rented out a small studio, and then slowly built my shop.

I cross the street to Black Bean just as my phone buzzes in my pocket.

Dion: Your drink and cinnamon bun are waiting for you on the counter.

I smile as I type back.

Me. Still stalking me, huh?

Dion: Ha-ha.

Dion: Maybe...

I laugh out loud, startling a lady who has just stepped out of the coffee shop, and walk through the door.

I smile at my screen as I text Dion back.

Me: I like it...

Dion: I know you do, little liar.

My entire body shivers. I love when he calls me his little liar.

Dion: I love seeing your cheeks go pink.

I halt my steps and twist around. *Is he here?*
My phone buzzes in my hand, surprising me.

Dion: Don't break your neck.

I scan the café for any sign of him, but he's nowhere to be found.

Me: Where are you?

Dion: Come and find me, wife.

My skin tingles with excitement.

So much has changed in the past few months. It feels like a lifetime ago.

Dion and I got married six months after he saved me from marrying Andrew. The relief I experienced seeing Dion that day was something I'll never forget.

I'm no longer chained to Andrew, no longer scared of his

threats.

I knew it would be a struggle to rebuild what was shattered, but with Dion by my side, I can face anything.

After everything with the arranged marriage and all the chaos, I couldn't handle the thought of having a big wedding. I wanted something simple, something just for us.

So, we decided to elope. It felt right, even if it's unconventional, especially in our world.

We couldn't wait any longer, and the thought of dragging out our union was unbearable.

Our lives are complex and often dangerous, but the love and loyalty we share make it all worthwhile. I'm happier than I've ever been and haven't had to use drugs or drink alcohol in almost a year. *I'm fucking proud of myself.*

I put my phone in my purse, heart racing as I walk toward the bathroom, hoping he'll be there. It's empty.

I push one of the stalls open, revealing nothing but the usual sterile tiles. A sigh of frustration escapes me, and I turn to leave the bathroom. Suddenly, a hand grabs me from behind, covering my mouth. I squeal, the sound muffled.

For a brief, terrifying moment, I panic, struggling against my captor. But then, a familiar scent hits me, and my body relaxes. Dion pulls me back into one of the stalls, away from prying eyes, and whispers for me to be quiet.

"What if we get caught?" I hiss.

"I don't fucking care," Dion replies, his eyes gleaming with mischief. "This is worth the risk." He leans in close, his breath warm against my ear. "I just want a little taste, baby."

"But I'm—"

Before I can finish, Dion presses a finger to my lips, silencing me. "Shh," he whispers.

I nod to give him the go-ahead, my heart still pounding in my chest.

He presses my back against the cool surface of the wall and his lips meet mine in a searing kiss.

I melt into Dion's arms, my hands instinctively reaching for his hair.

He plunges his hand into my leggings, and I hold my breath. *Here it comes...*

"Are you on your period?" He pulls away slightly and tugs on my tampon string.

I bite my bottom lip. "I tried to warn you."

"Well, fuck. This just got a lot more interesting," he says, a playful glint in his eyes.

"What are you thinking?" I whisper over the pounding of my heart.

Dion edges nearer, his words a soft whisper in my ear. "I'm thinking I'm going to take what I came for anyway." He nips my earlobe, and my knees threaten to buckle.

Oh, my God.

Dion lowers my leggings and panties just below my ass.

Heat creeps up my cheeks as he kneels in front of me, his fingers grazing my thigh. My body tenses for a moment when he gently pulls on my tampon to slide it out. I squeeze my eyes shut for a moment, before peeking at him through my lashes.

He dangles the red piece of cotton in front of me and my face burns with embarrassment. *I can't believe he's holding my bloody tampon.*

He stands and tosses it into the bin, his other hand moving to tuck a strand of hair behind my ear. "There's nothing to be shy about, Aria. I want *every* part of you—including your blood."

My heart skips a beat at his words. "Oh-kay," I say, jolting at the sensation of Dion's fingers going up my entrance.

My breath catches in my throat, my eyes widening. "Dion," I whisper.

His digits move slowly, exploring. "Relax, baby."

I let myself sink into the feeling. The shyness is still there, but it's being replaced by a growing warmth in my stomach.

Dion's fingers begin to move with a gentle beckoning motion, finding and stroking my most sensitive spot. A shiver runs along my spine, and my hips instinctively shift closer to him. The sensation is electric, a spark that starts deep inside me and spreads outward. I can feel my climax already starting to build, a steady, insistent climb that makes my breaths come faster.

"Dion," I gasp again. "Oh, God."

He leans closer, his lips brushing my ear. "Let go, *astéri mou*. I want to feel all of you."

His words send another shudder through me, and I can't hold back anymore. The tension inside me coils tighter and tighter until it snaps—and then I'm falling, my body shuddering from the force of my climax. I cry out, clutching his shoulders, lost in the sensation.

When it's over, I'm left trembling, trying to catch my breath. Dion slowly withdraws his fingers. They're full of blood. The sight makes my cheeks burn hotter.

He doesn't seem fazed at all. Instead, he lifts his hand, his eyes never leaving mine, and presses his fingers against my lips, smearing some of the crimson on them. My breath hitches, the metallic taste faint on my tongue.

Then, with deliberate slowness, Dion brings his fingers to his own mouth. His eyes remain locked on mine as he sucks them clean, savoring the taste of my blood and my orgasm.

"A fucking delicacy," he murmurs with a satisfied smile. "Now, I'm going to fuck you right against this bathroom stall and cover my cock with your blood, making me yours in every way."

He reaches down, unzipping his pants. Then, lifts me effortlessly, pressing me against the stll. A gasp escapes my lips, my body reacting on impulse. The pressure of the metal door against my back, combined with the intensity of our closeness, makes my pulse race. I clutch at Dion's shoulders, digging my nails into his skin.

He slides his dick inside me. "Oh!" I breathe, the feeling causing my skin to tingle and my nipples to harden.

"*Dikiá mou*. My woman. My *wife*," Dion growls into my ear. The possessiveness of his words makes my entire being pulsate with need.

"Please, Dion. Move," I urge, my head titling as I feel myself contracting around his hardened length.

Dion wraps my legs around his waist and drives into me mercilessly, and I bite my lip to stifle my whimpers. Every sensation is heightened, each stroke amplified, and I don't even care that I'm bleeding anymore.

"*Eísai poutána mono gia ména.*"

My pussy clenches.

"*Nai nai nai, moró. Mi stamatás,*" I plead.

In a few more thrusts, I come undone. My body tenses, a wave of pleasure crashing over me. I cry out, and Dion slaps a hand over my mouth to silence my moans. My muscles tighten and release in a rhythm of pure ecstasy.

Dion slows his movements as I gather myself, the intensity of my climax leaving me trembling, my legs shaking as I cling to him.

After a few moments, he gently lowers me. "Get on your knees, little liar," he commands, his voice husky with desire. I sink to the floor, meeting his eyes with a burning gaze.

His cock is covered in a mixture of my period blood and arousal. It only heightens my desire. It's fucking filthy. Dirty. *Primal.*

I grab Dion's shaft, the stickiness clinging to my palms.

He looks down at me, his chest expanding with every ragged breath. Then, opens his mouth to let a trickle of saliva fall onto the tip of his cock.

"Suck it."

Without sparing a second, I swallow him whole, teasing his swollen head with light suction before coming up for air.

Dion snakes his fingers into my hair, pulling at the nape, and my eyes water from the sting.

"*Riri*," he groans. "Baby." He plunges down my throat and I gag, tears now leaking down my cheeks. "You take my cock so well."

In and out, Dion fucks my mouth until he finds his release, shooting ropes of cum into my mouth.

"Don't swallow," he orders, and I obey.

Extending a hand, he helps me to my feet, his eyes still burning with raw intensity. He swipes his thumb over my lips. "*Omorfi*. You're fucking perfect. Swollen lips, mouth full of my cum. Your blood smeared all over your jaw. It's a fucking sight to be seen, Aria."

Dion hooks his thumb into my mouth, causing some of his release to trickle down my chin.

He pulls me close, our bodies pressed together, and he licks the trail of cum off my face. My breath falters.

His tongue finds its way into my mouth, the gentle brushing of lips becoming more and more urgent and consuming. I savor the flavor of his taste, mixed with the metallic tang of my blood. It's an intoxicating blend that ignites a fire within me. A soft moan escapes my lips.

Dion's hands cradle my face, tilting my head to deepen the kiss, exploring every inch of my mouth. My knees weaken, and I shudder against him.

My hands find their way to the back of his neck, fingers tangling in his hair, our bodies melting into one.

When we finally pull away, I immediately feel the absence of his lips. The heat of our shared breath lingering in the air.

My pulse races, and I feel my heart pounding in my chest.

I swallow a laugh. "This isn't normal. We just consumed my *period blood*."

Dion's smile widens. He takes my wrists and pins them against the cool wall behind me. The suddenness of it makes me gasp.

"I never said I was normal," Dion replies, his voice low and intense. "And if I were, you wouldn't love me the way you do. Because you're messed up too, little liar."

I look up at him, my breath coming in shallow bursts, and I know he's right. There's a part of me that craves this, that needs this connection, no matter how unconventional it might be.

"Maybe I am," I whisper.

Dion leans in, his kiss searing and possessive, smearing the last traces of my blood. "That's why you're perfect for me, wife."

ACKNOWLEDGMENTS

This book, guys! THIS. BOOK. I've never been as obsessed with my characters, plot, and spice as much as I'm obsessed with *The Sotíras*. Dion and Aria have my whole heart.

From the time I wrote *The Diávolos*, I was looking forward to writing their book. And it's finally here. It took so much time and effort to perfect their story, and I'm so proud of it. Proud of THEM. The angst, the trauma, the growth. It was so healing to write.

As usual, a HUGE thank you to my friend and editor extraordinaire, Jennifer! This is the fourth book we've edited together, and I'm looking forward to a thousand more. You've taught me so much, and my writing has improved because of you. I'll forever be grateful.

Danielle, my partner in crime. The best co-author and friend I could ever ask for! You were already indispensable, but now that you've formatted my books, you really can't get rid of me, LOL! Forever and ever.

To my amazing PA, turned friend for life, Abby. Thank you for being my handler and keeping me on track while I wrote and edited this book. I'm so thankful for you!

Finally, thank you to my incredible street team. Wowowow! I really don't know what I'd do without you. You always motivate me, praise me, hype me up. Without you, my books wouldn't have gotten the push they needed to end up in more reader's hands. You're all stuck with me! I appreciate you all so much. Special shoutout to Eleni, *angelóudi mou*. You were my go-to whenever I needed to make sure that my Greek was on point, and I have you to thank for the amazing Greek playlist.

ALSO BY NOUHA JULLIENNE

Godfathers of the Night Series - Dark Mafia Romance

The Diávolos: Part One

The Diávolos: Part Two

Sinners and Saints Series - Dark MC Romance

King of Sinners

If you don't want to miss out on future book releases, follow me on Instagram at novelswithnouha or subscribe to my newsletter! Click here for all my links: https://linktr.ee/NovelswithNouha

If you enjoyed The Sotíras, please leave a positive review on Amazon. I would greatly appreciate it!

Thank you for reading!